20040333F

53

✓

Death Penalties

'*Everybody* dies too soon,' Detective Chief Superintendent Luke Abbott tells his young colleague, Sergeant Tim Nightingale.

But Sergeant Nightingale, eager to prove himself a credit to the CID, decides to reopen the file on Roger Leland's fatal car crash. He discovers that Leland died not only too soon – but very inconveniently for someone. Leland's widow, Tess, has begun to put her life back together – but that someone seems determined to take it to pieces again.

A burglary, a break-in, cruel practical jokes, anonymous threatening phone calls – each more sinister and inexplicable – are putting her re-emergent career as an interior designer under pressure. When her son Max falls ill with rheumatic fever while at boarding school, he and his nightmares about his father's accident come home. Now Tess is frightened for his safety as well as her own.

Which of Tess Leland's old friends and new acquaintances is behind the campaign to harass and terrify her? Is it one – or more than one? And what terrible penalties for her husband's way of life – and death – will she have to pay in the end?

With characteristic flair and ingenuity, Paula Gosling weaves these separate strands together into a taut, gripping and suspenseful crime novel that will intrigue and delight her many fans.

DEATH
PENALTIES

A Mystery Featuring Luke Abbott

PAULA GOSLING

A Scribners Book

First published in Great Britain in 1991 by Scribners
a Division of Macdonald & Co (Publishers) Ltd
London & Sydney

Photoset in North Wales by
Derek Doyle & Associates, Mold, Clwyd.
Printed in Great Britain by
Mackays of Chatham PLC, Chatham, Kent

British Library Cataloguing in Publication Data

Gosling, Paula *1939–*
Death penalties.
I. Title
813.54 [F]

ISBN 0–356–19776–X

Scribners
A Division of
Macdonald & Co (Publishers) Ltd
Orbit House
1 New Fetter Lane
London EC4A 1AR
A member of Maxwell Macmillan Pergamon Publishing Corporation

This one is for Tess Sacco . . .
. . . and thanks to Ralph Spurrier.
A crime writer couldn't have two better friends.

ONE

'DAD! YOU'RE DRIVING TOO FAST!'

He didn't answer the boy. He *was* driving too fast, but he didn't know what else to do, because the dark green hatchback that had been following them since they left the house was gaining ground. He couldn't make out the driver's face, for light glared in his rear-view mirror, reducing the man in the car behind him to a menacing silhouette. He could just see the pale hands where they gripped the wheel.

Whoever he was, he drove very well, keeping pace, and closing the gap a little, every minute or so.

Maybe he was after Max.

They wouldn't. They couldn't be that angry. Could they?

He put his foot down harder.

It was a long, straight street, unusual in this part of London. Cars lined each side of it without a break, squeezed together right up to the crossing. Large ash trees overhung it, their branches thick with leaves. The warm summer rain that had been falling all day had ceased only moments before, leaving everything dripping and sparkling in new sunlight. The sky was opening, the gunmetal grey splitting like curtains to reveal vibrant blue. The sudden, unexpected illumination seemed even greater against the retreating clouds, each crest a cauliflower billow of fire-edged white.

Their brightness blinded him.

That was why he didn't see the old man step out.

When Max shouted, he straight-legged the brake and clutch pedals, twisted the wheel hard, too hard, felt the

1

wheels lock and the tyres skid on the wet surface, felt the jolt as they hit the front end of the last parked car, felt the roll begin, saw the street become the sky with the astonished face of the old man drifting past like a pink and white balloon, heard the incredible screech of metal scouring the asphalt with a scream not unlike his own, high and thin. The car landed on its side, still moving forward.

Clockwork, running down.

A film, frame by frame.

Suspended in his seat belt, he saw the rush of gutter water surge towards him across the bonnet, followed by the approach of the yellow-painted edge of the kerb with its overhanging fringe of grass, each muddy green blade sharp and distinct. Then came the cracked cement of the pavement, with a crumpled crisp bag, bright blue and red, lying on it.

The bag caught in the edge of the windscreen.

He stared at it.

Read the words 'Ready-salted'.

It was all so *clear*.

And then they hit the tree.

TWO

DETECTIVE SERGEANT TIM NIGHTINGALE STOOD with his
back to the window. Outside, a chilly late October rain was
curtaining across the overgrown rear garden of the house,
pushed by a fitful wind. He felt an annoying draft on the
back of his neck, and moved to one side. The room was
cold, and growing steadily colder. That might discomfit a
junior investigating officer from the CID, but it didn't
matter any more to its owner.

The old man was dead.

A limp wing of grey hair had fallen forward, obscuring
the upper part of his face, and below it the jaw had
drooped slightly sideways, giving a sardonic twist to the
otherwise blank expression. He lay curled on the floor,
making a comma beside the easy chair, his thin body
curving around a bouquet of flowers still visible on the
worn and faded carpet. His head was tipped forward, his
hands caught between his knees as if to warm them. A pipe
weighted the drooping pocket of his beige cardigan, and
some shreds of carefully hoarded tobacco had escaped
from a brown plastic pouch, trickling slowly out to make a
tiny pyramid on the floor.

Cartwright, the police surgeon, knelt next to the body.
He was a burly man who always seemed on the verge of
bursting out of his clothes, and his present position
emphasized the unequal struggle between burgeoning
flesh and grey gabardine. Beside him the local GP, a
neatly-dressed Pakistani, was like an exotic exclamation
mark, dark and thin and tense with impatience. It was past
time for morning surgery, and his usual partner was on
holiday, so the patients had been left to the ministrations

of a rather young and inexperienced locum. But he hadn't been happy about certifying death – hence Cartwright's presence. The tension between them was obvious.

The rush of traffic in the road beyond the walled garden was like a mechanical estuary, ebbing and flowing with the change of lights at the corner. It had been raining all night, and the passage of tyres through the puddles made admonitory whispers that filtered into the room, so that the two medical men unconsciously lowered their voices in deference to what seemed like municipal disapproval.

Despite his apparent calm, Tim Nightingale was eagerly waiting for the verdict concerning the cause of death of one Ivor Peters, first floor on the right, 78 Morstan Gardens, London W11. It was a large bedsitter, but even so it was crowded by its contents. A full-sized double bed with carved mahogany head and footboards stood in one corner and beside it a matching double wardrobe. The bed was neatly made up with a duvet, the contrast between Victorian and modern made even stronger by the pattern on its cover – a subdued tribute to Mondrian in blocks of brown, black and tan. One corner of the large room had been fitted out as a kitchen. On the sink lay a plate, some cutlery, a grillpan and a saucepan, washed and left to dry. A tea-towel was neatly folded over the ladder-back chair that stood with its rush seat tucked under a round mahogany table. In one corner was a large roll-top desk, so stacked with papers and notebooks that there seemed little room left for actual use. All the furniture spoke of having been culled from a larger house. The room was very clean, and its curtains and carpet were of excellent quality but worn and faded – like their owner.

While waiting for the two acolytes of Hippocrates to come to judgement, Nightingale had been trying to deduce the man from the room, looking for clues to Peters' life and death in the objects that surrounded him. It was something he did whenever the opportunity presented itself, trying to train his powers of observation and deduction. He had been in plainclothes for just a few weeks, and so far had done absolutely nothing to deserve

4

the title of 'detective', except pass his qualifying exams and find the shortest way to New Scotland Yard from his tiny flat in Putney.

He was tall and angular, with light brown hair, dark eyes, and a serious mouth not easily given to laughter, although he had a wry, dry sense of humour. Under his wool-lined mac he wore – as casually as possible – a new outfit of grey flannels and tweed jacket. He had tried leaving the jacket under the mattress at night and bashing it against the door of his wardrobe several times before putting it on each morning, but it remained stiff and unyielding, betraying both its recent purchase and his own lack of confidence. He had decided that on his next day off he was going along to the Oxfam shop to find something more lived-in. No suspect was going to be intimidated by such a newly-emergent detective, pegged out to dry in new clothes and naïveté. You had to obtain authority where you could, these days, and he was convinced it lay in a casual air of having been on the scene for years. Of not caring whether he lived or died one day or had his shoulder cried on the next.

Being a detective was important to him – it was one of the reasons he had joined the police in the first place, and everything he'd done from the moment he'd joined was to reach that end. Now here he was, at the scene of a sudden, unexplained death, ready to be brilliant in the unlikely event that someone asked his opinion. He continued his surveillance of the room.

The difficulty with his secret practice of Holmesian exercises was that he had few opportunities to verify his conclusions, so he kept them simple. The late Mr Peters had served in a uniformed capacity at one time – from his age probably World War Two – for both he and his surroundings were impeccably maintained and each item gave the impression of being aligned precisely for inspection. He had been a man of intelligence – the bookshelves were well-filled with books that looked as if they had been read and reread, and a chess board with a game in progress sat on a low table in front of the cold electric fire. Peters had been married and had fathered at least two children – photographs on the mantelpiece. He'd been a methodical man – witness the orderly if crowded desk, the very particular arrangement of tins and other items in the kitchen area, and the neatly ticked-off television page of the previous day's *Evening Standard* (he liked thrillers, wildlife programmes, and had heavily underlined the entry for a police documentary series). Perhaps he'd been a birdwatcher (the nature programmes), or a voyeur – there was a pair of binoculars by a rear window. He wore false teeth (denture powder on the shelf above the basin), which gave him trouble (soft foods dominated his store cupboard and refrigerator), and was a little vain (a tube of hair cream and a bottle of expensive after-shave sat beside the denture powder). He was reflective and quiet by nature – no bright colours in furnishings or wardrobe, not even a red tie kept for Christmas. He'd suffered from insomnia and migraines – both prescription and proprietary medicine bottles were crowded onto the table by the bed.

Nightingale noticed a framed certificate of some kind on the wall above the desk, and moved over to read it. As he did, Cartwright stood up. 'Natural causes,' he announced. 'Myocardial infarction, probably.'

For a moment the local GP looked as if he still might argue the point. His skin darkened slightly from either annoyance or embarrassment, but Cartwright's official presence looming above him, massive with the weight of experience, carried the day. He pressed his lips together, nodded, sprang to his feet, signed the appropriate form, and started out of the room to return to his waiting surgery.

'Excuse me, doctor,' Nightingale said.

The man turned. 'Yes?'

'Was it you who prescribed the sleeping capsules for Mr Peters?' Nightingale asked.

'Yes, he was my patient.'

'Had he been using them for a long time?'

'Oh, no – this trouble was recent. He witnessed a road accident some months ago, and it rather upset him. He was not eating or sleeping well. I prescribed only mild sedatives, of course, nothing addictive.' He did glance at Cartwright, then. 'No barbiturates,' he said, firmly.

'Because of his heart condition?'

There was a flash of something in the doctor's eyes, and he very obviously stopped himself from glancing towards Cartwright again. His chin lifted, but he spoke in an even tone. 'He had no previous indication of any heart condition,' he said, carefully. 'Aside from his migraines, from which he had suffered all his life, Mr Peters was a relatively healthy man for his age. Time was beginning to tell, of course, the little problems of digestion, fatigue, and so on. He had arthritis in the knees and hips, quite painful but not requiring surgery yet, and a troublesome bunion for which we have been awaiting a hospital appointment, but no overt indications of heart illness or circulatory problems.'

'I see. Thank you.'

'Not at all,' the doctor said, politely, and left.

Cartwright gazed at Nightingale with some disapproval. 'What was that all about, then?' he asked.

Nightingale shrugged. 'I wondered why he had hesitated to give the certificate, that's all.'

'Didn't want the responsibility,' Cartwright snapped.

'Mmmmmmm.' The fact that the GP had stayed on indicated otherwise, but there was no point in arguing with Cartwright. He was a truculent man who made up his mind and that was the end of the matter. Nightingale indicated the certificate on the wall. 'Mr Peters was one of ours.'

Cartwright scowled. 'What do you mean?'

'Metropolitan Police – retired as a sergeant in 1965, did the full thirty.'

'Hence the crooked knees and the bunion, no doubt,' Cartwright growled. 'Well, he died peacefully enough. Not bashed by a drunken lout or shot by some bankrobbing villain. Just look at the lips and fingertips. Heart failure – which is what it all comes down to, in the end.'

'Heart failure,' Nightingale echoed. So there would be no need to ask the Chief Inspector to call in the Scene of Crime team, after all, or to set up an Incident Room, or to

7

prepare statements for the Press. While he wished violence on no-one, certainly not on what appeared to be a blameless old man, there was no denying the disappointment in his voice.

'That's it. Last night, obviously. Rigor is established, but he was in his late seventies, rather undernourished, and probably hypothermic, judging by the temperature in this room.' Cartwright shivered and glared at the rather splendid electric fire which they had found switched on but cold. It had apparently gone off sometime during the night, when the money in the meter ran out. 'Unless I find something extraordinary in the autopsy, I still say it was just a matter of his heart giving out. It happens.' He was gathering his things together, snapping his bag shut.

'He seemed — '

'Damn it, hearts stop when they stop. They don't always blow whistles and send up flares ahead of time. No history of heart disease doesn't mean a damn thing. It just stopped. All right?' Cartwright was getting cross.

'Then why were *we* called in?' Nightingale asked.

'The landlady got over-excited,' said a bland voice from the door. Detective Chief Inspector Abbott had returned from interviewing the lady in question. 'She says the old man had a visitor last night. This morning she noticed he hadn't come downstairs for his milk, so she sent someone up with it. When they found Mr Peters like that, she immediately decided his mysterious visitor had murdered him, and dialled 999.' He grimaced. 'She watches a lot of television.'

'Does she know who this visitor was?' Tim asked.

'No. The front door is left unlatched until eleven at night, apparently, so the tenants can have visitors as and when they like. Although the rooms are bedsitters, there's no system for separate bells. There should have been, but her late husband never got around to it. Hence the open door policy.'

'Dicey,' Nightingale observed.

'Well, she has arthritis and claims she can't be bothered to get up and down all evening to let people in and out,' Abbott said. He had the knack of mimicry, and for a moment the old lady seemed to be in the room with them, creaky and exasperated by life's unfair demands. Abbott went on. 'She heard the door open, heard footsteps going up the stairs, heard them again going down the stairs about twenty minutes later, but she was watching *Coronation Street* and didn't bother to look out. She heard voices overhead in the old man's room – that's why she realized it was he who had the visitor. She says the voices were loud and she had to turn up the sound on her television, but doesn't think there was an argument. It was just that Peters was rather deaf.'

'Man or woman's voice?'

'Man's. She's absolutely certain about that.'

'Anybody else in the house hear anything?'

'There are only four bedsitters in the house, two on each floor. There's a basement flat, but it has a totally separate entrance. A middle-aged couple live there in exchange for doing the cleaning, maintenance and so on. The woman also shops for the landlady, who can't get out. She's the one who found Peters dead, but she claims she and her husband heard nothing unusual during the evening. The other room on this floor is empty at the moment, being redecorated. The two lodgers above on the third were both out. Peters and the old lady were the only two people in the house itself at the time.'

'And this didn't worry her?'

'She says it's often like that, and claims she's not bothered, but I think it does frighten her.'

'It should. This isn't the most salubrious of neighbourhoods.'

'No. But they get like that in the city, don't they? Either they put on ten locks, five steel bolts, and a drop-bar, sit shivering in their shoes expecting to be throttled at any moment, and then die because the firemen or the ambulance men can't get to them in time. Or they leave everything wide open because they can't be bothered. She's the last kind, partly because she's naturally bolshie, mostly because she's so disabled by the arthritis.'

'And what was Peters like?'

'I gather he was a reasonable old man, "very brainy",' she said.'

9

'He retired from the Met in sixty-five,' Nightingale said, again indicating the framed certificate. 'Sergeant.'

'Really?' Abbott said, going over to look for himself. 'Well, what do you know? I suppose we'd better notify somebody about it, then. They usually like to do something in the way of a memorial – flowers, representation at the funeral, that kind of thing.' He made a note in his book.

'Did the landlady say anything else about him?'

Abbott shook his head. 'She says his daughter was always after him to come and live with her, but he liked keeping his own hours, doing his own thing. He'd lived in the area all his life, and he felt comfortable here, even though it had changed so much. And he was fussy about his food, claimed the daughter's cooking was full of garlic and what he called "twigs". Herbs, I guess he meant. So he lived here and cooked for himself and watched his television and read and met his friends at the local day centre and generally was pretty happy, she said. Or had been until a few months ago. She finally admitted Peters had been unwell lately, not eating or looking after himself properly. Seemed to feel she should have done something about it, but hadn't. She said he'd been like that since the accident,' Abbott said, gazing down at the old man.

Tim frowned. 'The doctor said something about that.'

Cartwright stirred. He'd been waiting for an opportunity to interrupt Abbott's flow of words. 'Self-neglect,' he observed, brusquely. 'The old story. I see it every day. Delayed shock is more than enough to finish a man his age. Sudden shock even more so. But he certainly wasn't murdered,' Cartwright said, firmly. He picked up his hat and clapped it on his head. 'I'm finished here. You'll have to hang on until they come for the body, I'm afraid. I've got another elderly unattended death waiting in Ealing. God, I hate winter.' He left them to it.

'Did the old man have many visitors?' Tim asked Abbott.

'His daughter, two or three times a week, sometimes a friend from the local old people's day centre came around to play chess,' Abbott said, putting his notebook away. 'I expect that's who it was, last night. I took his name, but there's not much point.'

10

'We could go and ask him, just to round things off,' Nightingale said, eagerly.

Abbott shook his head. 'You heard him. Natural causes. That's it as far as we're concerned. No crime, no investigation.'

Nightingale nodded and looked down at the old man. 'We can't just leave him there like that,' he said.

Abbott looked, too. 'Because he was one of us, you mean?'

'I don't know,' Tim said, uneasily. 'It just doesn't seem right.'

'It never ceases to amaze me that you young ones still have some kind of cock-eyed romantic notion about the Job,' Abbott said. 'I understand you've done three years uniformed in some of the roughest districts, you've been beaten up twice and stabbed once, you were even assigned to football crowd control for three months to knock the stars out of your eyes, and still you think there's something splendid about being a copper.' He looked at Nightingale and Nightingale looked back at him. Abbott wasn't fooling him any more than he was fooling himself. This was a lecture from Abbott's mouth, not his heart.

Tim knew Abbott had been temporarily seconded back to the Met from the West Country, and was not happy about it. Tim, too, had been born to fields and hedgerows, and found the gritty grind of metropolitan life both confining and depressing. They shared that bond – but it was stretched thinly across the chasm of rank.

Tim had heard through the grapevine that Abbott was a good detective and a fair-minded man, but he and the other more junior officers had had to take that on trust. Ever since he'd arrived in London, Abbott had been short-tempered and ill at ease. It had been many years since the chief inspector had served in the Met – years he had thankfully put behind him. While he'd been endeavouring to re-assume the hard manner that armoured the city police, it was a cloak that did not settle easily on his shoulders.

'Oh, hell, come on,' Abbott said, impatiently. Together they picked up the thin, fragile body and carried it to the

11

bed. Rigor had set in, so they couldn't make him look more comfortable, but they laid him gently on his side and drew the duvet over him.

'The daughter will be coming, soon,' Abbott said, as if to explain why they should have done this simple, decent thing.

'I guess it doesn't take much when you're old and alone,' Tim said, softly. He looked down at the small mound under the duvet, and suddenly felt sad. He knew nothing about this old man, and yet was an official witness to his end. He'd had a family, a career, a life of nearly eighty years, and yet he'd died alone, with no-one to hear his final testament. It seemed unfair. Tim had an irrational desire to wake the old man up, ask him to talk about all the things he had seen and been and done, so they wouldn't be lost for ever.

But it was too late for that, now. And it was not the kind of attitude encouraged in a detective sergeant of the Metropolitan Police. Sentimentality was allowed, off-duty, but there were too many sad stories in London – and everywhere else – for him to spend the limited coinage of his emotions on every one. Save it for a rainy day, he told himself. For a dead child or a lost dog. At least Mr Ivor Peters had done it his way. Not so terrible, dying in your own home, even if it is on the floor with your pipe unsmoked. Better than in some institution, propped up in a nodding circle.

'I have to get back to the station,' Abbott said, glancing at his watch. He turned. 'Do you mind hanging on here until they come for him?'

'No,' Tim said, truthfully. 'That's fine.'

'Right.' Abbott headed for the door, slowed, then turned to look at his new sergeant with some curiosity. 'Why does your willingness to perform this lowly duty worry me?' he asked.

Tim smiled and shrugged. 'I have no idea,' he said.

Abbott continued to look at him with a raised eyebrow. 'It was natural causes,' he said, pointedly.

'Of course,' Nightingale agreed, blandly. 'Natural causes.'

12

Abbott stared at him a moment longer, then went out, just managing to hide the smile that came unbidden and unwelcome. As if he'd heard it announced, he knew what Nightingale was thinking. He knew how hungry he was to find 'his' first good case. But policing was a team effort, and a solitary explorer often stumbled into areas that weren't friendly to intruders. Nightingale's curiosity was something that *could* lead to trouble, and Abbott knew he should have ordered him away from the scene, assigned him quickly to something else, and finished it.

He clattered down the stairs, shaking his head. It probably wouldn't make any difference. And he felt no loyalty to the Met any more. The whole secondment had been a mistake, some Home Office psychologist's bright idea, no doubt, and he resented it deeply. The DCI who had changed places with him had been on the phone regularly, complaining. They were both out of place and functioning badly as a result. The hell with it, just put in your time and go through the motions, he told himself. Only another four months to go in London, and then you can go back to the Cotswolds, where you belong. You understand the people there, and they understand you. Nightingale's hopes and ambitions aren't really your problem.

Abbott opened the door and went out into the bluster of the day, lifting his face to the stink of exhaust fumes and the wet slap of the rain. God, he thought, for ten pence I'd just turn west and keep walking. The rain is soft there, and the wind smells of cut grass and woodsmoke. He teetered for a moment, imagining he could do that, pretending it was a real possibility, a matter of simple choice. Then he turned up his coat collar and climbed into the waiting police car.

As soon as he heard the downstairs door slam shut, Nightingale was across the room. He pulled out the swivel chair and seated himself in front of the cluttered roll-top desk.

He was still there half an hour later when the woman from the basement flat appeared in the doorway, bearing a tray. 'Mrs Finch says would you like a cup of tea while

13

you're waiting?' she asked, nervously, trying not to look at the bed and its forever silent occupant.

Tim smiled. 'Thank you,' he said, clearing a fresh space on the desk. 'That would be very welcome.'

keep her voice steady, but achieving only the predictable flutes and wavers of an adolescent boy. She cleared her throat and tried again. 'He had a cold a few weeks ago, but it seemed just the ordinary — ' Her voice seized, suddenly grown too large for her throat. 'The doctor says — ' She couldn't go on, decided not even to try, and gestured helplessly.

'Come outside for a moment,' Richard suggested.

The corridor was long and impersonal, with pale green walls and scuffed mock-marble linoleum. Benches were spaced along it at regular intervals, and nurses with rubber-soled shoes squeaked past carrying trays and bowls and mysteriously-shrouded objects. In the distance a trolley rattled, and someone laughed, the sound strangely distorted and somehow out of place. Richard sat down, took Tess's hand in his, and patted it awkwardly. 'Take a deep breath and then tell me all about it.'

She took the deep breath, and retrieved her hand. 'They're giving him antibiotics and other drugs, apparently, which will overcome the initial infection in a few days. There's no reason to think that he won't get through it all right – he's always been a very fit little boy. But . . . but . . . there may be heart damage.' She stopped for a moment, kept control, and went on. 'If he's very unlucky he may even have to have operations later on —' valve replacements . . . She felt the tears coming, tears she had held back before. Damn it. Stop this at once, she ordered. But it was no good. Old habits die hard, even when kicked hard, and knowing someone else was there to share the burden betrayed her into the old familiar reactions.

Her late husband's will had named Richard as co-guardian, so it had been only polite to notify him that Max was ill, but she had never expected him to appear like this.

Any more than she had expected to start crying.

Sit up, she commanded. Behave yourself.

But the troops were rebellious.

Damn. *Damn.*

When she eventually lifted her drooping head, she saw Richard deep in conversation with the doctor. She cleared her throat, and they both turned. 'Feeling better?' Richard smiled.

Don't patronize me, she thought. And smiled back. 'Fine, thanks,' she said.

His tone had implied failure on her part. Well, it hadn't been a faint, or anything like it. Just a moment of quiet reflection, that's all. A little rest, a gathering of loose threads, nothing more. What could have happened of importance in the world during those few minutes? What had she missed? Probably nothing at all.

Richard really did look concerned, and she felt momentarily ashamed of her resentment, but she was cross at him for rushing up here like some self-appointed knight in armour. She wanted to face this alone. It was so much easier to control yourself among strangers. Friends supplied too many excuses to the weak of will.

The consultant had glanced at the clock on the wall as covertly as possible, but it was obvious he had other things to do. 'Do you feel well enough to discuss Max's prognosis now?' he asked, tentatively.

'Yes,' Tess said, firmly. 'I want to know exactly where we are.'

The consultant nodded, approvingly, and came over to sit beside her. He had blue eyes, and one wayward grey hair curling out of his left sideburn, like a cat's whisker, giving the impression he was listening in to other worlds, receiving other messages. But his glance was direct and his voice was perfectly, wonderfully calm. 'A good convalescence will make all the difference to Max. A matter of damage limitation, I suppose you could say.' He carefully explained exactly what rheumatic fever was, how he would be treating Max for it, and what would be needed, once the crisis had passed.

Richard scowled when it came to the details of the boy's convalescence. 'That may not be as simple as it sounds. Tess is a widow on her own. She has a career as an interior designer and can't nurse Max during the day. Naturally, Max should have the best possible care, and I'll be glad to arrange it. If you could recommend a suitable nursing home, I'll — '

17

Tess interrupted, in a voice perhaps more icy than she intended. 'That's a very kind offer, Richard, but once Dr Shaw says Max can leave hospital, he's coming *home*. He's my son, not a parcel to be posted off to strangers.'

Richard had flushed at her rebuke. 'You try to do too much, Tess,' he said, impatiently. 'I wish you'd let me help you more, take some of the burden from your shoulders.'

It was a point of honour with him, as much as anything. Richard Hendricks had been her husband's business partner in what had been a most successful international public relations firm. But after Roger had been killed in that horrible car crash, it immediately became apparent that most of the company's success had stemmed from his brilliant creative abilities. Richard Hendricks' business expertise alone hadn't been enough to hang on to their clients – in PR it was ideas that counted. He'd practically wept when he'd had to tell her that the business was going to be wound up, and there would be almost no money from it for her and Max.

'I know you want to help, and I appreciate it,' she continued, using almost the same words she had used then. And almost the same mixture of feelings rose in her as she looked at his anxious, familiar face. Damn it, why did he have to look so worried? Why didn't he and everyone else just leave her alone to get *on* with things? Guilt, her constant companion these days, came to sit beside her.

It was Roger's fault, of course.

Blithe spirit, lately flown.

Oh, he'd made a will.

Once. When drunk. On a form from the stationers.

Everything to my dear wife.

Including all the responsibilities.

She had developed an inexpressible rage towards her late husband in the weeks following his death. As a grieving widow, how could she admit that, as each new problem presented itself, her secret anger grew at his intransigence, his grasshopper views on finance, his refusal to worry about tomorrow, his selfish determination to 'live for today', his casual assumption that he could take care of everything, manage anything, and would be around to do it for ever.

Because in the end – he wasn't.

It was true that when he died, the mortgage had automatically been paid off. For that she was undoubtedly indebted to some anonymous stranger at their building society rather than Roger himself. There proved to be two life insurance policies in Roger's desk. One, very small, had been taken out when he was still a student and subsequently left to the vagaries of the standing order system. It had barely covered the funeral expenses and their outstanding bills.

The other insurance policy had been taken out the day Max was born – to pay his school fees at Roger's old school. A typical Roger gesture. But fees were only the beginning. When Roger had won a place there, his parents had gone without so that he could dress well, take part in sports, go on school trips, and generally keep up appearances with the other boys. She'd been trying to do the same for Max, for he loved the school and would undoubtedly want to go back when he was better.

Tess had lived in England for fourteen years, but she had been born and brought up in Amity, Iowa, and her conscience was still nagged by stringent, contrary Iowa standards. Because she was an American, everything in her rebelled at the thought of élitist education. Equally, because she was American, something in her was impressed by traditional ways. And, because she was a mother, she conceded the undoubted advantages such an education gave to *her* child as he progressed from snotty-nosed schoolboy to future prime minister.

But, lately, she'd been losing both the moral and the financial battle.

'As a matter of fact, I'd been wondering whether I was right to send Max back to school so soon after his father's death,' Tess said, lifting her chin and keeping her voice firm. 'His housemaster has written to me several times about his nightmares. He's been very unsettled this term.' She thought of Max's face, flushed and small on the pillow, his mouse-brown hair clinging damply to his forehead. Damn it, Max was her *son*.

'Well, we'll want to keep him here for at least ten days – perhaps a couple of weeks. A matter of assessing damage, if there is any. I'm hopeful there won't be,' the doctor concluded. 'But this rather long convalescence afterwards is vital, I'm afraid. No question of his returning to school for quite a while. I expect he'll require tutoring as well as nursing if he isn't to fall behind.' He glanced at Tess and smiled. 'But I'm sure you'll manage to work it all out, Mrs Leland. You look a very capable young woman. I'll look back in on Max later this evening.' He nodded and smiled to them both, then hurried off down the corridor.

Richard watched him go, then turned. 'There's an answer to all this, Tess.'

'Only one?' she asked, and tried a shaky laugh that didn't quite come off.

'Only one that makes sense.'

She stared at him, wearily. 'No, Richard.'

'Tess, if you married me, you could give up work, stay at home, make sure Max was properly looked after.' He flushed, slightly. 'And you know I wouldn't pressure you about – anything. But I do care for you, and I'd do all I could to make you happy — '

'We've been over all this so many times,' she protested.

'Yes, I know. I was willing to let it ride for a while — '

'Decent of you, old thing.'

He grinned, suddenly, engagingly. 'Circumstances have changed, Tess. Even you can see that.'

'You mean even without my glasses?' She had to smile at him, the successful businessman who could never pass up a chance to make a sale, puppy enthusiasm contained by a firm jaw and handshake. Here is my product, he said, standing tall in his Gieves & Hawkes suit, Turnbull & Asser shirt, and Church brogues. How can you resist?

At first he'd left her alone with her grief, but lately he'd begun calling round, taking her out to concerts and plays, even going up to the school to visit Max. She hadn't known whether his attentions were out of love, kindness, or pity – and she still didn't. But, as appealing as he could be, she knew marrying him was no answer, not as far as she was concerned.

Not now, anyway.

Eleven years of being financially and emotionally dependent, of letting Roger make all the decisions, of playing the game of Letting Daddy Look After Me, had nearly proved her undoing. Because it was what Roger had wanted, because it fitted in with his self-image, she had adopted the rapidly-dating guise of a proper Englishwoman. She'd done the charity round, been a lady of leisure, a white-gloved drone, played the rôle of the successful Roger Leland's wife.

Then, without warning, she'd become Roger Leland's widow.

His death made her realize what she had forsworn, and lost – herself. For some days after the accident, she'd felt boneless, foolish, and weak. But, in the twenty minutes between leaving the limousine at the door of the crematorium and re-entering it to be driven home, she had made a resolution. She could – and would – take charge of her life again.

It had been hard, so much harder than even she had suspected, but gradually, doggedly, she had sorted, compartmentalized, organized her life and got it running again. Not smoothly, not always easily, but under control.

There had been, unfortunately, no compartment set aside for a seriously ill child. Measles or mumps she could have coped with, but this was more. She had a responsibility to herself, true, but an even bigger one to Max. Wouldn't it make sense to marry Richard? He was attractive and kind, and could provide them with a good life. Physical passion might arrive later, but its absence could well be a plus. Stability, in the upright and wonderfully English form of Richard Hendricks, beckoned her.

'You're very kind, Richard —' she began, but he held up his hand.

'That still sounds too much like a refusal. If so, I don't want to hear it.' He smiled his gentlest smile, and she detected definite signs of wavering within. No, she told herself. No.

'Look, Tess, I care for you very much.' He cleared his

throat and glanced up and down the corridor. 'More than I can say standing here.' He touched her hand, ran a finger over her wrist and into her palm. 'I have to go to Paris tonight, and I'll be away for some time. You concentrate on Max, because he needs you. But whenever you have a moment, think about marrying me. Just . . . consider it. All right?'

'All right,' she said. 'But no promises.' He squeezed her hand and Tess shivered – it was cool in the corridor. She got to her feet abruptly, despite Richard's anxious protest that she should rest a while longer, and hurried back to Max's room. Something felt wrong, suddenly.

Richard followed, and as they stood by the bedside Max half opened his eyes and gave a sudden whimper. He was only semi-conscious, and he stared at the wall behind Richard with a kind of horror, as if he saw something there, something awful.

'No, I won't. I can't. Dad? Dad – please don't go away, Daddy – please – you said you'll tell me what to do – please, come back . . . oh, please . . . I don't want to be bad . . .' Max's voice, which had risen practically to a shout, faded to a whimper, and then his eyes closed again.

'What was all that?' Richard wanted to know. His face was pale and he looked shocked. It had taken an effort of will not to turn around and look at the wall, so realistic had been Max's fear.

'Probably just the fever,' Tess said, unsteadily. She, too, had been unnerved by the passion in her young son's voice. 'It sounded like the nightmares his housemaster described. Apparently, they're always about the accident. He seems to feel some kind of guilt, I don't know why.' She leaned down. 'Max,' she whispered. 'It's all right. Mummy's here, darling. Everything's going to be just *fine*.' Max moved restlessly under the layers of white cellular blankets, and turned his head away.

She patted his hand, smoothed his cheek.

He knows I'm lying, she thought.

And so do I.

FOUR

'BUT, ADRIAN, THERE'S NO OTHER WAY,' Tess said, a few days later. She stood in the middle of the workroom, hands on hips, glaring at her boss. 'It's not just that Max needs care, he'll need to keep up with his schooling, too. An au pair would be useless when it came to lessons. I'll simply have to turn Mrs McMurdo's work over to you and — '

'Not me, love. The bloody woman makes me break out in hives,' Adrian Brevitt said, and gave an elaborate shiver. He picked up a block of damask samples and began flipping through them, while keeping a corner of his eye on her. 'Anyway, she specified you, remember? This is your big chance to make your name. And mine. I want Brevitt Interiors to rise right to the top. I'm not ready *just* yet to dodder off to my little cottage and rose garden.'

Tess had to smile, despite her problems. The image of elegant, fastidious Adrian Brevitt forking manure into the rosebeds was ludicrous in the extreme. He could never stray more than a mile from Mayfair without coming over faint.

'Adrian, you know how grateful I am. You were more than kind to take me back when Roger died, but — '

Adrian put the damask down with a thump. 'It had nothing to do with kindness and you know it,' he huffed. 'You needed me, and – after Jason's *treacherous* defection – I needed you. It might have been a coincidence, but it was a very happy one as far as you and I are concerned. Now that I have you back, I do not intend to let anything – not even the sickroom requirements of my beloved and precious godson – take you away from me without a fight.

23

Frankly, my dear, I *do* give a damn. We need the work to survive, and we need you in order to *do* the blasted work. You have a cachet, Tess – you're American. That's instant rapport for a lot of our expatriate and foreign clients.'

'And instant turn-off for others,' Tess reminded him, wryly.

'Well, there aren't many landed gentry left who can afford my prices,' Adrian sniffed. 'Anyway, of course we can manage your *smaller* assignments while you're staying with Max at the hospital, no trouble there, but *not* Mrs McMurdo. There must be a way around it, Tess. After all, we do have a little time.'

That was true enough, Tess acknowledged reluctantly. Mrs McMurdo, a wealthy Australian widow, had recently returned to 'the old country' to inspect her husband's 'heritage'. She had found it to be a rambling and nearly derelict Victorian house which sat in the midst of its overgrown garden like a huge toad, a warty and crumbling eyesore in a newly-gentrified area of London.

Perversely, Mrs McMurdo had fallen in love with the place. She decided to 'restore it to its former glory' as a tribute to her beloved husband's family, and she swept into the project with vigour.

Of course, nothing but the best would do. She made enquiries and appeared one day in the studio of Brevitt Interiors. After ten minutes of loud and cheerful conversation, she decided that Tess and only Tess was right for the task of restoring The House.

Glad of something which would absorb her and her grief, Tess had set to work. Rather like the man scheduled to hang in the morning, the task of restoring the McMurdo house concentrated her mind wonderfully. She had gone far beyond the remit normally given to decorators and, along with their usual consultant architect, was overseeing the physical reconstruction as well. This was due to be completed in another month, at which time she would be free to bring her magic to bear on the interior. Given a free hand and a generous working budget, it was – or could have been – her big chance. But the situation had changed.

She followed Adrian as he tried to avoid the issue by walking around the studio. 'Well, Mrs Grimble could hardly handle teaching Max, could she? The nursing would be hard enough what with running up and down the stairs fifty times a day, and her own health is delicate.' Mrs Grimble had been with Tess since before Max was born. She was eccentric, nosey, and opinionated. Tess put up with all her odd ways because by now she was the only one who knew how to find anything in the house.

'You mean her alcoholic level is variable,' Adrian sniffed.

'Don't be so damn snooty. She's been very good to me. She put up with Roger and — '

'And Roger put up with her, I imagine. Darling, the woman is a jewel – when she's sober. I quite agree that she's not exactly ideal to either look after or tutor Max. But neither are you. You don't understand the British way of education — '

'Very few do.'

He refused to be side-tracked. 'You haven't the patience to teach, and you're far more valuable elsewhere. Specifically, *here*.' He glanced at her sideways as he leant over a drawing pad and sketched in, quickly, another window treatment for a luxury houseboat he was redoing.

'I *could* take Max back to Iowa,' she said, slowly.

Adrian shuddered delicately. 'I shall ignore that,' he said, tearing off one page and starting another. 'There *are* other things coming along, you know, things you don't know about yet. When the McMurdo job is finished it will definitely get publicity for you. And us.' He flicked the pen over the paper and stood back slightly to see the effect. 'Get enough new commissions on the strength of it – and you will – and you'll be in a position to call your own tune, Tess. I might *even* be stretched to consider a partnership, one day.'

Tess stood watching him for a moment. She had known Adrian Brevitt for years, and found him now, as always, to be both exasperating and engaging. He was playing his high cards – something he rarely did – simply in order to keep her. She was flattered, and also tempted to kick him up his beautifully-tailored backside. Partnership, indeed. 'Richard has asked me to marry him,' she blurted out, as if in confirmation of his assessment concerning her intrinsic value.

'You're not accepting, of course.' It was a statement, not a question. He put his pen down and turned to face her, arms folded.

'I'm thinking about it,' Tess hedged. 'I know he's been lonely since his wife died some years ago and — '

'Ridiculous. I won't allow it. He's ten years older than you, and he'd never have time for you or for Max. He's one of those "go-getters" the media are always on about, thrusting and pushing and shoving and grabbing. Besides, he has absolutely *terrible* taste. I went to dinner there once with you and Roger, remember? The dining room wallpaper gave me indigestion for *weeks* afterwards.'

'Perhaps his wife chose it.'

'No, he did. He absolutely *bragged* about it. If it hadn't been for you and Roger, I would have quite happily peed on it just to force him to redecorate.'

Tess had to laugh, Adrian really was outrageous when he put his mind to it. The fact that he had a very firm grasp of the practicalities of plumbing as well as the lure of interior couture contributed to his success, of course, but it was the irrepressible and mischievous side of Adrian Brevitt that people remembered, and talked about. He was never cruel and always discreet when it was required, but he never left an inflated ego unpunctured, or a room unnoticed. Privately and recently, Tess had discovered that though he might try to hide it from public view, he was a solid and dependable friend in need.

He was also stubborn.

'What about that ethereal creature who lodges with you?' he asked abruptly. 'Couldn't she do bed-baths or geometry?'

'Miranda? She's drifted off to warmer climes with her latest boyfriend. He's "something" in movies, but I'm not sure what.'

She perched on a stool beside the drawing-board and hugged her knees. Some years ago, glorying in an

26

unexpected windfall from a grateful client, Roger had had the attic of their large terraced house converted into a studio. He said it would give him a place to work, provide extra guest accommodation, and increase the resale value of the house. The latter possibility was yet to be tested. Due to Roger's penchant for bringing home lame ducks and the walking wounded, they'd suffered a strange procession of visitors in the studio. Miranda had only been the last in a long line of non-paying guests. As for working up there – he'd used it only for designing and building conference displays too large for the office and, twice, too large to get down the stairs. Dear, fascinating, exasperating Roger. If only she'd smiled at him when he'd driven off that morning . . .

She sighed for all the might-have-beens. 'There's really only one way out of all this, Adrian, and that's for me to quit my job, sell the house as quickly as possible, buy a small flat, and live off the difference. I'll look after Max myself. I'll learn to be patient. I'll enjoy it.'

'Balls,' he said, uncompromisingly.

She went on, doggedly. 'Later, when Max is better and goes back to school, perhaps you'll have me back? I hope someone will.'

'You're assuming, I see, that I'll still be in business,' Adrian said in an irritated tone. 'Tess, the McMurdo thing is our first showpiece since Jason left. If you go, dear Dolly may well go, too, probably straight to Jason.' His voice cracked, slightly, and he walked away across the room, the very line of his shoulders shrieking perfidy, perfidy!

'Nonsense,' Tess said, weakly, but she knew it was true, which just gave her more to feel guilty about. Adrian spoke from across the room, where he now stood gazing moodily out of the window into the stylish depths of Knightsbridge.

'I'm accustomed to getting my own way, you know,' he said. 'I shall think of something, Tess, my love – never fear.'

And he did.

FIVE

'I THINK YOUR MOTHER WAS frightened by a copy of *Tales From the Round Table*,' Abbott suggested, wryly.

'Maybe. But I want to look into it,' Nightingale insisted. 'I think there's something there.'

'What?'

Nightingale tried to lean back in his chair and found it impossible, the chrome and plastic construction being astutely designed to prevent just such attempts at comfort. 'I think Ivor Peters was frightened to death,' he said.

'Oh?' Abbott raised an eyebrow. 'And under exactly what statute do we find this listed as a crime, pray?'

'None. That's not — ' Tim began.

'None. Correct. You might try to establish a case for Threatening to Kill, if you had a witness. But you don't have a witness. And you don't have any evidence. And he wasn't killed, he just *dropped dead*,' Abbott said, leaning forward and stubbing his forefinger rhythmically on his blotter. 'Cartwright did the autopsy and it was heart failure pure and simple. He uses a lot of medical terminology, of course, but the upshot is the poor old man dropped in his tracks approximately seven hours after consuming his evening meal, which – according to his landlady – was taken with clocklike regularity at six every evening, coincidental with the television news. This puts time of death after midnight, and his visitor had come and gone long before then.' He leaned back and regarded his junior officer with amusement. 'Unless, of course, you're suggesting the existence of some diabolically clever device which produces a delayed BOO and then self-destructs leaving no trace?'

28

Nightingale ignored that and seized on the one thing that seemed pertinent. 'You asked the landlady about his dining habits?' he asked in some surprise.

'Cartwright did.'

'Ah.' Tim seemed gratified.

'I gather Dr Cartwright likes things tidy. He probably got his secretary to ring the old girl up.'

'Oh.'

Abbott leaned back and wriggled slightly – his chair had been designed for a smaller man's comfort. He regarded his fledgling detective sergeant with benign exasperation. He liked Nightingale, he thought he was bright, and probably marginally mad. It was the university training that did it, of course. Abbott had long since decided, from his own experience, that university education merely fined-down craziness from the general to the specific and made it socially functional. Nightingale had taken his degree in history, so there was definitely a touch of the knights-in-armour there.

However, he reminded himself, Nightingale had been a late starter in the Job. Before he'd joined the police he'd been at Lloyds, working as a risk assessor, so he was an odds-on, odds-against man. Which meant he'd thought this through before risking a superior officer's inevitable sarcasm. Even *he* must have realized how crazy it sounded.

'What bothered you?' he prompted.

'The conjunction of the mysterious visitor and the unpredicted heart failure — ' Tim began.

'It was probably his chess-playing chum from the day centre,' Abbott interrupted, impatiently. 'He came around for a game, Peters told him he wasn't feeling up to it, which was hardly surprising seeing he was brewing up a heart attack, and so the friend left.' He saw Nightingale was shaking his head and found himself shaking his own in response. 'No?'

'No. I checked. He always played with one of two men, either Ralph Gleason or a character called Chatty Corcoran. He'd played Chatty that afternoon, and told him that he was spending the evening in front of the box.'

'Well, then — '

29

'He also told him why. He said he was frightened to go out at night.'

'He and I, both. Especially in that neighbourhood.'

'It had never bothered him before. He told Chatty he thought he'd "gone too far" about something, and that if he wasn't careful it was going to come back on him.'

It was Abbott's turn to say, 'Ah.' He said it despite a growing conviction that he was being sent up, and that Nightingale was either playing an elaborate practical joke on him, which seemed very unlike Nightingale, or was cracking up under the strain of trying to be the new Sherlock Holmes, which was possible and probably an indication that a transfer to Traffic was on Nightingale's cards. He'd be sorry to see him go.

'And did he say what it was?' Abbott asked, with some certainty as to what the response would be.

He was proven correct. 'No.'

'Inconvenient.' Abbott looked at his watch.

'But I know what it was.'

Abbott raised an eyebrow. 'I don't remember seeing "clairvoyant" on your personnel file.'

Nightingale grinned. 'It was under Nosey Parker.' He shifted forward in his chair. 'The reason I got on to it was because of what I read in the notebooks,' he said, rather desperately. He knew he had no case, but he wanted to spell it out and he wanted Abbott to listen – if only, perhaps, to help convince himself that what he suspected was worth going on with. Although he'd only seen him pushing papers around and staring out the window, he believed the gossip about the tall man from the West Country. Abbott was supposed to have cracked some really complicated cases, and they said he had the right instincts about people and their behaviour. Maybe he wasn't happy here, and functioning through clenched teeth, but to hold his attention at all might prove something.

'What notebooks?' Abbott demanded.

'On his desk. I looked through a few while I was waiting for them to take the body away,' Tim confessed.

'Oh, dear,' Abbott said. 'Invasion of privacy. I am shocked.'

Nightingale faced him down. 'And I took three away with me,' he said.

Abbott's expression altered. 'And *that* was thieving,' he snapped.

Nightingale sighed. 'I asked the daughter, when she arrived, and she said it was okay.'

'Did you give her an explanation?'

'I said I thought her father had been investigating something criminal, and that I would like to carry on for him.'

'And what did she say to that?

Nightingale shifted in his chair. 'She was a little too upset to say much about anything.'

'In other words, you took advantage,' Abbott said. Now his tone was censorious.

'Only because of what I'd read in the notebooks,' Nightingale said, defensively. 'As far as I could tell, he'd always kept private notes of things he worked on when he was on the Force. He kept up a diary of sorts after he retired, too, but it was mostly reflections, observations, that kind of thing. I got the feeling he was always meaning to write his autobiography, but never got around to it.'

'And so say all of us,' was Abbott's comment. 'James Herriot has a lot to answer for.'

'Yes. Well, the last three notebooks were altogether different – closer to those he'd done while working. He was investigating something in his spare time.'

'My God, a kindred spirit. No wonder you got sucked in,' Abbott said, not unsympathetically.

Nightingale looked injured, but went on quickly. 'It all started with that accident Peters witnessed. He wrote it up very carefully, regulation style. He'd been retired for fourteen years, but his instincts were still sound. According to him, the accident was triggered when he inadvertently stepped out in front of a car that was being pursued by another, causing the first car to swerve abruptly, turn over, and hit a tree, killing the driver. He felt responsible in a way, but he said the *real* culprit was the driver of the second car.'

'Not one of ours in close pursuit?' Abbott said in an alarmed voice. Recent publicity had left everyone sensitive on that subject.

'No. A Ford Fiesta, dark green.'

'Ah.' Relieved, Abbott picked up a pencil and began to rotate it between his right and left hands.

'Yes. Peters jumped back, naturally, and tripped over the curb, so at first he heard more than he saw. The second car screeched to a halt – to help, he assumed. But when he stood up he saw that the driver who had been doing the chasing was actually trying to open the boot of the crashed car instead of seeing if he could help the driver. Peters shouted, and the man ducked back into his own car, and drove off.'

'Drove off?'

'That's right. But Peters got the number, and got an old friend of his in DVL Swansea to put a name to it.'

'Naughty,' Abbott said, rotating the pencil a little faster.

'It was a hire car.'

'It would be.' Abbott sighed and put the pencil down.

'And the person who'd rented it had used a false licence naming him as "John Rochester" with an address in Leeds, gave his current address as the Mount Royal Hotel, and never brought the car back. They finally found it abandoned in the Park Lane underground car park. By that time he'd checked out of the hotel, paying his bill in cash. There had never been anyone named "Rochester" living at the address shown on the driving licence.'

'Life is like that,' Abbott nodded. 'Look, Tim — '

'But Peters kept on. He felt anybody who'd gone to such lengths to hide his true identity must have had something else to hide, too. He thought maybe this "Rochester" had planned to use some kind of accident to cover up murder from the beginning. Anyway, he had time on his hands, didn't he? It bothered him. It ate at him. So, he used his old contacts in the Force to get a look at the Accident Reports. They had it down as Reckless Driving, no mention of a pursuit car from any other witness except Peters, who did report it at the scene. The trouble was nobody else was on the street when it happened, and by the time people did come out to see what the noise was, the other car was gone.'

'A lot of people seem to have come and gone in all this,' Abbott said, standing up and turning his back to look out of the window. On the roof of the next building, a man in a uniform bearing the name of a television rental firm was checking out an aerial. 'For all I know that chap over there is planning to electrocute the next person to turn on his television set. If I ran downstairs and across the street and up the stairs again, he'd be gone, too.'

'Does he look suspicious? Do you think he's up to something?' Nightingale demanded.

Abbott turned. 'Don't be daft,' he said.

'But that's just it. You have a lot of experience, you're trained to spot the unusual, you've developed a sense of what's normal and what's suspicious. Peters was the same. And he couldn't get over the feeling that something was *wrong* about the accident – he says it again and again in his notebooks. He made a pain of himself at the scene. He made them open the boot, but it was empty. I've seen the report myself. The officer who did it said Peters was suffering from shock.'

'He probably was,' Abbott pointed out.

'Yes. But he was an ex-copper,' Nightingale stressed. 'He knew how to cope with shock — '

'He was also seventy-four years old,' Abbott said, gently.

'And still sharp enough to play good chess.'

Abbott shrugged. 'So? Make your point, Tim, *please*. My ulcer is getting restless.'

'According to the Forensic report there were no fingerprints in the abandoned car.'

Abbott's expression sharpened briefly. 'None at all?'

'None at all.'

They stared at one another. 'Go on,' Abbott said, slowly.

Nightingale shrugged. 'Nobody seemed to think anything of it. The report went into the files as Fraud towards the Avis people – naturally he never paid up – and that's that. They made a stab at tracking him down, but the car was undamaged and he'd only stuck them for a few days' rental, less the usual deposit since he didn't use a credit card. They gave it a try, and then put it in the back of the drawer.'

33

'You can't chase ghosts for ever.'

'But Peters did.'

'Tim — '

'He got a look at the reports – he had a lot of friends around here – and he talked to people at the hotel, especially one of the maids who had been friendly beyond the call of duty with this "Rochester" — '

'Tim — '

Nightingale speeded up his delivery. 'And she gave him an address, which led to another, and so on. He went on looking, and eventually tracked him down. Then, for some reason, he stopped the whole thing. In the last notebook he says something about "finding out more than he wanted to know", and being too old, that sort of thing. But he'd gone too far. I think this "Rochester" was alerted, somehow. He tracked *Peters* down, came to his place and either threatened or frightened him so badly that the old man had a heart attack.'

'*Tim.*' Abbott had got his attention at last. He spoke evenly and slowly. 'Did it ever occur to you that, far from being noble or enterprising, Peters' interest in this man might have been to blackmail him? And that when "Rochester" refused to pay up, Peters got angry and popped his valves?'

Nightingale shook his head. 'No. Never. If you'd read the notebooks, you'd understand. He wasn't like that at all.'

'I haven't got time to read the notebooks, or to go on listening to this. Neither do you,' Abbott said, wearily. 'In case you have forgotten, we have something called a Priority Points System for ranking this kind of thing – on which I would estimate this whole mess you've dreamed up would register as about a Negative Eight. We deal in Serious Crimes here in the CID. Put it down and forget it. I assume you gave a receipt to the daughter for those notebooks you "borrowed"?'

'Of course.'

'Of course. I don't know why I bothered to ask,' Abbott told his desk lamp. He looked at Nightingale, and his eyes were sharp and cold. 'What I *will* ask is whether this is some kind of bid for attention. Do you want to impress

34

everybody, make some kind of fancy investigation out of nothing because you figure it will look great on your record?'

'It's nothing to do with my "career",' Tim said, quietly. 'And if I messed up, it would hardly look good on my record, would it? I just think that, well, Peters was one of us. I looked into his record while I was at it, and I've talked to some of the older officers who worked with him. He was straight and he was smart and he was a good copper. If he had a feeling something was wrong, then I think there was something wrong.'

'So do I,' Abbott said, wearily. 'In particular, there's something wrong with you wasting so much time and energy on a nothing case that's going nowhere. Give the notebooks back, Tim. Forget it. Let it go. If you think you have so much time to spare from your present assignments, I can give you approximately twelve to fifty other cases that also require attention and energy devoted to them. Old cases, new cases, robberies, murders. You call it and you're on it.'

Tim sighed, and looked down at his knees. He folded his hands, inspected his thumbs, measured them one against the other. 'What do you want me to work on?' he finally asked.

The capitulation was complete and, if anything, too fast. Abbott, wrong-footed, looked around his desk for a quick inspiration. 'You're on that Primrose Street burglary, aren't you?' Nightingale nodded. 'Well, if you get stopped on that, there was a murder at a disco last night. They've got about two hundred suspects to sift through. Check with Detective Inspector Holliman if you want to lend a hand – I have no objection.'

Nightingale stood up. 'All right,' he said, quietly, and went out of the office.

Abbott watched him close the door, and, after a moment, confided in his desk lamp. 'He's not going to offer to help on the murder. And he's not going to give the notebooks back, either,' he said, in a resigned tone. 'He's going to *say* he gave them back, but he's not going to give them back. In two months I've learned just one important thing about Tim Nightingale, and that is that when he seems the nicest he's really planning to do his worst. On that basis, he'll probably go far. Meanwhile, he's going to sit at home and look at those bloody notebooks and think about poor old Peters. He'll read a little Sherlock Holmes or Raymond Chandler before going to sleep, and when he wakes up he's going to start investigating in his own time. That's what *I* would do, which proves that after all these years I haven't learned a thing.' The lamp was not much of a conversationalist.

Two months back in the city and I'm talking to electrical fittings, Abbott thought. Tomorrow during breakfast I will undoubtedly make a serious speech to my toaster concerning the front page news or the state of my shirt-collars.

He sighed, and thought about Tim Nightingale's apparently insatiable curiosity about people, his developing instinct for the 'wrongness' of things, and the years ahead in which these traits would grow and either drive his superiors crazy, get him killed, or make him a good detective. He considered the abundant energy and the refusal to be daunted that Nightingale displayed, and wondered whether the feeling he had might be envy.

He hoped not.

He'd been having enough trouble dealing with boredom.

'What do you fancy tonight?' he asked the lamp. 'Chinese or Indian takeaway?'

SIX

'PROBABLY BE ONE OF THEM weirdos with purple hair and leather trousers, flapping all over the place,' sniffed Mrs Grimble, making another stab at the sink drain with the plunger. Mrs Grimble and the drains had been waging war on one another ever since she'd first come to work for Tess over ten years before. The sink gave a sulky gurgle, surrendered some discoloured water, and slowly emptied.

With a triumphant smirk on her face, the old woman smacked the plunger down onto the windowsill and turned to face Tess, who was seated at the big kitchen table, peeling vegetables. She had been late getting home, and had hurriedly tied one of Mrs Grimble's huge aprons over her dark suit. She was wielding the peeler awkwardly, trying to keep the mess from staining her sleeves. Mrs Grimble picked up a paring knife in one hand and a carrot in the other. Busy hands did not stop her from speaking her mind, however. Very few things did.

'What did you want to say you'd see him for? We don't want the likes of him living in the house. Waste of time.'

'It's the least I can do,' Tess said, standing up and going over to tip the potato peelings into the bin. 'He's hardly likely to be weird if he teaches at Cambridge. He's a lecturer in history, and recently lost his wife.'

'Carelessness or divorce?'

'Neither, he's a widower.'

'Hmphh. They're all the same, thinking they're so wonderful when they can only put their pants on one leg at a time, like anyone else. What you want is a nice little retired *lady* teacher. Plenty of those around, I'll wager.'

Tess ignored this advice and went on, determinedly. 'Mr

37

Soame is taking a year's sabbatical to do research for a book on nineteenth-century London and needs a place to live. Anyway, Adrian talked to him — '

'Oh, my gawd, I might have known Fancy Pants was somewheres behind it,' moaned Mrs Grimble.

' — and Mr Soame is very interested in trading rent for tutoring Max. If we can work out complementary schedules, it should be an ideal arrangement,' she finished, triumphantly.

Mrs Grimble looked hard at the cooker in case it, too, decided to do something to make her life miserable. 'I hope you don't take it wrong that I can't help out more,' she muttered. 'But what with Walter's stomach and my back . . . ' she trailed off, meaningfully. Walter Briggs was Mrs Grimble's younger brother. He'd moved in with her the day after Mr Grimble died, and had remained ever since. According to his sister, Walter was 'delicate': particularly, it seemed, on the day he collected his dole money.

Tess reached out and squeezed Mrs Grimble's hand. 'I couldn't get along without you, but I certainly don't want to risk your health as well as Max's, do I? Who'd look after us all, then?'

The old woman looked at her fondly. 'You *need* looking after, you do,' she said. 'Too soft, that's your trouble.'

The front doorbell rang, startling them both. 'That must be Mr Soame now,' Tess said, wiping her hands hurriedly on the apron and then dragging it off over her head, causing her hair to stand up in errant spikes. 'Do you think you could be a darling and finish the vegetables before you go?'

'As if I wouldn't,' sniffed Mrs Grimble, reaching for a potato. 'I'll be right here if you need me,' she said, meaningfully, and waved the knife in a vaguely menacing manner.

Tess went down the long dark hall and opened the front door, expecting the worst. For a moment she thought she had got it.

On the top step stood an angular man in a wrinkled

tweed suit. He had a mac over one arm and a bulging briefcase in his free hand. Someone seemed to have been holding a party in his jacket pockets, and from their shape there was still a lot of clearing up to do in there. His features were somewhat obscured by heavy horn-rimmed glasses.

'Soame,' he announced. When she didn't reply, he seemed to shrink slightly. 'You *were* expecting me, weren't you? I'm almost certain we settled on Tuesday . . . ' His voice was hesitant and, despite his height, he seemed ready to bolt if Tess showed the least sign of disapproval.

'Of course we did.'

He rewarded her, or himself, with a sudden half-moon smile. For a moment Tess was reminded of the young Alec Guinness, and involuntarily smiled back. 'Come in,' she told him, and stepped back. He followed her down the dark hall and into the sitting-room. 'Won't you sit down?' She indicated the battered old sofa that sat like an elderly camel in the bay window. He perched on the edge of it rather warily, putting his brief-case down on the floor beside him and then – after jabbing it first towards the side table and then the coffee-table and then the lamp – he put his rather forlorn tweed hat on the cushion beside him. He seemed so ill at ease that Tess began to feel nervous, too.

'Would you like a drink or something?'

'I don't drink much,' he said apologetically. 'Wine with meals, occasionally, but nothing . . . ' He stopped himself and took a breath. 'Coffee would be very nice, though, if you had planned to make some for yourself, that is. There's rather a chilly wind outside and I walked from the tube station, not realizing it was quite so far . . . ' His voice trailed off.

'Of course, it won't take a minute.'

Tess fled to the kitchen, where Mrs Grimble was glowering behind the door, knife in hand. She'd obviously been playing Peeping Tom through the crack. 'I'm not leaving, don't you worry,' the older woman muttered, ominously. 'He's big.'

'He's also scared stiff, if you ask me,' Tess said, plugging in the kettle.

'Hmmmph,' Mrs Grimble said. 'That's just you being soft, as usual. And what's he been doing with that hat I want to know? Looks like someone sat on it.'

'He probably did,' Tess said. 'Poor lamb.'

Mrs Grimble snorted. 'You just remember what can be inside sheep's clothing, young lady. Don't be fooled by all that pardon my toe in your eye and pass the marmalade. I think he looks loony.'

'Nonsense,' Tess said, pouring boiling water onto the instant coffee powder she'd spooned into mugs – three mugs, not forgetting Mrs Grimble, who had an insatiable thirst.

'Don't tell me nonsense, because *I* read the papers. It's the meek ones that go berserk and chop people up,' Mrs Grimble said briskly, coming across to pick up her coffee, but not relinquishing the paring knife, which she dropped into her apron pocket. 'I'll be right here. Listening to his every cunning word.'

Tess returned to the sitting room with the coffee, much entertained by Mrs Grimble's suspicions. She found John Soame still perched on the sofa, absent-mindedly rubbing one knee over and over again as he looked around the room in a bemused fashion. Tess followed his glance, and understood his puzzlement. The rather nice wallpaper was loose in two corners near the ceiling, due to damp, and in several places above the wainscoting it still bore faint traces of Max's infant experiments with crayons. The curtains in the bay window were newish, but clashed terribly with the faded carpet – she'd been shopping for its replacement on the very day Roger had been killed. She hadn't had the heart – or the money – to complete her mission since.

The furniture was a mixture of solid old pieces she'd picked up at various auctions and sales. She'd stripped and renovated them as they came along, always in a hurry, always with a new colour scheme in mind, and always intending to redo everything to match – one day. The entire effect was more that of a room created by a near-sighted colour-blind junk dealer than a highly trained artist and experienced interior decorator.

'You know the tale of the cobbler's children, don't you?'

she said. 'The same thing applies here. This is the place I have always *meant* to make wonderful, but I never seem to find the time to do it.'

Soame shook his head. 'Actually, if I were rich, I would commission you to create one just like it for me.'

She laughed. 'You're not serious.'

'I am. You see, when Adrian said you were an interior decorator, I thought it would be so perfect that I'd be afraid to sit down.' He leaned forward, confidentially. 'I tend to spill things.'

'So I see,' Tess smiled, as a few drops of coffee escaped his mug and disappeared into the carpet.

'Sorry, sorry,' he said, jerking it back so quickly that even more spattered out, this time hitting both his knee and the sofa. 'Oh, Lord,' he muttered, brushing ineffectually at the spots.

If I don't do something to distract him, he's going to fall apart at the seams, she thought. Leaning down, she picked up the black and white quilt she was working on and began to stitch.

'That's very attractive,' Mr Soame said.

'It's called a Widow's Quilt,' Tess said. 'It's a traditional American pattern: always black and white, and always made to fit a single bed. I believe the theory is that by the time you've finished it, the worst of your grief is over.'

'And will it be?'

The needle slipped. 'Damn.'

She saw that he looked stricken. 'The worst of it is over already,' she assured him. 'I just jabbed my thumb, that's all. I do it frequently. Whatever I sew always has my blood on it, one way or another. I find patchwork very soothing, hand-quilting even more so. But this particular pattern is a bit boring, I must say. I don't know what made me start it.'

But she did know. It was a penance for all the wicked thoughts she'd had towards Roger since his death. Not being Catholic, and confession not being available to her, she had found her own punishment – the sewing of this damned quilt.

There were many examples of her handiwork around the house, covering all the beds, hanging on the walls, even curtaining the downstairs cloakroom. But those patchwork pieces were bright and vibrant, done to her own designs. Working this traditional quilt was monotonous, and dull, and she was determined to finish it, even if it killed *her*.

'Are the black arrows supposed to represent something?' Soame asked. 'Or are they your own creation?'

'Oh, they're traditional, too. They're called the Darts of Death.' And they are many, she thought. They cause the wounds that come after: longing, loneliness, frustration, remorse, reproach, resentment, rage, the constant wish to live the time over and repair the wrongs of the past, the bitter knowledge that such a wish will not be granted. A widow's mite. A widow's pillory.

'I see,' he said, quietly. And, remembering belatedly that he was himself a widower, she thought perhaps he did. He watched her for a minute, then looked around the room again.

'Is there something wrong?' she asked, deciding she could stand it no longer. He was making her nervous, too. Working the quilt wasn't helping, and neither was the coffee.

He gazed at her through the heavy-rimmed lenses and spoke with utter sincerity. 'I have faced many things, Mrs Leland, but none of them compare with the prospect of pleasing a small boy and his mother with my somewhat limited teaching credentials.'

'I'd hardly call them limited,' Tess protested. 'Of course, Adrian told me about your research and why you need to be in London for the next twelve months. Did he also explain my situation to you?'

He nodded vigorously, causing his glasses to slide down his nose. He peered at her over them. 'Oh, yes. Adrian said you need a combination tutor and baby-sitter.' He flushed slightly, and rushed on. 'As for me, all I require is' peace and quiet, a place to sleep, and a large table on which to lay out my reference books. At present I am in a bed and breakfast hotel which is on a very busy street. I'm not very happy there. Most of the other inhabitants seem to be foreigners on holiday. All very jolly, of course, but they are constantly asking for directions which I cannot give, or translations which I cannot make. The very few permanent residents all seem to be subject to fits. There is usually someone *shouting*, or crying, or falling down the stairs.'

'Oh, dear,' Tess said.

'Yes. I've only been there a week, mind. It could have been an unusual seven days for them, I suppose.' He didn't sound convinced. 'In the place I stayed before that, someone deliberately set fire to the dining-room.'

'Good heavens.'

'Yes.' He reflected. 'I think it was out of pique, really, the bacon was always burnt, so why not everything else?'

'Why not, indeed?' Tess said, faintly.

He warmed to his refrain. 'On another memorable occasion there was a fistfight between two very large and angry women at three in the morning. I got a black eye trying to separate them — they both turned on me, you see. People *will* do that.' He sighed. 'It is all so exhausting, and hardly conducive to serious study. In addition, London is proving to be very expensive and I'm not exactly wealthy at the moment, what with . . . one thing and another.'

He paused, swallowed, and took off his glasses to polish them, oblivious to Tess's efforts to keep a straight face. His eyes, thus revealed, proved to be dark blue and oddly unfocused, like an infant's. She thought she recognized him at last – a fellow sufferer at the hands of wilful fate, one to whom things happened without warning, and without explanation.

She'd heard there were natural victims, but until Roger's death she had never considered herself in that category. Yet, for the past few months she had definitely been got at. She'd been burgled, for a start. And then there were the little things, like silent phone calls, people staring at her and then turning away, letters that looked like they'd been opened by someone else first, deliveries of things she hadn't ordered, lost deliveries of things she *had* ordered. All petty, all ridiculous – probably just the vagaries of life in a big city – but unsettling.

13

From the expression on Soame's face, he too felt gnawed by the rats of misfortune.

He sighed, replaced his glasses, and went on. 'But all that's neither here nor there.' He cleared his throat. 'If you and I can come to some satisfactory mutual arrangement, it would be a great relief to me. Of course, I'd have to meet your son first.'

Tess stiffened, defensively. 'He's a perfectly nice little boy,' she said.

Soame nodded. 'I was thinking more of whether *he* would approve of *me*, actually.'

'Oh, I see.' She felt embarrassed at having misunderstood, and decided theirs was probably doomed to be a relationship of continuous mutual misapprehensions. She was already resigned to it. 'Well, if you can spare the time, we can go up together the day after tomorrow to see him. I'll pay for your ticket, of course. It's not far out of London. I'm staying over, but there are plenty of trains back.'

'Very kind,' he said, quickly. 'Very kind.'

There was a pause.

'How old is Max, by the way? Adrian probably told me but I can't remember . . . '

'He's nine.' She felt a stab of concern. 'Won't it be boring for you to teach a youngster after teaching university students?'

He leaned sideways to put his empty mug down on the end table and gazed earnestly at her. 'Mrs Leland, it would be sheer delight,' he said. 'That is, I assume he's the usual kind of nine-year-old boy? No long hair, no beard, not given to beer-drinking contests, pot-smoking, arguing theories of genetics, demonstrating rugger tactics at four in the morning, making anarchistic plans for revolution, playing the guitar badly, or bringing aggressive feminist girlfriends to tutorials?'

'Not so far,' Tess grinned. 'He collects stamps.'

John Soame sighed deeply, leaned back, and produced again that engaging half-moon smile. 'A proper boy,' he said, in gratified tones. 'I'll take the job.' Then he leaned forward, apparently startled by his own enthusiasm. 'That is, if you'll have me?'

44

SEVEN

TIM NIGHTINGALE LEANED BACK IN his chair and opened the notebook. Slowly and carefully, with *déjà vu* born of what felt like a thousand previous examinations of the same facts in the same file, he read over the information that had been accumulated by Ivor Peters.

It didn't take long.

'Are we going out to lunch or staying in?' It was Tom Murray, standing by his desk, looking harassed. 'Because if we're going out, we'd better get a move on or we'll never get a table, and if we aren't we'd better get a move on or all the decent food in the canteen will have been snapped up.'

'That wouldn't take long,' Nightingale said, leaning down to put the notebook carefully into the bottom drawer of his desk, which he then locked. Murray raised an eyebrow.

'You still crooning over that?' he asked, in surprise.

Nightingale shrugged. 'It bothers me.'

'Lately they all bother you,' his friend said.

'Only the ones that don't make sense,' Nightingale said, with a wry smile.

They walked out of the office they shared with two other detectives and started down the hall. 'But it was days ago,' Tom protested, shrugging into his coat. 'I thought Abbott told you to shelve it.'

'As far as I'm concerned, it's still open,' Nightingale said. 'Still very much alive.'

'Which is more than the old man is.'

'Yes.' Nightingale pushed the lift button and the indicator lit up, showing it was high above them. The light did not change. They glanced at one another and then

45

turned and started for the stairs. As they clattered down, Nightingale spoke over his shoulder. 'By the way, you didn't see me looking at that file. It wasn't there, all right?'

'I don't know what you're talking about.'

'The no – oh, right. Thanks.'

'But I reserve the right to think you're nuts.'

They emerged from the stairwell and made for the street. A slight drizzle was misting down, and the prospect of the busy, grimy, soggy thoroughfare did not please.

'God, I hate the city,' Nightingale said, turning up the collar of his mac. 'The only green thing I've seen lately is the mould on my last piece of bread when I got it out of the wrapper this morning.'

'Country boy.'

'So?' Nightingale glanced at him. 'I'm not ashamed of it. I grew up in beautiful surroundings, and I miss it. We weren't rich, God knows, but we could look up and see hills and trees and sky. If an old man dropped dead there, people would be upset, people would want the thing explained, settled, tied up. Here, we do nothing but make a report, and then we have to shove it to the back of the shelf, because another one comes along. And another. They're all human beings, they all deserve more than that. A little anger, at least.'

'Which you seem to be supplying.'

'Which I'm tired of supplying,' Nightingale grumbled.

They went out into the drizzle and made for the Italian restaurant they both favoured. The traffic moved slowly past them, tyres peeling stickily from the wet tarmac, windscreen wipers thunking in many rhythms. Windows were steamed because the drivers were complaining and cursing one another, their lips moving silently behind the misted glass. The gritty shuffle of pedestrians was the only sound from the pavement. An occasional umbrella forced them to dodge or duck to one side, otherwise their progress was steady. Nobody wanted to linger outside any longer than they had to today.

They reached the restaurant, went in, and were instantly enveloped in exotic aromas of pesto, tomato, garlic, cheese, and sharp red wine. Relayed softly through speakers placed with merciful discretion were Neapolitan love songs. There was one table left – the smallest one, of course, in the corner, where their elbows would knock the wall and waiters would constantly pass and mutter, but it would have to do.

'What are you on at the moment?' Nightingale asked, when they'd settled themselves as well as they could. 'Still that camera shop break-in?'

'Yes. Personally, I think it was the owner himself, looking for the insurance pay off, but I can't make it out enough to hold up in court.'

'Law's old sweet song,' Nightingale smiled. It was not a happy smile.

'For the next hour let us forget our work,' Tom suggested. 'Let us wine and dine and talk of cabbages and kings.'

Nightingale eyed him. 'It's beginning to get to you, too, isn't it?'

'What is?'

'Everything. The city, the frustration, everything.'

Tom shrugged. 'Maybe. But if you're going to start in again about transferring to one of the Regions, forget it. I am not interested. I will never be interested. I am a city boy. Down today, up tomorrow – swings and roundabouts, that's the way it goes. You'll get used to it.'

'You could get used to hills and trees.'

'And having to drive twenty miles to the nearest town to get a meal like we're about to have? In fact, having to drive twenty miles to the nearest town to get *everything*? Forget it.'

'I can't forget it. I can't forget anything.'

Tom leaned forward and put on a German accent. 'Dat is your trrrouble, Herr Nightingale, you cannot vorget anyting. Lie down on ze couch und tell me about zis compulllsion you have to valk in se hills vot are rrround like breasts, and see the trrees vot are tall and strraight like — '

'Like zis bread stick vot I will place in your eye?' Nightingale opened his menu and gave Matt a dangerous look across the top of it. 'Let's order this meal. I think your blood sugar is getting low.'

'Just trying to cheer things up.'

47

'I don't want to be cheered up. I want to get back to the office. I have an idea.'

Tom Murray looked disgusted. 'Great. Have your idea. Me – I'll have spaghetti.'

Nightingale grinned. 'They have something in common, at that.'

'What?'

'Loose ends.'

EIGHT

THE OLD MCMURDO HOUSE WAS in a tree-lined street in west Ealing. The street began with terraces, but these stopped at the edge of a small park that had been preserved against years of onslaught by eager developers. This minor piece of civic salvation had come about because the small park had originally been part of the McMurdo estate. It had been bequeathed to the borough on the understanding that it would never be built upon. This endowment on the part of the family was less than altruistic – the McMurdos did not like to be overlooked.

The McMurdo family tree had sprung from strong roots, but its later growths were better at making money than sons. By the middle of this century, the only remaining branch was that which had sprouted from a young twig who had emigrated to Australia to make his fortune. Sheep and opal mining, mostly, but a bit of timber, too, had been the basis of his endeavours, and he had prospered. However, Australian weather being what it can be, even that McMurdo branch eventually withered down to one man – Burdoo McMurdo, a successful (of course) manufacturer of plumbing fixtures. It was Burdoo's childless widow who had come to Britain to trace her husband's roots and claim his heritage.

Dolly McMurdo was what generous friends might call 'a character', and what everyone else called a case of all mouth and no taste. Dolly's saving grace was that she knew she was loud, knew she was gauche, and knew she was laughed at, but didn't give a damn. She was rich enough to soothe any ruffled feelings she might engender through an unkind but truthful observation or a misjudged slap on

49

the back, and rich enough also to buy the good taste she lacked from those who had it and were willing to sell.

In short, an interior designer's dream and burden, in one.

Dolly had swept into the Savoy like a bleached, beached whale become woman. Large in girth and gusto, she'd won over the staff with her good humour and large tips, and the other guests by involuntarily becoming a source of delicious disapproval to one and all.

One horrified look at the old McMurdo mansion – now occupied mostly by wasps and black beetles – had convinced Dolly that she had a mission in life, and that was to renovate this fallen symbol of the family's former power and prestige. No matter what it cost.

'My God, would you look at the rotten heap!' she had trumpeted on alighting from her rented chauffeur-driven Rolls. 'Burdoo always told me it was a mansion, a dream of old England, and all that dingo dribble.' Apparently she had then fixed the heavens with a mean eye, and had spoken to the sky. 'Burdoo, you always were a liar – I should have flushed you down one of your own toilets when I had the chance, bless your little dried-up heart.' On the chauffeur's later telling of it, she had marched up the path through the nettles, given the front steps an almighty kick, then leaned back and looked up at the scabby paintwork and sagging roofline.

Again, she had addressed a passing cloud. 'Burdoo, I guess I'd better make an honest man of you and get this place back in shape before I die. Mind you, another shock like this one may send me along sooner than I think. Enjoy yourself up there while you can, you old wowser.' She had then turned to the chauffeur and demanded to be driven to her friend Noelene Arletta Hanks's house in Chelsea. Noelene was always bragging how she knew the finest interior decorators, wasn't she? Well, here was the chance to prove it.

The task set by Mrs McMurdo was a daunting one, for the structure of the house had suffered through many transformations (bedsitters, ever-decreasing in size and ever-increasing in number), encrustations (wallpapers

50

from William Morris through Art Nouveau, Art Deco, wartime austerity, the New Look, the frankly fundamental Fifties, the hallucinogenic Sixties, a brief flowering of Laura Ashley, and finally flat buff paint over all when it served, even more briefly, as a hostel for recently-released sexual offenders), and visitations (families, single women, soldiers, students, young marrieds, the above mentioned ex-prisoners, and at last – through broken windows – the British weather). But it was a task that Brevitt Interiors – or, rather, Tess Leland – had taken to with gusto.

And now it looked as if she would be able to complete what she had taken on, after all. After a reassuring phone call to the ward sister and a brief chat with Max, she spent the next morning talking with the men working on the house, getting firm commitments as to when she could begin scheduling the various stages of her own work. Then she met Adrian for lunch, and told him about her interview with John Soame.

'I think it will be fine,' she told him. 'We're only a ten-minute tube ride from the British Museum. We should be able to work out our schedules pretty easily, since we both work to our own hours. Max won't be able to do much except read at first, so Mr Soame intends to use the next few weeks to make a start on his basic research. Then, as Max gets stronger, they'll start proper studies. Max's school is going to give me a syllabus, the appropriate books, and a suggested work schedule.'

She reached for another roll and buttered it enthusiastically. Adrian watched her with approval. She had got so very thin so very quickly after Roger died, and then again when Max first fell ill. He leaned back as the waiter set down their first course. 'You must be sure to take advantage of him,' he advised.

Her eyes widened. 'I beg your pardon?'

'His expertise,' Adrian said. 'He knows a great deal about the entire Victorian era – particularly architecture – and you could do worse than ask his opinion if you come up against something in the McMurdo house you know little about. I mentioned it to him and he was very interested. He has a great eye for detail, and he's made some unusual contacts in the antiquarian world.'

Tess paused with her soup spoon in mid-air, considering John Soame in this new light. 'Well, he may be an expert, but I don't think I've ever met a grown man so lacking in self-confidence,' she finally said.

Adrian nodded, spreading pâté on a piece of thin toast. 'His wife was one of the most unpleasant women I've ever known – and, my pet, I've known a few. I know one shouldn't speak ill of the dead — '

'That's never stopped you,' Tess commented.

He ignored that. 'Alicia did a proper demolition job on poor John, something about him seemed to bring out a vicious streak in her.'

'You sound as if you knew her very well.'

'She was my youngest sister.' Adrian smiled sadly at Tess's astonished expression. 'Hers was a destructive soul. In the end she left him, went on a trip to India with a "friend" and was bitten by a rabid dog – which seemed to me simple justice.'

'Adrian!'

He eyed her over his wire-rimmed glasses. 'She was as lovely as a flower to look at, but as deadly to the soul as cyanide.' He sniffed. 'There is no law that says you have to love your own family, especially when it throws out a dud like Alicia. My father suspected the milkman, of course, a narrow-eyed goat of a man who was always leaving extra cream. However, I have recently come across an engraving of his great-aunt Beulah who was the image of Alicia in a bustle. Besides, Mother may have been *tempted* by the dairyman – she was a woman of earthy appetite – but she was far too worried about what the neighbours might have thought to have actually succumbed to his ungulate charms.' He waved to the waiter and indicated that they were ready for their next course. 'Well, even if dear old John *is* a bit edgy, I still think he'll be ideal for your situation.'

Tess pressed a large bite of Chicken Dijon onto her fork. 'Oh, so do I,' she agreed. 'He could probably use a bit of comfort and appreciation.'

Adrian raised an eyebrow and inspected her more

closely while refilling her wine glass. 'Oh, dear,' he said, smiling mischievously to himself. 'What *have* I done?'

'You've made certain Max will be tutored and I will have a man – albeit a nervous one – around the house. You've therefore made certain I'll be free to protect *you* from the Monster McMurdo,' Tess said briskly. 'And that was just what you set out to do, wasn't it?'

'Why, Tess, you make me sound quite *ruthless*,' Adrian said in a hurt tone.

'You *are* quite ruthless, Adrian, when it comes to your own peace and survival. But never mind, we love you, anyway.' Tess grinned and blew him a kiss across the flower arrangement. 'All of your devoted slaves adore you, we always clank our chains when you pass.'

Coming home that evening, weary but content, Tess hung her coat in the hall and then kicked off her shoes, moaning with pleasure and relief. She had walked about twenty miles since lunch, choosing plumbing fixtures and getting solid delivery dates out of four different suppliers and looking through a warehouse full of junk for just one little table that she finally found under the stairs, and then discovering that nobody had nineteen rolls of 'Daisychain'. Two had fifteen rolls each, but of course they had totally different batch numbers. Now she had to convince the client to have 'Fieldflowers' instead.

She started up the stairs, then had to come back down again as the phone began to ring. 'Hello?'

Silence.

Again. 'Hello!'

Silence.

Tess felt familiar fury boiling up in her. This had been going on for weeks now. The phone rang at random times, but the result was always the same – silence. No giggling, no heavy breathing, no obscene suggestions. Just silence. Not the silence of a broken connection or a dead phone, either. Oh, no.

It was the silence of someone listening.

She had complained, of course. Her phone and her line had been thoroughly checked. No fault. And, as nothing was said of either an obscene or threatening nature, it was not a matter for the police. The phone people were sympathetic, but the only alternatives on offer were an interception service that would only ask what number had been dialled and who the caller wished to speak to by name, or changing her number, which would cost money she could not spare. Going ex-directory was free, but wouldn't be effective until the new phone books came out next year.

Tess reached for the whistle she had bought recently and hung by the phone. 'Damn it, who is this? I'm sick and tired of being called at all hours of the day and night.'

This time, just as she was bringing the whistle to her lips and taking a breath, just as if she could be *seen*, the silence was broken. A sense of movement from the other end of the line, and a whisper, like a snake shedding its skin.

'We want the money, Mrs Leland.'

The whistle dropped from her fingers and rolled under the bench. She was so dumbfounded she could only say, 'What?'

'The money, Mrs Leland. Give it back.'

There was a terrible rasp and slither in the voice, and Tess felt the skin of her back and arms raise up in gooseflesh. A cold draft seemed suddenly to swirl down the hallway.

'I . . . I . . . don't have any idea what you're talking about. What money?'

Now it was worse. Not a whisper, but a chuckle.

'You know. *You* know.' Like a cruel child, pointing a finger on the playground, chanting, chanting. '*You* know.'

'I don't . . . I don't . . . ' Tess felt her throat closing, as if an invisible hand had encircled it.

'It isn't in the house – we looked. And you haven't spent it – we checked. So you've got it hidden somewhere, right? If you don't give it back, *someone* is going to be very, very cross.'

Still a whisper, but now a gleeful, maniac whisper.

And then a click. Dead line.

Tess stood staring at the phone, as if she expected it to strike at her, but it was only a white plastic handset, silent again, connection broken.

Slowly, Tess replaced the handset and stood staring at the

phone. It had to be children, or some pubescent teenager trying to exert power in a threatening world . . .

Boy? Girl? Man? Woman? It had no gender, no age.

But it had known her name.

Suddenly she whirled, ran up the stairway, down the hall and into her bedroom. Slamming the door behind her, she twisted the key in the lock and stood, panting, with her back against it.

All was normal here.

The white curtains, the delicate flowered wallpaper, the brilliant intersecting patterns of the patchwork quilt that covered the king-sized bed, the warm dusky pink carpet, her slippers and robe, the dried flower arrangement on the bedside table. All untouched, and her own. Safe.

Eventually she calmed down sufficiently to move away from the door. Slowly she unbuttoned her suit jacket and went to the wardrobe for a hanger. A bath, some supper, a book in bed . . . she would not think about the call. She would *not*.

She pulled at the door of the wardrobe – it seemed a little stiff – swung it wide, and began to scream.

Things flew at her, moth-like, fluttering, and cold hard pellets poured over her face and body as she flailed about her, screaming and crying . . . and over it all . . . laughter.

The wild, unceasing laughter of a demented old man.

NINE

WITH AN ALMOST IMPERCEPTIBLE JERK, the train began to move out of the station. The train beside them seemed to slide backwards – an impression which always disconcerted Tess – and then they were out from under the roof and into the rain. In a moment the windows were covered with running drops and ribbons of moisture that converged and spread, blurring the world beyond.

'If you'll pardon me for saying, you look as if you haven't slept well. Has something happened to Max?' John Soame was asking, patiently. He seemed to have been asking it for some time.

Tess shook her head and sipped some of the tea he had brought her. It was scalding, but tasteless. 'No, he's doing fine. I was frightened by the wardrobe.'

'I beg your pardon?'

She shook her head again, and put down the tea in order to explain about the phone calls, the shower of confetti and fresh red cranberries that had cascaded out of the wardrobe, and the mechanical toy called a laughter-bag that had gone on shrieking long after she had stopped. 'I felt like such a fool,' she said. 'It was just some terrible practical joke.'

'But who do you know who would do such a cruel thing?'

'No-one, as far as I know. I mean, I don't have all that many friends of my own. We mostly entertained Roger's clients or contacts in the business if we entertained at all. None of the people I know are given to that kind of "humour".'

'But when could someone have got into the house?'

56

'Well, the house was empty all morning. But I called Mrs Grimble, and asked her about it. She arrives at two o'clock, and stays on until five, most days. She did the bedroom first, apparently, and there was nothing in the wardrobe then, because she hung up some dry-cleaning that she'd collected for me, and nothing happened. She was there all afternoon, except for about forty minutes when she went out to do my shopping – if I'm pressed for time on a particular day, I usually leave a list and the money on the kitchen table. Whoever it was must have got in during those forty minutes.'

She was suddenly aware that a middle-aged woman sitting opposite them was listening avidly to their conversation, and lowered her voice. The woman looked away, making a pretence of non-interest, but her ears seemed practically to glow with attention. Well, let her listen, Tess thought. Let everyone listen. A sudden recklessness overcame her – this was too important to worry about eavesdroppers or what the neighbours might think.

'You say you'd been getting phone calls before this?'

'Yes, frequently. But only silent ones. Last night was the first time anyone spoke to me.'

'And the first time anyone has got into the house.'

Tess nodded, her mind still filled with that terrible moment, when she had looked down and seen the carpet dotted with red berries and thought it her own blood. 'Just when I realized what it all was, the telephone began to ring again.'

'Did you answer it?'

'I was afraid to. Eventually it stopped.'

'I see.' Soame was lost in thought for a minute, then spoke diffidently.

'When your husband died, did you *inherit* any money, aside from insurance and so on? I'm sorry to pry, but someone seems to think you have some available.'

Tempted to have a look at a possible heiress, the woman opposite risked a glance at them and met Tess's eyes. Flushing, she turned away again, pressing her lips together. Tess felt some sympathy: the poor thing couldn't have known that when she sat down she would be forced to share these intimacies. To get up would be to admit she'd been listening. And, of course, to get up would be to miss the rest. What price Hollywood when you could get all this drama for free on the 10:38?

'I wish we had inherited something,' Tess said, ruefully. 'In a sense we lived from hand to mouth all the years we were married. I don't mean we starved. I mean we lived up to and frequently beyond our means. Everything that came in went right out again – Roger was a real grasshopper – he never seemed to think about the future, because he found here and now so interesting, I guess. When he and Richard Hendricks started up their PR agency they did it with a bank loan – Roger was always amazingly good at talking to bank managers. Even when the agency started to thrive, every penny they made seemed to go straight back into the business. Roger had no secret accounts or deposit boxes.'

'As far as you know,' John Soame said.

'I know that Roger couldn't hold on to money at all,' Tess protested. 'I'd certainly have known if — '

'I don't mean to be rude,' he interrupted, firmly. 'But the fact is, the newspapers are always full of stories about wives who are astounded to discover things about their husbands after they've died or run away.'

That was certainly true, Tess thought, ruefully.

John Soame spoke again. 'Was he a secretive man?'

Tess thought about that. 'Not in a sly way, no. But he did like to surprise people. He was very generous, always bringing home unexpected little gifts and things.'

'What about this – Richard Hendricks, did you say? Your husband's ex-partner? Would he know about any money?'

Tess shook her head. 'I'm sure if Richard had known about any money that Roger had, he'd have given it to me long ago. He's been very good to us.'

'Did you ask him about this?'

'I rang him last night but there was only the answering machine. When I rang the office this morning, his secretary told me he's still out of the country on business.

58

He's gone into partnership with someone else now, doing
market research, I think. He and Roger handled a lot of
international accounts, and now that we're in the Common
Market, anybody with that kind of experience is in demand.
I believe he's doing very well, already.'

'Have you told him about these calls?'

'No. I just thought it was a crank. Mrs Grimble knows
about it, she's taken a few of the calls. She thinks it's one of
the neighbours. Or the greengrocer or the butcher –
depending on who she's had her latest argument with.
That's more or less what I assumed, too.'

John nodded. 'Well, if Max approves of me, you'll soon
know there's someone in the house all the time. And
perhaps the police can convince the telephone people to
cooperate.'

Tess's eyes widened. 'The police?'

He glanced at her. 'Of course. You've been threatened,
and threatening phone calls must be against some law or
other. I'll ring Scotland Yard when I get back to London
later this afternoon and find out the position.'

The middle-aged woman in the blue hat and coat had
stopped pretending not to listen. So had the two men in the
seats across the aisle. Tess stared at John Soame in some
confusion. Why was he doing this? He saw the question in
her eyes and smiled that oddly infectious smile of his.

'Blame it on Clark Kent,' he said.

The meeting between Max and John Soame went very well.
As soon as they discovered mutual passions for cricket,
stamps, Sherlock Holmes, and World-War-One flying
machines, the relationship was solid.

While they talked, Tess went over to the window and
looked out. Maybe it would be all right, after all. Mr Soame
would teach Max, she could look after Mrs McMurdo's
house, Mrs Grimble could look after *her* house, and everybody would be happy. A thin shaft of sunlight penetrated
the gloomy overcast sky, and touched a vase of brilliant
yellow roses that stood in the window of a room in the
opposite wing, seeming to set them alight. That's a hopeful
sign, isn't it? she thought.

There was a tentative knock on the door, and a young man poked his head through the gap. 'Hello? Oh, sorry, Max, didn't know you had visitors.'

'It's only my Mum,' Max said.

'Thank you very much,' Tess laughed.

The young man came in a few steps, and smiled. He was dressed in jeans and a bright red pullover, and resembled a plump robin. His hair was a fluff of light brown curls that surrounded his high forehead like a halo, which may have been appropriate, for his shirt had a reversed collar.

'Hello, Mrs Leland?' He extended a pale hand. 'My name is Simon Carter. I've been visiting your son – I hope you don't mind.'

'Not at all,' Tess said, shaking his hand, which was surprisingly warm and firm of grip.

'He's a vicar,' Max said, in pretended disgust.

Simon grinned. 'I've only just been ordained,' he said. 'Doing a bit of hospital visiting until I get a parish assignment. Max is trying to convince me that rugby is a much finer vocation. We are fighting the good fight across a chessboard.' He produced a folded board and a box of chessmen that he had been holding. 'Mind you, we haven't finished a game yet, but . . . early days, early days.'

'I'm going to beat you before I go home,' Max said, with pathetic determination. He looked very tired now.

'Perhaps. But not today,' Simon said, gently. 'How about tomorrow, after lunch?'

Max looked as if he was going to protest, then sank back on his pillows with a sigh. 'Okay,' he said. 'Tomorrow.'

Carter smiled engagingly at them all, and departed.

Tess walked John Soame to the lifts. After he'd prodded the button to go down, he smiled at her. 'I'm sure we can get to the bottom of this business with the phone calls, you know. The police must deal with this kind of thing quite regularly.'

She'd almost forgotten, but he obviously hadn't. 'I'll bet they've never dealt with a vicious wardrobe before.'

He frowned. 'I must admit, that was worrying, if only because it shows someone got into the house.' He prodded the lift button again, rather viciously. 'You must leave the dirty work to those who are good at it,' he told her.

She had to smile. 'Meaning you?'

'Don't I look the type?'

'Frankly, no.'

He nodded, accepting her sympathetic assessment. 'Ah, well, you see – that's my secret strength,' he informed her, solemnly, and limped away down the corridor towards the stairs, his awful mac flapping around his long, thin legs. The lift arrived then, but it was too late.

The caped crusader was gone.

TEN

NIGHTINGALE HAD BECOME ACCUSTOMED TO hospitals, but was still a long way from liking to be in one. Their internal workings were akin to those of a small city erected to the glory of some mysterious and undeclared religion. The gleaming instruments and machines glimpsed through half-open doors seemed manufactured for arcane ritual, the various uniforms of doctors, nurses, technicians and workers were worn like vestments to delineate both status and function. The whole edifice was riddled with intersecting corridors leading to unlabelled destinations, and surrounded by a seemingly random and organic encrustation of outbuildings, annexes, and chambers, many of which emitted sudden unexplained bursts of noise or steam. Most of all, there was a peculiar sound that flowed down every hall – a humming pulsation of hidden machinery, overlaid by the susurrus of unseen people speaking softly in secret rooms, using words you could not quite catch, but which seem filled with important meaning.

He might have enjoyed learning about it all, were it not for the pain.

He could feel it as he walked down the corridors. Not just the pain of the patients, but the pain of their families as well. Worst of all, he had a heightened awareness of Death hovering in the corners and on the stairways, watching for its chance. To enter a hospital may be to enter a city, he thought, but it is a city at war with battalions of nurses, doctors and technicians on one side, and the dark, invisible shadow of mortality on the other. For Death is a guerilla fighter, and will dart in through any

62

door, any window, given even the briefest opportunity. He'd seen its work, and knew he would see much more in the years ahead.

A haggard-looking young doctor passed him in the hallway.

Death is our common enemy, Nightingale thought. But you're the soldier, and I'm just one of the dustmen, one of the ones who come to clear up after the battle is lost. You might stop Death; I only trace its footsteps back to its instrument.

And I'm here to do that, now.

He found the room number he'd been given. The door was open and he looked in to see a woman sitting in a chair beside a bed in which a small boy was sleeping. She was holding a magazine open on her lap, but was not reading it, gazing out instead at the rain clouds scudding low above the trees.

'Mrs Leland?' He spoke softly, and she turned, startled. 'Yes?'

Nightingale introduced himself and showed her his identification. 'I wonder if I might have a few words with you?' he asked. 'Perhaps over a cup of tea? I noticed a visitors' cafeteria as I came in.'

She stood up and glanced at the boy. 'Yes, that would be nice. He's just had his medication and will probably sleep for another hour or so.' She smiled at him.

He was startled by her American accent, which was still strong. Despite constant evidence to the contrary, his image of American girls was of long-legged blue-eyed blondes who were incredibly efficient and laughed a lot.

Tess Leland had long legs, yes, but she was a brunette with dark eyes, and had a fragile beauty that aroused every protective male instinct. Police detectives are no more immune to that than any other man. She was pale, and her skin had a translucency born of skipped meals and bruised nerves. As a result, her wide-set eyes seemed even larger, and her mouth more vulnerable. And yet there was strength there, too, in the way she held herself, chin up and shoulders back, in unconscious imitation of a soldier facing danger. The fact that she was dressed in a jumper

63

and skirt that accentuated her slenderness made her rigidity of purpose and backbone all the more appealing – and sad. Because the thinness was not natural, and the bravery was assumed. This was a frightened and weary woman.

The visitors' cafeteria was newly-decorated, and obviously popular, but they found a corner table empty. Nightingale brought over a tray of tea and biscuits. He draped his rain-soaked coat over a chair and watched her fill their cups.

'I must say, you don't seem very surprised by a visit from the police,' he said.

She glanced up briefly from her task. 'Well, I'm surprised by the speed of it,' she admitted. 'Mr Soame must have made quite a scene to produce such quick results.'

Nightingale stared at her in some puzzlement. 'Mr Soame?'

She put the chrome teapot down and pushed the sugar bowl towards him. 'Yes.' It was her turn to frown. 'Aren't you here because of Mr Soame?'

'No, I'm here about your husband's death.'

She sat back and stared at him. 'But that was months ago.'

'Yes, I know.'

'Then you're not here because of someone asking you to come?'

'I'm afraid not.'

'Oh.' She seemed quite taken aback. After a moment's reflection, she focused on him again. 'I really don't understand. You said it's about Roger's death?'

'Yes. I'm very sorry to cause you any distress, but I need to ask you some questions about Mr Leland.'

'Why?'

This was the sticky part. Particularly as it was his day off and he had no official sanction to question her or to make any other enquiries. He didn't want to upset her, but usually the truth was best. 'Because I have some cause to believe his death was not just an accident.'

Damn, he'd seriously shocked her. 'Of course it was,' she said. 'He was going too fast and lost control of the car on a

64

wet street. There was no question at the time, and the insurance company was perfectly satisfied.' Her voice rose a little.

'Yes, I know. But there was a witness.'

'Was there?' Sudden weariness seemed to sweep away her initial alarm. 'Oh, yes, I seem to remember them saying there was someone . . . ' She sighed and rubbed a temple, then sipped her tea.

'He was a retired police officer, and he had the distinct impression that another car was chasing your husband's, and that was why he was speeding.'

Her eyes widened. 'Someone *chasing* Roger? But that's crazy. Who would do that? Why?'

'That's what I'd like to find out.'

'Even so – it would still be an accident, wouldn't it? I mean, Roger was a good driver, but . . . ' She paused. 'Like a teenager or something, is that what you mean? Because Roger had challenged him at the lights? He'd do that, sometimes, rev the engine and so on. He liked to win, you see.'

Nightingale sipped his tea, then shook his head. 'I don't think it was like that, exactly.'

'No, of course not, because Max was in the car. Roger would never have played games with Max there.'

'Max?'

'My son.'

Of course, it had been on the report, a child in the car. Nightingale was horrified. 'You mean he's still in hospital because of the accident? I had no idea he was so badly — '

'No, no, Max wasn't hurt at all,' Tess said quickly. She could see this was a nice man, that he'd been instantly upset to think of Max being hurt. She didn't know what it was all about, why he should be coming along to talk to her after all this time, but perhaps it was just bureaucracy, the slow grinding of the paper wheels. 'They had to cut him out of the car, it's true, but he was wearing a seatbelt at the time of the crash. It was an adult seatbelt, though, and he slid out and ended up under the dash, sort of cocooned. Bruised and shaken up, and shocked, of course – but whole.'

'He's ill, then?'

She nodded. 'Yes. Rheumatic fever. He's at school near here.' She stared at the sugar bowl, then looked up at him anxiously, and seemed to be seeking some kind of approval. 'I wanted to keep him home, but everyone said he should go back to school, that it would be better for him to be busy and distracted. It seemed so – so *English*, stiff upper lip, all that. I wasn't sure.'

'Did *he* want to come?'

'He said he did. In the end I could see that probably it would be better for him to go back to school than stay at home and notice the . . . ' She raised and lowered her shoulders. 'The emptiness. And I had to go to work, anyway. So, I sent him back.'

'Children are resilient.'

She nodded. 'Yes. But the accident and Roger's death must have upset him far more than he let on – he still has nightmares.' She took a deep breath and let it go in a rush around her words, as if she had to get them out quickly. 'And I think that he got sick like this because he was trying too hard not to show how much it hurt, so his body – sort of – gave him a way out. Does that make any sense?'

'Shock does strange things to people. We see a lot of it, I'm afraid, and it's not always just a matter of a cup of sweet tea. There's something called delayed shock, that could lower someone's resistance, I expect. I don't know if it could give him something as serious as rheumatic fever, but I guess it could make him more vulnerable to the germ or whatever when it came along.' (Or make an old man vulnerable to fear, he added to himself.)

She nodded, apparently satisfied with this, and drank her tea.

Nightingale ate a biscuit, giving her time. When she'd topped up both their cups, he spoke. 'Did your husband have any enemies, Mrs Leland?'

She frowned, but there was a trace of amusement in her eyes. 'Good heavens, you really do say that.'

'I beg your pardon?'

'Oh, I'm sorry, but it did sound like something from a television series.' She scowled and put on a husky voice. ' "Did your husband have any enemies?" '

He smiled, but shrugged. 'I can't think of any other way to ask it,' he admitted. 'Does it upset you?'

She shook her head. 'No. If you mean talking about Roger, that is. I'm over the worst now.' She sighed. 'As to whether he had enemies, I imagine he had quite a few.'

'Can you remember their names?' Nightingale reached for his notebook.

But she was shaking her head. 'No. I didn't mean I knew of any specific ones – just that it wouldn't surprise me if some people hated Roger, that's all. You see, he was very competitive. More than anything, Roger liked to win. He never meant to hurt people, though, there was no cruelty in him. He was always surprised when they got angry or sulked. People didn't understand or believe he was just out to win for the sheer joy of it, but it was true. Maybe a psychiatrist would argue the point, but I think he was like that because he was always trying to prove to *himself* that he could win. That was what mattered, not beating other people down, but seeing that he could succeed at whatever he took on.' She smiled to herself, ruefully. 'Roger was like a child in many ways; he believed in living for the minute, and enjoying everything – it was all games, really. That's why I asked about the car race – what do they call it, a "chicken run" or something?'

'I don't think it was anything like that,' Nightingale said. He looked down at his empty teacup, and moved the spoon back and forth in the saucer.

'But you suspect someone was trying to . . . to . . . what?' She was groping for a sense of what he was after. 'Catch him? Hurt him? Frighten him?' She paused, then spoke in a whisper. 'Kill him?'

Nightingale shook his head. 'Any of those, all of them, none of them. I just don't know. Ivor Peters just said there was something wrong, and I believe him.'

'Who is Ivor Peters?'

He explained who Peters was, and what he said had happened at the scene of the accident. He added that Peters had since passed away, but supplied no details.

'Poor old man. What did he say this man looked like?'

He gave her the description from Peters' notebook – it

67

was all he had. 'About six feet tall, brown hair, regular features, slim-built, wearing dark blue trousers and a light blue windcheater over a white shirt, no tie, no glasses, no distinguishing marks.'

She looked at him. 'That could be you, if you were wearing the right clothes . . . ' She looked around. 'Or quite a few men in this cafeteria. Or Max's consultant, come to think of it.'

'I know. Peters only caught a quick look, and his glasses had come off when he fell. But the description was more or less the same from the girl who rented the car, and the hotel maid. Except they added that he was attractive. Of course, Ivor Peters was retired, and the official verdict was Accidental Death, so he wasn't in a position to arrange a photo-fit session or get a police artist to draw the man.' (And neither am I, damn it, he thought.)

'Did anyone say anything about his voice?' Tess asked, casually.

He stared at her. 'His *voice*? No, I don't think that was mentioned by anyone. Why?'

She told him about the phone call, and the silly game with the booby-trapped wardrobe. 'Although it didn't seem silly at the time,' she admitted. 'It frightened me half to death.'

'Anonymous threats are always scary,' Luke agreed, sympathetically. 'It's not the threat itself so much as the feeling that it could be anybody – a stranger in the street or, even worse, someone you know and trust. You feel the floor isn't solid any more.'

'Yes, that's it exactly.' She was grateful for his under-standing. She had been feeling so very foolish about it all, behaving so weakly when it was so important to stay strong for Max.

'And you say there have been other calls?'

'Yes, but they were only silent ones. Nobody ever spoke.'

'It does seem odd, especially when you add it to that burglary of yours —' he said, slowly.

She was astonished. 'You know about that?'

'Oh, yes. Computers are wonderful things,' he smiled. 'I gather it was on the day of the funeral.'

'Yes. That was the cruellest thing about it, to have your house torn apart when you're at your own husband's cremation. I could hardly bear it. Fortunately, after the service, I had sent Max to stay with a friend for a few days, and we managed to clear it all up before he came back. I just didn't want him to know about it – on top of everything else. He was shocked and upset enough as it was.'

'I'm afraid it's not all that unusual,' Nightingale admitted. 'Houses are often left empty during funerals, and burglars can read the obituary columns just like anyone else.'

'I suppose so,' she sighed.

'The pattern of the break-in seemed rather unusual to me, though,' he said.

'It seemed just awful to me.' Tess shivered. 'I felt there wasn't a room they hadn't invaded, a thing they'd left untouched.'

'And yet they took very little and destroyed nothing.'

'Yes. The insurance man told me I was very lucky that they hadn't broken up the house instead of just dumping out drawers and so on.'

'It seems more likely to me that they were searching for something,' Nightingale said, leaning back and regarding her from grave, dark eyes. She felt she was being explored and assessed. His glance seemed to travel along hidden veins and nerves, following them to her heart and brain, but she did not feel the sense of invasion she'd felt from the burglary. Had she been approved of – temporarily – or not? It was impossible to tell. She returned his gaze, steadily, but he was not open to a similar evaluation. His personal doors and windows were closed and curtained, she could not discover him that way. Just a tall and attractive young man doing the job he was trained to do. Nothing like Kojak at all. Or the town sheriff back in Amity. How much of his kindness stemmed from his own personality, and how much from his training? Was that smile just Lesson Three on how to put a person at ease? Was Lesson Ten how to soften up someone with gentleness, then pin her with a sharp and unexpected question?

'Do you think they were looking for this money the man on the phone asked you about?' he asked, suddenly.

69

Ah, Lesson Ten. She hadn't expected it so soon. Steady, now. 'But there *isn't* any money. I told that to Mr Soame. Roger had an insurance policy that paid off the mortgage, and another to cover Max's school fees, but very little personal insurance – even less, once they found out he hadn't been wearing a seatbelt.'

'Was that usual – his not wearing a seatbelt?'

A shadow of some distant annoyance crossed her face. 'I'm afraid so. Roger was not one to be confined, unfortunately.'

'I see. Go on.'

'Well, after I'd settled all the outstanding bills, there was hardly anything left. Enough to set aside as an emergency fund, but certainly not enough to live on. Not even enough interest from it to cover poll tax, in fact. I had to go back to work, if we wanted to stay fed and clothed. There was no other way. The house is big, and a drain to keep up, but I wanted to hold on to it if I could – because I thought eventually I could sell it to provide a start for Max or something.'

Nightingale nodded, but his expression had become faintly sceptical. Tess felt oddly let down. Nobody seemed to believe her. She only wished there *was* some money.

'So you don't know anything about any sum of money that your husband may have had at the time of his death?'

'No, I don't. I really don't.'

'I see.' He had opened his notebook, but had found no need to write anything in it. Now he closed it and put it back into his inside jacket pocket, watching her face as he did so. She seemed genuine enough. Was this story about the phone calls true? About the booby-trapped wardrobe? She'd said the cleaning lady had taken some of the 'silent' calls. Had they come when she herself was home or conveniently away?

It was not uncommon for lonely, grief-stricken women to behave oddly, to do things to draw attention to themselves. There was the further complication of her son's illness, the stress and strain of it all, the need for comfort and support from any direction, through any excuse. Was she like that?

He could believe her, he *wanted* to believe her, because it tended to vindicate Peters' conviction that there was something wrong about Roger Leland's death. And, by inference, his own similar conviction about Ivor Peters' death. And yet . . .

There was no proof. No proof for any of it.

And he only had so much spare time.

He looked again into Tess Leland's eyes. She could be imagining things.

So could he.

And somewhere in the back of his mind, he could hear Abbott's dry, quiet voice. 'Two wrongs don't make a case.'

ELEVEN

MAX ARRIVED HOME FOUR DAYS later. He was thin, and his pale cheeks were flushed with excitement at having travelled such a distance in an ambulance.

Tess's heart contracted when she and Mrs Grimble helped the ambulancemen transfer Max to his bed. Although reasonably fit for his age, he had never been a robust child, and now his body seemed all skin and bones. He looked around the room, as if checking that it had not changed while he was away, and his eyes widened at the sight of the big television set and matching video recorder sitting on his desk. 'It's a present from your Uncle Richard,' Mrs Grimble informed him.

'He's not my uncle,' Max objected.

'No, nor mine, neither,' Mrs Grimble agreed. 'But he meant well, and you should write him a note to say thank you.'

'Okay, I will,' Max said, resignedly. He'd propped himself first on one elbow and then the other, in order to get the full circle of inspection, and now he flopped back onto his pillows with a thump. Mostly his movements were slow and listless, but he seemed more weary than ill. His joints were still slightly painful, but he didn't complain. Tess started to murmur sympathetically, and he glared at her. Apparently she wasn't supposed to say anything about her 'poor baby', *especially* in front of the ambulancemen.

Mrs Grimble glanced across the bed at Tess, her eyes brimming with unshed tears at the sight of Max's thin body. She'd only heard about his illness, not seen it first-hand. Now she realized how sick he'd been and how

72

poorly he still was. 'Poor mite,' she murmured, as they left the room.

'He'll be fine,' Tess said, with more confidence than she felt. 'All we have to do is feed him, look after him, and love him.'

'All any mother ever wants to do,' Mrs Grimble observed. ''Cept these days nobody lets her.'

Tess looked at the old woman with deep affection. Mrs Grimble had brought up two sons, both of whom had turned out almost too well, for they were now abroad making careers for themselves. One day, when they'd settled, one of them might send for her, but Tess selfishly hoped it wouldn't be for a long time.

Of course, Mrs Grimble might refuse to go to a new and unfamiliar life among the palm trees or mountain ranges, far from the London she'd known all her years. And there was always her 'baby' brother Walter to consider. Rarely-seen but ever-present Walter, the charmer, the weakling, the pay-day drunk. Although Tess had only met him a few times, and had never really talked to him, she felt she knew Walter Briggs and his unfortunate history only too well. She didn't think the Grimble sons would be sending for *him* one day.

Tess saw the ambulancemen out, thanked them for their care of Max, then waved them goodbye. Closing the door seemed, suddenly, a monumental task. It signalled the end of one phase and the start of the next. Max was her responsibility now, not the doctors' or the nurses', or even the school's.

As she came back down the hall, the phone rang. Tess picked it up, glancing in the mirror as she did so, and brushing back some wisps of hair. 'Hello?'

'Hello, Mrs Leland.' It was the same horrible whisper, distorted, weird. 'I'm still waiting for the money.'

She froze, her hand still caught in her hair. 'Who is this?' she demanded, more bravely than she felt.

'Watch over that boy of yours,' the voice advised.

'Who is this?' she repeated.

Silence.

'Hello?' she demanded.

Mrs Grimble, who had come down the stairs behind her, spoke up, making her jump. 'Give it to me,' she said, firmly, and took it from Tess's grasp. 'Hello?' After a minute she spoke again, more impatiently. 'Hello?'

Apparently her authoritative challenge evoked no response. As she held the receiver out in front of her and glared at it, there came the unmistakable click of a phone being hung up at the other end.

Mrs Grimble slammed the receiver down in disgust. 'Fish feathers,' she said, furiously. It was her worst expletive. 'I'm sick and tired of it.'

'What did he say?'

Mrs Grimble looked startled. 'Say? Said nothing, as usual. Never spoke a word. What did he say to you?'

Tess started to speak, then thought better of it. 'Just nonsense,' she said.

'Hmmph,' Mrs Grimble said. A bright pink flush of annoyance suffused her cheeks. 'Wretched kids.' She marched back towards the kitchen, mumbling. Tess stared at the phone, black and silent now.

It had been no child who spoke to her.

That evening, as Tess sat in her favourite rocker, looking through dealers' catalogues, there was a knock at the door and John Soame looked in. He had been moving his things into the flat gradually, dividing his possessions and his days between London and Cambridge. Now he was settled in upstairs for the duration of his researches, but he had been out all that day.

'Everything all right?' he asked. His hair had been ruffled by the wind, and raindrops spattered his spectacles. He took them off and rubbed them absently on the front of his mac.

Tess smiled. 'Yes, thanks. The king is in his counting-house and, when last seen, was going over his stamp books and checking over his airplane models to make certain everything was intact. Apparently I have committed the sin of "tidying up".'

'Something no boy can tolerate.' He returned her smile, then glanced at the large book she had balanced on the

74

edge of the table. He came across and peered over her shoulder. 'What year did you say the McMurdo house was built?'

'1875.'

He indicated the reproduction wallpaper collection she was considering. 'Those didn't come in until the nineties.'

She sighed and closed the book. 'I know, but it is so difficult to be exact. Sometimes you just have to settle for what you can get, and trust that the ambience of the whole will satisfy the customer, who doesn't know dates from figs, anyway.'

He made a disapproving sound, but there was a twinkle in his eye. 'Bad history, but good decorating, is that it?'

'Something like that. I could, of course, have some paper made specially – I have done, for the three large rooms – at a cost you wouldn't like to know about. But this is just for a small bedroom. Unlimited budget or not, I hate to waste a client's money unnecessarily.'

He nodded, then glanced up at the clock on the wall. 'Is it all right if I go in to say hello to Max on my way upstairs? I won't tire him, I promise.'

'Of course.' She watched him start for the door, and found herself wishing him back. 'Ummmmm – ' She hesitated.

'Yes?'

'There was another phone call this afternoon, just after Max came back,' she said.

He frowned and came a few steps into the room. 'And?'

'That's all. The same nasty whispering voice. He said he was still waiting for the money. And then he told me to look after my son. Then, just – silence. But not very nice silence, somehow.'

He came a little further into the room. 'No instructions about where this mythical money was to be given over, anything like that?'

'No.'

'No specific threats?'

'No. It was more in the nature of a second reminder,' Tess said, wryly. She picked at a loose thread on her sleeve. 'By the way, I forgot to tell you, a policeman came

75

to see me at the hospital the day after you came up. He wanted to know about Roger's accident.'

'Oh?' John Soame came a few steps more into the room.

'He said there had been a witness to the accident – an old man – who thought Roger's car was being chased by another car, and that was what caused him to crash. He saw the man driving the other car, and tried to find him.'

Soame stiffened. 'Why should he do that?'

'Apparently he was an ex-policeman. Instinct, maybe? Or perhaps just curiosity. The detective wasn't sure, I don't think. Not really.'

'I see. And has he found him?'

'I don't know. He's dead now, anyway, so — '

'Who's dead?'

'The old man. The witness.'

Soame sighed, shrugged, smiled. 'So it came to nothing, then.'

'Yes.' She looked down at her lap, then up at him again. 'I told the detective about the telephone calls. I don't know whether he believed me or not,' Tess said. 'He left looking very bemused and I haven't heard from him since. It was all rather – upsetting.'

He regarded her through his misted glasses. 'I should have said you've had more than enough to upset any six people during the past few months,' he said, gruffly, and went out.

Tess listened to his footsteps going up the stairs, and felt relieved. Although it might mean resigning from the feminist movement if it got out, she was glad to have John Soame living in the house. She could lean on him without being emotionally involved. It might seem an odd arrangement, but it made her happy.

Unfortunately, it didn't please everyone.

TWELVE

'I CAN'T BELIEVE YOU'VE DONE THIS!' Richard Hendricks said, reproachfully. He'd tracked her down to the McMurdo house, and was now following her from room to room as she took measurements and jotted down her latest ideas on colours and patterns. He was very upset. 'I got home late last night. This morning I called the hospital to find out how Max is, and they tell me he's gone home. Wonderful. So I go around to see him, and discover you've actually *installed* a complete stranger in your home, and turned Max over to him.'

'Mr Soame is highly qualified,' Tess said, calmly, stepping over a pile of bricks and broken tiles. 'He's a Cambridge professor, for goodness' sake. Adrian knows him very well.'

'Am I to gather you think *that's* some kind of recommendation?' Richard asked. 'Honestly, Tess, you are so naïve it sometimes frightens me. Adrian Brevitt might be a fashionable name in interior decoration, but he has some very odd friends along with it.'

Tess stopped to look at him. Outside there was a cheerful chuckle of workmen and the sloppy churn of a cement mixer. From above there came the intermittent tap of a hammer, and a persistent scraping noise as someone removed years of accumulated wallpaper. Traffic rumbled distantly, and a jet growled its way across the sky to Heathrow. Here, however, in what would eventually become a breakfast room, there was silence. When Tess finally spoke, her voice was cold. 'Just what do you mean by "odd friends", Richard?'

He looked uncomfortable, obviously not expecting quite

this reaction from her. 'Oh, just gossip, I suppose. But gossip has to start somewhere – and it's said he's popular at a certain kind of party.'

'I had no idea you were so narrow-minded. Adrian makes no secret of being gay.'

'I didn't mean *that*. What he does in bed is his own business. I meant he's popular because of what he brings with him.'

'I don't understand.'

He sighed in exasperation. '*Drugs*, damn it. Marijuana, cocaine, Ecstasy, that sort of thing. Oh, come along, Tess, don't tell me you never suspected it?'

'I never thought about it one way or another,' Tess said, slowly. 'Particularly in connection with Adrian.'

'Exactly!' Richard pounced on this evidence of her naïveté. 'Any more than you thought about getting involved with this Soame character.'

'I am not "involved" with him,' Tess snapped. 'He's a lodger.'

'He comes into your part of the house, doesn't he? He sees Max, alone, every day. God knows what might happen. Especially if he's a "friend" of Adrian's.'

Tess felt like slapping his face. 'In fact, he is – was – Adrian's brother-in-law. And you have absolutely no right to make such insinuations about a man you've never met. He's a good, kind man — '

'They often *seem* like good, kind men — ' Richard began.

'Oh!' Exasperated, Tess turned away and stalked into the area that would eventually become a dining room, but which at present was simply another rectangle surrounded by walls of lathe hung with loops of unconnected wiring cable. Richard followed her.

'You took Adrian's word, I suppose. Did you bother to check up on Soame? Did you find out if he was really from Cambridge, or if he'd been fired from some little school or other – or even whether he was a teacher at all?'

'No.'

'Lord, Tess, you are a fool. He could be anything.'

She stopped her pacing and faced him. 'Now you are getting totally ridiculous, Richard. What would be his

78

point in taking on a task for which he was totally unqualified? And Adrian would never do anything to hurt Max. The decision is made, and that's an end to it. It's my choice, not yours. My life, not yours. I'm sorry if you don't approve.'

'It's not that I don't approve. It's not a matter for approval. The whole arrangement simply horrifies me.' He ran his hands through his hair and then stood before her, reproach on his face, pleading in his voice. 'And then there is this other thing hanging over you. Why didn't you come to *me* when these silent phone calls started?'

'Because I thought they were just one of those cranky things that happen in a city,' Tess said, irritably, knowing he was probably right. She should have told him, if only because he knew so many people in useful positions. 'How did you know about them, anyway?'

'Your gorgon of a housekeeper told me, this morning. My God, I thought she was bad enough before, but since Roger died she's got positively bizarre. I swear she was wearing a tea cosy on her head.'

'She's fine. I like her just the way she is.'

'And what about that sleazy brother of hers? I suppose you like him, too?'

'I hardly know him.'

'Well, he had his boots under your kitchen table this morning, and very expensive boots they were, compared to the rest of his get-up, which owed more to Oxfam than Oxford Street. Looked like he felt right at home, drinking your coffee and eating your pie.'

'Oh?' Tess was momentarily startled. 'Well, I don't mind if Mrs Grimble has him around now and again,' she said, casually, not wanting to let him see that it was a surprise to her. Mrs Grimble had never mentioned Walter coming to the house when Tess was out. Or feeding him, either. Not that Tess begrudged her the privilege, or Walter the pie, but she was rather sorry to learn of it this way. It would no doubt give Richard even more reason to fret and think her unreliable if he realized it had been done without her permission. 'I'm just grateful she gives me as much time as she does. I really depend on her.'

79

'Well, she's no protection against people threatening you, is she? I mean, suppose they don't stop at phone calls? You're a woman alone — '

'But I'm not alone, now, Richard. That's the whole point. I've organized it all, and neither I nor Max are ever alone now.'

'Temporarily. And questionably.' His voice softened, 'Why don't you just let *me* take care of you and Max, instead of blithely turning yourselves over to some stranger? I'm earning good money again, and my house is more than large enough for a family. You could stay at home with the boy, be a proper mother, a proper wife. You wouldn't have to come out and work in all . . . this . . . mess.' He gestured around at the half-finished interior.

Tess smiled, and looked around, too. 'What you don't seem to understand is that I *like* working in all this mess, as you call it. What's more, I'm very good at it.'

'That's all very well, but — '

She didn't want to seem unkind, or ungrateful, but his persistence was beginning to make her feel a little claustrophobic. 'Look, Richard, I'm grateful for your concern, but it is not needed. Truly.'

She went into the kitchen and he followed, doggedly, trying another tack. 'What does Mrs Grimble think of this Soame? Does she like him?'

'She wasn't sure, at first,' Tess admitted, picking up some quarry tiles that had been stacked on the old stone sink. She held them closer to the window, to get the colour fixed in her mind. 'But then she doesn't like most people. At first.'

'Hah. Don't dismiss that, first impressions are important.' He seemed to have forgotten his own opinion of Mrs Grimble and her questionable freeloading brother. He was off again, pacing and thinking aloud. 'You said he was Adrian's "ex"-brother-in-law. Divorced or widowed?'

'Widowed – if it matters.'

'Oh, it matters, all right. Don't you see the pattern? All right, you had a few odd phone calls before, as you said, it happens in the city. But I'll bet they only started to get unpleasant when Soame appeared on the scene.'

'Not at all — ' But her voice was hesitant.

He pounced. 'Ah, I *am* right, then. You must have mentioned the silent calls at some point in your first conversation with him. Did you?'

'I don't think so. I don't remember, to be honest.' He was talking so fast he was confusing her.

'You must have, and it probably gave him the idea. I bet he wasn't in the house when the threatening calls came, was he?'

'No, but — '

'I knew it. Don't you see? He probably wants to frighten you, to make you dependent on him and get some kind of hold on you.' His expression was almost gleeful.

'*Richard*. What on *earth* is the matter with you?' Tess stared at him. 'John Soame is a quiet, simple man. When you meet him you'll see that all this is just *nonsense*.'

They glared at one another across the sink.

When Richard spoke again, his voice was icy. 'I have met him, as it happens, and he was neither quiet nor simple. I was greeted first by your loony housekeeper, and then by this Soame, who was prancing around Max's bed with a twisted coathanger, pretending to be a swordsman.'

Tess grinned. 'Wish I'd seen that.'

'It was not edifying – and the boy was far too excited. He's supposed to be convalescent, isn't he? That kind of thing could easily affect his heart.'

'What kind of thing?'

'Laughing, getting excited, talking too much. If you ask me — '

'I didn't.'

' — Soame is bad for the boy. I talked to him for ten minutes, and he struck me as very odd indeed.'

'He's shy — '

'Shy a few marbles.'

Tess glared at him. 'Do you think I am a complete cretin?'

'Well, of course not, but — '

'Then why do you insist on questioning everything I do where Max is concerned? He's my son, not yours.'

'But I *am* a legal co-guardian,' Richard reminded her. 'Roger trusted me to look after Max's interests. He must have had a reason for that.'

She turned away. 'Roger had a false image of me that he'd built up in his own mind. Perhaps it was my fault for letting him think I was the clinging, dependent wife – it seemed so important to him. But it was not a true image, Richard, and I think you know it. I am not a fool, and I would never do anything to endanger my son.'

'Not consciously, no. But you're too trusting. You always believe the best of people — '

'And you always believe the worst,' she interrupted.

'I've had good cause,' he snapped. 'I came up from poverty, Tess. The real, grinding thing, with a father broken by unemployment and a mother driven into a mental ward by despair. It wasn't an easy climb for me, and I encountered some real bastards on the way. I learned how to recognize them, and I learned how to deal with them. They don't always wear their colours on their sleeves, but the signs are there if you know what to look for.'

'Especially if you *want* to find them.'

His expression became bleak, and he seemed genuinely wounded by her flare of anger and resentment. 'I'm sorry, Tess, I really am. But I intend to make it *my* business to find out more about Soame, since you won't.'

She put down the tiles, and brushed the reddish dust from her hands. 'You may do what you like, I am sure you'll find nothing wrong.'

He stood watching her. When he eventually spoke, his voice was soft. 'Oh, Tess, I don't want to quarrel about this. I want to marry you, remember? I want to look after you.'

Tess was unconvinced. She glared at him above crossed arms. 'Well, you're going the wrong way about it. Anyway, since you're usually in Amsterdam or Paris or Nigeria or America or God knows where, doing deals, I don't see how you could find *time* to work a wedding into your schedule.'

Richard's face brightened – he had only heard the words, not the tone. 'Just give me a date, Tess, any date,' he said, eagerly.

'Miz Leland?' It was Ernie Flowers, one of the workmen. He'd often done renovations for Adrian's firm and knew something of her requirements. 'We found this under the moulding in the upstairs hall,' he said, holding out a long thin scrap of paper. 'I reckon it's the original wallpaper.'

Tess took it from him, grateful for the distraction. 'Red. I knew it! And not flocked, either. Thanks, Ernie.'

'That's okay.' Ernie eyed Richard doubtfully. 'Anything else you want, just call out. I'm not far away.' He wandered out into the hall, slowly, whistling under his breath.

'You don't seem to lack for protectors,' Richard said in a thin voice.

She looked at him. 'Some are more welcome than others,' she replied evenly.

He went over to the bay window and stared out into the unkempt rear garden. 'Did you tell Max about the calls?' he asked, after a moment.

Tess stared at him in surprise. 'No, of course I didn't. He's still very weak, and I refuse to upset him in any way. That includes not telling him about stupid threatening phone calls or any other problems of any kind. The doctor said he must have rest, and rest he shall have.'

He turned on her, his voice harsh. 'Then it must be Soame who has turned him against me.'

'Why on earth would he do that?' she asked, astonished.

'I don't know,' he said, bleakly. 'But when I saw Max this morning he was very distant, almost cold. Max and I were good friends before your precious "lodger" came along. Now I can see I am going to be systematically shut out.'

'Oh, Richard, that isn't true.'

He jammed his hands in his pockets and scowled at her. She'd never seen him untidy or upset before – not even when Roger died. It gave him a new dimension, somehow. Controlled, careful Richard Hendricks apparently had a weakness – and it was for her. All the dinners and the attentions she had thought mere kindness were apparently much more, otherwise why was he so angry, so hurt? She was annoyed by his anger, and even more annoyed to discover she was excited by it. It made her feel foolishly valuable – with the accent on foolish, she told herself, abruptly.

'Richard — ' she began, in a gentle voice.

He interrupted, glancing towards the shadow of Ernie

Flowers, who was ostentatiously lingering nearby. 'Why don't we finish this over dinner tonight? Is eight o'clock still all right?'

'Oh. Oh, dear.' She felt herself flushing, and looked down at the floor. Presumably this was some previous arrangement, but she couldn't for the life of her remember making it with him. When she looked up again, his expression was wary, as if he knew from the set of her shoulders exactly what she was going to say. But she had no choice. 'I'm sorry, Richard, I hadn't realized that was a firm date. As I hadn't heard from you I'm afraid I've made other plans. You see, John felt we ought to have a working dinner . . . '

Richard Hendricks' face went white. 'I see very clearly.'

'Well, Max *is* getting better, and his lessons have to be organized — '

'I don't think it's only Max who needs lessons, Tess. I think you have a lot to learn about people, and how foolish it is to take them on face value. Well, I wish you both luck in your education. Perhaps, when you find out more about this Soame – as I firmly intend to do – you'll ring me and admit you were wrong. Until then, I leave you in charge of your life, since that seems to mean so much to you. I hope you – and Max – don't have reason to regret it.'

THIRTEEN

TESS STARED AFTER RICHARD HENDRICKS' retreating figure with resentment. His outburst was simply wounded vanity, the lion growls of a self-appointed king of the jungle who'd got a thorn in his paw through grasping the wrong end of the stick. Of course, she would pay no attention to it, none at all. It was outrageous to suggest that there was anything sinister about John Soame.

Wasn't it?

And Richard Hendricks was a jealous, possessive *idiot*.

Wasn't he?

'Hey, how ya goin'?' asked a soft Australian drawl from above her left ear.

Startled into a sideways leap that nearly ended in a broken ankle, Tess found herself confronted by a lanky, sandy-haired man in very large suede boots. He'd appeared so suddenly and so quietly that he might have been a ghost. He was dressed in a bright brown suit that matched, almost perfectly, his bright brown eyes. He was tall, tanned, and handsome – a lad from Ipanema by way of Bondi Beach.

'I'm Archie McMurdo,' he told her, with a devastating grin. 'And I don't think Aunt Dolly is going to be very happy with the kitchen windows you're putting in.'

Ten minutes later, Tess was in the phone box on the corner. From its cat-scented confines she could see Archie McMurdo deep in conversation with Ernie Flowers, who looked less than enamoured of this new source of irritation.

'But Adrian, why didn't you *tell* me Mrs McMurdo was leaving London?' Tess demanded, when she'd finally got through to her boss.

'I did,' Adrian said, absently. 'I'm sure I did.' He sounded preoccupied.

'No, you didn't. I just called the Savoy and they said she'd gone abroad. Where is she, may I ask? And how long will she be gone?'

Adrian sighed heavily to convey that she was causing him pain and suffering. Again. 'Dolly McMurdo has gone to Italy, dear Tess. She'll be back in three months or so. She phoned me last Tuesday, I think it was. Or Wednesday.'

'But how am I to get on without her?' Tess demanded.

'A great deal more easily, I should imagine,' came the bland reply. 'She gave you *carte blanche*, darling girl. Use it.'

'And do I have *carte blanche* to deal with darling Archie, as well?' Tess asked, drily.

Adrian's attention was finally caught. 'Who?'

'Archie McMurdo, Aunt Dolly's dear nephew. He showed up here at the house a few minutes ago and said he was deputizing for her. He then proceeded to complain about absolutely everything.' She bent slightly and peered out of the callbox. 'In fact, he still is.'

'Never heard of him,' Adrian said. He was trying to sound breezy, but a fretful undercurrent in his voice betrayed him. 'She gave us complete authority, my dear. In writing, if you remember, at my very cautious and obviously necessary request. Are you certain he said he was her *nephew*?'

'Yes. He seemed to know quite a lot about her – and he showed me some letters from her.'

'About the house?'

'No, just personal letters. But that's not the point, Adrian,' Tess continued in exasperation, spacing out her words as if she were speaking to a recalcitrant six-year-old, which, in a way, he was. 'I think you should get in touch with her and clarify the position. If he's speaking for her, fine, we'll have to do our best to keep him happy. But if he's not, I want her to say so, preferably in writing, before he drives all the workmen crazy – to say nothing of me.'

'Well, I'll do what I can, ducky.' He sounded rather doubtful.

'Thank you. In the meantime, what do you suggest?'

There was a short pause, during which she was certain Adrian was doing something other than considering her problem. Like reading a book or filing his nails. Finally, he spoke. 'Charm him.'

'What?' She wasn't sure she'd heard correctly.

'Charm him, I said. Tell him how clever he is, and that you'll think over everything he suggests, and perhaps when it's all done Aunt Dolly will invite him round to see it. Bat your eyelashes, dear. Stick out your boobs. Swivel your hips.'

'Unzip his fly and suggest we go upstairs?' Tess asked, in honey and vinegar tones.

'That was unworthy of you,' Adrian clucked.

'Well, so was your suggestion unworthy of you.'

Adrian sighed – he was a world-class sigher. 'I am absolutely certain you can manage him. Now run along and leave me to wrestle with this ghastly list of new requirements from the Sheik's secretary. Would you believe he wants *solid* gold bath taps?'

'Yes, Adrian, I believe it,' Tess said, resignedly. 'I also believe you will be shortly called to court in order to bail me out for assaulting Archie McMurdo with a deadly weapon – probably a brick.'

She hung up on his 'tsk-tsk' and marched back up the street to Number Eighteen to confront Archie, who now stood alone, having been deserted by an impatient and disgusted Ernie Flowers.

'Your little man seems to think he knows best,' Archie said, with maddening insouciance.

'I am sure he does,' Tess said. 'Unless, of course, you have a degree in architecture, structural engineering, or are a qualified surveyor?'

He beamed down at her, but said nothing.

'Well?' She demanded. 'Are you any of those things?'

'Nope.'

'Have you any practical experience in building or construction work of any kind?'

87

His smile widened – she was amusing him. 'Nope,' he said, cheerfully. 'Do you?'

Tess felt her blood pressure start to rise. 'I have a degree in art history and over eight years' practical experience in the field of interior decoration, particularly in the restoration of older properties. What is more, all the structural work on this house has been under the direction of a qualified architect whom we consult for all our renovation requirements.'

He was grinning, now. 'Aunt Dolly said you were a beaut sheila, all right,' he said, admiringly. 'Peppery, too. Never told me you were a Yank, though. Generally, I like Yanks. Sympathetic to 'em, you might say, seeing as we all kicked over the Pommy traces in our time. Fact remains, that kitchen needs bigger windows. Putting on the style is all very well, but it kind of spoils the effect to have your client cut off a thumb the first week in residence because she can't see what she's doing, don't you think?'

'I'll speak to the architect about it.'

Archie smiled expansively, showing wonderful teeth and two dimples. 'There you are, that's all I ask. I just want Aunt Dol to be happy in her new home.'

'Very considerate of you.' Tess was still nettled.

'Aw, now, don't go snaky on me. Let me buy you some lunch. We should get to know one another, because I intend to be around a lot from now on.'

'You do?' Tess asked, faintly. She envisaged weeks of fruitless argument with this antipodean alarmist. Handsome he might be, but he hadn't the first idea about Victorian authenticity. Or kitchens. But Adrian had spoken.

'All right,' she conceded.

It was a very long lunch.

They found a small Italian restaurant nearby. There Archie McMurdo talked of many things – carefully avoiding the subject of interior décor. He told her of his travels, his property in Australia, his hobbies, his ambitions.

In fact, Archie spent so much time and energy

88

systematically attempting to charm her that Tess hardly had a chance to follow Adrian's suggestion that *she* charm *him*. Concerning smiles and graces, the lunch was a definite contender for the Annual Sweetness and Light Award, providing the judges could keep from throwing up.

He *was* very attractive, of course.

Nice voice, nice hands.

Shame about the clothes.

Still, by the time they'd reached the strega and cappuccino, she'd decided to let him win the charm contest. Why not? He was neither Max's edgy neuter tutor nor her late husband's suddenly possessive ex-partner. (She still felt cross, remembering Richard's demands.) Here was a handsome stranger who thought she was lovely and kept saying so. It is very soothing to be told you are lovely, especially when you are feeling hot and cross and frustrated. If Richard wanted to be jealous, well then, she'd give him reason. Damn him.

After the meal, she thanked Archie, deftly evaded enquiries about her plans for the coming evening, and fled homewards. There had been a great deal of icy white wine with the spaghetti vongole, and while being charmed was one thing, being seduced was quite another. One man in her new life had been pleasant, two had been interesting – but three could be confusing, if she wasn't careful. She needed time to think.

And lots of black coffee.

Mrs Grimble was in a hurry to get away, and John Soame had gone to spend the afternoon in the British Museum Reading Room, so there was only Max to tell about the initially annoying (but eventually delightful) Archie McMurdo. Max listened to her description with deep interest.

'Why don't you get Mr Flowers to brick him up in the basement?' he suggested, with all the ghoulish delight of a nine-year-old.

'Don't tempt me,' Tess said, and started to laugh despite herself. 'I think Ernie would enjoy doing it, though.'

'Never mind, Mum. These things are sent to try us,' Max said, and sighed wheezily, like Mrs Grimble. 'We have to rise above them,' he said, in a fair imitation of the housekeeper's lugubrious tones.

'I guess I have to admit it wasn't all that trying, in the end,' Tess admitted. 'He took me to lunch and told me I was a lovely sheila.'

'I see.' Max eyed her censoriously. 'And did you believe him?'

'Shouldn't I have?'

He thought about this, and folded his arms across his chest. 'You're not too bad looking for your age,' he said, in a judicious tone.

'Oh, thanks very much.'

'But I don't think you should go around flirting with men you hardly know, Mother.'

'You're too young to be so pompous. And anyway, what makes you think I flirted with him?' Tess asked, defensively.

'Because you're going red, and because your voice went all weeny and horrible when you told about him saying you were lovely. Yeuchhhhhhh. Disgusting.' He made as if to poke his finger down his throat and pantomimed vomiting.

'That's quite enough,' Tess said. She considered him for a moment. His colour was better, and he seemed restless. 'Are you getting bored up here all alone?'

'A bit,' he admitted.

'Did you have any visitors, today?'

'Mr Hendricks came around,' Max said.

'Can't you call him Uncle Richard?' Tess asked. 'He's very fond of you, you know.'

'But he's *not* my uncle,' Max said, firmly. 'Any more than that other one is.'

'What other one?' Tess asked, alarmed. Who had been there?

Max looked sheepish. 'I guess he's Mrs Grimble's brother.'

'Oh. Walter Briggs.'

'I don't think I was very polite to him – he woke me up

and I didn't know who he was. I think he was a little bit . . .
you know . . . pissed.'

'Max!'

'Well, he was. He scared me, at first, sort of leaning over
me and staring the way he did. I thought he was going to fall
right on top of me.' He went a bit pink. 'And he smelled. So
I said "Who the hell are you?" and sort of scrumpled up the
covers over me. And he laughed.'

'Oh, dear.'

'He said he just wanted to say hello. He brought me that.'
He pointed to a jigsaw puzzle at the foot of the bed. 'I *did* say
"thank you".' His tone was defensive.

'Good. Richard said he was here.'

Max looked grim. 'Does Mr Hendricks own this house or
something?'

'No, of course not. I own it. Why?'

Max shrugged. 'You'd think he did, the way he stomped
around, shouting and everything. It was pretty embarrassing.'

Tess straightened the coverlet. 'Is Mrs Grimble's brother
here often?'

'How should I know?' Max asked, grumpily. 'I was away
at school and now I'm stuck up here, aren't I? There could
be a herd of elephants drinking lemonade in the sitting
room for all *I* know about it.'

'Maybe you should start your proper lessons, if you feel
so left out of things,' Tess suggested.

Max groaned piteously. 'No, no, I'm too weak. Watching
old movies on the video is all I can stand. My brain is fuzzy,
my mouth is dry, I have dry rot in my wooden leg. In fact, I
feel a whole new attack coming on,' he said, clutching his
forehead dramatically. 'Oh, the pain!'

Tess laughed. 'You *are* feeling better. I'll tell Mr Soame to
set you an essay when he comes in.'

Max slid down under the covers. 'Tell him I've gone to
Timbuctoo,' came the muffled suggestion. 'Tell him I've
turned into a frog.' He pushed down the duvet suddenly,
and produced an uncanny imitation of his late father. 'Tell
him I'm in a *meeting*,' he growled.

'I'll tell him you're impossible,' Tess said, pulling the

duvet back up around her son.

'He already knows *that*,' Max said. 'He said I have a mind like a grasshopper – jumping around nibbling everything and digesting nothing. He said I was a challenge.' This judgement seemed to evoke deep satisfaction.

Tess stood up and walked around the room, straightening things idly. 'Do you like Mr Soame?'

'Sure. Why shouldn't I?'

'Was he in here for long, this morning?'

'I don't know. We watched *The Flame and the Arrow*,' Max said. 'It was medieval and had a sort of motte and bailey castle in it. Did you know that Burt Lancaster used to be an acrobat in the circus?'

'No, I didn't.'

'John said that when I'm stronger — '

'John? You call him John?'

'He said I could. It was his dumb idea, not mine,' Max said, negligently. 'Mostly I call him "sir" because we have to at school, and it's hard to break the habit.'

Tess leaned against the windowsill and regarded him thoughtfully. His hair was sticking up in spikes and his eyes were like Roger's – long-lashed and slightly tilted at the corners. He'd be quite pretty, she thought, if it weren't for that jaw and those freckles. As it is, even thin and pale, he's all boy. 'I think calling him "sir" is good,' she said, casually. 'It shows you respect him.'

'Hmmmmm. Anyway, he said when I'm stronger maybe I could do some fencing. Fencing isn't medieval, though, they used broad swords then and hacked bits off one another until they died. But modern fencing is good, he said. Did you know that one year in the Olympics somebody cut somebody else's ear off? A German or a Russian or somebody. Snick, snick, just like that – it flew off and landed on a judge's lap!'

'Oh, nonsense.'

'It did. And then he cut off his nose and then — '

'All right, all right. What do you want for dinner?'

'Fried ears and chips,' Max said. 'And ice-cream!' he shouted after her, as she went down the stairs.

Well, it all sounded pretty normal to her, Tess thought,

92

as she went into the kitchen. And Soame was obviously getting a few facts into Max along with the snickersnees and varlets. What was a varlet, anyway? Villains in historical films were always calling people varlets. Or was it vartlet? She must look it up.

Putting on an apron, she began to get out pans and plates.

Richard said he would be looking up things about John Soame. Where would he look? How did you go about, what did they call it? – oh, yes – 'positively vetting' someone? She stopped in the middle of the kitchen, a frying pan in one hand and a potato peeler in the other.

Perhaps he would hire a private detective.

Would a private detective find out anything terrible about John Soame? Was there anything terrible to find out about him? Or, if there wasn't, would Richard make something up? From the way he had been behaving that morning, she wouldn't have put it past him. Honestly, saying that John had been the person making those nasty phone calls. Why, the voice had been nothing like his.

She continued across the kitchen and banged the pan down on the sink. Men were impossible, absolutely impossible. They said one thing but meant another.

You never knew what they were *really* thinking.

FOURTEEN

THAT NIGHT, MAX HAD ANOTHER NIGHTMARE.

Tess had been awakened a few minutes before by a faint noise, and had been lying in the dark trying to figure out whether it had been one of the neighbourhood cats doing a fandango on the dustbins, or just another of the creaks and cracks the old house was heir to.

And then Max screamed.

Jumping from bed, she grabbed her dressing gown and fled down the hall to his room. She found Max sitting bolt upright in bed, his eyes open. But she knew he was still asleep, caught somewhere in a subconscious limbo of horror. His face was a blank mask, but his eyes were dark with fear.

She and Mrs Grimble had moved his bed to the bay window that overlooked the back garden and the bird table he and Roger had built together two years before. The afternoon sun would warm him, they'd thought, and the birds would give him an outside interest. His binoculars hung conveniently from the bedpost, and a bird book sat upon the windowsill, ready for consultation.

But now, in the stillness of the night, moonglow streamed over the patchwork quilt she had made years before, while waiting for him to be born. The squares of bright primary colours she'd chosen looked washed out in the strange, pale light. Only the appliquéd tumbling clowns were visible, their frozen antics somehow eerie and ominous.

And then Max began to speak.

'No . . . please . . . don't make me do that. Please . . . I won't . . . I can't . . . please . . . no . . . '

94

Tess stood, stricken, afraid to waken him too suddenly, but John Soame, coming into the room behind her, didn't hesitate. He stepped around her and spoke quietly and firmly, with the unmistakable voice of authority.

'Max, it's all right. No-one is going to make you do anything you don't want to do. It's all right, Max. You can wake up now. You're safe now. Nothing bad is going to happen.'

He didn't touch the boy or even go close to the bed, but stayed near Tess, still and watchful, talking steadily and evenly. Gradually the fear was erased from the small, thin face. Max slumped in the bed, his eyes closed.

Tess went to him and took him in her arms, cuddling him as she had done when he was very young, feeling the bird-flutter of his heart against her, his soft breath feathering her throat. She looked up at John Soame, and smiled her thanks.

Standing there in his pyjamas, without his spectacles, he looked rumpled and young and suddenly embarrassed. He turned away abruptly, and said something about making them all a cup of tea. A few moments later there was a sound of cups and clatter from the kitchen below.

Max gave a long shuddering sigh, and snuggled closer to her. He was awake now, she could feel his eyelashes brushing her collarbone as he blinked away tears he would rather have denied. He sniffed. 'Mum?'

'Yes, darling?'

'I didn't mean to be a baby.'

'We all feel like babies when we have bad dreams.'

'It was bad. It was all . . . ' His voice trailed off.

'It was what? It might help you to talk about it, you know.'

He was silent for a moment, thinking this over, then shook his head against her shoulder. 'I can't remember. When I woke up . . . just for a minute I remembered . . . but now it's gone.'

Tess, feeling the tension in his body as it rested against her, decided not to press the point. She was quite sure he *did* remember, and equally sure he didn't want to tell her about it.

Why?

What was it that he so feared both sleeping *and* waking?

John returned, then, with three steaming mugs on a tray. Deftly, as they drank their cocoa – which he had apparently decided was more soothing than tea – he led the conversation into general channels, keeping it cheerful. They left a more relaxed Max behind when the cocoa was gone, tucked up and smiling, his eyes already closing.

Tess and John walked down the hall towards the stairs. 'It must be the accident,' Tess said. 'It can't be anything else.'

John stood outlined against the light from below. He held the tray with the empty mugs awkwardly before him. 'I'm not so sure,' he said, slowly. 'Come downstairs for a minute.'

Puzzled, she followed him down and into the kitchen. He put the tray down on the table and turned to face her. 'When I came down to make the cocoa I found the back door wide open,' he said, quietly.

'What?'

'Take a look,' he suggested. 'The lock has been forced.' She went over and looked at the splintered wood around the lock, and felt the hairs rise on the back of her neck, just like in books – only this was real. Burglars, again.

Burglars?

Or someone else?

'It might be a coincidence that Max had a nightmare at the same time as some intruder was sneaking around the house. Or it might be the very thing that gave him one. Perhaps he heard something, or sensed something . . . ' John said.

Tess just kept looking from the door to him and back again. It was too much to take in. Someone in the house? Someone in Max's room?

John went on. His voice was calm on the surface, but she thought she heard anger there, too. 'I looked around the house and garden before I wedged the door shut. I didn't find anyone, obviously. As far as I can tell, nothing has been taken, but you'd know that better than I would. The question is – do we call the police now, or in the morning?'

FIFTEEN

THE POLICE CAME PROMPTLY, TWO uniformed constables arrived within ten minutes of the call. They were thorough – they inspected the door, looked around the yard and did a quick tour of the immediate neighbourhood. They asked a lot of questions: who had keys to the house, were neighbours or friends in the habit of dropping by, had there been any repairmen in the house recently, or insurance salesmen, or vicars of unknown denominations, or charity callers, or people claiming to represent the local council? Did the dustmen come into the garden or collect from outside the gate? Did she know the faces of the regulars? What about itinerant window washers? Television aerial installers? People claiming to be searching for lost dogs or cats? So many questions, so many possibilities. They were kind. They were sympathetic.

But they were not all that helpful.

'About twenty or thirty break-ins a week now, in this area,' the big one said. He seemed almost proud of it.

'You're sure nothing was taken?' the smaller one said.

'I think he was frightened off before he could,' Tess said, and explained about Max's nightmare screams.

'Ah, well,' the smaller one nodded. 'If there was something taken – something of value – I'd say call in the CID for fingerprints and all that palaver. But I doubt they'd take it on, seeing as how things are so backed up with real — ' He paused. 'With bigger crimes. We had a jeweller's broken into in the High Street last week, they took maybe ten thousand's worth out of there, neat as you please.' He glanced at his partner. 'What do you think on this one?'

'I think they would let it pass,' the big one said.

'But Mrs Leland has been threatened,' Soame protested.

Interest flared momentarily in their eyes. 'Oh?' the big one said. 'Have you reported this?'

'Yes,' Tess said.

'No,' Soame said.

She looked at him. 'But I thought you said you went to the local police,' she said.

He looked uncomfortable. 'I rang them up and explained the situation, but I didn't give your name or go in to make a formal complaint. They didn't seem very interested, you see.'

'This a person you know making threats?' the smaller policeman asked.

'Well, no,' Tess said, hesitantly. 'It's phone calls, really. Silent ones at first. Then he spoke, but it wasn't what he said, more the tone. He demanded some money – I didn't know what he meant, though. And then there was the confetti and the cranberries.' She told them about the wardrobe. Even as she was speaking she understood what Soame had been up against, it sounded so feeble and foolish. 'Actually, he hasn't called for some days. Maybe he won't now.'

'And maybe he will,' the big one said.

'Maybe,' the smaller one said. 'Maybe.'

'Then you do believe me?' Tess asked.

The smaller one smiled. 'Of course I believe you, Mrs Leland. We can ask the exchange to intercept your calls, or to change your number. Would you like us to do that?'

She was momentarily taken aback. 'Well, changing numbers is such a big fuss, notifying everyone and . . . all that.'

The big policeman and the smaller policeman exchanged a glance. 'It's up to you, Mrs Leland,' the smaller one said.

'I think you should,' Soame said. 'I know it costs money, but I think you should do something to put your mind at rest. It would be worth the expense, really.'

'Change the number and keep a list of the people you tell,' the big policeman advised. 'That way you can narrow it down if this geezer calls again, see?'

'Y . . . y . . . yes,' Tess nodded. 'All right.'

'It would be faster if you did it yourself,' the smaller policeman said. 'Tell the phone people to call us if they want confirmation or anything like that. Here, I'll give you our names.' He took out a notebook, wrote, tore out the sheet and handed it to her. 'Tell them either Constable Sims or Constable Cole – or Sergeant Reeder. We'll leave details with him at the station. All right?'

'Yes, all right. Thank you,' Tess said.

They gave her a pamphlet on home security, suggested a few improvements concerning locks and routines, and then they got another call. When they had gone, she sank into her rocker and closed her eyes. 'They didn't believe me,' she said. 'They were just humouring me.'

'Nonsense,' Soame said. 'It's all paperwork for them. If they made some kind of official request for your phone number to be changed or calls to be intercepted it would probably take days and days to go through. I'm sure they were right, it will be quicker for us to request it.' ·

'Yes, but — '

The telephone rang. From the darkness of the hall its jangle cut through Tess's words like a knife, a cold sharp knife. She glanced at the big old store clock on the wall: two a.m.

'It's him,' she said. She knew it as surely as she'd ever known anything. 'I know it's him.'

'I'll answer it,' Soame said. 'I'll put a stop to this.'

'No!' Tess sprang to her feet. 'He'll just hang up on you. Let me answer it – you listen.'

He stood beside her, reassuringly close, as she picked up the receiver. 'Hello?' she quavered. She tipped the earpiece away from her slightly so Soame could hear, too.

There was only silence. Soame stirred beside her. 'Hello? Who is this? Answer me!'

Silence.

Tears of frustration started into her eyes, and she balled her fist and stamped her foot. 'Answer me!'

Soame took the phone from her. 'Mrs Leland has no money of her own or anyone else's. There is no point to this persecution when . . . ' He stopped. His shoulders

99

slumped, and he put the receiver back in its cradle. 'Gone,' he said.

'You shouldn't have interfered,' Tess said, wildly. 'He might have said something if you hadn't interfered. Now it will just go on and on until I go crazy!'

'I know, I'm sorry,' Soame said. 'It was just the look on your face . . . if you could have seen your expression . . .'

She shivered. 'I'm cold,' she said, wearily. 'I'm going back to bed.'

'I really didn't mean to — ' Soame said.

'I know, I know.' She managed a smile. 'I expect I looked pretty desperate, at that. Blame Clark Kent, again, I suppose.'

He flushed. 'Perhaps I've never really grown out of hoping to be a hero to someone, someday. On the evidence so far, I think I'd better stick to printed history.'

She wanted to say something reassuring, but nothing came. 'Good night,' she said.

Warmth came from the electric blanket, but it was a specious warmth, and did not reach her bones. She took a deep breath, sighed a long sigh, and shivered.

You wanted to be independent, you wanted to prove you could run your own life, she told herself. *Do it.*

After a few minutes of this inner pep talk, she fell into a restless sleep, and awoke the next morning with a headache. Never mind, she thought, swinging her legs over the edge of the bed and reaching for the paracetamol. We have no time for headaches, Mrs Leland. We have to Get On.

And the first thing we are going to do is call that detective who came to see us in the hospital, aren't we?

Atta girl.

Mrs Grimble conducted Nightingale and Murray to the kitchen. She scowled at them each, in turn, and then went out of the room. Moments later, the roar and clatter of the old vacuum cleaner started up in the dining-room. Vigorous sweeping sounds could be heard, along with an obbligato of muttering.

100

Nightingale and his partner dutifully peered at the splintered wood beside the lock, looked at the lock itself, inspected the garden, and then looked at Tess.

'You seem to have been very lucky, Mrs Leland,' Nightingale said, accepting a mug of coffee. 'If your boy hadn't shouted out with his nightmare, you might have lost some more valuables.' He took a swallow of the coffee. He'd risen too late for a decent breakfast, and had left a fresh, steaming cup of tea and a jam doughnut on his desk. Now, having rushed out without his mac, and proceeding unvictualled, his turn round the garden had left him chilled.

'The local police seemed to think we should be used to this sort of thing, count it in a day's expectations,' Tess said. 'Do you? I mean, considering everything?'

'By everything I suppose you mean your husband's death, the burglary, those phone calls you mentioned?'

'Yes. You said you were suspicious about Roger's death — '

'Indirectly, yes, I was.'

She caught the past tense. 'But you aren't, any more?'

'I didn't say that. Not exactly. It's just – well – it's difficult for me at the moment.'

'We have a lot of work on at the moment,' Murray put in, trying to be helpful. He wasn't certain why Tim had dragged him along on this – whatever it was – but he felt he should say something. Anything.

'Oh.' Tess felt deflated. 'I'm sorry, then, to have called you out here. I remember now, you said you were doing it on your own time, didn't you?' She blinked quickly, and stood up. 'I hope I haven't made any difficulties for you, calling you at your office and everything . . . '

'Not at all. You see — '

The kitchen door swung open. John Soame stood there, hair still uncombed, shirt half tucked into his trousers, and wearing mis-matched socks. He held a coffee mug in one hand and a slightly-burned piece of toast in the other. 'Mrs Grimble told me the police are back,' he said. 'Have they come up with anything?'

Nightingale turned. The two men stared at one another.

'I know you,' Soame said, peering at him.

101

'Yes, you do,' Nightingale agreed.

'Why do I know you?'

'Because I used to ask awkward questions,' Nightingale said. 'If it helps, I usually sat in the front row, on the right. Your left, of course.'

Soame considered him. 'You had a beard?'

'For my sins. A beard, a moustache, and a chip on my shoulder.'

'But you weren't in my tutor group.'

'No. In Jon Chappel's. For *his* sins.'

'And now you're a police officer?' It seemed almost too much for Soame to take in. Sometimes, Nightingale thought, it was too much for him to take in, too. All those cloistered years, all those dreaming spires, and now this. His parents, were they still alive, would be startled, too, he supposed. Chappel, when he'd bumped into him a year or so ago, had been stupefied.

'I am.'

Tom Murray smiled, grimly. 'For everyone's sins.'

'I see. Well, you've seen the damage?' As Soame gestured towards the rear door, a few crumbs flew out from his toast and a spot of marmalade fell to the floor beside his left shoe. 'Of course, you've realized this wasn't a burglary attempt at all, but a further example of what has been going on all along. Somebody is systematically trying to frighten Mrs Leland into handing over money. It's obvious.'

Nightingale raised an eyebrow. 'Is it?'

'Come along, you were taught better than that by Chappel if no-one else,' John protested. 'Examine the evidence, for goodness' sake.'

'I have, sir,' he said. He kept his face neutral, but winced within. The situation might be clear to Professor Soame, but it was far from clear in police terms. About as clear, in fact, as his own position. Officially, he was not connected with this at all. Officially this had been logged locally as a burglary attempt. Officially, he was at his desk in New Scotland Yard drinking tea and wishing himself back in the country.

Unofficially, of course, he was up to his ears in it.

'What is your place in this, sir?' Murray asked as politely as he could, while eyeing Soame's state of dishabille. 'Are you a relative of Mrs Leland?'

Tess Leland explained, and as she did, Nightingale covertly examined John Soame. His being here was another coincidence, of course, but surely not one related to the case at hand. If there was a case. Soame must have faced thousands of undergraduates in his time. That he should re-encounter one of them as an investigating officer was not all that startling. He just wished he could remember more about Soame than he did. Wasn't there something about him having an unsuitable wife, somewhere?

'I'm sure Mrs Leland is glad to have you on hand, sir,' Tim said, politely.

'I'm not so certain of that, myself,' Soame said. 'I seem to have frightened off the phantom caller last night, before he could even speak.'

'I see,' Tim said. That was interesting.

So many interesting things.

He glanced at the broken door jamb. Was this just an attempted burglary, thwarted by a child's thin cry of fright in the darkness? The local men were quite correct. This neighbourhood, marginal, semi-residential, showed quite lively statistics in the fields of car-theft, burglary, assault, and assorted mayhem. And this was just the kind of house a thief on the prowl for the quick chance would fancy – single occupancy, slightly up-market, potentially filled with the kind of small, portable shinies that could be quickly and easily exchanged for cash across a pub table, no questions asked. After all, it had already happened once.

There might be a pattern, yes. But it also might be that, in their twitchy state, this woman and Soame were *imposing* a pattern on events that were really quite unconnected.

What was worse, *he* might be doing the same thing himself.

Leaping to the wrong conclusion now might mean manpower being expended to no good end, hours wasted, resources drained, all in looking for a little man who wasn't there. And on his recommendation. Very bad for the record. Especially the unwritten record.

His problem was simple: was there a problem?

Murray looked uncomfortable, as well he might. He hadn't the least idea what was going on – Tim had carefully refrained from telling him anything on the way over. He wanted clear first impressions from a disinterested party. From Murray's expression, dragging him in on this would cost Tim a lunch, at least.

He looked around the kitchen. A nice room, with the comfortable cluttered feeling of something that had grown organically over many years of various family requirements rather than something that had been imposed according to an ideal of modern efficiency. What little wallpaper there was showed a simple red on white pattern of small flowers. The many glass-fronted cupboards on the wall were, he thought, contemporary with the building itself. Beside the splintered rear entrance door was another door, slightly open, through which he could see liberally-stacked marble cold shelves – an old fashioned larder, then, still enthusiastically in use and so far unconverted to the omnipresent 'downstairs loo'. The sink was stainless steel, the taps modern, but the whole unit had been dropped into the existing structure of battered floor cupboards. Their original tops had been covered with butcher blocking, which had the effect of raising the actual work surfaces higher than the ordinary. That made sense – both Mrs Leland and the loony cleaning lady he'd met on the way in were taller than average. All the cupboards, high and low, had been painted a pale cream with red accent lines, but it had been done some time ago. Scars showed, dents and bruises, and the chips thus incurred showed many layers of old paint beneath. There was a big pine table in the centre of the room, scrubbed clean but heavily scarred, with four chairs placed around it. There were plump red printed cushions tied to each one, but the chairs themselves – although of pine and roughly similar in size – didn't match.

What did all this tell him?

That Mrs Leland, although a professional interior

designer, was one of those rare people who knew the value of *not* rushing in, of staying her hand, of letting be. She'd probably moved in, made the changes in her new kitchen that were necessary for efficient and pleasant function, and had then done no more. Perhaps she was not a dedicated cook and milkbottle washer. A practical woman who kept the more modish aspects of her imagination for her work. Even, possibly, a lazy one. Would such a woman imagine dragons where none existed? Worse, would she manufacture them, either consciously or subconsciously?

He drank more coffee and looked at her over the rim of the mug. Now that the burden of the child's illness had been lifted she looked younger than she had in hospital. A pretty woman, once, who could be again, given time and love and security. Not, he thought, over-emotional, but not invulnerable either. She would stand up to a great deal – but only for a certain time. Watching him quietly, standing up to his inspection and concomitant calculation, she was waiting for his verdict on her, and on her predicament.

If there was simply an attempt here at frightening Mrs Leland – and she was obviously frightened, for whatever reason – then finding and scaring the hell out of the person responsible might be all that was necessary. With the young, the half-hearted and the amateur, realization that the authorities 'knew' of their efforts was often sufficient to stop them from continuing a campaign of intimidation against their chosen victim. If the little man *was* there, a brisk outline of the possible consequences resulting from prosecution might do it.

But who was the little man?

And, most importantly of all, was he the *same* man who had chased Roger Leland to his death, and – still a conjecture – frightened Ivor Peters into a heart attack when he'd got too close?

In all things criminal, evidence – usable evidence – was the prime factor. If a chargeable offence was committed, then it came down to whether the charge could be proven. Going off half-cocked more often than not provided the defence with all they needed to get a case thrown out

105

before it even came to full trial. The Force knew all it wanted to know about *that* kind of case.

'I can see what you're getting at — ' he began, cautiously.

'Well, then, what are you going to do about it?'

'John, please.' Tess could see that Nightingale was having an internal struggle of some kind, and she felt embarrassed by John's insistence on immediate action. 'Perhaps there's nothing Sergeant Nightingale *can* do.' She felt a wave of desolation sweep over her. Perhaps there was nothing anyone could do, she thought. You are alone. This is not your country, many things are strange to you here. And you are seen as a stranger, too. There is no-one. Accept it. Live with it. Get on with it.

Nightingale saw the defeat in her eyes, and wished there was a way to remove it. 'While all these things are unpleasant, there is no proof that they're connected in any way. Not necessarily.'

'It would be an amazing coincidence if they weren't,' Soame muttered.

'Not amazing at all. Coincidences *do* happen, and frequently. Mrs Leland says she has no enemies that she knows about. Mrs Leland says she has been threatened, but the threats have not been followed up. Nothing at all has come of it. No lines of communication have been arranged, no instructions issued, nothing specific has been indicated or requested.'

'What about the break-in last night?'

'What about it?' Nightingale countered. 'A broken door-jamb isn't enough to convince a judge, much less a jury.'

'But there was another call last night, within minutes of the police leaving the house,' Soame said. 'Someone must have been watching the place, waiting for the right moment. It's a campaign of intimidation, I tell you.' His voice rose up, verged on – something. Desperation?

Nightingale shook his head. 'One of the great modern compulsions is to answer the telephone. Most people think they have to respond instantly to it. That's what phone freaks count on. This caller may be an adolescent with criminal fantasies. Making threats gives him a sense of

106

power. Or a crank – we get plenty of those – someone seeking sexual thrills from an intake of breath, or the sound of fear in a woman's voice. It isn't *necessarily* a dangerous person, or even a person connected with this attempted break-in. Your caller could just be a neighbour who saw your lights on and decided to take advantage of the moment. Failing evidence to the contrary, that's how we have to look at it. I'm sorry.' And he was.

Tess looked at Nightingale and tried to imagine him younger, with a beard, and couldn't. But he was recognizably a police officer. Why? She looked at his partner, sitting quietly at the table, listening and watching. A closed face, that was it. They all had it. Eyes never still in ever-still faces, and carefully, professionally, unimpressed by anything or anyone. Would it help if she flew into hysterics? Screamed, threatened? She thought not. They would change mode instantly, trained to do the right things, say the right things, 'sit down, drink this, calm down, it's all right', but nothing would change within them as they went through the rituals. Impervious, waterproof, seamless. The very best materials, the very finest workmanship, head to toe. She crossed her arms, settled herself. 'Suppose I say something was taken. Suppose we did report a burglary. What then?'

Nightingale shrugged and put his empty coffee mug down on the table. 'Then it would go into the files as a reported burglary. The item or items taken would go on a recovery list.'

'And?'

'That's it,' Murray said. 'That's what would happen.'

'And, of course, it's a very long list,' Tess said, resignedly. 'Don't you see, John? It's no use. There has to be some actual blood shed before they can do anything.'

'No,' Nightingale said, firmly. 'There only has to be a clear connection, a clear and specific threat to someone's safety, or clear criminal activity or intent.'

'I'm not making it up, you know,' Tess said.

Nightingale felt the sharp edge of her bitterness. It made a thin incision in the carefully-maintained envelope of his self-respect. He stood up. 'I didn't say you were,' he told her, evenly. 'But neither am I. That's simply the position as

107

far as we're concerned.'

The kitchen door banged back and Mrs Grimble erupted into the room. 'I knew it. I told her. I told him. All mouth and no trousers, the police,' she announced, glaring at the detectives. 'Ready enough to accuse when it suits you, I'll wager. Ready enough to push people around, yell at them, lock them up just for being alive.' She turned to Tess, who saw with surprise that her eyes were filled with tears. 'Local rozzers come round at seven o'clock this morning, for Walter, and it wasn't a friendly call, neither. Wanted to know where he'd been last night, wanted to know what he was doing for money, wanted to know why, what, and wherefore.'

Tess was stricken. 'I'm sorry, that was my fault.'

'Why would it be your fault?' Soame asked.

'They asked us about who'd been in the house. I told them Walter was here, yesterday,' Tess said. She looked at Mrs Grimble. 'I forgot.'

She felt a vague guilt, because Walter Briggs had an old count against him. Years ago, at the age of twenty or so, he'd been convicted of grievous bodily harm against another boy, and had served five years for it. There had been some mention of homosexual advances, counter-charges of intimidation and theft. Mrs Grimble maintained the conviction was a false one because Walter had been too drunk to know what was happening, but the record – however old and however questionable – remained. What was worse, Walter's life since his release did not bear close scrutiny, mostly because of his repeated backslides into alcoholism. He had learned some questionable skills in gaol, and made some less than honest friends. He came and went in Mrs Grimble's life, his presence kept vaguely alive in Tess's mind by Mrs Grimble's occasional outbursts of despair on his behalf. Tess had always sympathized with the old woman's frustration.

Roger hadn't been easy, either.

'But he *was* here, wasn't he?' she asked, gently.

'Well, yes, he was,' Mrs Grimble admitted. 'What of it? Aren't I allowed — '

'Of course you are,' Tess said, quickly. She put out a hand, but the old lady went right over to Nightingale and glared up into his face. Though she was not small, the flowers on her hat came just to his nose, and he had to lean back to avoid being tickled by them.

'It seems to me you police spend so much time hassling people like Walter, there's none left for doing what you're supposed to, which is protecting the public. Mrs Leland's a member of the public. What's more, she's a woman alone with a little sick lad to look after and money to earn. But you're just leaving her to it. Never mind people keep breaking in here and calling her up and all the rest of it, oh no. What's so important that you haven't got time for her, hey? What else have you got to do?'

'We *are* investigating a murder — ' Murray began.

Mrs Grimble whirled on him. 'I'll give you murder,' she said, in a dangerous voice. Her eyes fell on the coffee mug he'd put down. 'And look at the ring that mug's leaving on my kitchen table. Isn't it enough vandals try to break in, but we have to *invite* them in as well. You ought to be ashamed.' She snatched up the mug and took it over to the sink. Soame had to leap out of the way to avoid being splashed as she ran hot water at full pressure and added far too much detergent, squeezing the plastic container as if it were someone's neck.

Nightingale had turned slightly pink across the cheek-bones. 'We'll tell the local men to maintain their drive-bys. You know their telephone number, and ours. Sorry we can't do more . . . '

'Certainly couldn't do much less,' Mrs Grimble snorted over her shoulder, and jabbed the dishmop into the mug so hard the wooden handle split from end to end.

SIXTEEN

BACK IN THE CAR, MURRAY BREATHED out. 'Whew,' he said. 'I haven't been screeched at like that since my mother caught me smoking in the garage.' He shook his head. 'Women's voices,' he said. 'God, how I sometimes hate women's voices.'

'The damnable thing about it is, she had a point,' Nightingale sighed.

'I'd like to make a point,' Murray said. 'My point is this, what the hell was that all about?'

Nightingale smiled. 'I wanted an objective observer.'

'Well, you got an observer who objects, instead. Come on, give. It has to do with that file you've been crooning over, doesn't it? The one that I'm not supposed to know about.'

'It does,' Nightingale agreed. And he outlined the trail that had led from one old dead copper to this particular house. 'Perhaps Soame is right, Mrs Leland – and her son as well – may well be in danger.'

'But from what?' Murray asked. 'And why?'

'If we're to go by the phone calls – and they are the only specific we have – because of some unnamed amount of money she insists she knows nothing about.'

'Do you think she's lying?'

Nightingale thought about it. 'I don't honestly know.'

He looked back at the house, which was the end terrace in a line that curved around the remnants of a crescent garden. Once, perhaps, there had been flowerbeds and benches where there was now simply uncut grass plus a great deal of litter beneath two defeated-looking lime trees. The railing around this tribute to municipal neg-

110

ligence was rusting badly, and the gate which implied admittance to only a favoured few was wired shut and obviously admitted nothing.

The windows and door of the Leland house had been painted bright red, but the handle and knocker of the door were still the old, plain steel. No expensive reproduction brasswork. No doorside flower urns, no coy china numberplate. And the brave red paint was beginning to chip.

The other houses in the terrace were a mixed lot. Two had been 'done up' in the full and accepted manner, and four or five looked neat and respectable, but many of the others had been allowed to disintegrate to such a degree that the contrast was painful. Several had multiple door-plates and bells, indicating bedsitters within. A mixed prospect, then. Neither a good neighbourhood nor a bad, exactly, but something awaiting the inevitable slide into one or the other.

How long had the Lelands lived here? Judging by the condition of the paintwork trim, about ten years. No doubt there had been a moment, back then, when Kingfisher Terrace had looked about to burst into gentrification, and a local estate agent had got several people to buy on that promise, the Lelands among them.

Even so, it wouldn't have come cheaply. Newly or recently married, perhaps, he looking for an investment, she looking for a home to make, they'd taken the plunge. And they had been happy, no doubt, those ten years ago. Full of hope for the future and one another, the way young people persisted in being no matter what they saw around them.

But the estate agent's hope for the neighbourhood had died. Why? Absentee landlords, most likely, who continued to profit from those bedsitters. Or perhaps owners too poor or too old or too uncaring either to maintain their homes or move from them. The city was moving outwards, a tentacle here, another there. Once-genteel neighbourhoods that had dragged their petticoats in the mud for years were now rising again, and where broughams had been replaced by bangers, Porsches and BMWs now parked. But not in Kingfisher Terrace.

111

Although he was hardly an experienced observer of marital patterns, Nightingale thought hope had died in the Leland marriage, too. The evidence was clear. Their first expenditure had been the last. Because after the first flush of ownership they had never bought the brass doorknob, or modernized the kitchen, or planted the garden out. They had converted the top floor to a flat. For added income? For company? To increase resale value? What had gone out of the Leland marriage that was reflected in the Leland house? If he'd had money in the beginning, and his business had been doing well at the end, where was the money now?

He had met Tess Leland, but Roger Leland was beyond his recalling. What had been his true character, the inner persona that his wife had discovered, as all wives do, over their years together. Profligate or miser? Had he hoarded? Had he gambled? Maintained a mistress? Played the market? Did it have a bearing on his death? On what was happening now? And, most importantly, was it worth pursuing? He kept coming back to that, over and over.

Was this a suitable case for investigation or not?

Murray broke into Nightingale's reflective silence with a reflection of his own. 'Loneliness and grief can make women do strange things, Tim. She could have staged the first burglary, broken open the back door herself any time before the boy woke up. You have only her word for the words spoken in the phone calls – all the calls picked up by the housekeeper were silent. As was the one Professor Soame heard last night.'

'But what would it get her?'

'Company. Sympathy. A reason to fail. Who knows? Maybe somebody else has some money she thinks she should have, and she's trying to smoke it out,' Murray suggested. 'Or, if we're to believe this phantom caller, it's the other way around – she has some money somebody else thinks *they* should have.'

Tim sighed. 'Where would she have it?'

'How about a safety deposit box?' Murray said.

'But she's gone to a lot of trouble to get Soame in to teach the boy so she can keep on working. Why would she do that if she has money?'

'Camouflage. She has it, and means to keep it.'

'Where would she have got it?'

'From her old man, I suppose. Or maybe there's somebody else we don't know about. Maybe she was playing around before he got killed, maybe she was into something he didn't know about – or found out about. Yeah, how about that? Maybe he got killed because of something *she* was up to.'

'And maybe cops could fly,' Nightingale said, as he put the car into first and, glancing back, pulled away from the terrace. 'Looks like there's a lot more to do before this is finished. I certainly want to check up on the housekeeper's brother and find out what kind of "list" he's on, for a start. If that's a dead end, I can see about four different directions to go in if I'm right.'

'And if you're wrong, the only direction for you is down.'

Nightingale banged the steering wheel. 'It stinks, Tom. Peters sensed it and so do I. Something is going on here, and I want to find out what it is.'

'For Peters' sake, so to speak?' Murray asked, wryly. 'Well, if you're going on with this, you'd better clear it with the Inspector.'

'Don't nag.'

'That's not nagging,' Murray said. 'That's insurance.'

The wine bar was very crowded, and Nightingale had to hold the two glasses high to avoid the heads of his fellow-imbibers. He managed to return to the table without dousing anyone, and sank into his chair with surprising gratitude, seeing as it was too small for him and very unsteady. He'd been on his feet most of the day, doing follow-up interviews on the Primrose Street robbery, and had not enjoyed it.

Being on your feet presumably included access to and use of the mind – his employers paid him on that basis – but his had been elsewhere. He hoped it didn't mean he'd missed something vital, probably the clue and the arrest of a lifetime.

He froze for a moment, did an instant replay of the day's confrontations, then relaxed. To hell with it.

'Well, what do you think?' he asked the blonde girl sitting opposite him. She was tall and sleek and clever, and they had been conducting an on–off affair for the past few years, emotional weather permitting. He had met her during his time at Lloyds and knew her to be adroit in bed, hopeless in the kitchen, and a demon at the bridge table. She was personal assistant to one of the medium-powered underwriters, and loved her work more than she loved Tim. He found this a source of great comfort, as he felt the same way about his occupation. Neither saw their relationship going anywhere, but neither – at the moment – saw another relationship coming from anywhere. And so it went on. Her name was Sherry, and her eyes were that colour, too.

'I think you work hard enough without doing unpaid overtime,' Sherry said, sipping her claret and raking the crowd with a comprehensive glance to check there were no clients among the throng that might merit a smile. Her eyes returned to his, and he saw they were amused. 'Don't you?'

'I work hard, sure. So do you. That doesn't mean I can't have an outside interest.'

'In an inside subject? You risk becoming a law and order obsessive, Tim. Pretty soon you'll be reminding me to renew my car tax and put a better burglar alarm in my flat.'

'All praiseworthy things. Consider yourself so advised.'

'Oh, get stuffed,' Sherry said, with a grin.

'Come on, come on. You have an opinion. You *always* have an opinion, and this one is ripe. I can see it trembling on your luscious lips.' He picked up the battered bar menu and made a pretence of scanning it. She watched him, then sighed.

'Okay. I think you're probably right, there was something wrong and there probably *is* something wrong. One coincidence: "isn't life strange". Two coincidences: "wait a minute". Three or more: uh-oh, forget one and two. But as far as I can see, what you can do about it on

114

your own is damn-all. Don't murder investigations require lots and lots of people? That's what it said in the last mystery book I read.'

'*Mary Poppins Meets the Bad Person*? Loved it. Very sound, technically.'

'Well, then.'

'I can look into it a little.'

'How little?'

'Too little.'

'Exactly.'

He fixed her with a flat expression. 'Or I can wait around to see if Mrs Leland gets beaten up or killed – that might alert DCI Abbott that something is amiss.'

Sherry frowned. 'Do you think — ' Her last words were lost in a roar of manly guffaws from a group of pin-striped young things at the far end of the bar.

'What?' He leaned forward.

'I said, do you really think she's in danger?' As usual, a silence had followed the outburst at the brass rail, and Sherry's question turned heads in their direction.

Tim waited until curiosity died, and then nodded. 'But how much and from what or whom, I can't say. That's what makes it so damnable. She could have some money in a building society somewhere under a false name — '

'The book would be in the house, that burglar would have found it.'

'She might keep it in a safe deposit box somewhere.'

'But you said she seemed genuinely puzzled by the phone call demanding money.'

Nightingale made a wry face. 'She did. I must admit, she was very convincing. But then, I've only spoken to her once before, so I have nothing with which to compare her attitude. She might be the greatest actress the stage has ever lost, or a pathological liar, or have several personalities – maybe Tess Leland is also Griselda Leland, and only Griselda knows about the money.'

'You're tired,' Sherry said.

He rubbed his face. 'Of course I am. Coppers are congenitally weary, wasn't that in your book?'

'Yes, Chapter Four – Mary Poppins Goes To Bed Alone

Again.'

'I've never been *that* tired,' he protested. 'Not yet, anyway.'

'You will be, if you insist on following every hunch that pops into your head.'

'It's more than a hunch.'

'I see.' She leaned her elbows on the table and ran her hands through her hair, dislodging the last of the pins that had held it in place. The glossy, deep golden strands tumbled down over her ears and she shook it back carelessly. It was a moment he always looked forward to with pleasure – when she shrugged off the office and became a girl again. He wished he could perform a similar shrug of responsibility, but hadn't learned the knack as yet. Maybe his hair was too short.

'Could you do a little detective work for me?' he asked.

Sherry looked at him in some surprise. 'What could I do?'

'Well, you could find out about Hendricks & Leland Limited. Or it might be Leland and Hendricks. They were a public relations company with quite a few international clients, according to Mrs Leland. What I'd really like to get hold of is their client list, and the names of any financial backers they might have had, and their general financial history. It would give me a slant on at least one side of his life. Contacts, things he might have got to know about, secrets he might have had, trouble he might have been in or caused, enemies he might have made – particularly the latter.'

'You say the company is now defunct?'

'Yes. I gather Hendricks closed it down a month or two after Leland died – he's started up again with someone else. Leland was the creative side of it, Hendricks the administrator.'

'What's he called now? Hendricks & Something Else, presumably?'

'I have no idea. It might be one of those other kind of names – Prometheus Unbounded, or Zippy-Nifty Fixers, for all I know. I'd be glad of anything you could pick up: facts, rumours, gossip – anything at all.'

116

She made a little face, funny but not unattractive, and pretended to glare at him. 'You mean now *I* have got to have the Outside Interest Blues, too?'

'Call it companionship,' he smiled.

'I call it damned cheek,' she said. 'What if I get caught?'

'Doing what? All you have to do is make a few phone calls and tap out a few enquiries on your magic computer.'

Her face tightened. 'I'm not supposed to — '

'I know your boss, remember? I know you do half his stuff for him, that you use his access code, act for him when he wants to play golf, even commit funds — '

'Shhhhh.' She looked really alarmed.

'I wasn't shouting,' he said, mildly. 'I was using a focused voice and only you could hear it.'

'My God, you're really serious about this.' Her attitude had undergone a sea change.

'Somebody should be.'

She leaned back in her chair and studied the absolutely fascinating edge of the elderly table. Around them swirled the after-closing crowd, now well into their third and fourth glasses and considering the dash to Waterloo or the possibility of a few sausages to aid digestion. A rich aroma of claret, mustard, and bangers filled the room, even overcoming the day's last vestiges of Paco Rabanne and Trader's Muck Sweat. Nightingale could smell Sherry's familiar perfume, too, reactivated by her warmth and the wine. He knew what it cost – he'd bought her some the previous Christmas – and blessed the blender while cursing the packager. Its sudden presence told him she was worried.

'All right, look, it was just an idea. If you don't want to do it, fair enough. I understand,' he said, carelessly. 'Really, let it go.'

She raised her eyes to his face. 'She has a little boy, you said?'

'Yes. About nine. He was in the car with his father when it crashed.' He left out the part about the rheumatic fever, thinking it might seem a little over the top.

'The crash that your old policeman thought was deliberate?'

'He thought it was a result of Leland being chased, he never said it was intended. There's no way of knowing whether it was intended. Not with what we have now.'

'We?'

'Sorry, not with what I have now.' He waited.

She gnawed her lower lip, rather prettily, then seemed to make up her mind. 'All right. I'll poke around a little.'

'Thank you.' He meant it. 'More wine, or are you ready to toy with a little filet mignon?'

She chuckled. 'Those were the good old days, my love. On your present salary, it's more like a little hamburger.'

'Nothing wrong with hamburger, is there?'

'Nope.' She stood up. 'Especially when you can pick it up in a bag and take it home with you.' She momentarily transfixed him with a raised eyebrow as she reached for her coat. 'Coming?'

SEVENTEEN

TESS STAYED CLOSE TO MAX FOR the rest of the day.

She lay only half asleep that night.

And nothing happened.

The next day, leaving Mrs Grimble and John Soame on duty, she went back to work on the McMurdo house, argued with Archie McMurdo, soothed the workmen, shopped at a local supermarket. She came home, cooked dinner, spent the evening with Max, watching television. Slept lightly, waking frequently at the slightest sound.

And nothing happened.

Work, again. Research at the V&A. Initial interviews with two new clients, each with different requirements, different expectations, and widely differing budgets. Lists and drawings. An argument with a supplier, happily resolved by a switch to an alternative small-bore central heating system. A sales rep from a German fabric manufacturer with a tumble of rich colours and textures that covered her desk and filled her office with a kind of visual singing. Another rep from a Berwick-upon-Tweed pottery, offering imaginative shapes, amusing ideas, and an excellent discount for bulk purchase. Home again, dinner again, praise for the model castle, edgy laughter, edgy sleep.

And nothing happened.

Max had a bit of excitement when his friend from the hospital, the newly-reverend Simon Carter, appeared on the doorstep with a chessboard under one arm. He and Tess gave one another a nasty moment when, on her way out, she opened the front door and found him standing there with his other arm upraised.

119

'Good Lord,' he gasped. 'I was just about to ring the bell.'

'I'm glad to hear it,' Tess said, breathlessly. 'I thought you were about to strike me down.'

Carter chuckled and lowered his arm. 'Sorry,' he said. 'I don't usually go around frightening innocent women. Or even sinful women, come to that. Not that I've encountered many.' He sounded rather disappointed about it. 'I've been assigned to a parish in Peckham, actually. Start my duties next week, but I came down a bit early to get used to London. Frightening place.'

'Aren't you from the city?' Tess asked, stepping back to let him in.

'No, no . . . a small town lad, that's me,' Carter beamed. 'So, I thought I'd call round and see how the invalid was getting on. I hope you don't mind.'

'Not at all. He'll be delighted to see you, he's at the very bored stage.'

'Ah, then my timing is good, for once. Perhaps I'm getting the hang of vicaring at last,' Carter said, engagingly, removing his coat and unwinding a very long scarf from around his throat. There was a pink rash around the edge of his collar, and a small piece of plaster under his chin where he'd apparently nicked himself shaving. He seemed very young, and eager as a puppy to please. 'Is he up or down?' he enquired.

'Up. I'll show you,' Tess said, temporarily removing her coat and dropping it over the balustrade as she led him up the stairs.

Mrs Grimble was waiting for her when she came down. There was a burst of laughter from Max's room.

'Mr Soame went to the London Library half an hour ago. Who's that up there with Max?' she demanded. Tess explained. 'Well, just so's I know who's around the place,' Mrs Grimble said. 'All these people coming and going . . . '

Tess was putting on her coat again. 'It was very nice of your brother to bring Max the jigsaw puzzle the other day.'

Mrs Grimble flushed. 'I never invite him,' she said, defensively. 'He just comes.'

'Oh, that's all right. I don't mind it if you have your brother or a friend around for a coffee. But I do like to know . . . the same as you do . . . who's around.'

They exchanged a glance of perfect understanding.

'Do I give this person upstairs a cup of coffee?' Mrs Grimble wanted to know.

'If you're having one yourself,' Tess said, with a smile. 'I'm sure he'd appreciate it.'

'Don't hold with Church, much,' Mrs Grimble conceded. 'But I got nothing against it, neither.' She headed back towards the kitchen. 'Might make some biscuits this morning. Got everything in yesterday.'

Tess smiled to herself and went out. She was beginning to think, reluctantly, but gratefully, that Detective Sergeant Nightingale may have been right – the phone calls, perhaps even the booby trap in the wardrobe – had been meaningless attempts by some unknown enemy to cause her pain. And the other things were quite unrelated to it or to each other. Her nerves still twanged with the sense of being watched, manipulated, threatened; she grew annoyed with herself for leaping into the air when someone dropped something, or seizing up with panic whenever the phone rang. She began muttering 'Pull yourself together' so frequently that she wondered if she should have it set to music.

Things were settling down to a familiar routine.

Why, they even had a vicar visiting.

Life was returning to normal.

It would be all right.

A week after the supposed break-in there was a call from Richard. 'Still happy with your lodger?' he asked. 'Noticed any of the heirloom silver missing, yet?'

'No.'

'Any more nasty phone calls?'

'No,' she said, and wondered why she was lying.

'So everything is perfect?'

'Yes, everything seems to be just fine, thank you.'

He pounced like a cat on a mouse, familiar enough with the sound of her voice to detect doubt. '*Seems* to be?'

121

'Well, there *was* someone sneaking around the house the other night. But there was nothing tak — '

'What do you mean, sneaking around?' His voice was sharp.

Already sorry she'd mentioned it, she explained about the break-in, and Max's nightmare. 'The police think he was scared away before anything could be taken. They're keeping an eye on the house now, but Sergeant Nightingale doesn't seem to think there's any connection between that or anything else.'

'Oh, doesn't he? And who is Sergeant Nightingale?'

'He's been looking into Roger's accident.'

There was a moment of silence. 'What do you mean, looking into Roger's accident? That was months ago.'

'I know. He came to talk to me in the hospital about it. So, when the local police didn't do anything about our prowler, I called him. He's Scotland Yard, you see.'

'And he says what?'

She sighed. 'The same as the local police – just a crank caller, an interrupted burglary, and a lot of coincidences.'

'I see. So much for the Met. Tell me, did you find this broken door or did Soame?'

'Oh, John did – when he went down to make some cocoa for all of us.'

'How cosy,' Richard said, snidely. 'And how do you know dear, kind John didn't do it himself and tell you about it later just to make himself look like a hero? Did he offer to spend the night in your room – just to make sure you were "safe"?'

'That's a rotten thing to say.'

'Not when you take a look at his financial position,' Richard said.

'What do you mean?'

'I've had one of my banking friends asking a few pointed questions of some old school chums.' He sounded unabashed, smug, ready to impart triumph. 'I've just had his report. Want to hear it?'

'I'm not interested,' she said, picking up a pencil and beginning to doodle on the margin of an invoice from D.H. Listerman, Limited, manufacturers of ceramic ware for the

122

discerning (fancy basins and toilets).

'Oh, yes you are,' Richard purred. There was a rustle of paper. 'According to my impeccable source, Soame is in a world of financial trouble. And not for the first time either. Apparently his late wife was quite the spender. His bank is making legal noises about his overdraft, which is in the high hundreds. There are some large withdrawals of cash that might be to cover gambling debts. Apparently your new friend likes a flutter now and again.'

'He told me that he had financial problems,' Tess said. 'He's been very open about it.'

'And there is a tidy sum paid regularly to a Miss J. Wickham. She could be his mistress. Or a blackmailer.'

'Or his dental hygienist. Or an elderly aunt in Brighton.'

'Her cheques are cashed on a Barclays branch in Cheapside, actually.'

'I don't want to hear any more, Richard,' Tess said, quickly, certain there must be some perfectly rational explanation for all these things. Of course there was.

'I'll bet you don't,' he said, harshly. 'Mr John Soame is obviously not the paragon you thought he was.'

'Neither are you,' she snapped.

There was a brief silence. 'And what is that supposed to mean?' Each word was frozen into a separate icicle.

'All this suspicion, all this sneaking around – I never knew you were like this,' she said.

There was silence on the line, and then Richard spoke, repentantly, 'I'm sorry, Tess. Blame jet lag, if you like. I came back, saw this report, and just snapped. I only had it done because I'm really worried about you. All this sudden determination to make decisions – any decisions – to do things for yourself, to plunge ahead helter-skelter. It scares me, it really does. Whether you like it or not – and for some reason you suddenly seem not to like it – I care about you, Tess. I care very much. I'm still waiting for an answer to my proposal, you know.'

'Well, if you want an answer right now — ' Tess began.

'I don't,' he interrupted. 'Not when you're in this mood.' He sighed, and his voice became plaintive. 'Max's illness seems to have changed you overnight.'

'If anyone has changed, it's you,' she said, tightly.

He immediately adopted a brisk but cajoling tone, undoubtedly developed for use when facing an awkward client. 'Look, talking on the phone like this is silly. How about dinner tonight? Unfortunately I have a plane to catch at ten, so our time will be limited, but — '

'My goodness, which country are you conquering this week, Richard?' she asked, before she could stop herself.

Silence. Then, 'Very funny.' He slammed down the phone.

By the end of the day Tess decided she hated men.

All men.

Adrian was in one of his most peevish moods, having heard that his former friend and partner, the renegade Jason, had secured a very desirable contract to do an entirely fresh interior design for the flat of a rich, newly-arrived American oil executive who had somehow — the mind boggled — secured rooms in Albany. Adrian had been counting on the commission, having been introduced through a mutual friend to the wife of the executive in question — a malleable lady who, it now proved, was less than reliable in her promises. According to Adrian's contact, a minor Embassy aide, she had been 'swept away' by Jason's ideas.

'Well, she'll want to sweep them away when she sees them, that's for certain,' Adrian huffed. 'My God, Jason in Albany, it doesn't bear thinking about. He has no sense of continuity or respect at all; he'll Art Deco the woman to *death*, mark my words. It's his latest craze, he does it *everywhere*. With *anyone*. Silver walls and silver balls and little triangular dadoes, that's how *his* garden grows.' And then, whirling on an unsuspecting assistant who had just entered bearing a stack of newly-covered cushions for the window display, he shrieked, 'I said Delft Blue, not Dark Blue! Take the hideous things out and burn them immediately!'

The assistant rolled his eyes at Tess, and turned without a word, bearing the offending items away. Twenty minutes later Adrian was stalking around demanding that they be returned with equal alacrity, why didn't anyone do what he asked around there? Who was in charge, anyway? *Who made the decisions?* WHO PAID THE BILLS?

At four o'clock, weary, frazzled, and slightly deafened, Tess was sorting things into her briefcase when a shadow fell across her desk. Looking up, she saw Archie McMurdo standing there, watching her. 'G'day,' he said.

She stopped and glared at him. 'Well, what's wrong now?' she demanded, slamming her briefcase shut and preparing to do battle. 'Picture rails not level? Floorboards too dark? Windows too small? Come on, out with it.'

He looked deeply hurt. 'I thought maybe you'd like to have a bit of tucker with me,' he said. 'But, seeing as you're packing it in early, maybe you'd prefer tea at the Ritz?'

'Why?'

'Does there have to be a reason?' he asked, a plaintive note in his voice. 'It's a beautiful afternoon, isn't it? I don't know many people in London, and I have a craving for those little sandwiches and some scones with cream and strawberry jam. Someone told me tea at the Ritz is definitely the bonzer thing to do, so I thought why not do it with someone who's nice to look at? Sure wouldn't want to go there with Aunt Dolly, would I?'

Tess tried to visualize Mrs McMurdo in the marbled and mirrored vastness of the Ritz, bending over one of the little tea tables with pinkie upraised, her red curls frizzing energetically from under an expensive and totally unsuitable hat, her corncrake voice rasping out over the tinkle of the teaspoons and the piano. The visualization was successful, and she giggled.

Archie beamed down at her, a ray of sun from the window gilding his curly hair and sparking the devil in his eyes. 'Exactly,' he said. 'And, frankly, you look pretty jacked. I figure you could use some little sandwiches and a cup of that God-awful perfumey Earl Grey tea they probably serve there. Am I right?'

Tess sighed. He was very right. She looked at him speculatively. Was this a man with secrets? Did that open countenance and B. Lancaster smile go all the way through, or was what she saw exactly what she got? 'Give me a

125

minute,' she said, and reached for the phone.

A few minutes later, assured by John Soame that he and Max were deeply, happily – and literally – glued to their model-making, she allowed Archie McMurdo to take her to tea at the Ritz.

It was all that he had promised, but he impressed her more than the pillars and the confections. Gone was the loud-mouth complainer, the opinionated boor, the troublesome gadfly. Like some antipodean chameleon, he changed his colours to suit the background, and proved to possess all the polish necessary to negotiate the maze of tiny tables, the spindly legs of the gilded chairs and the ostentatious flurries of the waiters. He ordered exactly the right things in exactly the right voice, but did no more. He sat beside her in his dark suit and cranberry tie and seemed to glow, quietly. The heads that turned belonged only to assessing females, and she met several pairs of covetous eyes with, she hoped, total disdain. He poured her tea and treated her like some rare and valuable visitor from another world. She forgot her wrinkled suit and decidedly tired silk blouse. Gradually the images of peevish Adrian and possessive Richard and impecunious John faded from her mind. She was somebody, after all. Somebody who *deserved* tea at the Ritz.

In short, this particular Archie was both a balm and a revelation.

He caught her watching him and grinned.

'Forgiven?' he asked.

'For what?'

'All the strife I've been causing out at the house,' he said. 'I know you didn't like it – you're a hard-hearted sheila, and you can cast a mean eye on a man when you want to.'

'Can I?' Tess asked.

'Scared hell out of me,' he smiled.

'I doubt that very much.'

'Well, all that's over. We're going to get on beaut, now, aren't we? We're going to declare a truce.'

He looked so earnest, so contrite, that she couldn't resist him. 'Oh, all right,' she relented. 'Let frivolity reign.'

'Absolutely. Have another cucumber sandwich.' He held

up the plate for her selection. As she chose, she chanced to glance up at him and saw him staring fixedly at the people passing down the main corridor below the steps that separated the tearoom from the lobby. When she followed his gaze, she saw an older man had paused, hand on a chair as if seeking support in a crisis, and was staring back at him. His face was pale above the velvet collar of his dark blue coat, and his mouth slowly thinned as he pressed his lips together.

'Good Lord, do you think he's unwell?' Tess asked.

'Who?' asked Archie, casually, replacing the sandwich plate on the crowded top of the small table that sat before them.

'That man you were looking at, he seemed about to faint.'

He looked at her in some puzzlement. 'Sorry?' he asked.

Tess looked over at the wide, carpeted corridor. Many people thronged there, going right to the cocktail bar or left to the dining-room. The high-backed blue upholstered chair was still there. The frightened man was not.

'Oh,' she said, blankly. 'He's gone.'

'More tea?' asked Archie.

EIGHTEEN

'SECRETS,' TIM SAID, ABRUPTLY.

Murray spoke without looking up, turning a page and keeping his place with one finger. 'Whose secrets?' he asked.

'Anybody's secrets. It's secrets that lead to all the trouble in the world, secret thoughts, secret caches of arms, secret scientific developments, secret political moves, secret agreements to do or not to do — ' He had been pacing back and forth between the desks for over an hour.

'Listen, if people didn't have secrets, we'd be out of a job,' Murray said. 'I'd be stuck in my mother's antique shop, and you'd be . . . what would you be?'

'Much happier,' Tim said, coming to a stop and a decision at the same time. 'Much, much happier.' He went to his desk, picked up the file that had been weighing down his blotter all afternoon, and went out of the door.

Murray looked after him, smiled, and went back to revising for his promotional exams.

'Well, Nightingale?' Detective Chief Inspector Abbott looked up from his paperwork.

'Could I have a word, sir?'

Abbott threw his pen aside with every evidence of relief and leaned back in his chair. He seemed in an expansive mood, and Tim was encouraged. 'What can I do for you this time?'

'It's about the Leland case, sir.' Tim sat down and placed the file on his lap, ready to hand.

Abbott's forehead wrinkled. 'Is that something new?'

'I'm afraid not.'

Abbott gazed at him for a moment, then closed his eyes and groaned slightly to himself. 'It's still this Peters thing, isn't it? You didn't give the notebooks back.'

'Oh, yes, I did.'

'Ah.'

'After I'd photocopied the relevant pages.'

'Oh.'

'And I've been looking into things in my free time.'

Abbott started to show anger, then shrugged. Free time meant just that – he really couldn't stop Nightingale going around asking questions while off duty, as long as he didn't abuse his position. 'Let me guess,' he said, cautiously. 'You have a hunch.'

'More of an itch, really.' Tim explained about his interview with Tess Leland and his discovery of her situation: the burglary, the phone calls, the interrupted break-in. 'I've said to her that it's all coincidence, but frankly I think there's just too much of it to ignore. Peters stirred something up, and whether it killed him or not, it's still stirring. Roger Leland's death could have been a beginning rather than an ending. Or it could be part of something much, much bigger.'

'And so now you want to scratch this Leland itch officially, is that it?'

'I think it should be looked into, yes.'

Abbott shook his head in what looked like regret. 'We've got too big a case load to go chasing butterflies, Tim.'

'And we always will have. But if it turns out that Ivor Peters was right and I'm right and Roger Leland's death *was* more than an ordinary accident, and his widow and son suffer through our negligence, we'd look very bad. And feel even worse.'

'Hmmmm.' That possibility was not pleasing to Abbott. He scowled. 'But the Leland woman could be an hysteric, looking for attention.'

'I've considered that. But Soame believes her, and I respect his judgement. He was there when the latest phone call was made, he saw her reaction.'

'Who the hell is Soame?' the DCI demanded.

Patiently, Tim explained how John Soame had recently

129

entered into the Leland household. 'He's a well-known historian. I used to attend his lectures at university. He was very sound.'

' "Sound", was he?' Abbott asked, with only slight sarcasm. It was an awkward moment. Abbott was a good DCI, but only at the Yard temporarily, and thus lacking the aggressive edge that ambition honed so sharply in men who were out to make themselves known to those on the top floors. He liked Nightingale – most of the men liked Nightingale – but he was hesitant to trust his judgement completely. It was always expensive to trust young Detective Sergeants completely, and there'd been so much fuss about budgets, lately. As far as he could tell, in fact, almost everything up here was about budgets.

'Well, I really can't justify it, you know,' he finally said, with a sigh.

'It would be a lot more expensive to investigate Mrs Leland's murder,' Tim persisted. 'And we are supposed to prevent crime as well as detect it, aren't we?'

'Theoretically.'

'Well, this might be doing both. We can't be blamed for trying, can we?'

Abbott regarded Nightingale thoughtfully, thinking of the DCI who would return to this desk in a few months. The man he was temporarily replacing was an officer of the old school, who'd come up through the ranks, whereas Abbott himself – like Nightingale – had received Accelerated Promotion because of a university degree. He understood Nightingale's impatience with Yard politics, and the niceties of rank, privilege, and rumour. He didn't think DCI Spry, when he returned, would be so sympathetic. If he encouraged Nightingale, he might only be making future trouble for Spry and the boy himself. If he *dis*couraged him, however, he could nip in the bud the very qualities that were already lifting Nightingale above the others in the Service. Which responsibility should he honour first: loyalty to the Service and its concomitant infrastructure; or loyalty to the future, where officers like this one could create better and more sensitive policing? He glanced at the clock again, swiveled his chair to look

130

out of his window, and considered. Finally, he turned back and slapped his hands on the desk. 'Just keep it down,' he said.

'Sir?'

'Get on with whatever you want to set in motion, but keep the costs down and keep your head down, too. We've only got so much time, only so many hands, we've got to do it all the best we can.' He stood up. 'Unless and until something bigger or more urgent comes along, that is. Understood?'

Nightingale nodded, stood up, and turned to leave the office. He wanted to get out before Abbott changed his mind or put any limitations on him or said anything else, but he wasn't fast enough.

'Nightingale?'

Tim turned in the doorway. 'Sir?'

'What do you intend to do next?'

'I want to run up to Cambridge and talk to a few people.'

'Why?'

'I've only heard Soame lecture, sir. I know nothing about his private life. He *is* new on the scene, and he *is* right there in the house and — ' he paused.

'And?'

'And telephones can be rigged to ring on an electronic command – the technology can be picked up in half a dozen shops along Tottenham Court Road. You can be in the same room and call yourself, so to speak. You can also rig a phone to relay taped messages on command, all kinds of things. Just because he was beside her when she got one of the calls doesn't mean he wasn't behind it.'

'I thought you said he was "sound".'

'He is – on the nineteenth century. And anyway, that was a long time ago. That doesn't mean he's perfect. Or honest. Things may have happened to change him since I was up there. I don't know what his motivation might be, or if he has any connection with Mrs Leland, but some answers might be available in Cambridge.'

'Not trusting anyone is a bitch, isn't it?' Abbott said.

'Yes, sir.'

'But good policing, all the same,' Abbott said, approvingly. The door began to close. 'Tim?'

131

'Yes, sir?'

'Make it a day trip, I'm not authorizing any overnight expenses so you can have a piss-up with your old school ties.'

Tim grinned. 'All my old school ties are now rich merchant bankers or pop group promoters. If I do make contact in Cambridge it will probably be with other coppers. And you *know* we industrious, trustworthy coppers only drink tea, sir.'

Tess and Archie moved on from the Ritz to a small Italian restaurant just off Dean Street, where the food was superb and the wine ambrosiac. She had far too much of both, and found herself telling Archie all about the phone calls and the mysterious burglar who wasn't there.

'And they're after this money of yours, is that it?' he asked, offering her a breadstick.

'Yes. Except that there isn't any money,' Tess said. 'If I knew what they were talking about, it would make sense, but I don't, so it doesn't.' She paused. 'Any more than that sentence does. I don't think I should have any more wine.'

'On the contrary,' he said, filling up her glass. 'It's just what you *should* have.' He topped up his own glass and then raised it to her. 'Here's to nonsense.'

'I wish I agreed with you,' she said. 'It would be funny if it wasn't so frightening.'

'It looks to me like maybe it has something to do with your husband,' Archie suggested. 'Maybe he had some money. Maybe he put it some place and didn't tell you – how about that?'

'Well, maybe, but that wouldn't have been very like Roger. He *was* secretive about some things, but — ' she paused.

'But?' he asked, encouragingly.

She shrugged and sipped more wine. 'If there was any money hidden in the house, I expect the burglars found it weeks ago.'

'Not necessarily,' Archie said. 'Maybe your husband hid it in some really terrific place. What kind of things interested him? What did he do with his time?'

132

'He didn't have much time of his own, really. He was a workaholic. But when he did take time off, he liked to walk, and drink wine . . . and read . . . '

'Maybe he hid some money in a book.'

'I don't think so,' Tess said, sadly. 'He played squash, sometimes. He was quite good at that.'

'Doesn't sound very promising,' Archie said.

'No,' Tess agreed.

'Hey, cheer up. Have some more wine. You're supposed to be having a good time, here, remember?'

When they emerged, around ten o'clock, it was raining. They began to walk along the pavement towards Shaftesbury Avenue, where taxis would be patrolling to catch the after-theatre crowd. 'Just like Melbourne,' Archie said, moving her around a puddle.

She glanced sideways at him. 'I thought you said you came from Sydney.'

'Oh, sure, but I grew up in Melbourne,' he said.

As they passed the open mouth of a dark and noisome alley, there was a sudden clatter of bins and a shout. A few yards within, two men were grappling together in a drunken argument.

One knocked the other down and stood over him, shouting obscenities. The reek of alcohol blended with the stench of dirt and decaying garbage as the fallen man struggled up from a heap of split black plastic sacks, shouting in turn, waving his arms. He glanced towards the mouth of the alley and saw them. Abruptly his venom was turned on them rather than his more recent adversary.

'Come on, this is no place for you,' Archie said.

As they moved on hurriedly, the man leaned down, picked something up, and hurled it towards them. 'Piss off, piss off!' he shouted. 'Mind your own effing business!'

'Jesus, it's a rat!' Archie exclaimed, as the small black missile fell at their feet and began to twitch.

'No, it isn't, it's a cat,' Tess said, stooping down to pick it up. 'A kitten,' she amended, as the tiny, soaking wet little body squirmed and mewed in her hands.

'Cripes, it's filthy,' Archie said, with distaste, pulling her away as the man began to come towards them. 'Drop it and

133

come on.'

'No, he'll hurt it. He's a vile man,' Tess said, blurrily, allowing herself to be propelled along the pavement towards the lights of the avenue ahead, but still clutching the squirming, mewling little body. 'Throwing this poor defenceless animal at us like that. He could have killed it. Ouch.' Needle claws had dug into her hand as the kitten sought freedom.

'Defenceless, hell. It's probably covered with fleas,' Archie said. 'Oh, for crying out loud, let it go. We can't take a cat into a bar.'

'We're not going to a bar,' Tess said. She opened her briefcase and carefully inserted the bedraggled kitten, closing the bag gently over its spiky, muddy, reeking head.

'But it's only a little after ten,' Archie said, in some consternation.

'Time to go home,' Tess said, carefully.

'Oh,' Archie said, as if a light were dawning. 'Oh. Right. Got you. Home it is.' He seemed pleased suddenly, she couldn't imagine why. She'd had far too much wine. Her throat was sore from talking so much, and her feet hurt. Maybe his feet hurt, too.

She came to a different conclusion in the taxi.

All traces of the wine, the cocktails, and the candlelight were dissipated from Tess's brain as Archie McMurdo made his expectations plain. 'No, Archie, please — ' Tess protested in a low but audible voice, prying away his busy hands and leaning back from his looming face, which cut off the light and made her feel trapped and claustrophobic.

He glared at her for a moment, then pushed her away abruptly. 'I thought Yank women were liberated,' he said.

'Not all of us,' she snapped. 'And liberated doesn't mean — '

'Leave it out,' Archie said brusquely, and turned to stare out of the window. His Australian accent, softened during the tea and dinner interludes, had reappeared under the influence of this apparently unexpected and certainly unwelcome wound to his self-esteem.

'It's just that — '

'I know, I know, you're not that kind of sheila,' Archie

134

said, turning back to face her and leaning into the corner of the seat. 'Forget it. I didn't read you clear, all right? Let's leave it at that.'

'I did enjoy this evening with you,' she said, quietly.

He patted her hand in an avuncular manner. 'Well, that's good, girl, that's fine. Glad to have been of service, as they say.'

And he spoke no more during the rest of the journey through the gleaming streets. Window displays and traffic lights reflected off the wet asphalt and made puddles of colour on the pavements, but once they'd left the theatre district there were few pedestrians about to appreciate the rainbowed duplication. The bright rectangles containing heaped merchandise or mannequins frozen in fashionable poses became fewer and fewer, the gaps between them longer, until only the occasional gleam from restaurants, pubs and late-night takeaways lent warmth to the grey, slanting shafts of rain and the patent-leather sheen of the road. Other cars, secret and sleek, moved beside them, occasionally punctuated by the red wall of a bus or the half-seen and indecipherable lettering on the side of a passing lorry. In front, the driver was listening to a radio phone-in on the decline of public morals, but in the dark cube of the rear seat there was only an intermittent squeak and scrabble from within Tess's briefcase.

Now secure in her corner of the taxi, Tess looked at Archie sideways and tried to free herself from the last, seductive strands of alcohol. It wasn't Archie's fault at all, but her own. He'd read the signals correctly – she *was* attracted to him. The trouble was, she was physically attracted not only to Archie, but also to Richard, to Sergeant Nightingale, to John Soame, to that lovely young curate who came around to play chess with Max, and – it seemed to her – practically every male she passed in the street. Even ever-so-elegant Adrian gave her odd moments of speculation. My God, she thought, I'd better be careful. If the taxi-driver turns around I'll probably manage to find something devastating about *him*, too. Was this a result of hormone build-up or a reassertion of her own sensual persona?

Clearly, Mother Nature was not a feminist.

135

Well, she was not going to give in to Mother Nature any more than she was going to give in to Archie McMurdo's apparent conviction that women were supposed to pay for their dinners, albeit not with Visa. Unfortunately, there were other wishes to be considered, and other obligations. She wrestled with the dichotomy, and then her nerve snapped.

'Perhaps you'd like to come to dinner one evening?'

Archie glanced across at her, somewhat startled by this apparent reversal in her attitude. 'Well, sure. Maybe. Why not?' He began to smile again. After a minute he began humming to himself, and reached over to pat her hand, allowing his fingers to linger. 'Why not?' he repeated.

I'm doing this for Adrian, she thought.

I really am.

NINETEEN

TESS'S BRIEFCASE WAS NEVER THE same again.

She got rid of Archie in the nicest way she could, and carried the case inside at arm's length, for it had developed a leak from one corner.

She ran down the hall with it, and plunked it into the sink. John Soame, who had been reading on baby-sitting duty, appeared with a worried expression. 'Is there anything wrong?' he asked. 'You ran in so quickly — '

The briefcase gave a squeal.

He looked at it and then at her with an owlish expression. 'Your briefcase is haunted,' he said. He inspected her, gravely. 'And you are — '

'Perfectly all right,' she said, not realizing that her struggles with Archie had left her make-up smudged and her hair rather corkscrewed over one ear. 'But if they breathalyse me I may be taken in for being drunk in charge of a pair of shoes. Which hurt.' She kicked them off, and sighed. 'Better,' she said. '*Much* better.'

The briefcase squealed again. Soame raised an enquiring eyebrow.

'He threw it at me,' she explained.

'Did he?'

'Yes. He was a mean, drunken old tramp.'

'Really. I was under the impression he was a client.'

'Oh, not Archie. *Archie* didn't throw it.'

'That is a relief.' There was a pause. 'Then who — '

'The man in the alley.'

'Ah.'

'Outside the restaurant.' She looked at him crossly. For a

college professor he seemed rather dim. 'He was having a fight with another man and he saw us and he threw the cat at us. Didn't hit us, though,' she finished, triumphantly.

'It's all in the footwork,' Soame nodded. He went over to the sink and inspected the briefcase, which had ceased to leak but had begun to rock. 'May I?'

'Watch out,' she warned him. 'It's very fierce.'

He gingerly opened the briefcase to reveal the very small, very bedraggled kitten crouching in one corner. 'My God,' he said. 'He *is* a dangerous beast. You're lucky to be alive.'

'It was a close thing,' Tess smiled, sinking on to the rocking chair in front of the old Rayburn range. 'But I thought maybe Max would like it. He isn't happy.' She closed her eyes and leaned her head back. 'He should be happy.'

'I know,' Soame said, softly, and then watched her fall asleep in an instant. He put a quilt over her, then went down to the local high-street shop which was run by a hard-working Asian family who knew no night. He returned bearing flea powder, a litter tray and litter, a few tins of cat food, and a tiny bright red flea collar.

He ran a few inches of warm water into the sink and extracted the kitten from the briefcase for a bath. During the following few minutes Tess awoke. In fact, she was surprised the entire neighbourhood didn't awake. After most of the water in the sink had been redistributed over the kitchen floor and the two bath attendants, there was a brief pause for TCP and plasters. There followed an interlude of relative peace concerning flea powder and a saucer of milk, and the evening's entertainment was concluded by the ceremonial fastening of the collar.

The exhausted kitten was settled down in an apple box beside Tess's bedroom radiator, and the equally exhausted bath attendants retired to their respective corners for the night. Tess, now plagued equally by doubts about Archie McMurdo and indigestion from the veal piccata, was convinced she would never sleep and dropped off instantly.

Had she remained awake she would have been aware of John Soame pacing back and forth above her head, until very, very late.

*

In the morning the kitten's thin cries awakened Tess. She put on her robe and padded over. 'Good morning,' she said, and gathered up the box to present to Max, discovering in the process that she had a hangover for which bending over was definitely not a cure.

'What's that?' Max asked, wearily, when she entered his room. 'More books to read?'

'No. Guess again.'

He turned his head away and looked out of the window. 'Something Educational,' he said, in vast disgust.

'Absolutely,' Tess agreed.

Though he had been healing in body, Max was still unsettled in mind. He would cheer up after a visit from Simon Carter, who seemed always able to make him laugh. And he would be mentally lively after a lesson with John. But there were still too many moments when she would catch him staring into space with a frown. He had begun asking questions about his father, as if he were a stranger he'd never known. More than once she had caught him crying over the stamp collections or the aeroplane models he had made with Roger, or going through the box of snapshots of them all together on holiday and stacking them in various and apparently arbitrary combinations, or rereading a childhood story book rescued from the bottom of his pine chest. But when she'd tried to comfort him he'd become offhand and cross, telling her not to treat him like a baby. He was just bored, he said. Sick of being sick, he said.

And she guessed he was still having nightmares, for she often found his bedlight had been turned on in the night, and shadows would come and go beneath his eyes.

They were there now.

Without another word, she put the box on the bed beside him, and went down to the kitchen to make breakfast.

She spent the morning at the Victoria and Albert museum, sketching and taking notes, researching the final details for the McMurdo interiors. It was the part of the job she most enjoyed, reconciling the stylistic demands of the past with

139

the practical realities of the present. Fortunately for her – and for Mrs McMurdo – Victoriana was now very much in fashion, and there were many companies reproducing the lovely curling lines of early William Morris designs in both lighting and plumbing fixtures, basic areas in which anachronistic clashes most often occurred.

Tess had also renewed many contacts in the antiques trade that she had made before her marriage, and asked several dealers with whom she had a good relationship and whom she could trust to find her authentic pieces to feature in the large rooms of the McMurdo mansion. Proportion was very important here she felt, and wherever possible she wanted to use original things rather than reproductions, which were often scaled down slightly to fit into the reduced dimensions of modern homes.

In some cases she'd had no alternative but to find craftsmen willing to reproduce the items she'd chosen, and she spent the afternoon with one of them, a cabinetmaker who would be building the special wine-racks for the basement. Tess was determined to carry authenticity even to those dark regions.

She arrived home at three thirty, told Mrs Grimble she could leave early, and made tea for Max and the kitten, whose name was apparently Albert. Leaving them mutually absorbed and quite transformed by their new friendship, Tess sank into a scented bath, enjoying the rare luxury of being pleased with herself and her day's work. She was just drying her hair when the phone rang.

She froze for a moment, then squared her shoulders and went downstairs to face the worst.

But it was not the mysterious caller.

It was Adrian, and he was in a foul temper.

'Don't tell me that's really you,' he said, sarcastically. 'How nice to know you're still breathing. May I assume, despite finding you at home at this hour, that you are still working for me and have not resigned to go into business for yourself?'

'You knew my schedule for today – or you would if you'd bothered to ask Maud. I phoned her and told her I would be at the V&A this morning, which I was, and with

Mr Greenslade this afternoon, which I also was, skipping my lunch-hour, by the way, so I am taking it now.' She dropped into the chair beside the phone and inspected her toes. 'What is it, Adrian?'

His tone was measured, small doses filtered between clenched teeth. 'I have been having a long, heart-to-heart talk with Mr McMurdo, who kindly called into the studio this afternoon.'

'Oh, really?' She was amused, imagining how Archie would have impressed Adrian. 'Beautiful, isn't he?'

'I hardly noticed.'

She laughed. 'Oh, come on — '

'His attractions are not in question, here. What is in question is *you*, Tess.'

'Me?' She was startled.

'Indeed. He seems to think *you're* not "up to the job".'

'What?'

'He told me some mad tale about burglars and unpleasant phone calls and you having a lot of money. That was quite a revelation, my sweet.' There was nothing sweet about his tone. 'I was under the impression that you were as stony as me.'

'I am. He had no ri — '

'He says you're too "burdened" by your private concerns to give the restoration of the house your full attention, and that the work is being skimped or not done at all.'

'That's not true!'

'He says he's going to ask his Aunt Dolly to name another decorator. Or, preferably, allow *him* to do so.'

Tess had been slowly sitting up as Adrian spoke, and was now fully erect and at full attention, her spine stiffened by dismay. 'And what does Aunt Dolly say to that?' she demanded.

'How should I know?'

'But I told you to get in touch with her, to ask — '

'Yes, yes, yes.' Adrian was in full flow, ignoring her protests, concerned only with what he saw as betrayal and a considerable loss in income. 'But the damage is done, Tess, and *you've* done it. I told you to charm him, I told you to handle him. I have enough to do just keeping

141

Brevitt Studios *afloat* these days . . . ' Self-pity was beginning to creep into his voice.

The scene in the taxi came back to her, in every detail. Apparently Archie really hated taking 'no' for an answer, after all. 'Adrian, there's more to this than you think. I think you ought to look into Mr Archie McMurdo's motivations a little more closely, because — ' she began, angrily, but he gave her no chance to continue.

'That is not all,' he continued, his voice growing heavier with each word. 'According to our irreplaceable builder – and I underline the word irreplaceable, which does not apply to *everyone* in this organization – the good Ernest Flowers, with whom I've just spoken, Archie continues to turn up at the house and tries to get them to change things.'

'What kind of things?'

'Oh, doors, windows, ceilings, floors – just *small* items of that nature. He's apparently underfoot at every turn, getting into everything, and generally making a nuisance of himself. I'm afraid Ernest became rather heated on the telephone. He wants to know whether to treat Archie like a client, or throw him off the site. We are at risk here, Tess, Ernest and his fellow workers are threatening to down tools if the situation isn't clarified.'

'Then clarify it, Adrian,' she snapped. 'I can't believe this is — '

'Oh, really? I find it dismayingly easy to believe,' Adrian said. 'It is a direct result of a slack hand at the tiller, Tess dear. Of *somebody* not tending to business.'

'I have been working hard on the McMurdo house,' Tess said, hotly. 'I have rearranged my life entirely so that I can concentrate on the work – you begged me to do it, remember? And I'm doing it.'

'I'm beginning to wonder if I wasn't too hasty about all that. I shall be going over to the house myself, tomorrow, to see exactly what you've been doing.'

'You *know* what I've been doing. I've showed you all my sketches, from the beginning. It's not fair that you — '

He interrupted. 'I haven't time to be fair, Tess. I only have time to survive, and however fond I am of you

142

personally, I am not going to let that cloud my judgement. I'm not going to let even you destroy what I've taken years to build up.' Within his wrath, Tess could detect the sound of imminent tears.

'Adrian, dear, you *know* that I — '

'I don't know anything, Tess, but I will know more tomorrow, that is certain. Goodbye.'

TWENTY

STUNNED BY THE SUDDEN FEROCITY of Adrian's attack, Tess sat back and stared at the small group of framed Bateman cartoons on the far wall. One was slightly crooked, and she noticed that the heavy embossed wallpaper she had chosen so carefully – so long ago now – had begun to curl away from the wall in the lower corner near the sitting-room. It seemed appropriate to her mood that little things which had formed the solid background of her life were becoming skewed and worn. She thought about straightening the picture. She thought about finding some paste and sticking the paper down. But she remained, immobile, on the bench beside the telephone.

Adrian had sounded almost hysterical.

Although he had a temper and temperament, she had never heard quite that degree of angst in his voice. Could it be she *was* doing a poor job at the McMurdo house? It was true she hadn't gone there in the past few days to see what progress was being made, but that was because she trusted Ernie implicitly.

Had she been wrong? Had she made errors of judgement as to concept, overall design, small details? No, she refused to believe it. She knew her work was good. Better than good.

She sat there for a very long time, until the hall grew dark, and beyond. Wind suddenly shook the windows in the sitting-room, and there was a mutter of thunder. A little while later, she could hear rain falling, and above it, the sound of Max's television set. Still she sat there, staring without seeing. She was so absorbed in her reflections that the doorbell, going off without warning above her head, made her jump in alarm. Perhaps Mr Soame had forgotten his key. Wearily, she got up, pulled her old, comfortable dressing-gown around her, tied the belt in a knot, and went to the door.

Suddenly overtaken by caution, she stopped before opening it and called, 'Who is it?'

The clamour of the bell, which had continued, abruptly stopped, and an equally loud voice replaced it. 'G'day! Is that my sweet little sheila? I've come to bring you joy and merriment, as promised.'

Anger swept through her. Taking a deep breath she opened the door. Archie McMurdo stood on the doorstep, grinning, his hair wet and his mac dripping rain. He was carrying a bottle of champagne under one arm, and had a bunch of roses in his hand. As he stood there he wavered a little from side to side – clearly he had fortified himself for the anticipated rigours of the evening ahead.

Tess glared at him, firmly gripping the front of her robe as an alternative to his throat. 'How dare you go behind my back to my boss and tell him I was *incompetent*.'

His face fell, comically. 'Why, the old galah promised he'd let me talk to you first. Damn his eyes.' Archie's voice carried clearly above the hiss of the rain, and Tess glanced nervously at the neighbouring bay windows. Archie leaned forward, and a gust of beery breath hit her full in the face. 'I ought to have a chance to explain, don't you think?'

'I'm not interested.' She began to close the door.

'Here, wait on, sweetheart,' Archie bellowed, jamming a foot in the opening. 'You and me have got to come good over this. That old wowser only gave you his side of it, I'll bet. I've got a few points to make, too.'

'I don't care to hear them.'

'Then I'll just stand here and shout them through the door.'

She assessed him. He was grinning, again, and she decided he would do just what he said, if only for the sheer hell of it. He seemed the sort who enjoyed such little scenes of macho courtship. 'Five minutes,' she said in a steely voice. He followed her in, his eyes bright, smilingly certain that he could overcome all obstacles in his way,

145

including her anger and the knot in the belt of her dressing-gown.

'That's better. Not used to all this rain in Adelaide,' he said, shaking himself like a dog.

'I thought you said you came from Sydney,' she said, standing with hands on hips while he put down the champagne and roses, after offering them to her without success.

'Adelaide first, then Sydney,' he said earnestly.

'But — '

'You look real beaut,' he went on, oblivious to her expression. 'And you smell good, too.' He came closer. 'Just stepped out of the bath, I'll bet, and nothing on but that little robey thing . . . '

'Was it in Melbourne, Adelaide, or Sydney that you learned to be such a . . . such a . . . *creep*?' she demanded, sidestepping his advance. It had been a mistake to let him in, to worry about what the neighbours might think, and she already regretted it. Why, for all she knew, that boyish grin could be the very expression he wore when pulling the wings off flies.

'Now don't go all snaky on me, sweetheart,' he pleaded, as she dodged him.

'I have every right to "go snaky" on you,' she snapped. 'You've been a bit of a snake, yourself, if you ask me. You promised not to interfere at the house, yet I find out you're still hanging around out there annoying Ernie and the other men. Now you've gone behind my back to Adrian and told him I shouldn't be working on the house — '

'You shouldn't.'

' — and threatening to write to your aunt suggesting that she hire another interior decorator. How dare you!'

He stopped his clumsy but apparently good-natured pursuit and scowled. 'Not a matter of dare, sweetheart. Matter of fact. You've got too much on your mind these days. Your kid. The money. People threatening you. All that. Takes a girl's attention from her work. Changes her priorities.' He beamed suddenly. 'So, I think you should forget the house and all the rest of it and concentrate on

146

me. Much nicer for both of us when we've got time to enjoy it.'

She stared at him. 'Do you mean to tell me that you did that just so we could be together?'

'Sure. Aren't you flattered? Just shows how much I think of you, sweetheart.'

Drawing herself up, Tess went from stare to glare. 'On the contrary,' she said, coldly. 'It shows how little you think of me and how much you think of yourself.'

Anger flared in his eyes. 'Now, wait a minute — '

'No, *you* wait a minute,' she said. 'I am a mother and a working woman who is hanging on by the skin of her teeth to her home, her child, her career, and her sanity. Contrary to general opinion, I do not need a man to complete my life. Get out!'

'The hell I will. Not until you and me get a few things straight.' He lunged at her, still apparently under the impression that a few deep-tongued kisses would transform her from independent career woman to supplicant, and convert hostility into panting hunger.

She struck him, hard, across the face.

It had a strange effect on him. He went red, then white, and then a terrible expression came into his eyes. She saw, too late, that he was far more gone in drink than she had thought. And that slap had been one mistake too many.

She backed away, knocking over a small pine chair which in turn collided with the small hall table near the front door. A vase teetered and went down onto the scuffed parquet floor with a splintering crash.

Archie McMurdo laughed. It was a vicious laugh – he was enjoying himself now. 'Uh-oh,' he said. 'There goes the furniture,' he added, gleefully, and returned to his relentless pursuit, moving as suddenly and unpredictably as a spider, scuttling first one way and then another. Dodging around her own hallway, Tess would have felt foolish if she hadn't been so frightened. 'Time to squirm for your supper, sweetheart,' he grinned, reaching for her. 'Time to give old Archie what he deserves.'

'I'd rather do that myself,' said a voice from above them, and Tess looked up to see John Soame standing on the

147

stairway, arms crossed and staring down. His face was very pale.

Archie, startled into immobility, stared at him. 'Who the hell are you?' he demanded. He turned to Tess. 'Nobody said anything about a boyfriend. Who's he?'

He was still waiting for her answer as Soame descended the last few steps, took hold of him from behind, and started propelling him towards the front door. Caught unawares, Archie seemed to forget for a moment that he was taller and stronger by far than the other man.

Then he remembered.

'Let go of me, you little bastard!' he howled, and twisted out of Soame's grasp, then went for him, wildly. Tess put her hands to her mouth, horrified, as the two men began to grapple in the hall. Seeing violence on television or witnessing it in a Soho alley was one thing, having it in your own home was quite another. The grunting, the sudden bitter smell of violence, the wordless struggling was eerie, shocking, and made infinitely more terrible by taking place within familiar walls.

'Oh, John, be careful, oh, darling, *please* stop, please be careful – oh, no – don't . . . ' She could hear herself babbling, as she moved around them, plucking ineffectually at their straining shoulders, mesmerized by the enraged grimaces on their reddening faces as they pushed and shoved one another backwards and forwards, like animals jockeying for superior position and leverage, or like boys in a playground. It was silly, and it was absolutely awful.

'Open the door,' John grunted, through clenched teeth.

Tess edged past them and did as she was told. Cold air and rain swept in. She wanted to close her eyes and ears to the sight and sound of the two men, but she couldn't.

A moment later, she was glad she hadn't, for she might have missed the sight of an astonished Archie McMurdo being suddenly thrust through the open front door and thrown down the front steps on to the wet pavement below. It was so quickly done, so adroit and unexpected, that she could only stare at the man who had done it. John Soame stood panting but unmarked in the open doorway,

148

staring down, quite oblivious to her presence in his moment of triumph.

Archie, however, was not. He got up, staggered slightly, brushed at himself and stared up at her defiantly. 'Did you enjoy that, sweetheart? Don't laugh too long, because we haven't finished with you, yet. We still have business together. And next time I'll make sure you're alone.'

John slammed the door shut and then leaned his head against it, panting slightly, his shirt taut across his thin shoulders, his tie dangling over one shoulder, his hair ruffled up at the back like a boy's.

'Damn,' he said, under his breath. 'Damn, damn, damn.'

TWENTY-ONE

JOHN SOAME TURNED AND STARED at Tess. 'Are you all right?'

She was suddenly aware of her scrubbed face, her old bathrobe, her straggly hair, and her acute embarrassment at having been the cause of a scene.

'I — I'm fine, really,' she stammered, feeling the flush rising up her throat and flooding her naked face, like a unfurling banner of shame. 'I'm sorry about – it's so – '

'I'm sorry if he was a friend — ' He glanced at the abandoned roses and champagne, and managed to imbue the word 'friend' with a great complexity of meaning.

'No . . . not at all. He's my client's nephew, the man I had dinner with last night. He's been causing a lot of trouble at the house, and Adrian thought my being friendly might change his attitude.'

He offered a wry smile. 'Apparently it did just that.'

'Yes.' She pulled her dressing-gown closer around her throat. 'But I really gave him no reason to suppose — '

'I'm sure you didn't,' he said, rather too quickly. And rather too coldly for comfort.

'In fact, I made things worse. He went to Adrian today and told him he thinks I can't handle the job, said he wants another decorator. And Adrian *listened to him*,' she said, miserably. 'He's angry with me . . . I don't understand anything, any more.'

He came to her then, and put an arm around her shoulders. 'Don't worry, Adrian is always flying off the handle about something. You know he has faith in you – he wouldn't have been so determined to keep you if he didn't.'

She looked up at him. 'Even to the point of inflicting me and my troubles on his poor, unsuspecting brother-in-law.'

He in his turn flushed slightly. 'Poor, yes, but hardly unsuspecting. Nobody who has taught adolescents is unsuspecting – quite the reverse, I assure you. And as for —'

'John? What's wrong? What on earth was all the shouting about?'

It was a woman's voice – a young woman's voice, light and soft as gossamer. Startled, Tess sprang away from Soame's encircling arm and looked up. There, outlined in the entrance to the attic flat, was a lovely girl; slender, blonde, and barefoot. She was wearing a man's silk dressing gown, presumably Soame's. Suddenly Tess realized that when he had first appeared on the stairs he, too, had been dressed rather more casually than usual. That his tie had been loosened and the first few buttons of his shirt had been undone before his encounter with Archie. Her heart, which had been thudding and fluttering a moment before, closed up and went as hard as a fist.

'It's all right, Julia,' Soame said. 'Just a drunken intruder who needed to be shown the door.' He glanced uneasily at Tess – his turn now to be embarrassed. He started to say more, but Tess didn't want to hear it. The situation was all too obvious.

'I'm sorry, I hope I haven't spoiled your evening,' she said, stiffly. 'Thanks again for the rescue.' She wrapped her faded robe around her, feeling very foolish, very tired, and very, very old. She fled to Max's room, before she made it all worse.

Max looked up as she came in and closed the door behind her. His freckles stood out against the pale skin, and his hair was standing up in spikes, needing a wash. His pyjamas were all wrinkled, and he had a smear of jam on his chin, a teatime leftover. 'Hi,' he said.

It was enough.

She sat down on the side of the bed and, taking him into her arms, she wept into his spiky hair. 'Oh, Max, I'm sorry.'

151

'What for? Gosh, Mum, you're strangling me,' he said, squirming in her arms until he was free. He stared at her, startled by her tears. 'Hey,' he said. 'Stop that.' He patted her arm and smoothed the top of her head awkwardly.

She wiped her eyes on her sleeves. 'Oh, rats,' she said, crossly, blinking rapidly to recentre her contact lens. She sniffed hugely, and sighed. 'It's just that sometimes I'm so – so – *dumb* about things. People and . . . things. You know.'

'Oh, that.' He was half disappointed to find the crisis so small.

'What do you mean, "Oh, that"?'

'Well — ' He shrugged. 'You are a bit of a klutz, Mum.'

'Am I?' she asked, in some astonishment.

'Never mind,' he said, patting her hand with an unconscious air of benign superiority. 'Girls are *always* hopeless.'

'Oh, really?' She gazed at him speculatively, and blew her nose. If that was the attitude his father and that damned school had been inculcating into him, perhaps it would be a good idea if he *did* go to the local comprehensive, at that. From what she'd seen of the little ladies of the neighbourhood, he'd soon have that patronizing attitude knocked out of him, and a good thing, too.

'This has been a momentary aberration,' she said, giving her nose a final wipe. 'Normal services are now resumed.'

She began plumping his pillows and straightening his blankets. There was a resentful squeak and Albert appeared from beneath the covers, his cosy nest disturbed by her sudden burst of housekeeping. 'I think you should have a bath and a hair-wash before you go to sleep,' she said, firmly. 'And you need fresh pyjamas, too, you've had these on for days.'

'I've just got them nicely broken in,' he protested.

She plucked at a hole in the right sleeve. 'Broken out, you mean. This top is a diary of disasters – I can see glue, ketchup, gravy, ink, and poster paint, all down the front. Come on, stop moaning. No, leave Albert here. He might fall in and drown.'

Grumbling over the unfairness of it all, Max deposited Albert in a huge cardboard box of balled-up newspapers.

'Simon made that today to keep Albert from knocking the pieces off the chessboard,' Max said. 'It kept him quiet – sort of.' As if to prove the efficacy of the young vicar's unusual gambit, the kitten immediately began a mad scrabble, picking out a ball and chasing it around the box, then changing direction when another took its eye. Max grinned. 'That's his crazy-box.'

Tess looked down at the kitten as it excitedly continued its manic, circular pursuit. 'I know just how he feels,' she said.

During a humiliating night of waking and sleeping, Tess confronted herself and was not impressed. What an idiot she'd been. What a fool. Why hadn't she seen it before?

All her troubles had to do with the McMurdo house.

They must do.

She thought back to Mrs McMurdo and their first trip to the house all that time ago. Hadn't Dolly said something about 'Harry's little treasure'? At the time she'd thought the woman was being sarcastic about the house itself, but could there have been more to it than that? Suppose there had been some family story about the old man having a secret hoard of money, which Dolly only took half-seriously, but which Archie had taken to heart?

Suppose he'd followed his aunt to London and, when she made no fabulous discovery, decided to do a little exploring of his own? Ernie had said, just before they started the restoration work, that he thought 'kids' had been in the house at night, disturbing things. What if it hadn't been kids, but Archie, searching for something?

And then she'd arrived on the scene, and got in his way.

What would he have done then?

Decided to get her *out* of his way, of course. He could easily have pumped Dolly about Tess: heard all about Roger's death and then Max's illness, and decided to use the situation.

Because he thought she'd found what he'd been searching for.

'We want the money back, Mrs Leland.' That's what the

153

caller had said. It seemed so obvious now.

The burglary, the phone calls, the threats – they had to have been Archie. When they hadn't worked, he'd decided to try criticizing the restoration work. But no luck. So he'd turned to charm. That hadn't worked either. So he'd gone to Adrian and tried to get her fired. That would have got the work suspended, and while he pretended to be choosing another decorator, he'd really be searching for the money, unobserved and unimpeded.

But where was it?

The house had been almost literally torn to pieces while they installed new wiring and plumbing and put in the central heating system. The attic had been completely exposed when they'd put on a new roof. All the window frames had been removed and replaced, the chimneys swept and repaired, even many of the walls had been stripped right down and replastered. What was *left*, for goodness' sake? She frowned in the darkness, and then her eyes flew open and she stared into the shadows. Of course.

The cellar.

TWENTY-TWO

WHILE THE VISTA OF CAMBRIDGE under sunlight is uplifting and noble, Nightingale felt that in mid-morning rain the town revealed its true nature – quiet, enclosed, introspective. Steamy windows in teashops and cafés bespoke earnest conversations within, lights glimmering in the various libraries told of shoulders hunched over books and hurriedly scribbled essays, while brief flares of blue light, random metallic ticks and deadly silences emanating from within the Cavendish laboratories told of heaven knew what next.

He walked slowly across Trinity's Great Court, practically alone in the vast expanse. He passed one or two hurrying scholars and a muttering academic, all head-down into the rain. In the distance two gowned figures marched in almost military tandem beneath a large blue umbrella. The stormy sky pressed down, with torn rags of smaller and darker clouds moving quickly beneath a pale grey canopy.

The line between town and gown was a sharp one, as always. In contrast to Trinity's peace, the street beyond was as clotted with cars as any London thoroughfare, and a horde of Saturday-morning shoppers jostled over the pavements. Around and between the road and foot traffic wove the bicycles, their riders for the most part encased in waterproof ponchos, rain speckling their spectacles and dripping down from hatbrims or noses. In their baskets or trapped over rear wheels under elasticated ropes, rode awkward bundles of books, haphazardly encased in layers of plastic carrier bags. Under the banners of Gateway, Safeway, Sainsburys, Marks and Spencer, and Gupta's

Groceries, were transports of Herodotus, Thucydides, Darwin, Donne, and Drucker, safe from the rain, but still – and always – vulnerable to undergraduate attack.

The cheekbones of the cyclists were flushed with exertion, but otherwise they looked pale and waxy with cold and damp around the jawline. They seemed, for the most part, unbearably young, and he envied them – knowing that his envy stamped him forever old and severed at last his tenuous connection to that age which parents think wonderful but students know to be fraught, confusing, and full of strain.

He'd been happy here.

He was not happy to be back.

Not, at least, on this mission. Always behind him he could hear the Yard accountants' footsteps drawing near. He should have had a week to suss out John Soame – to talk casually to academics, students, his bank manager, his landlady if he had one, and so on. The bits and pieces that reveal a man are rarely found in a hurry – one day would never be enough.

It gave him only one real option.

Bardy Philpott.

Bardy had been head porter at Brendan College, Tim's alma mater. Brendan was one of the 'newer' additions to the university, being less than two centuries old. Brendan bore its nouveau stigma gracefully. The blatant red bricks chosen by its founder had long since been hidden behind trembling ivy. The panelled rooms and hallways had gradually acquired the desirable patina of age by the simple expedient of successive Masters allowing smoking everywhere until well after World War Two.

Nightingale made a stop on his way to Little Badger Lane, to acquire a small offering of Bardy's favourite tobacco and malt whisky. The old man was retired, now, and living in a very bijou residence acquired for him by his son, who had 'done well' after leaving Trinity with a First and going on to become a QC much given to annoying the Met by gleefully picking holes in their evidence.

Nightingale was astonished to discover that Bardy actually remembered him by name and corridor. When he considered the numbers of young men who had filtered through Brendan before, during, and since his own stay there, it seemed an impossible feat, and he said so.

' "Memory is the warder of the brain",' intoned Bardy, proving he, at least, had not changed during the intervening years. His speech was still larded with quotes and misquotes from Shakespeare. He was always to be discovered reading the Bard in the Porter's Lodge – hence his nickname – apparently thinking that such a scholarly pursuit was one befitting his position in the college. Bets had been taken as to what other book might be hidden behind the rubbed blue cover of his massive *Complete Collected*, but despite furtive forays into the P'lodge taken as dares, no rogue copies of Raymond Chandler or *Playboy* had ever been discovered.

Bardy Philpott was unusual in other ways, too. Unlike most porters he was tall, and cadaverous in appearance, his long and melancholy visage convincing callow undergraduates that he lacked a sense of humour. Certainly he was strict in his application of the rules, but those who took the trouble to know him better soon discovered a wry, dry slant of mind lurked behind his lowering brow. But while he was firm, he was not entirely unyielding, and had often turned a blind page of his Shakespeare while a late returnee skulked past the P'lodge.

He accepted Nightingale's offering of tobacco and whisky with grave appreciation, and led him past his retired bowler – which hung in honourable estate on a separate peg in the hall – through to his snug sitting-room. He loomed oddly against the chintz and exposed beams, and when Tim commented on the room's attractions, Bardy snorted.

'Daughter-in-law did it all. Never asked me. When she finished, there wasn't a chair in the place I could sit in.' He sank into the one jarring item in the room, a huge and ugly club chair covered with cracked brown leatherette which Tim remembered had taken up a great deal of the space in Bardy's lodge. 'Bursar let me take this when I retired,' he said, tapping his large bony fingers on the worn arms. 'Probably would have had to talk to visitors while lying on the floor, otherwise.' He grinned, exposing large, even teeth. 'Does my heart good to see her wince at it every time she drops by. Which fortunately isn't often.'

They spent a few minutes exchanging vital trivia, filling in the cracks between the years. Although it was still early, Bardy had provided them both with a stiff drink, and now raised his glass and an eyebrow. 'I never would have placed you with the constabulary. You must have changed a lot.'

'I hope so,' Tim said. 'Looking back, I'd say I was pretty much a self-righteous prig in those days.'

'Would have thought that was a prime qualification for policing,' Bardy said, slyly, but there was no rancour in it. The old man leaned back and searched his memory for something suitable. ' "In every honest hand a whip to lash the rascals naked through the world",' he said, finally. He opened his eyes and looked at Tim with lively interest. 'I'm assuming the honesty, mind.'

'Depends on your definition, doesn't it?' Tim smiled. 'So far I don't think I've been too bad.'

'And tomorrow?'

Tim shrugged.

Bardy nodded. 'I suppose that's honest, too,' he conceded. He took another sip of his drink. 'What particular rascal are you after today?'

'John Soame,' Tim said.

'Has he killed someone?' Bardy asked, in some surprise.

'No. Why? Would you have expected him to?' Nightingale asked, rather startled by this leap to the worst possible conclusion. Was he more right to suspect Soame than he'd thought?

'Most people expected him to murder his wife,' Bardy said, obviously worried that he'd said the wrong thing. 'But as bad as she was, he never raised a hand to her that we heard of – and we would have heard.'

Exactly. Tim's decision to come here had been based on just that. 'Was she so terrible?'

'Yes,' Bardy said, flatly. 'I would have murdered her, if she'd been my wife. "A most pernicious woman." '

'You're speaking in the past tense, I notice.'

158

'She died out east somewhere, in the end. Let him off the hook. Funny thing was, he was upset by it.' Bardy paused to consider this aberration. 'Maybe he felt guilty because he wished it would happen, but never could bring himself to do it. Maybe it was regret. Or annoyance, even. No satisfaction in having her drop dead where he couldn't see it.' He began to fill his pipe. 'If not for that, then what?'

Tim explained a little of the Leland case, naming no names, and that he was short of time. 'As he's new on the scene, I want to find out as much about him as I can,' he said.

'Fact or fiction?'

'As much of either as possible.'

Bardy smiled. ' "If a lie may do thee grace, I'll gild it with the happiest terms I have." I take it you know about the two girls.'

'Two girls?'

'Yes. The reason he's not here now is because the master suggested a sabbatical. It was thought better to get him away until the gossip died down. He wasn't really due for one for a few years, yet. They were embarrassed, of course, but they didn't want to lose him.'

Slowly the story came out. Two girls – close friends it later turned out – had alleged that John Soame had subjected them to sexual harassment in order to ensure good grades. He'd denied it strenuously, and had – in the end – been exonerated. But the damage had been considerable, both to him and to the college. 'They should never have let women into Brendan,' Bardy concluded. 'These two were not good scholars, and he'd been tough on one of them – to the point where she put her friend up to siding with her, figuring it would excuse her poor performance in her first-year exams.'

'What happened to her?'

Bardy sucked the flame down from four matches before he spoke. 'Father is a magistrate,' he said.

'So nothing happened to her,' Tim concluded, wearily.

'Just finishing her final year.' He sucked again, blew smoke, seemed satisfied and leaned back. 'Not many friends, though. Just the one, now. Just the one.'

159

'And they sent Soame away.'

'He was pretty shaken by it. Went a little odd, which is hardly surprising, what with the life his wife had led him for years, and then her dying, and then these girls. And money troubles, too, I hear. Started to drink a bit. Got into a fight with a senior tutor from Trinity – bit of a sarcastic bastard, as it happens. Still, no excuse for public fisticuffs, is it?'

'I don't know,' Tim said. 'It might be.'

Bardy regarded him with some amusement. 'You accept excuses, do you? Even in the Met?'

'I hope so,' Tim said.

' "Nothing emboldens sin so much as mercy." '

' "Some rise by sin, and some by virtue fall," ' Tim countered.

Bardy grinned – an unnerving sight – and nodded. 'Anyway, the master decided to grant him this sabbatical so he could pull himself together. But if the Met are interested in him . . . ' He waited.

'As far as I know he hasn't done anything criminal,' Tim said. He didn't specify further. 'You say he went "a little odd". What do you mean by that?'

Bardy shrugged. 'Thought people were ganging up on him, conspiring against him. Not just the girls – although it was them that set it off, I suppose – but the other tutors, the dean, even the master. I believe it's called paranoia, is that right? Suspicious of everyone.'

'Was he "odd" to the point of imagining things?'

Bardy shifted uncomfortably in his big chair. 'I don't like to speak ill of the man, Tim. I liked him, and felt sorry for him. We all did – it wasn't his fault.'

'To the point of imagining things?' Tim persisted.

Bardy sighed. 'Some.'

Tim leaned forward. 'To the point of doing something about it?' he asked.

There was a long pause.

Finally Bardy Philpott spoke. 'He gave us a few rough nights,' he said, slowly.

'Had to admit him to Addenbrookes for a couple of days,' Detective Sergeant Flynn told Tim that afternoon, in the

160

lounge of the Eagle. 'They sedated him, made him sleep it off, so to speak. And to give him his due, he stayed quiet after that. Must have put him on tranquillizers, I suppose. We didn't want to bring charges. We like to be discreet about goings on in the colleges. God knows, there are enough batty ones wandering around to fill a loony bin and overflow into the Cam – we can't arrest them all or there'd be no-one to lecture, would there? But barricading himself in his rooms and shouting that he'd kill anyone who came inside – we had to do something about that.'

'Did he have a weapon?'

Flynn smiled. 'He had a carving set – you know – big knife and fork. Kind of thing you give as a wedding present. Knife was as dull as a breadstick, but the fork could have done a bit of damage. Never used it – never intended to use it, in my opinion. Two minutes after we broke down the door he collapsed and started to cry. Poor bastard. He'd just had too much put on him, that's all. More of a danger to himself than anyone else. My chief inspector thought the same, and decided to let it go. We have to be flexible, here, you know. We get heavy with them, they'll get heavy back. Too many of them, too few of us. Not worth it.'

'Can you tell me anything else about Soame?'

Flynn shrugged and picked up the other half of his ham sandwich. 'My sister-in-law Edna is a bedder at Brendan. She often brought back stories about his wife running around with other men and that, and a rotten tongue on her, to boot. One of the kind that likes to stir things up for the hell of it, know what I mean? Enough to turn God himself into a woman-hater, apparently. A few years of that must have affected Soame somewhere inside, but Edna says he was "always lovely". She thought the world of him – all the women on the staff did, according to her. Not what I'd call a Cary Grant to look at, but something about him appealed to them.' The last bite of sandwich disappeared. 'Mind you, if they'd seen him swinging that carving knife, they might have thought otherwise.'

TWENTY-THREE

WHEN TESS ARRIVED AT THE McMurdo house it was locked and apparently empty. She'd expected to find Adrian here, after his pronouncements on the telephone, but he was nowhere in sight. As it was Saturday, there were no workmen around either.

The prospect of prowling the house alone was not an attractive one, but she'd gone to some trouble to get over here, and was determined to get to the bottom of all this.

The answer had to be here, somewhere.

She opened the front door and entered the unlit hall, which felt cold and gritty. If there *was* something hidden in this old house, something valuable and still undiscovered, it would be pretty amazing. Workmen were here every day, and the place was locked at night. Of course, it could be broken into like any empty house, but she had a feeling – also formulated during the previous long night – that something more was needed.

Archie had changed his tactics. Maybe his original thought was to get her out – but now it was to get her *in*. Perhaps he accepted that Tess hadn't found what he wanted, but knew how and where to find it, and was just biding her time.

The oak stairway rose ahead of her, and broad arches opened into rooms on either side. Normally the place was filled with the sound of hammers pounding, boards creaking, the slop of plaster, and the whistling and chat of workmen. Now all was still and quiet – and yet there was a feeling that someone was here. Somewhere.

'Adrian?' she called, in a tentative voice. It had started to rain again on the way over, and the house had a dank and

162

gloomy atmosphere. As she went through the empty downstairs rooms, thunder grumbled disapprovingly overhead. She shivered in her damp coat.

They had begun decorating the dining-room at last. It had been the least damaged of all the rooms, and one of particularly graceful proportions. She had chosen a rich but darkish paper with a pattern of peacock feathers against a green background, and the minute she entered she saw that it had been a mistake. Even with only one wall completed she could tell she had misjudged the mood of the room, had hoped for too much light from the deep bay windows that overlooked the rear garden. Luncheon as well as evening meals would be taken in the dining-room. In an evening glow of candlelight the peacock paper might seem mysterious and exotic, but at midday it would probably depress both appetite and conversation.

My goodness, she thought to herself. I hope Adrian didn't see this. Maybe Archie was right, maybe she was losing her grip. She took out a pencil and wrote in large letters beside the last strip: ERNIE – DON'T CONTINUE – WANT TO CHANGE PAPER.

Still thinking she might encounter an Adrian too sulky to answer her call, she went upstairs. Things were not so far advanced here, and in many places the plaster was still too wet to be painted or papered. Wires stuck out of the walls, awaiting the arrival of the special light fittings she'd ordered copied from a pattern she'd come across in an old catalogue in the V&A. Such a luxury, having an absolutely unlimited budget. Mrs McMurdo might be annoying, and her absence might be awkward, but if she had interfered the way her damned nephew insisted on doing, the job would never be done.

After an unsuccessful tour of the upper floor, Tess went up to the attic, still with the expectation of meeting someone. Whether it was the rain or just the sounds of the old house adjusting to its new arrangements, she kept thinking she was not alone. But here, too, there was only empty space. She hadn't been up here since her first survey of the house with the architect. She remembered her disappointment when the long dusty area had revealed only cobwebs and spiders, instead of a treasure-trove of trunks and old furniture.

They had discussed the possibility of converting the attic to another living floor, but the house was so large there was really no need. Since there were very few cupboards in the bedrooms below, the attic would really be needed for its original use – storage. If Mrs McMurdo did employ servants, probably only one or two would live in. There was already provision for a small flat off the new kitchen, and there were three good-sized rooms over the garage that could be converted into an easily-accessible flat, should the need arise for further employee accommodation.

She walked the length of the attic, which derived only limited illumination from the original dormer windows. This was supposed to have been augmented by the discreet installation of several windows on the rear roofslope, but the overcast sky and the sluicing pattern of raindrops on the slanting glass reduced this benefit considerably. Still, there was sufficient light to see that there was nothing here to interest her – or anyone else. The floor had been up because Ernie and his men had replaced some boards when they rewired the first floor ceiling circuit, and the entire roof had been removed and replaced, so any secret rooms or hidey-holes would have been exposed long ago.

If there were any secrets left in the McMurdo mansion, then her midnight thoughts had to be correct – they were in the cellar. And she couldn't avoid going down there any longer.

Uncle Harry had written to his Australian relatives begging for money to 'protect our precious family heritage'. McMurdo had sent a few thousand Australian dollars, and asked for details, but had heard no more until the solicitor's letter arrived, announcing Uncle Harry's sudden demise. Mrs McMurdo had thought it a great joke, and told Tess with some glee how her husband had been fooled. 'The old wowser probably blew it all on beer,' she'd said. 'That's probably what killed him, in the end.'

Or had Uncle Harry been telling the truth?

Had he wanted the money to 'protect' something valuable, and then died before he could tell his nephew about it?

Gold? Jewels? Paintings?

And what kind of protection? The more Tess thought about it, the more she was drawn to the idea that Uncle Harry had had some kind of safe installed in the cellar. Installed and concealed.

At some point in the house's chequered history, the cellar had been converted from kitchen and storage to a small flat. She seemed to remember Mrs McMurdo muttering something about Uncle Harry living 'like a mole' – so, presumably when the place had been converted to bedsitters, he must have spent his last days down there in solitude.

There was an outside entrance, at the side of the house, where tradesmen would have called on the cook who ruled the huge basement kitchen in the old days. There the coalman, the wine merchant, the greengrocer, the butcher, the baker, and the iceman would have cometh. The inside staircase that Tess descended also led directly into this old kitchen, now devoid of everything except dirt. The windows that overlooked the small front areaway were thick with muddy grime, and very little light came through. Tess had come prepared with a torch, and was glad of it.

Behind the kitchen, a long passage led back into darkness. The first door Tess opened revealed a very primitive toilet. Other small, windowless rooms opening off the passage had probably been used for the storage of vegetables and preserved comestibles, and possibly for servant accommodation. The scullery maid would have slept down here, certainly, the air of her unventilated room half-poisoned with the fumes left on her clothes by the various polishes she was expected to use daily on grates, cutlery and brasswork. Towards the rear of the passage was a larger room. It had a small fireplace that used the same chimney which served the large and elaborate dining-room fireplace above. Although this back room was dark, it had a pair of wide, shallow windows that looked out on a steeply rising slope now overgrown with weeds. Next to this room, and sharing the chimney on the other side, was a smaller room, also with windows, although these were tiny and almost blanked out by overgrowth. These two potentially pleasant 'garden' rooms would have undoubtedly comprised the cook's accommodation – parlour and bedroom. If the original McMurdos had employed a couple, it would have been for both butler and cook – a common and useful domestic combination.

At the very end of the long passage was a wooden door, and Tess knew that behind it lay the wine-cellar, hollowed out beneath the garden, and so far untouched by the workmen. When she turned the handle and opened the door, it came towards her accompanied by a cool, earthy breath of dark air.

Like a grave.

'Oh, for goodness' sake, stop trying to scare yourself,' Tess said aloud, and the echo of her voice made everything immediately worse. It seemed to stir rustles and whispers in the rooms behind her, causing her to glance back over her shoulder in some trepidation. But no-one was there. Back at the beginning of the passage, beyond the old kitchen, the sound of a car driving by on the street impersonally confirmed her solitude, its occupant humming past in total ignorance of her existence, the warm purr of its engine coming, passing, gone, leaving an even greater silence behind.

Of course, she should have waited until Monday, when Ernie and the men would be around to assist her. The floor within the cellar was uneven, she could sprain an ankle, lie there for days, there might be rats, there definitely were spiders . . .

But she had wanted to meet Adrian, counter any disapproval or disappointment he might feel about her work. In order to be here to do just that, she'd had to call Mrs Grimble to come over and look after Max, because John had previously arranged to meet someone at the V&A this morning. So for better or worse, she was on her own.

166

'Good God, woman, get on with it,' she muttered, and entered the vast but strangely oppressive space beyond the wooden door.

Almost immediately she came up against the end of the first empty rack, crumbling and grimy. Beyond it stood another, and another, rank and file, some ten in all, their cobwebbed honeycombs now empty where once hundreds of green, brown, and crystal bottles had glittered and waited in the cool dark for a summons from above. After all, Victorian gentlemen prided themselves on their cellars, and according to Mrs McMurdo the builder and first owner of the mansion had been a noted collector of fine vintages.

All gone now.

Just the empty racks, sentinels of an earlier grandeur, guarding an empty treasury. For wine was valuable – and old wine, fine wine, even more so. But of course, that was it. 'Harry's little treasure'!

Poor old Harry, writing blearily to his relatives in Australia about the family 'heritage' could simply have meant the hoard of wine kept here. The last of the English McMurdos probably drank his way to oblivion on some of the rarest wines in the world. Many might have turned to vinegar during their long incarceration, but perhaps he'd been beyond noticing. Or perhaps he'd been cannier than that – perhaps he'd found out the value of some of them and had sold them off to an eager dealer. That certainly made sense. And if that was true, it meant that Harry's little 'treasure' was no more – for not a bottle remained. She played her torch over each rack to verify what she knew already to be true. Not one produced a reflected wink of glass.

Tess frowned. If the wine had indeed been the 'treasure', she need look no further. But if it was not, there was not much further she *could* look, for the wine cellar was the last room in the house.

True, she had stood in the doorway – as she did now – to do her sketching, and had not explored the room further, leaving that to the architect. But he, too, had seemed reluctant to remain in the oddly claustrophobic room, and so their examination had been rather superficial, a matter of quickly estimated measurements, no more.

'Last hope,' Tess muttered, and reluctantly entered.

She walked between the first two racks to the rear wall, and then did a quick perimeter of the room, counting her steps out of habit.

The left wall was five steps shorter than it should have been. And on the floor below it, there was a scraped mark just visible under the accumulated dust of years.

So, she'd been right. A false wall had been subtly built in on a slant in front of the original wall, creating a wedge-shaped space between them. But how to get into it? She played her torch across the stone work, and saw that it was not stone at all, but some kind of modern artificial surface that had been rubbed over with dirt to aid concealment. She caught a brief, reflective flash in a line of 'mortar', and leaned closer. A ring was embedded there, made of steel or brass. It had been painted over in an attempt to blend in with the mortar, but the paint had flaked away. She rubbed at it, then inserted two fingers and tried twisting it. No. She pulled and was rewarded with a scraping sound. She pulled again, harder.

With a groan of unoiled and unused hinges, the wall swung towards her. It was surprisingly light for its dimensions, which in a way confirmed its modern construction. When there was space enough, Tess stepped through and used her torch.

More racks. Not for wine, but for books.

Shelf upon shelf of books. Her heart gave a thump. First editions? Rare illuminated manuscripts? Now that she thought back, wasn't there something about the original McMurdo who built this house being some kind of collector? Where had she seen it, that oblique reference?

She went forward and, propping her torch to give her light, she took a book at random and opened it. Turned a few pages. Returned it to the shelf and took one from another shelf. And another.

After a while, she began to laugh.

And laugh, and laugh.

There was a step behind her.

168

Behind her.

She turned, went to the opening between the real and the false wall, and saw the dark silhouette of a man outlined in the entrance to the wine cellar. But she was not afraid.

'Here's your "treasure", Archie,' she giggled, holding out a large, copiously illustrated volume. 'Uncle Harry's family heritage. No wonder he wanted to keep it hidden. About two hundred dirty books. As fine a collection of Victorian pornography as I've seen. I don't know what they're worth, but you're certainly welcome to them.'

'Bitch.'

She couldn't have heard correctly. 'What?'

'Stubborn, stupid, silly bitch!' The voice was like a rasp against her, the hatred in it was salt in the wound. The figure took a step forward, out of the faint twilight of the corridor into the blackness of the wine cellar. She could hear his shuffling steps, and tried to put the torch beam onto him, to find his face, but before she could, there was a grunt, and then a most extraordinary sound.

Like huge dominoes, falling.

And she knew, although she could not see them, that the wine racks had been pushed and were falling towards her in the dark. She cowered back against the crumbling white-wash of the stone wall behind her.

There was a splintering, crunching, thudding sound as the wine racks began to hit the side wall and one another, still falling towards her. Some instinct made her look up into the darkness over her head and she saw, for an instant, in the light of her rolling torch, the loom and rush of a great dark shape. She held up her arms for protection, but they were not enough against the weight of the rack. Broken, rotten wood cascaded around her as the massive bulk of the rack crashed against the frail barrier of the false wall, but kept falling, taking the new wood down with the old.

She screamed, but her voice could not be heard over the splintering crash of the successive wine-racks as they broke over her, one after another.

Afterwards, there was only silence.

And then footsteps, walking away.

169

TWENTY-FOUR

TESS OPENED HER EYES AND saw only roses and honeysuckle – a bright flowery print on the folds of waving curtains. Turning her head, and clenching her teeth against a wave of pain and nausea, she encountered a barrier of chrome bars through which the calm blue eyes of a nurse were watching her carefully.

'Hello,' the nurse said, with a smile. 'Decided to rejoin the living, have you?'

'Wha — what happened . . . ' Tess's throat was raw and her lips were dry. The nurse stood up and lowered the bars to cradle her head while she sipped some water. Then she moved the protective sides back into position.

'You just rest and I'll fetch the doctor,' the nurse said. 'You've been in an accident, but you're safe in hospital now, and you're going to be just fine.'

She went out, and there was a brief and confusing pause, during which Tess was certain her head had fallen off. Then the curtains moved aside and John Soame stood there, white-faced. 'Thank God,' he said. 'I thought you were never going to wake up.'

'What happened?'

He came over to stand awkwardly beside the high table onto which she was both blanketed and fenced. 'We're not exactly certain,' he said. 'We expected you back well before tea. We waited and waited, but when you hadn't appeared by four, and hadn't called, I left Max with Mrs Grimble and went over to the house. I finally found you under about five hundredweight of fallen wine racks.' He took a deep breath. 'You were so damned lucky, Tess. The racks fell against some kind of false wall, propped themselves

170

over you like a house of cards, supporting each other and leaving you trapped but pretty well untouched, underneath. I called the fire brigade. I could see you under there in the light from my torch but I couldn't shift the damn things. An ambulanceman crawled in to make sure you were alive . . . '

'Sorry I missed all the excitement,' Tess said, in a dry voice.

'More like it all missed you,' John pointed out. 'How did you manage to pull it all over on yourself like that?'

'I didn't,' Tess said. It was coming back now, the shadowy figure in the wine-cellar, the crash, the sound of the footsteps going away, and then the blackness closing in. 'Archie did it for me.' She told him about the dark figure in the doorway. 'I don't understand why he didn't bother to look at what I'd found, because I'm certain that's what it's all been about.' She explained the theory that had taken her to the house in the first place. 'Instead he seemed incredibly angry, for some reason. He knocked over the racks out of sheer bad temper. That's what it seemed like, anyway.'

'Well, he's obviously mad. He might have killed you.'

'Well, in a way he did us a favour – the racks had to be demolished anyway,' Tess said, wryly. 'Did you see the books?'

He smiled. 'I was more interested in making sure you were alive, but I couldn't resist a quick glance at one or two, since I assumed they were why you were there.'

'And?'

'An interesting collection. Possibly quite valuable.'

'What does Adrian say about it?'

An odd look crossed John's face. 'Nobody seems to know where Adrian is,' he said. 'Once they were certain you were alive, I called him, but there was no answer at his house. I tracked down his secretary at home. She was under the impression Adrian had also intended to go to the McMurdo house this morning, but there was no sign of him when I arrived.'

'Or when I arrived,' Tess said. 'One of the reasons I went over there was to talk with him. I thought if I could

171

find what Archie was after, it would prove to him that my work wasn't the problem at all. He was so cross and almost frantic about the possibility of losing Mrs McMurdo as a client.'

'Well, he's been having real financial difficulties since his partner left.'

'But we've got lots of commissions,' Tess said, in some puzzlement. 'We're very busy.'

'Are you? Or is it just Adrian flapping around the place saying there isn't enough time to do anything, that he must get on, must get on?'

'Oh.' She had forgotten how well John knew his ex-brother-in-law. His picture of Adrian was a familiar one. Perhaps too familiar. 'He hasn't fired anyone – he even took me on when he didn't need me.'

'Oh, he needed you, all right. It's been a long time since Adrian did a full commission himself, and he wanted someone "special" to give him the cachet he'd lost when Jason left.'

'I'm no replacement for Jason,' Tess said.

'Ah, but you're American, and attractive, and – according to Adrian – very clever. But his problem is more immediate than that. As I understand it, the perfidious Jason took quite a chunk out of the company's bank account when he left, saying it was a return on his original investment. It might have been, I suppose. He was the one who handled the books. Adrian doesn't know anything about keeping accounts. I gather some creditors have been baying at the door. Adrian is getting desperate.'

Tess was confused – and it was getting worse. She felt very odd, talking to him while lying down like a baby in a cot, and her head was thudding painfully. He kept fading away, like a bad television picture. 'But he never said anything about all this to me.'

John nodded. 'It's a Brevitt trait, I'm afraid, keeping your actions – and your intentions – a secret. They're not exactly the most stable of families, either.'

His tone was both sad and bitter, and she remembered his wife had been a Brevitt. Suddenly another and very horrible thought occurred to her. What if the figure in the

172

doorway hadn't been Archie at all?

What if it had been Adrian?

The curtain was swished back, and a white-coated doctor appeared with the announcement that there was no skull fracture, but because she had been unconscious for so long they were going to keep her in overnight for observation.

'No,' Tess said. 'I want to go home.'

The doctor, a young man with a top-knot of very curly blond hair that made him resemble a benign sheep, told her that would be very dangerous under the circumstances. 'Should there be a lesion, there might be subdural bleeding, a build-up in pressure — '

'I think you should do as he says,' John advised.

'I'm sure you do, and I'm sure he's right,' Tess said, struggling to sit up. 'But I'm still going home.' She got down from the examination table and struggled to get her feet into her shoes. Why was it so difficult? They were just shoes. Damn. DAMN!

For another thought had come plunging unbidden into her aching brain. What if the figure in the doorway had been neither Archie, nor Adrian, but the owner of the voice on the phone? The one who had said 'look after your little boy'?

John Soame's hand was under her elbow as he put his key in the lock of the front door. 'I'm sure everything is just fine,' he told her, soothingly.

'But she didn't answer the phone,' Tess wailed.

'Perhaps they were watching television and she didn't hear it — ' John began, then stopped. The door had swung open onto chaos.

'My God,' Soame gasped, and held Tess up as she sagged against him, her eyes wide with disbelief.

'Oh, no, no, no!' she moaned.

The house had been torn apart. Pictures had been taken from the walls and smashed, furniture was slashed and stripped, rugs were up as well as floorboards. There didn't seem to be a single thing left whole or untouched anywhere.

'Max!' Tess screamed.

There was an answering wail from upstairs. John

Soame's long legs took him up the stairs three at a time, and he was in front of Max's door in seconds. The door was locked. 'Max! Mrs Grimble!'

'Saints alive, it's the Perfessor. We're all right!' He could hear Mrs Grimble within, and there was a scrabbling as the door was unlocked. He was nearly knocked flying as she erupted like Vesuvius into the hall. 'Where is he?' she shouted.

Tess had managed the stairs, and her heart nearly stopped at the old woman's words. Then she saw Max's face peering around the doorjamb, and she sank down onto the top step, suddenly legless with relief.

'What happened?' Soame was demanding.

Mrs Grimble glared at him, as if it had all been his fault. 'About ten minutes after you left, he come. We were playing Snap, and I heard the front door open. I called down, but there was no answer. Something warned me. Something told me!'

'*I* told you,' Max said, clinging to Tess. It was difficult to see who was comforting whom.

'I heard noises, footsteps coming up the stairs. I didn't like it, so I slammed the door and locked it,' Mrs Grimble announced, melodramatically. Two red spots of colour shone high on her thin cheeks, and the flowers on her hat seemed to tremble with indignation and excitement. 'He come to the door, he rattled the knob, he said he wanted to talk to Max. Said he wanted to take him to his mother, because she was badly hurt and was asking for him. Well, if that had been true, he would have been a policeman, wouldn't he? With a woman constable, because of the boy. Even *I* know that. So we didn't say a word, Max and me. We just sat there, and he just stood outside the door there for a while. It was as if we could hear him thinking. I suppose he could have knocked the door down, but he didn't. He went away. A few minutes later, the crashing and the banging started up.'

'Did you recognize the voice?' Soame asked.

'No,' said Max, over his shoulder.

'What's he done?' Mrs Grimble demanded, starting towards the stairs. Now assured of personal safety, she

174

could afford to enjoy the dramatic aspects of the situation. Her name might even get into the paper. Weeks of being the centre of attention at the launderette beckoned her on. She paused by Tess.

'We might have been killed in our beds!' she announced, rather inaccurately, and edged past her, grumbling.

'You'd best get back into bed,' John said to Max.

'I don't want to get back into bed. I want to look after Mum. What happened to her? Who was here? Who . . . '

'Hooligans! Hooligans!' Mrs Grimble was shrieking from down below. 'Omygod! Omygod!' She could be heard going from room to room, freshly shocked by every new discovery.

Max looked at John and then at his mother. His face was drawn and he looked like a fretful little old man. He went to look over the balustrade, then turned back. 'What's going on, anyway?' he asked suspiciously. He looked at his mother. 'You look scared,' he said. 'Who hurt you? Was it the same person who was here? Why did he mess up the house?'

Soame answered for Tess, who was leaning against the balustrade and looked in no condition to answer questions. 'Your mother is fine. There was an accident at the house she's been restoring, and she got knocked out, but the doctors have X-rayed her all over, and she's not badly hurt. I don't know what happened here, but I'm going to find out. Okay?'

He and the boy locked glances. 'Okay.' It was clear that it wasn't okay, but Max didn't quite know how to argue about it. Where to start? His face was pale, and his eyes were shadowed as he looked at his mother. 'Mum?' He spoke softly.

'It's all right, Max.' Tess straightened up, blinked her eyes clear. 'It's my opinion that we have been visited by a poltergeist.'

'Oh, sure,' Max said, totally unconvinced.

'And it's also my opinion that we should have a cup of tea before we do anything else.' She managed to stand up – probably the hardest physical thing she'd ever done. 'You go back to bed, and we'll bring it up. All right?'

175

He nodded, and slowly, reluctantly, he did as she asked. But he knew, they all knew, that it wasn't all right at all.

When Soame returned from the kitchen, where Mrs Grimble was wailing as she worked, Tess was still sitting in the rocking chair where he had left her, her face paper-white under the slow-running tears. He patted her shoulder, but there was no response as she stared blankly at the overturned and gutted sofa.

It hadn't been much of a house, she thought, but it had been home, full of the small and silly things that had no intrinsic value but were precious to her. Every piece of furniture had a history. Junk-shop prowls with Roger, or early-morning visits to country markets on the rare weekends when they stole away together, afternoons of searching for the right materials, evenings of re-upholstering, with Roger handing her the nails while he kept one eye on a televized soccer match. And the pictures, also bought in junk-shops or markets, occasionally even on a visit to a friend's gallery when times were good, discussed over a paper cup of tea from a stall or a glass of white wine at a preview, choices narrowed, prizes carried off and hung in various places until the right spot was found. The hugs when they knew they'd been right, the giggles when they admitted they'd been had – all part of it. All important. All still Roger when Roger was gone. Grief overwhelmed her as it had not upon his death, because all that they had had together, all the marriage had been in the beginning and through the years, was tied up in these broken bits of wood and cloth and paper. Roger had still been here, somehow, his presence triggered and maintained by those memories, and now all that had been torn apart.

Now he was *really* gone.

And there was just Max. Thank God, there was still Max.

Seeing she was in a dark world of her own, Soame went into the hall, dragged the telephone out from under the overturned bench, and called the local police. They told him to sit down and touch nothing. It seemed only

176

minutes before they arrived, bringing a sense of order to the scene, their sensible voices and confident manner briskly blowing away the miasma of violence and violation that hung in the rooms. It was a damn shame, they agreed, in tones that indicated they knew lip service to convention was not going to help, but was very necessary. They'd seen it before and they'd see it again, and they knew how to deal with it, so not to worry. Anything taken? How about a list? No hurry. Who's your insurance agent? You look absolutely shattered, Mrs Leland, would you like us to call your GP? They were sympathetic and efficient. While two of them surveyed the damage, a woman constable comforted Tess with practical suggestions for salvage and a hot mug of tea conjured somehow from the shattered kitchen and the equally shattered Mrs Grimble, who was now blaming herself for the entire thing.

When she had finished her tea, Tess looked so absolutely devastated that Soame sent her to bed and agreed with the police that calling her GP would be sensible, under the circumstances. The doctor could look in on Max, too, who was now getting a little too flushed and bright-eyed as he waited for an explanation and some kind of comfort. A forensic team arrived from the local police station and began photographing the scene and attempting to find fingerprints. They had to take Tess's prints (she hardly noticed), Max's (who was thrilled and was given a copy of his own to keep), Mrs Grimble's, and John Soame's – all for elimination.

John then made another phone call. An hour later Detective Sergeant Tim Nightingale and Detective Chief Inspector Abbott were standing in the doorway, looking around, as the forensic team finished their work. Soame glared at Nightingale with a mixture of anger and appeal.

'*Now* will you believe that Mrs Leland and the boy are in danger?' he asked, grimly. '*Now* will you take this seriously?'

TWENTY-FIVE

TIM NIGHTINGALE GLANCED AT HIM. 'I always have taken it seriously,' he said calmly. 'But there wasn't much for me to go on, was there?'

'Is this enough?' John demanded, waving an arm around at the heaps of material that had once furnished the Leland home. 'It was planned, the whole thing was planned.'

Chief Inspector Abbott raised an eyebrow. 'What makes you say that?'

'It's obvious, isn't it? She was attacked by Archie McMurdo. He knew I would have to go out to look for her, or to identify her body, or whatever, and when I did he got in and tried to get at the boy, who he probably thought would have been left alone. When he couldn't get at the boy, he did this.'

Abbott looked confused. Sergeant Nightingale had returned from Cambridge and brought with him some interesting information – interesting enough to jolt Abbott from indifference to intrigue. He now understood why Tim had become caught up in the case – the people and the situation were ambiguous and somehow did not mesh comfortably. There was a feeling of jagged edges, a picture out of focus, and pieces missing. They had been discussing Soame when the call came through concerning the Leland house. And now a new element was being introduced. He glanced at Nightingale and saw that he, too, seemed puzzled. 'And just who is Archie McMurdo?' Abbott asked, slowly.

'Oh, Archie is — ' Soame paused. 'I thought you knew about Archie,' he said to Nightingale.

178

'He's news to me.'

With a visible effort at self-control, Soame explained about their visitor of the previous evening, the trouble he'd been causing Tess at the house, and the threats he'd made after he'd been thrown out.

'You threw him out bodily?' Abbott asked. He gazed at John Soame with new interest.

'I had no alternative, the man was drunk and objectionable. I felt Mrs Leland was in some danger from him.'

'Fair enough.' Abbott sent Nightingale a glance, and Tim went into the hall, where he had a low-voiced conversation with one of the other policemen. When he returned, Soame was standing with his fists clenched by his sides, and Abbott was gazing into space reflectively. 'So you think the scenario is as follows – just let me talk this out, if you will,' Abbott was saying.

'Go on,' Soame said tightly. He apparently had mixed feelings about the appearance of a superior officer on the scene. While he welcomed the presence of rank as an indicator of the importance of the situation, he resented the authority so represented. It had been easier dealing with Nightingale.

Abbott was reciting for his own benefit as much as anyone else's. There had been too many cases crossing his desk, too many investigations in progress, and he needed to know exactly where they were on this one. 'A few months ago, Roger Leland was killed in a car accident. His son was in the car with him, but was uninjured. Since that time he has suffered with nightmares, and on top of that he caught rheumatic fever and is now convalescing here at home. In order that Mrs Leland may continue her work, you have been hired to tutor the boy in exchange for accommodation. Right so far?'

'Yes.'

'In the past few weeks Mrs Leland has received several "silent" phone calls — '

'Some of them were threatening. They threatened her, and her son, and demanded money.'

'Unfortunately, you have no proof of that, other than

179

Mrs Leland's word. Anyone else who has picked up the telephone has heard only silence.'

Soame looked stunned. 'Are you saying she's *lying?*'

'Mrs Leland felt confident enough to go to a large empty house on her own,' Abbott pointed out.

'In broad daylight. And she expected Adrian to be there.'

'Adrian being?'

'Her employer, my ex-brother-in-law, Adrian Brevitt.' Soame was obviously not happy with Abbott's attitude. 'And you're forgetting the intruder we had the other night.'

'Oh, yes – the intruder, who forced open a door but didn't come in.'

'He might have — '

Abbott ignored him and continued his resumé. 'Now, in addition to all that, you tell us that for the past few weeks, a man named Archie McMurdo has been harassing Mrs Leland at her work – a mansion she is restoring for his aunt, Mrs Dolly McMurdo. He annoys her and the workmen, so naturally she goes out to dinner with him.'

'You make it sound irrational,' John muttered. 'I think she was trying to put the relationship on a friendlier basis – for Adrian's sake.' Obviously agitated now, Soame began moving around the room, trying to put a few things back in place. Abbott stayed where he was and continued. Nightingale, fascinated by the older officer's technique, watched and listened. There *was* a case here. He'd been right. And now Abbott was taking it, and him, seriously.

'She was co-operating for her *boss's* sake, then, rather than her own,' Abbott said, slightly annoyed at Soame's pedantic interruption. 'But then this Archie McMurdo shows up here at the house — '

'Drunk.'

'Drunk, and makes an unwelcome pass at Mrs Leland, which you interrupt. You throw him out. He makes threats and accusations, which unsettle Mr Brevitt and, through him, Mrs Leland. So she suddenly decides to go to the house today.'

'Yes.'

'When Mrs Leland doesn't return, you decide to go to the house to find her.'

'Yes.' Soame was continuing to pick up objects, as if searching for something.

'You leave the boy in the charge of the housekeeper.'

'Yes.'

'And not ten minutes after you leave, someone arrives here and tries to get to the boy.'

Soame whirled. 'Exactly my point! As if he'd just been waiting for his chance.'

Abbott looked at him and nodded. 'Yes. But when the housekeeper locks the door and refuses to come out or to answer him, he doesn't shout, or argue, or attempt to break it down, but goes away and vents his anger on the house itself.' Nightingale glanced at Soame, gauging his responses to Abbott's questions. 'Does that sound like he really wanted to kidnap the boy?' Abbott asked, with what sounded like sincere interest.

'How would *I* know what he really wants?' Soame demanded. 'How can you? How do we know he's even sane?'

Nightingale shifted his position, leaning against his other shoulder, arms folded. He was looking at the professor with new eyes. 'Just where is the McMurdo house?' he asked, abruptly.

In a voice that trembled with exasperation, John gave him the address. He explained Tess's sudden suspicion that there might be something hidden there. 'Which, as a matter of fact, there was.' He told them about the false wall and the collection of Victorian pornography. 'I didn't take time to really assess it, but it's probably quite valuable,' he concluded.

'Is it?' Nightingale asked. His eyes were hooded as he looked at Soame. 'Of course, you'd know more about that than I would – that period is your speciality, isn't it?'

'Yes, but that's not the point,' Soame argued. 'The point is, this mad Australian followed her there and tried to get her out of the way – either by killing her or putting her in hospital.'

'To what end?'

'To get at the boy, obviously.'

'Why would he want the boy?'

'To force her to hand over what he thought was his.'

'Which she had just found and offered to him, anyway? That hardly makes sense, Mr Soame. You can't have it both ways – either he wanted what was hidden in the house or he wanted the boy.'

'Well, then, *you* tell me what's happening, here,' John practically shouted, as he moved towards Nightingale. 'Give me *your* theories. Give me *your* explanations.'

'Take it easy, take it easy,' Abbott said, taking hold of his arm. Soame glared at him, struggled for a moment, then stepped back.

Nightingale was being patient, but it was difficult. Considering all he had learned in Cambridge about Soame, from both Bardy Philpott and the friendly local sergeant, it wasn't surprising the man's nerves were so shot. On the other hand, he was reacting rather strongly to someone else's troubles. If they *were* someone else's troubles. He got out his notebook and opened it. 'Let's go over it a step at a time and see what we've got, all right?'

'You just *did* that. You're wasting time, damn it!'

'I don't think so, Mr Soame. What we have here is agreement on the facts and disagreement on their interpretation.'

'No,' Soame said. 'What we have here is people being pig-headed, obstinate, and dangerously lax in doing their duty!'

'That's a matter of opinion, too,' Abbott said, sharply.

'Then why aren't you looking for Archie McMurdo?'

'We are,' Nightingale said.

'We're checking with the biggest hotels,' Abbott explained, patiently, knowing without having to ask that that was what Nightingale had put in operation during his whispered colloquy with the constable in the hall. It was the obvious step to take. 'Then we'll move down to the smaller — '

'Fine, yes, fine,' Soame said, barely controlling himself. 'Good.'

'Right. Now, Mrs Leland went to the McMurdo house this

morning, leaving you in charge of the boy.'

'No. Her decision to go was unexpected, and I had made other arrangements for this morning, so she called Mrs Grimble and asked *her* to come over and stay with the boy. Which she did.'

'Very obliging of her. So you left here at what time?'

Soame frowned. 'About ten thirty, I suppose. My appointment was for eleven.'

'And that was with?'

'Clarissa Montague – she's a specialist at the museum.'

'A specialist in what?'

'Oh, for . . . ' Soame gritted his teeth. 'Does it matter?'

'It might.'

'Well, in Victorian architecture, then.'

Abbott raised an eyebrow. 'Really? And what did you discuss?' He paused. 'I *can* check with Ms Montague, you know.'

Soame's shoulders sagged. 'We discussed the McMurdo house.'

'Oh, really?'

'I thought I might be of some help to Mrs Leland. And it pertains to the research I'm doing as well.'

'I see. Interesting.' Nightingale wrote it down and seemed to dismiss it. 'And Mrs Leland left the house – when?'

'Shortly after I did, I suppose. I know she was just getting her coat out of the cupboard when I closed the front door behind me.'

'Fine. And she went straight to the McMurdo house?'

'I expect so.'

'How long would that take her?' Abbott enquired.

'I have no idea. You'll have to ask her.' Soame was restless. He picked up a picture and looked at the wall above where it lay, searching for the hook that had held it. He hung the picture back up, but as he did so, the last piece of its broken glass fell out and shattered at his feet. 'Damn.'

'What time did you leave the museum?'

'I don't know. About twelve thirty or so.'

'And you arrived back home at what time?'

'Again, I can't be certain. About three, I suppose. I stopped for a quick lunch at a café somewhere in Knightsbridge, and browsed around Harrods for a bit. Walked part of the way home.'

'I see.' Abbott stared at Soame and Nightingale made another note. 'But when you arrived back here, Mrs Leland hadn't returned?'

'No. Mrs Grimble was worried, she had expected her back for lunch. We waited and waited, and then I decided I'd better go to the house and see if anything had happened to her.'

Nightingale finished writing and waited for Abbott's next question. 'What time did you arrive at the McMurdo house?'

'What?'

Abbott repeated the question, and Soame frowned. 'Somewhere around five, I suppose.'

'And how long did it take you to find her in the wine cellar?'

'I have no idea. About twenty minutes.'

'But the 999 call was logged at five fifty-five,' Abbott said, in a flat voice. 'We checked it before we left the Yard.'

Nightingale felt a jolt go through him. He saw it now. The way Abbott had set it out made it clear that it could have been Soame himself who caused the accident at the McMurdo house, because he had only a vague alibi for the relevant time. Equally, it could have been Soame who vandalized this house after pretending to leave it – thus arriving at the McMurdo house later than he'd said. Now *that* was a new and interesting kettle of fish.

Had Soame built up – on the basis of a few crank telephone calls – an entire edifice of threats and dangers surrounding Mrs Leland, all because of his own paranoia? Was this another manifestation of his mental breakdown, seeing monsters in other people's lives as well as his own? And was this Archie McMurdo just a convenient scapegoat or a real villain?

Soame didn't seem to see the dangerous course Abbott's questions were taking. He stared at him blankly, then shrugged. 'Perhaps I arrived later than I thought. Or the

184

search took longer than I thought. Christ, what does it *matter*? I found her, and she was *alive*.'

'Yes. That was fortunate, wasn't it? The way the racks fell just so. They are extremely heavy, but luckily – very luckily – Mrs Leland was only trapped under them. Not badly hurt.'

'Would you rather she had been crushed to death?'

'Obviously not.'

Soame scowled. 'Do you think she *arranged* for the racks to fall on her like that?'

'I think somebody could have.'

'But not Tess . . . Mrs Leland. Why should she?'

'Indeed, why should she? You see, Mr Soame, I *can* make a case for Mrs Leland creating this situation – either consciously or unconsciously – to call attention to herself.'

'That's ridiculous.'

'It's been known.'

'She's not that kind of woman.'

'How well do you know her? You, on the other hand, insist that the phone calls, the intruder, the attack on Mrs Leland and now on this house are part of a pattern. Well, I could make a case for *you* creating that pattern – consciously or unconsciously.'

Soame's chin came up. 'Why would I do that?'

'You've done it before.' Abbott's voice was perfectly calm.

Soame's face went paper-white. 'You —'

'Yes. Sergeant Nightingale has been to Cambridge and asked some questions about you. He got some very interesting answers.'

Soame looked at Nightingale, shocked and angry. 'But why?'

'It was *necessary*,' Abbott said. 'He was proceeding sensibly. It was sound investigation. There can be no exceptions in a case as vague yet complex as this – a good officer who senses wrongdoing must suspect everyone.'

Soame turned away, and stood rigid, facing the windows. Although he did not seem to move, both Nightingale and Abbott could sense the struggle he was having with himself. When he turned back, they were both

185

tensed, prepared to cope with any reaction – except the one he showed.

'Quite right,' he said, quietly. 'That's also good scholarship, Nightingale. One really can't draw a sound conclusion any other way.'

TWENTY-SIX

'TIM.'

Sherry stood in the open door, running one hand through her dishevelled hair, and using the other to hold her pale pink terry cloth robe closed. Now she reached behind her for the trailing belt and managed to cover herself properly – but not before Tim had seen she was naked underneath.

'I'm sorry it's so late,' he said. 'Maybe I should have rung first. But you always said — '

'Well . . . yes, of course,' she said, and stepped back. 'I thought you were going to Cambridge this weekend.'

'Went and came back,' he said, proceeding down the hall and into the large sitting-room. 'Fare was courtesy of the Yard, but everything else I had to pay for myself, and there wasn't much more I could do. Just as well I came back, too, because there's been a Development. Any chance of a coffee?'

She had followed him through and now glanced at the ebony and brass clock on the wall as she closed the sitting-room door behind her. After eleven – she had begun to doze off when the doorbell had roused her again.

'Yes . . . yes, sure.' She went into the kitchen and reached for two mugs. Dirty dishes were stacked in the sink and on the counter – plates, cups, bowls, cutlery – hurriedly rinsed but not yet inserted into the dishwasher. 'You'll have to have it black, though – I ran out of milk about three hours ago and was too lazy to go out and get any. I thought I'd pick it up with the Sunday papers.'

He sat down on the sofa and stretched out his legs. 'I can do that,' he said, yawning. 'You can have a lie-in. Least I

187

can do after waking you up, right?'

She stood in the kitchen, holding the jar of instant coffee high in the air between cupboard and counter, pausing for a moment before completing its transfer. 'Mmmmm,' she said, after a moment, and began to unscrew the top.

'You remember that case I was worried about – the widow and her little boy?' he said, as he loosened his tie.

'Mrs Leland?'

'That memory of yours never ceases to amaze,' he said. 'Mrs Leland it is. She nearly got herself squashed under about five hundredweight of assorted lumber this afternoon. It all fell on top of her – but she escaped with only scratches, bruises, and possible concussion.'

'Lucky woman.' The kettle gave its little characteristic internal moan as the water began to simmer within. Sherry added sugar to Tim's mug and ducked her head to glance in the small hand-mirror set on edge in front of the spice jars on the rack. She made a face at her messy hair and chapped chin, remembered that she had an old lipstick in one of the drawers, and began to root among the spoons for it.

'Maybe.' He was silent for a moment, listening to the comfortable clatter from behind him. 'But while she was lying unconscious, somebody tried to lure away her little boy, and when that didn't work, he vandalized her house.'

'How awful!' she called. 'Was the boy hurt?'

'No. And neither was his kitten, which was found safely shut in the bathroom.'

'What has a kitten to do with it?'

'I'm not sure. But it bothers me. Why would someone who vandalized a house stop short of hurting a kitten?'

'Even killers are kind to their mothers,' Sherry observed. 'Maybe the vandal is a cat-lover.'

'Maybe. Or maybe he isn't a vandal at all.' He told her some of what he had learned in Cambridge, and some of what he thought about Soame, and Tess Leland. Not all, just some. He also threw in what he knew about Archie McMurdo – whom they had so far been unsuccessful in locating at any hotel. But hotel searches take time, and he

188

was patient. There were so many possibilities to consider. He sensed her coming up behind him, and recalled another more distant aspect of the case. 'By the way, did you manage to dig up any of the information I asked you to get for me? On Roger Leland's business?'

She put the coffee mugs down on the table in front of the sofa, then perched herself opposite in the easy chair. He raised an eyebrow. 'That's not very friendly – am I in the doghouse for coming around so late?'

'Of course not,' she said. 'But I feel a bit . . . you know . . . messy and unprepared. Caught with my pants down.' She heard her own words and raised a hand. 'No gratuitous remarks – I'm too sleepy to keep up.'

'Fair enough.' He picked up his coffee and sipped at it, burning his tongue. 'Ouch.'

'No milk, remember?' she said.

He put the mug back onto the table and leaned his head against the back of the sofa, grateful for a little support at last. It had been a long day. 'Well, did you?'

She'd been watching him with an odd expression that mingled affection, concern, and something else. 'Did I what?'

He lifted his head and looked at her directly. 'Get any information on Roger Leland's business?'

'Oh, yes. Quite a bit.' She untangled her long legs and got up to go over to her desk unit, which obliquely filled one corner of the large flat. Beyond the desk huge windows overlooked the Thames, giving a view rather like that from the bridge of a ship. The building in which Sherry lived had been a sugar warehouse which some clever architect had converted to flats. When she'd invested in it, Tim had protested. He hadn't much liked the idea of her living down here, where the streets were dark and lonely. But the architect (who still lived on the top floor) had had visions of the area developing one day into some kind of premier riverside village complex. In the event, Tim had been wrong, and the architect had been right. Sherry's original brave investment would net her a hefty profit when she decided to sell. If she decided to sell.

189

She often teased him about missing his chance at a similar place and now being stuck renting a tiny flat in Putney. He absorbed these shafts with equanimity because he could, he pointed out, have been right. The odds had been even, and predicting fashion trends – whether in couture or property – was a risky business. Almost as risky as becoming a copper.

Now she returned from her desk bearing a large folder. 'Here you go,' she said, handing it to him.

'My God,' he said, hefting it. 'This will take me all tomorrow to get through.'

'It's Sunday,' she told him. She glanced at the clock again. 'Or it will be, in twenty minutes or so.'

'Can't you give me a précis?' he pleaded, putting the folder down beside him and trying the coffee again. 'Better still, can't we go to bed and you can tell it all to me as a bedtime story?'

'Too many details,' she said. 'You have to look at the figures to get the idea.'

'And what is the idea?'

'Well, *my* idea is that it was a very peculiar public relations company,' Sherry said, resettling herself in the easy chair, but not looking much at ease in it. 'On paper it was doing really well. A lot of money was going back and forth between here and the Continent, for example, but there weren't that many clients.'

'You got that far into it?'

'Oh, it wasn't difficult. I know a lot of people in the City,' she said.

'So I remember,' Tim said.

She avoided his eyes. 'Yes. Well, you have to admit, it's useful. Apparently Roger Leland was a real charmer, shot out creative ideas in all directions, really produced for his clients. There's no question, in his hands the company was a real goer. You get the feeling from the figures that they would have been in a terrific position when the Common Market really opens up. But there was some talk just before he died – nothing you could put your finger on — '

'Saying what?'

She shrugged. 'Odd stuff. That maybe he was losing his edge, or he was ill, or something.'

190

Tim raised an eyebrow. There had been no evidence of serious physical illness revealed by the post mortem. 'You mean mentally ill?'

'Maybe. It was more like terminally pissed-off.'

'With his partner?'

'I don't think so. More like with the world. You know – ratty, irritable, slamming phones down, storming out of meetings, that kind of thing. For no apparent reason. I think that was what worried the people over at Philadelphia Mutual.'

Tim made a dismissive sound. 'Typical insurance company, balking at paying out a measly few thousands to a widow.'

'More like half a million. But it wasn't to the widow – it was to Richard Hendricks. Partnership insurance.'

'Half a million?' Tim said, incredulously.

'It was based on Leland's "unique creative ability", apparently. They paid in the end, but not without a fight. They raised the question of suicide, based on Leland's apparent "depression".'

'Oh?'

'Yes. But it was pointed out to them that suicide was pretty unlikely, because Leland's son had been in the car with him, and it was decided a devoted father like Leland would never have risked injuring or killing the boy.'

'I see.'

'Anyway, once Hendricks got the money out of PM he closed down the old business, which was really built around Leland's talent, and used the insurance as seed money for his new company, which, by the way, is called Salescan. It specializes in profiling prospective international markets. It's doing all right, but it doesn't have anything like the potential his partnership with Roger Leland had. Hendricks is respected but not particularly well-liked. A good numbers man, but *not* a genius.'

'Yes.' Tim was still absorbing the fact that Richard Hendricks had been paid off handsomely for Roger Leland's death, but his widow had been nearly impoverished. Of course, Hendricks was under no obligation to give her any of the partnership insurance money – that

191

had been a normal business arrangement. But it wouldn't have hurt him to drop her a few thousand, would it? On the other hand, maybe he had, and she was hiding it – say from someone in Leland's family? Or from his past? A former wife, perhaps? He knew so little about the dead man, but he did know that in any victim's personality or lifestyle or history there were always the clues to why someone wanted him dead. The trouble was, they were often buried deeper than the victim himself.

'Well, that insurance pay off gives us a motive for Hendricks.'

Sherry shook her head. 'Not really, Roger Leland alive was a lot more valuable to Hendricks than he was dead. In the long run, anyway.'

'Maybe Hendricks needed money fast, for some other reason.'

Again, she shook her head. 'The man is fairly solid in his own right. He could have managed to finance the new company out of his own pocket – it just made good business sense to use the insurance payout. That's what it's *for*, Tim.'

'I know, I know.' He scowled. 'And then there's Soame.'

'The nutty professor?'

'Yes.' He scowled.

'You like him.'

'Yes, I like him, but . . . ' He paused. 'I like Tess Leland, too,' he murmured, half to himself, as he idly turned the first few pages in the folder. 'Good Lord.'

'What?' Sherry leaned forward slightly.

'It says here that Leland and Hendricks part-owned Brevitt Interiors.'

'I told you, Hendricks is a good numbers man. He knew the value of outside assets, especially for a firm that was so dependent on the talents of one man.'

'What would have happened to that interest when Hendricks closed down the company?'

'He could have transferred the asset to the new company, or sold the interest to someone else – any number of things. It may be in there, somewhere.'

'Could he have brought any kind of pressure on the people in Brevitt Interiors?'

'Pressure to do what? And why? L&H's interest wasn't the major one, from the look of it. Maybe it was sentimental. It wasn't a big asset, and certainly not their only asset. It wouldn't be worth the bother, I shouldn't have thought.'

'Unless there was something else there. Say maybe that Brevitt Interiors had hidden assets of its own. Do you know anything about them?'

Sherry laughed. 'Good God, Tim, you must think I'm omniscient or something. I only know what's listed there – their name, their value, and the amount of L&H's investment. You said to look into Leland and Hendricks, not investigate everyone else in the City or out of it. It would take weeks to check them all out. I do know Adrian Brevitt is considered sound, rather than flashy. His boyfriend was the flashy one – but they've split up, of course.'

'Oh? When was that?'

'A few months ago, I think.'

'About the time Roger Leland died?'

She stared at him, and shook her head. 'That's pretty far-fetched, Tim. What possible connection could there be between that and Mrs Leland? You sound like a man grasping at straws.'

'Got it in one,' Tim said. 'But Mrs Leland now works for Brevitt Interiors. She worked for them before she was married, too. Brevitt took her back eagerly – I gather she's pretty good on restorations.'

'And all this kerfuffle, all this "case" you're trying to shape, revolves around her, doesn't it?'

'Yes.'

'And now somebody tried to squash her – she says.'

'It was a pretty lucky escape.'

'Luck – or careful planning?'

'I don't know. I really don't know. I can't see any advantage to anyone for persecuting her in the way she claims, yet I do believe someone is.'

'And why do you believe that?' she asked, playing devil's advocate.

'Because *she* believes it, I suppose.'

'What's she like?'

He thought back. 'Scared. Tired. Defiant. Stubborn. A

193

little naïve.' He paused. 'And innocent, damn it. If I ignore her, or dismiss it all as Soame's paranoia, and I'm *wrong*, I'll never be able to forgive myself.'

Sherry shook her head. 'I told you when you left Lloyds, and I'll say it again – you've got too much damn conscience to be a cop.'

'And you're a cynic.'

She sighed, and glanced again at the clock. 'Never denied it, love.' There was a shade of something in her voice that was almost bitterness, and it surprised him. 'Most of us vote the straight bitch ticket, these days,' she said. 'That's the price for getting what you want.'

'What's that supposed to mean?' Tim asked, in some confusion. What was it about her? She was looking nervy, and seemed restless. Somehow exasperated with him. Somehow – uneasy? 'Look, maybe I should have left this until morning,' he said, getting slowly to his feet. 'I didn't mean to wake you up.'

She stood up too. 'Oh, you didn't wake me. I was just lying there, thinking,' she said. Now he got what the sound in her voice was – some brand of sadness he hadn't encountered there before. She glanced towards the closed sitting-room door. When she spoke again her voice was soft, but very clear. 'You didn't wake either of us, Tim.'

He looked at her for a long time, and she let him look, meeting his eyes levelly, waiting. After a while he edged out between the sofa and the low table, went down the hall to the bedroom door and opened it, very quietly. He looked in, then closed the door again. Very quietly. He came back to the sitting-room and, without looking at her, picked up his jacket, put it on, then leaned over and collected the folder containing the information she'd gathered about Roger Leland's business life.

Only then did he look at her.

Her face was pale, and there were tears in her eyes, but her chin was high. 'I'm really sorry,' she said. 'But I think I'm going to marry him, Tim.'

He just managed a smile. 'Then there's nothing to be sorry for, is there? We made no promises.'

'I know, but — '

'We made no promises,' he repeated. 'Forget it.'

She followed him to the door. 'Shall I send you an invitation?' she asked, trying to keep it light and failing.

'No,' he said. He raised the folder. 'Just send me the bill for your expenses on this.'

She looked as if he'd slapped her. 'That was unfair,' she said, reproachfully.

'Yes,' he agreed. 'Unfair.' The word bounced back and forth between them, and she couldn't meet his eyes.

He opened the door into the chilly concrete corridor that betrayed nothing of the income received or spent by the trendy tenants of this vast and peculiar edifice. At the end of the hall a tall narrow window gave a slightly more angled view of the black river that divided one diamond-spangled bank from the other. The reflections on the water made it look oily, slow, and full of menace.

'I feel like I'm a long way from home,' he said, softly.

'Putney isn't so far.'

He glanced at her. 'That isn't the home I meant,' he said.

And left.

TWENTY-SEVEN

TESS NEVER DID REMEMBER MUCH about Sunday morning.

The clink of a cup in a saucer woke her from her exhausted sleep, and she opened her eyes. Mrs Grimble stood beside her bed, holding a large tray.

'What time is it?' She struggled up against the pillows, and looked at the clock on the bedside table, but avoided looking at Roger's face in the photograph beside it. She didn't want to have to explain to him what had happened to his house, his wife, his son, their life. Twisted, torn, all of it. Gone.

'Near noon, as you can see.'

'Where is everybody?'

'The professor's upstairs. That blonde bit of his is here again. Or still, maybe I should say. She arrived yesterday while the coppers were grilling him.' Her tone of disapproval only just covered a deep and salacious satisfaction at sin uncovered and proven. 'Disgusting, I call it. Her only a slip of a thing, probably no better than she should be, and him old enough to be her father, if you ask me.'

From the attic flat overhead there came a sudden burst of music, quickly muffled. Then silence.

'Perhaps she helps him with his research,' Tess said, weakly. Oh, Tess, grow up, she told herself.

'Research, is it?' Mrs Grimble sniffed. 'That's a new name for it.'

'How's Max?' Tess asked.

'Max is proper wore out, that's what he is. White as a sheet and too weary to complain, poor mite, what with the police and all making him so excited he was up half the

196

night. He's gone back to sleep.'

'What did the police do?'

'Which police, you might ask.'

'Which police?' Tess responded dutifully.

'The police from around here, they did this and that, poked about a bit, took photos, threw some kind of powder all over everything, just more for me to clean up, *they* don't care. Them from Scotland Yard, all they did was ask questions. Put Mr Soame through it, proper. Asking him when did he come, when did he go, why did he this and why did he that. All sorts.'

'But why should they do that?'

Mrs Grimble shrugged. 'Why do they do anything? To make themselves look good, that's all. They talked to Max. Wanted to talk to you, but I said you was asleep, and that was that. I said you'd had enough, and showed them the door. They're coming back this afternoon, so eat your breakfast. You'll need your strength.'

Mrs Grimble thumped the tray down onto Tess's knees. 'Come on, get it down, while I run you a bath.'

She went into the bathroom and there was a sudden rush of water thundering into the old lion-clawed bathtub Roger had brought home in a taxi one evening, rescued from a skip near King's Cross. A scent of peach and primrose filtered out in a cloud of steam that hung around the bathroom door and dampened the edge of Tess's dressing table. Condensation formed on the glass top and one side of the mirror.

'Not too hot, I don't want to faint in there,' Tess called. She ate a little, just to be able to say she had, and spread what was left around the plate. 'About the mess downstairs —'

Mrs Grimble reappeared in the doorway. 'Oh,' she said, archly, arms folded across her scrawny bosom. 'Don't you worry about that.' She pointed upwards at the ceiling, presumably in reference to John Soame rather than the Almighty. '*He's* going to arrange for some special firm to come and deal with it tomorrow, he tells me. Bunch of hippy students, like as not, probably steal you blind. That's why I'm staying on. I made up the guest room for me.

197

Somebody has to keep an Eye On Things.'

'That's very kind of you.' Tess was beyond protest and very grateful. Mrs Grimble had 'stayed on' when Tess was ill on various occasions over the years, most notably after Max was born. It was bliss for Tess, but Roger would usually lose his temper after being told for the fifteenth time to eat up his greens, and would send her home in a taxi. 'But, what about Walter?'

Mrs Grimble looked uneasy at the mention of her brother. 'He's gone to stay with his son and snooty daughter-in-law in 'ampstead.' The old woman's glance slid away, then returned. 'Well, they'll be after him again, won't they?' Mrs Grimble said, defiantly. 'It wasn't him did this. You know that, and I know it.'

No, Tess thought, I don't know that, but I hope it's true.

'Anyway, he's old, now. He can't take all that questioning and knocking about.' Mrs Grimble went on, as if to excuse the warning she had very obviously passed on to her brother.

'They wouldn't knock him about, would they?' Tess asked.

'Well, they've done it before. Like to keep their hand in, that lot do. The trouble is, Walter won't stand up for himself any more. In fact, he's been real quiet lately. Wonder if he's sickening for something nasty?' She frowned, thinking back, then continued briskly. 'Be a bit more grateful for all I do for him when he comes back, though, you can be sure of that – he'll be locked in his room out there, like as not, and fed scraps under the door, if *she* has anything to say about it. Stuck-up cow. *Her* family isn't exactly royalty, neither, come to that, seeing as how her old man made his pile scrapping cars that weren't always his. Bet her la-di-dah friends would be interested to hear about *that*.' Mrs Grimble smiled grimly. 'Anyway, here I am and here I stay until you're better, and I don't want a word said about it, so just finish your breakfast.'

Tess looked down at the scrambled egg, which was coagulating on the soggy toast, and the greasy strips of bacon which bracketed the pale yellow curds. There was an aroma rising from it all that was faintly reminiscent of school dinners. That, combined with the sweet steam from the bathroom, was too much for her. Her head was pounding and her stomach was clenching in protest.

Thrusting the tray aside, she threw back the covers and made a dash for the loo. As she closed the door behind her, she heard Mrs Grimble gathering up the tray and muttering to herself something about 'keeping it warm'.

It was in the nature of a threat.

After her bath she slept again; mercifully spared the reappearance of her breakfast or any other offerings. When she awoke she was aware of bustle and conversation downstairs, interspersed by the tinkle of glass and the occasional thump. She slept and woke again, several times. In between the blanks, she caught glimpses of Max peering around her open door, looking worried. She saw John Soame standing over her, she saw her doctor standing over her, she saw Sergeant Nightingale standing over her, and once, just for a minute, she thought she saw Roger standing over her, looking sad. She smiled and spoke to them all, but never knew exactly what she said. Or they said. She would have liked to know what Roger said.

At four she awoke completely.

Simon Carter was sitting beside her bed, watching her. He smiled brightly, and closed the book he was reading – from the cover, a fairly lurid thriller. 'Hello,' he said.

'Hello.' Alarm shot through her. 'Is anything wrong?'

'No, no, no,' he said, quickly, and patted her hand reassuringly. 'Everything is just fine. Mr Soame is talking to the police downstairs, and Mrs Grimble has gone home to feed her canary and fetch some fresh clothes. Max and I had a nice chess game, and now he's asleep again.'

'Is he all right? He hasn't got a fever or anything?'

The young curate shook his head. 'No, Mrs Grimble keeps checking, but it's just exhaustion, poor lad. I'm afraid all this has really upset him. He's found out about the other things that have been happening – he's rather cross at being left out of that. Mostly, I think, he's worried about you.'

'That's precisely why I *didn't* tell him about all the other

199

things,' Tess said, bleakly. 'Losing his father was bad enough – I didn't want him to think the other props of his life were being rocked, as well. Was that wrong?'

'Well, in my limited experience I've found that children generally prefer the truth, however difficult it may be. That was certainly the case in the hospital,' Carter said. 'And it seems to matter a great deal to Max. He is troubled, you know.'

'I know,' Tess said, feeling exhaustion sweep over her. 'The nightmares and everything. I just don't know how to help him.'

'Perhaps he'll just have to help himself.' He smiled. 'With God's support, of course. Max is stronger than you think, Mrs Leland. He's bright, and he's clever. And he loves you very much.'

'I'm very grateful to you for giving him so much of your time.'

Simon Carter flushed a becoming pink. 'One reaches out, you know. Stuck with the impulse, can't stop it, really. Too squeamish to be a doctor, too lazy to be a lawyer, too impatient to be a social worker – Church the only thing left. Embarrassing, sometimes, not much for incense and all that.'

'A worker priest?'

'Mmmmm, but don't tell the bishop.' Carter grinned. 'Speaking of work, I thought someone should be with you in case you needed anything when you woke up. Do you?'

She badly needed to go to the loo, but she could hardly tell him that. He looked so eager to please, so hopeful of some kindly assignment, that she requested a cup of tea. As soon as he bounded off, she slipped to the bathroom. When she came out again, it was not the young curate who awaited her return, but Detective Chief Inspector Abbott. He seemed entirely undismayed by the sight of a woman in a rumpled nightgown, with toothpaste on her chin and the beginnings of a black eye.

'Good afternoon, Mrs Leland. Do you feel up to answering a few questions?'

'Yes, I think so.'

But there were more than a few.

200

Some time that night, Max came and got into bed with her. Waking in the semi-darkness she discovered him beside her, curled tightly against her ribs. She murmured to him sleepily and wrapped her arms around him.

'Mummy, can I ask you something?'

'Yes, lovey, of course you can.'

It was a long time coming, and when it did it was a past midnight question, perhaps not quite what he meant to say. 'They can't put children in gaol, can they?'

Simple reassurance rather than a semantic discussion seemed called for. 'No, of course not.'

'But they can take them away from their mothers if they're bad, can't they?' His voice was very small in the dark.

'They *can* – but they try very hard not to. It depends on how bad the children have been, and how often.'

'If they've been very bad?'

Tess started to wake up. 'Have you something you want to tell me, Max?'

'That's what *he* said.' He took a deep breath, and it caught somewhere in his throat.

'Who?'

'The really tall one with green eyes.'

So Abbott had been questioning Max, too. She wondered if he'd used the same tactics as he had with her – going over and over the same ground, asking for the same things again and again – the times, the words spoken, a hundred small details, things she'd forgotten, things she hadn't known she knew. And always, always, with that oh-so-patient air of faint disbelief that kept you babbling, rushing to testify, fretful of mistakes.

'He's only trying to help us.'

'Maybe.' Tess felt the shivering begin, and held him more tightly. She waited, giving him a chance to continue, but he was silent, and the silence stretched. Tess sighed, blowing his hair gently away from her mouth, like feathers lifting and falling. 'Go to sleep, darling. We can talk about it all in the morning. Mummy's head hurts, now, and we're both pretty tired, aren't we?'

201

He twisted around and kissed her on the chin, which was all he could reach. 'Don't worry,' he said. 'Don't cry any more. They won't take me away, I promise. I won't let them.' He hugged her and snuggled down again, his arms around her as protectively as hers were around him. His breathing steadied, slowed, and became softly even.

She was puzzled and worried by his questions. What could be bothering him? She frowned, and found that her face was stiff with dried tears. Realization swept over her – she must have been crying in her sleep. Ill and exhausted as he was, Max had heard and come to her – not only seeking comfort, but offering it as well.

For a long while, until she herself was overcome by sleep, she lay in the dark, holding the solid little shape, silently apologizing.

On Monday morning, when she awoke, Tess gritted her teeth and stretched, all over, until she knew the worst. It was not so bad. Except for her head, of course, which was no longer muzzy, but still ached dully.

There was a pale, diffuse light in the room. She rolled over and looked at the clock – nearly ten thirty, yet it was dark enough to be much earlier.

She could hear Max's voice down the hall, talking to Albert in a scolding tone. Apparently the kitten had committed some small, furry crime, and was being chastized. Feathers and pillow seemed to come into it, but there didn't seem to be much anger in Max's voice.

Tess stretched again, remembered, and groaned.

Mrs Grimble, who was either psychic or lurking in the hall, immediately appeared in the doorway. 'They've Started,' she announced, ominously, and disappeared. After a moment she stuck her head back around the door. 'Breakfast in ten minutes. Brush your teeth.'

Tess stared at the empty doorway, and then, hearing noises and men's voices from below, realized the firm that John Soame had engaged must have arrived to put the house to rights.

Tess hauled herself to the bathroom, groaned again at the sight of two no longer faint black eyes, and decided to

202

do more than brush her teeth. She was back in bed, towelling her hair carefully by the time Mrs Grimble returned with a breakfast tray.

'They're thorough, I'll say that,' she announced with grudging approval. 'But they won't find any cobwebs in *my* corners.'

Tess crunched a piece of toast and found it good. 'What are they doing?' she asked, in a muffled voice, as she cut her bacon.

'Well, two are picking up pieces and putting them together, so to speak. There's one sewing up upholstery, and another one is sweeping and chucking out. Don't worry, I gave him a box and everything he *thinks* to chuck out I tell him to chuck in, instead. Up to you, I said, what goes out. Even a piece of something might be important to you, sentimental the way you are.'

'Am I?'

"Course you are. Why not? Them little things might seem like junk to other people, but they have memories attached, don't they? Worth more than the price,' she said. After a moment, she added, 'Have to be.'

'Where's John?' Tess asked.

'If you mean Mr Soame, *he's* gone to Scotland Yard to play with the detectives.' The scorn in her voice could have been usefully employed removing tarnish from the copper pans hanging on the kitchen wall. 'Full of investigating, he is, all mouth and magnifying glass.' She paused, then plunged ahead. 'His lady friend was here again. Left last night about eleven, made a big noise of it so's I'd hear.' She sniffed. 'Wouldn't be surprised if she crept back, after, though. Butter wouldn't melt her.'

'I'm sure she's very nice,' Tess said, keeping her voice carefully neutral.

'Hmmmm. Well, I don't care if he is some sort of professor, sometimes I think he's not quite right in the head. This morning he announces they're going wrong down at Scotland Yard, and off he goes to put them right. Honestly. Maybe *I* should go down there and tell them about what I found him doing this morning. Maybe they'd be interested in *that*!'

Tess pushed the tray away, and was surprised to see that someone had eaten everything on it. 'What was he doing?' she asked.

Mrs Grimble leaned forward as if to grasp the tray, but merely glared at short distance into Tess's eyes. 'He was *measuring*.'

Tess felt inclined to laugh at the menace with which this announcement was imbued, but managed to control herself. 'Measuring what?'

'The *walls*,' Mrs Grimble said, and snatched up the tray. 'He was measuring the walls, as bold as glass.' With this announcement, and the tray, she departed.

Tess slid back down in the bed and decided she was not going to think about anything, ever again. Everybody else could take over her life – like the men downstairs, other people would have to put it all back together. She felt heavy with fatigue, and her headache was tightening again. The nausea she had felt yesterday was gone, but she still felt empty – hollow in arms and legs, dreamy in mind, and sad throughout.

She allowed herself to be cocooned by weakness, and stayed that way for another hour or so, listening to the mutter of the radio beside her. She tried to concentrate on a short story about an elderly cat burglar making a comeback and a programme on the virtues and value of double-glazing in saving energy. Supine and defenceless, she received a stern talking-to from a man with a squeaky voice about the waning butterfly population, and a warning of bad visibility from several coastal stations. But when asked to consider the dangers of allowing the present government to continue on its wayward course unchallenged, she lost her nerve and switched off.

No solace there.

None anywhere.

Except from Max.

She sat up, suddenly.

Max, who had asked her about children going to gaol. Despite her efforts to remain unconnected to the real world, the memory of those small troubled questions had snaked past her defences and was now hissing in her ear.

204

Sending children to gaol?

'Max?' she called out. 'Can you come here a minute, lovey?'

There was no reply, although his room was only down the hall. Perhaps he'd gone downstairs to watch the men working. He was allowed up for brief periods now. That must be it. Throwing the covers back, she got up, put on her dressing-gown, and went along to his room.

Empty. Not even Albert in sight.

A little wobbly, she went slowly downstairs. The men in the sitting-room looked up at her approach, and smiled encouragingly. 'Coming along, ma'am,' one said. 'Be back to normal in no time.'

'Thank you,' she smiled, and went on down the hall to the kitchen, where she discovered Mrs Grimble rolling out pastry for a pie. 'Is Max with you?' Tess asked, looking around the big kitchen. Mrs Grimble put her rolling pin aside and headed for the cooker.

'No. He's in the garden with the kitten.' She came back with a coffee pot and a mug with red and blue frogs on it. 'Now, don't you fuss. He's dressed up warm, and I told him it was only for ten minutes. Can't come to harm in his own garden, can he? And a few breaths of fresh air will do him the world of good. Here, sit down and have some coffee.'

But Tess was heading towards the side door.

'Now, stop that. Don't go out in your dressing-gown, it's damp and chilly.' She slapped the mug down on the table for emphasis, but her orders were ignored.

Tess stepped out onto the damp flagstones of the patio. The garden was garlanded with drifting wisps of mist that had broken away from the thick fog that hung over the roofs and shrouded the treetops of the park beyond the next street. There was a still, dank heaviness in the air – fog was flowing in to weigh down the afternoon. The birds were silent, and the fat brown rosehips glistened with moisture.

There was a soft touch at her ankle. She looked down to see Albert, his fuzzy kitten-coat glittering with mist, weaving small, intricate patterns around her slippers. She picked him up and nestled him under her chin. He began to purr.

'Max? Time to come in, love. It's cold.'

Her voice seemed to hang in the air, the words pegged out like washing drooping limp from the line. 'Max?'

She stepped further along the patio, emerging from the shelter of the vine-covered trellis. The garden stretched away to the rear, hedged in by tall laurels on one side, and the weathered brown board fencing Roger had put up on the other. At the far end, the garden gate stood open.

Wide open.

And Max was gone.

TWENTY-EIGHT

THE FOG HAD FLOWED UP the river from the sea, flooding across the Essex marshes and creeping over the city stealthily, silently, under hedges and over rooftops, curling around chimneys and eddying at street corners as the cars moved cautiously through it, their engines strangely hushed, their drivers shadowed and mysterious within. Pedestrians moved, isolated, within the circles of their own limited vision. Sounds were distorted, seemed to come from nowhere, anywhere – a drift of conversation, a ping, a thud, a footstep, a whistle, a whisper – all floated within the moist and suffocating shroud. Untouchable, uncatchable, inescapable: the fog was everywhere.

And Max was somewhere within it.

Was he alone?

'How long has he been gone?' It was John Soame, coming through the front door at a run, followed by Abbott, Nightingale, three other detectives, and several uniformed police officers from the local station. Tess's call to Scotland Yard had been both rushed and hysterical, but had produced immediate results.

Mrs Grimble, wringing her flour-covered hands, told him about forty-five minutes. 'I shouldn't have let him go out,' she wailed. 'But he kept pestering me, and I thought — '

Already the men from the cleaning firm were out, calling Max's name, moving away from the house and down the misty streets, but the cotton-wool of the fog deadened their voices, twisted their words into useless

207

echoes that summoned no-one save the occasional curious cat or dog.

Beyond the next street stretched the park, its great-headed trees hanging still and shadowy in the mist. They were the only things visible within the perimeter of the fence – everything else was hidden, secret.

Everything.

Everyone.

Quickly, Abbott produced a street map, and they divided the neighbourhood up into sections. 'He may just have gone for a walk, to get sweets or a comic,' he said. But there was no real conviction in his voice. There was, instead, the bitter awareness of failure, and the memory of all those threats and 'coincidences' Nightingale had produced and he'd dismissed. Until now.

Tess Leland stood in the middle of the hall, as if standing watch over entrances front and back, a slight figure huddled into a faded blue chenille dressing-gown, her arms crossed over her chest. Nightingale watched her throat convulse as a sob struggled with a scream, and felt his own chest tighten – not because of her pain, but because of her courage in trying to overcome it. He had seen a lot of pain over the past few years, had learned to face it without flinching, but bravery always undid him.

Stable doors, he thought. Regrets, apologies, but the boy is gone and I am here too late, with too little. I can say nothing that will provide either comfort or hope, nothing that she will believe, because I don't believe it myself. And with all the possibilities we have, all the things we know or suspect, there is the additional ever-present danger of a purely chance encounter with a pervert. Every family it touches once lived in complete certainty that it would never happen to one of their own – until it did. Until its foul darkness fell for ever on them. That chance was as real here as with any other child. All the other dangers that hung over his small tousled head did not provide any immunity for Max Leland from the lying smile, the quick grab, the fumbling hand, the knife, the rope, the shattering blow.

How long does it take for that twisted hunger to

overcome self-loathing and caution, for the fog to offer its rare and cloaking opportunity, to take a child, to rape a child, to mutilate, stab or strangle a small body, to thrust it under a bush, to run and run and run, haunted, breathless, sated for now. But only for now.

He knew, as every policeman knows, that it takes only a few minutes. Only minutes.

And they were passing so quickly.

Abbott was ordering Max's description to be circulated immediately to all car and foot patrols in the area, with underlined urgency. Out of the corner of his eye he saw Tim Nightingale, as unobtrusively as possible, slip a photograph from a frame which still held shards of glass broken the day before, and pass it to one of the patrolmen to take back to the station for duplication. Their eyes met, and Tim's mouth tightened in a face already pale with anger. He, too, was blaming himself.

And it was worse for him, Abbott realized. Because there would always be one terrible thought within him – did I cause this by asking too many questions? If I'd left this whole thing alone, would the boy be here now, and safe? This was the bad part, he wanted to tell Nightingale. This is the hard part, where you watch the pain and wonder what you should have done, could have done, to prevent it. You did your best, you scented danger, cried out on discovery, and were not believed. That is my fault, and I'm sorry I let you down.

Whether here temporarily or permanently, I am your superior officer because I am supposed to know my job. Most of all, I am supposed to listen. But in the busy day, so many dangers walk past us wearing disguises, whistling casually, looking like promises or excitements or security. There isn't time to follow them all, stop them all, put them through the tests. We try, of course. And in this pursuit we may even, quite innocently, catch the eye of Death and cause Him to turn our way. He doesn't notice everyone, but He has a special soft spot for coppers. You might as well learn that now as later. We have a stink He likes.

He went over to Nightingale, and though he wanted to say that, all he could manage was, 'I should have listened

209

to you sooner.' For a moment it seemed to ease the pain in Nightingale's eyes. But only for a moment.

'Perhaps if I'd — ' he began.

The phone suddenly rang, louder and more insistent than any phone ever rang, and they all froze where they stood. Tess was closest, and, stiff as an automaton, picked it up.

It was Richard Hendricks. His voice was casual, relaxed.

'Tess, I've just got home from the airport. I've been going through my post. I know you won't like this, but I wasn't satisfied with what my banker friend found out, so while I was away I've had a private investigator looking into Soame's background, because I never quite — '

'Is Max with you?' Tess interrupted. Her voice came out in a croak, emerging from a throat that felt as if it were closing forever.

Richard was silent for a moment. 'With *me*?' he finally asked. 'Why on earth would Max be with me? He doesn't even know where I live.'

'No special reason. Look, Richard, I can't talk about this now. Maybe if — '

It was his turn to interrupt. 'Is Max missing?' he demanded. 'I *am* his guardian, too, Tess. I have a right to know what's going on. Is he missing?'

'Yes.' There was no point in denying it, and Richard might be able to help. He'd always been so good, before. So strong, so very strong. Why hadn't she listened to him? Why hadn't she realized he cared so deeply? 'He disappeared from the back garden about forty-five minutes ago.'

'Oh, I see.' There was relief and indulgence in his voice. 'Well, I would hardly call that *missing*, Tess. For goodness' sake, he's almost ten, he's quite capable of going to the shops on his own — '

'Not without telling me,' Tess said, flatly. 'It's a house rule he's never broken. We always say where we're going, we *always* know — ' Her voice broke, and Abbott gently took the phone from her. He talked quietly to Richard while Mrs Grimble took Tess over to the sofa and sat down beside her, patting her hands as she wept.

John Soame, watching her with concern, spoke quietly and firmly. 'You ought to go back to bed, now, Tess. You're still wobbly from that blow on the head — '

'No!' She rose up, braced herself, and her eyes blazed in her wet face. 'He's *my* child, *my* baby, and if you won't do anything, I will. I'm going to look for him myself.'

Abbott had replaced the phone and came over to her. 'I wouldn't do that, Mrs Leland. When we find him we'll only have to come looking for you. It's best if you stay here, Max may well come home on his own, you know. He'll expect to find you waiting for him.'

'Let them do their job,' Soame urged, reaching out to take her arm. 'They know what to do and how to do it — '

'Oh, yes, they know what to do,' Tess said, bitterly, shaking him off, backing away from his touch. 'They know that everything is coincidental, that you have to wait until you have *proof*, that hysterical women don't make sense, that there are rules and regulations — ' She knew it was untrue and unfair, but their oh-so-reasonable tones infuriated her. She didn't care, she couldn't care now, not with Max gone. She drew in a quick, sharp breath. 'What if somebody took him?'

Soame looked uneasy. 'If you mean Kobalski, I don't think kidnapping is quite his style.'

She stared at him. 'Who?'

Abbott explained. 'That's why Mr Soame's been with us down at Scotland Yard, Mrs Leland. When I spoke to you yesterday — '

'Did you?' Tess's voice was vague. 'I don't remember.'

'You didn't make much sense, I agree. But you did say one or two things that needed looking into. Particularly about this Archie McMurdo. He was a puzzle-piece that didn't fit.'

'It looks like Archie isn't a McMurdo, after all,' Soame said. 'I thought his accent slipped a little the other night – you said he was Australian, but he sounded more like Brooklyn to me – so Sergeant Nightingale arranged for me to look at some pictures. We aren't sure, but we think the man who *claimed* to be Archie McMurdo was actually an American named Kobalski. He's . . . '

211

'A twisty son-of-a-bitch,' one of the other detectives muttered, then stifled a grunt as Nightingale kicked him in the ankle.

Tess had heard his comment, though. She looked at the circle of men around her. 'You mean he's some kind of criminal?'

There was a brief silence, which Abbott finally broke. She might as well have the truth, she would go on demanding it, more and more loudly, anyway. 'It's remotely possible, Mrs Leland. And now that we know about Kobalski, there could be some kind of pattern showing up here. Possibly something to do with the drug trade.' He looked at her, and there was compassion in his eyes. 'Were you ever aware of your husband having any connection with drugs?'

She was astonished. 'Drugs? You mean . . . real drugs?'

'Yes.'

On this she could be completely clear. 'Absolutely not. You see, Roger's younger brother was a registered addict and . . . well, he died. Roger loathed drugs and everything to do with them. Why would you think he had any connection with drugs?'

'Because of Kobalski,' Nightingale said. 'If this man who calls himself "Archie" really is Kobalski, then there *has* to be some drug connection. He is a bright and ruthless operator, and he works for one of the main American drug syndicates. They use him over here because he speaks several languages, and can mimic dozens of accents.'

Tess took a long breath. 'Such as Melbourne and Sydney?'

'That would be easy for him,' Nightingale said. His tone was almost apologetic.

'I see.' But she didn't. She didn't *want* to see.

'We think Kobalski was sent to pose as Archie McMurdo by a third party. Perhaps with the help – unwitting or otherwise – of someone who knows all about your work and your life and the boy and all the rest of it. Someone who would know where you were at all times, and possibly had access to your house keys.'

212

Irresistibly, Tess found herself looking at Mrs Grimble, who had gone white as a sheet and was sinking down onto the telephone bench, horror in her eyes. And Tess knew she was thinking of Walter.

Nightingale hadn't noticed – or if he had, he gave no indication of it. 'It may be someone who is involved in drugs in some way, either using or distributing. Perhaps someone who has got into financial trouble and is looking to you to get them out of it. Someone who is desperate. Someone in need of money. Someone you trust.'

The doorbell rang and Mrs Grimble, her steps unsteady and her face stricken, went to answer it. They all turned and went to the archway that led to the hall, waited as the door swung back.

Adrian Brevitt stood on the top step, dapper in his fur-collared overcoat, his pale pink and white striped shirt gleaming behind his rose silk tie, his white hair silvered by the mist. In his hand he carried a colourfully-wrapped parcel, banded and bowed in blue ribbon.

'I have come to visit my godson,' he announced.

The stunned silence by which this was greeted puzzled him. He frowned, then caught sight of the faces behind Mrs Grimble. He brightened. 'Are we having a party?' he asked.

'I tell you, it's impossible!'

Tess was precariously seated on the edge of her recently-reassembled mulberry chair, and she was outraged at the suggestion that Adrian Brevitt was the mysterious person behind all her persecutions, leading up to and possibly even including Max's kidnapping. 'Why you might as well accuse Simon Carter!'

'It's interesting you should mention him, Mrs Leland. We're looking into the very helpful Mr Carter, and the recently solvent Mr Walter Briggs,' Abbott said, smoothly. 'In fact, we're looking into the background, whereabouts, and habits of everybody who has been in this house or had anything to do with you or your family over the past six months. We have a great many people to do this, but it still takes time. At the moment we are interested in Mr Adrian Brevitt.'

John Soame, although obviously angered by the sudden and rather rough reception that had been visited on his ex-brother-in-law, was nonetheless listening to Abbott's explanation. Tess seemed to have stopped just short of clapping her hands over her ears.

'He knows you well, and his company is in financial difficulties,' Abbott pointed out.

'Companies like Brevitt Interiors are *always* in financial difficulties, until they make the big breakthrough or until they find a backer who will cushion them,' Tess snapped, briefly distracted by this attack on another pillar of her existence. 'We work on long-term arrangements, and all too frequently our creditors do the same. Adrian has come up the hard way, with just his talent to work with. No private fortune, no titles in the family, no millionaires willing to sponsor him. At least, not any more – there was one, but Jason took her with him when he went solo. I suppose Adrian has been struggling a bit since then, but I'm certain that if there's a problem it's only temporary and can be straightened out. He *works* for his keep. He's a genius, not a businessman. And he's one of my oldest and dearest friends.'

'But are his friends your friends?' Abbott asked, in a reasonable voice.

She hung her head. 'That's what Richard said,' she mumbled. And maybe, she thought, Richard had been right. About everything.

Abbott glanced towards the kitchen, where Tim had taken Adrian for questioning. 'What else did Mr Hendricks have to say about Mr Brevitt?'

'I don't remember.' Tess would have stamped her foot if she had been wearing shoes instead of slippers. 'And I don't care. I just want my son back, safe and sound.' Tears of fear and frustration again overflowed, but she paid no attention to them – her entire concentration was on Abbott, willing him to make Max re-appear.

John Soame put his arm around her, reassuringly. 'The search is going on right now, believe me. The police are doing everything they can in that direction, leaving us free to look in other directions. There have been these threats and the break-ins, Max has been upset and having nightmares – there may be some connection there that will give us a lead. He may know something without realizing it, and so might you. Chief Inspector Abbott is only trying to find it.'

'Well, he's looking in the wrong direction if he thinks Adrian is behind it,' Tess said, standing up and shrugging Soame's arm away from her shoulders. She had no time for sympathy now – she didn't deserve it. Why hadn't she paid more attention to Max? Why hadn't she *seen* the danger?

Abbott was looking out of the bay window at the front. At the kerb stood two police cars, the men inside acting as co-ordinators for the various search parties. Neighbours, at first limiting themselves to peering around the edges of curtains, were now standing around openly staring, talking to one another, pointing, nodding or shaking their heads. The streetlights had come on, adding a false yellow glow to the scene. Condensation dripped from the trees in the gardens on the opposite side of the road, and the fog seemed even thicker than before, blurring the houses, obliterating the ends of the crescent.

'There's been some question concerning Mr Brevitt's circle of friends,' Abbott said, slowly, turning back to face Tess. 'He attends parties where cocaine is available — '

Tess sighed. 'So do half the people in London, it seems to me,' she said. 'Coke is the latest in-sin for the soft-headed. People who can afford interior decorators can also afford cocaine. Naturally they come in contact, but that doesn't mean that Adrian — '

'See here, am I under arrest?' came Adrian's voice. He stood in the archway, hands on hips, glaring at Abbott. Nightingale stood behind him, looking frustrated. 'If so, I demand to see my solicitor *immediately*. If not, I refuse to sit in that kitchen any longer to be glowered at by your sergeant here and that gorgon in the chintz apron. Tess, my dear, my poor dear — ' He swept across the room and took her hands. 'Have they found our wandering boy, yet?'

'Not yet, Adrian,' Tess said, thinly.

John looked at him in some exasperation. 'By the way, where have *you* been? I've been looking for you everywhere.'

Adrian took a deep, dramatic breath. 'I have not *been* everywhere. I have been somewhere, which is quite a different thing. And Max is somewhere, too.' He whirled on Nightingale. 'Get out of here, young man. Climb on to your white steed and comb the byways for that innocent child. Whatever interest you have in me can wait. *I* shall wait, as a matter of fact, until Max is found and restored to his mother's arms.'

Adrian went over to the rocking chair and sat himself elegantly down, crossing one knife-creased trouser leg over the other and placing both hands on the top of his silver-headed cane. After a moment he raised one hand in a fluttering, scattering motion. 'Get on with it, get on with it,' he directed grandly.

'Adrian — ' John began.

Adrian fixed his ex-brother-in-law with a sceptical eye. 'I should have thought you had sufficient experience in dealing with students to keep track of one rather small one, John.'

'He was at Scotland Yard,' Tess said.

'Oh?' Adrian looked at John with interest. 'And what were you doing there?'

'I was looking into the activities of an imported crook called Kobalski,' Soame told him.

'Also known as Archie McMurdo,' Nightingale volunteered.

Adrian glanced from one to the other. He looked suddenly crestfallen, and much, much older. 'Oh,' he said, in a small voice. 'So you *know* about him.'

216

TWENTY-NINE

TESS HAD RETREATED TO THE kitchen to drink coffee, away from the questioning, and, more importantly, away from the temptation of the stairs that led upward to her bed and oblivion. She had only been there a few minutes, it seemed, when the door crashed back and Richard Hendricks strode in.

Tess flew into his arms, and clung to him, all ambitions to be independent lost in the terror of what might be happening to her child. 'Oh, Richard, Max is gone . . . '

He held her close. 'It will be all right, Tess. I promise, it will be all right. I'll make sure they find Max, I'll look after you both from now on . . . don't fret, love. Don't fret.'

'Hmmph!' snorted Mrs Grimble. She began banging pots and pans about, but she kept glancing over her shoulder at him. She didn't seem able to decide whether to smile or sneer.

Tess stood quietly while he whispered reassuring phrases into her hair and patted her over and over again. She was grateful to be encircled with care and love, if only for a minute or two. She was still there, her face blank and her eyes closed, when the kitchen door swung back again, and John Soame came in. He glanced at the pair of them, but his face remained as blank as Tess's.

'Hendricks, the police would like to talk to you,' he said, after a moment.

'Oh, really?' Richard relinquished his hold on Tess. 'Running errands for them, now, are you? If they knew what I know about you, they might not be so trusting.'

'They know all they need to know about me,' Soame said.

217

'Oh, really? I wonder.' Richard's tone was threatening.

Soame's mouth tightened, but he said nothing, just stood holding the door open, waiting.

Richard turned to Tess. 'I won't be far away, my love. Don't be afraid. I'm certain we'll find him soon.' He gave John a malignant glance, and then walked out.

'Going out looking himself, is he?' Mrs Grimble asked the cooker. 'Get his expensive shoes dirty? Not likely.'

Soame cleared his throat and spoke to Tess, who was standing where Richard had left her, as if she had no more will of her own, not even enough to sit down again at the kitchen table and finish her half-drunk mug of coffee.

'Why don't you take just ten minutes, Tess?' he said, in a quiet voice. 'Even ten minutes' rest will do you some good.'

'He's right, for once,' Mrs Grimble agreed, grudgingly. While she was desperately worried about Max, she was also a practical woman and accepted that others could search better than she. Her concern here and now was Tess. 'I'll come up and get you the minute we hear anything, I promise you that. Anything at all. You can trust me.' She put a hand on Tess's arm. 'Go on, lovey. Do as he says.'

When Tess spoke it was in a dead, empty voice. 'What is Adrian saying now?' she asked, tonelessly, her eyes looking between them at the blue and white porcelain jelly moulds arranged on the wall beside the door.

'Still nothing. He just sits there, glaring at them. He says he's waiting for his godson and his solicitor, in that order.'

'Oh.' She reached up and rubbed her temples with vague irritation, as if something within annoyed her. 'Why won't he speak?'

'I really don't know,' John said, helplessly. 'I've never seen him like this before.'

'It is an unusual situation,' Tess said, in an oddly formal tone, like a newsreader giving the latest headlines, or a teacher instructing recalcitrant students. 'None of us have been like this before.' She walked past him, down the hall, and up the stairs. She did not even glance into the sitting-room, where Abbott was talking to Richard and Nightingale was looming over Adrian, apparently trying to intimidate him by telepathy.

218

Soame and Mrs Grimble watched Tess ascending the stairs, as stiff and erect as a model in a fashion show, her face blank, her throat taut above the turned-in collar of the old chenille robe. When she had disappeared, they looked at one another. 'She's going to crack soon,' Mrs Grimble said.

'I know,' Soame said. 'I know.'

'Why haven't you put Soame in a cell?' Richard Hendricks demanded.

'Because we have no evidence of his committing any crime,' Abbott said. 'No reason to bring a charge.'

'I can give you evidence,' Richard snapped, reaching into his inside coat pocket and producing a thick envelope. 'He's a psycho. It's all in here.' He handed it to Abbott, who gave a quick glance at the name in the corner, and put it into his pocket.

'Aren't you going to read it?' Richard asked, annoyed that his offering was being ignored.

'At the moment, my main concern is for the boy,' Abbott said. 'Have you any idea where he might be?'

Richard flushed. 'Why should I? Despite my best efforts, I don't know him well. I don't know his friends or his habits or — '

'I thought you were planning to be his stepfather,' Abbott interrupted.

'I have asked Tess to marry me, yes,' Richard said.

'Dear God in Heaven, what a prospect,' Adrian muttered.

Hendricks glared at him. 'It has damn all to do with you, you old poof.'

Adrian took this calmly. 'He *is* my godson,' he said.

'Do you know a man who calls himself Archie McMurdo?' Nightingale asked Hendricks. 'Or Kobalski?'

'Never heard of them,' Hendricks said, over his shoulder, still concentrating on Adrian Brevitt. 'If he is your godson, and I do marry Tess, I shall have you exorcised, or whatever it is they do to sever an unsuitable godparent.'

Adrian managed a smile. 'The bishop will hear of this, do you mean? I am *terrified*, absolutely *beside myself*.'

'Mr Hendricks,' Abbott said, loudly, before further

219

fighting broke out. 'I want to know more about Roger Leland.'

Hendricks turned back, slowly. 'What about him?'

'Why was he upset just before he died?'

'Was he? I didn't notice anything.'

'Philadelphia Mutual did. Or perhaps you've forgotten the fight you put up for your half-million pound payout? A payout, I might add, that Mrs Leland apparently knew nothing about and did not benefit from in any way.'

Hendricks went white, then bright pink, then white again. 'That was a straightforward business arrangement, it had only to do with the partnership. I did nothing wrong, it was all — '

'Half a million?' Adrian Brevitt said, standing up so suddenly that Nightingale nearly fell over. 'Do you mean to say you were paid half a million pounds in insurance when Roger died? And you let Tess suffer, let the boy suffer . . . '

Hendricks turned on him. 'It had nothing to do with them,' he said, biting off the words. 'It was a perfectly standard business arrangement. As to letting them "suffer" – I have repeatedly offered to marry Tess. I've also begged her to let me look after her and the boy, but she has always refused my help *and* my money, by the way, which was also offered freely and frequently. For some reason, she was determined to survive on her own – she's a very stubborn girl. And she was encouraged to do it, no matter what the consequences.' He glared at Adrian, and Soame, then turned back to Abbott. 'I'm not ashamed of taking that insurance settlement. I paid heavily enough in premiums over the years, and so did Roger. If *I* had died in a car crash instead of him, he would have done with the money exactly what I did – used it for business purposes.'

'And you're a very good businessman,' Abbott said.

Hendricks drew himself up. 'Yes, I am, damn it. I don't see why I should be pilloried for it. Tess had insurance — '

'A pathetic five thousand pounds,' Soame said, abruptly. 'And bills to pay out of it.'

Richard's glance went to him, and his lip curled. 'Well, you know all about having bills to pay, don't you? You know all about being in debt, don't you, *Professor* Soame?'

220

'I am not a full professor,' Soame said, evenly. 'I do not claim to be.'

'And you never will be, with your history — '

'This is not relevant,' Abbott said, loudly.

But Hendricks was in full, self-defensive flow. Allowed back into the situation by Tess's apparent capitulation and gratitude, he spoke with authority. 'As for Tess suffering, I could hardly call living in this house suf — ' He stopped and seemed to glance around for the first time. 'What on *earth* has happened here?' he demanded, in some dismay. 'Is Tess redecorating?'

'What's the matter, Hendricks?' Adrian said. 'Not to your taste?'

Tess sat down on the bed, but she did not lie down. Instead she folded her hands in her lap and gazed at them. They looked old, like her mother's hands. When she flexed her fingers the skin on the back of them became marked with hundreds of tiny lines – a phenomenon she hadn't noticed before. After a moment her glance travelled down to her slippered feet. She saw that a thread had begun to come loose around the appliquéed flower that adorned each scuffed toe. There was a star-shaped asterisk just above her ankle bone where a capillary had burst during her pregnancy. Her feet and ankles looked white, like those of a person in hospital. She felt white all over, drained and parched and almost weightless. Moving her body – in the interest of purely scientific enquiry – she found her joints were slippy and moved unpredictably. It was disconcerting. She felt she was held together by taut and tangled wires, she would not have been surprised to have her head drop into her lap and turn to grin up at her, or to see her kneecaps slide slowly down her legs and roll like empty teacups onto the floor.

She waited quite patiently for everything in her to unsnap, unbuckle, fly apart into every corner of the room like an overwound watch flinging itself into spare parts.

When nothing of the sort happened, she stood up and got dressed.

THIRTY

THE STREET STRETCHED BEFORE HER, long and diminishing to invisibility between the grey curtains of the fog. On her right, in the vast and silent expanse of the park, the sentinel trees loomed dark and motionless, their outlines blurred by the twisting skeins of the fog. The fog, the fog – damp against her face, betrayer of light and sound, clammy fingers sliding down her throat, encircling her legs and hands, muffling the scream she could not, would not utter.

She had waited at the top of the stairs, listening to them all talking, arguing, wrangling downstairs. They all sounded so angry. Doors crashed open and slammed shut, voices rose and fell – and what good was it doing? What point did it have? All that mattered was Max.

When the moment had come, it had come quickly, without warning, and she had lost a precious second or two in realizing that Mrs Grimble had gone into the sitting-room with coffee, and had thoughtfully closed the sliding doors behind her. Down the stairs, through the hall and kitchen, out the back door and through the garden gate: the way Max had gone.

Just to be away, to be moving, to be doing something was better than lying on her bed, wide-eyed, pretending to rest when there was no rest to be had, pretending to be passive and good when she was filled with rage. No. Her head throbbed with each step, but she just dug her hands deeper into the pockets of her coat and went on.

Such a long street. How strangely empty it seemed. And then the next street, and the next. Empty? Or were there footsteps following? She turned once, twice, three times –

but there was never anyone there. Perhaps it was her own footsteps she heard, held high in the fog and then dropped, gritty, furtive, faster and faster, like scuttling rats gathering behind her.

But no shadows moved there, high or low.

Only one car, at the far end of the street, a moment of motion, a glitter, a hum, and then only the blank, dank, unembroidered hanging of the fog. She shivered and went on.

All around there seemed to be a low thrumming, the sounds of the city wound together into one steady purr, a perfectly level harmonic pierced now and again by the stab of a car horn, the rumble of a Tube train emerging momentarily into the open, the snap of a twig, or the disconsolate chirp of some stranded bird clinging to a branch or chimney, caught high over invisible ground.

She turned corners, moving instinctively, imagining herself a ten-year-old boy and going – where? Now the street was a narrower one, the next narrower still. Away from the park the buildings diminished, becoming more and more mean, frowning closer and closer to the pavement, crowding in on her.

How dead the houses seemed. As if no-one lived within, had ever lived or moved in those rooms, looked out of those windows, tended those small squares of garden. The fog hung them all with cobwebs, like Miss Havisham's room, caught and suspended in time. This strange little street was as silent as the rest she had passed along – as if everyone in London was elsewhere, attending some celebration or party to which she hadn't been invited.

Now she realized where she was heading. At the far end of this street there was a cul-de-sac containing a line of derelict buildings that had always fascinated Max. She'd mentioned them to the police and they'd added them to their list of special haunts. Perhaps the police had already been there, found nothing, and gone on. Perhaps it was pointless to hope, but she was determined to find out for herself. Max had been told never to go into the houses, but he'd been so odd lately, so moody and strange. Maybe he'd just been sick of being cooped up. Maybe it was just defiance. Maybe she would find him exploring the empty rooms, full of his own mischief.

She prayed for a naughty child.

A living, laughing, naughty child.

She looked at her watch. Nearly five o'clock, and the day was darkening. It would probably be pitch-dark in those houses. The street-lamps were only creating useless pools of sickly light, deepening the shadows in between, so that her progress was stroboscopic. She visualized herself flickering on, off, on, off. She slowed, hearing again that odd echo of footsteps, and whirled around. Nobody, nothing. Just the empty street hung with misty curtains and, far away, the hum of the growing rush hour.

A car passed down the street, and then another, seeking a short-cut around stalled or slow-moving traffic, the drivers intent only on their journeys home, hunched over their steering wheels, androgynous silhouettes, as unknown to her as she to them, and as uncaring. They could not help her find her child.

Maybe they'd taken Max away in a car.

Who?

Don't think about that, she told herself. Think about finding a naughty little boy in a bright red anorak and school scarf. Expect to see him any minute, every minute, around this corner, around the next, here, there, anywhere, everywhere.

Now.

Yes!

As she turned the final corner she thought she saw a flash of red in the distance, going into one of the derelict houses.

'Max! *Max!*'

She began to run.

The house was the last in the row, at the end of the cul-de-sac. A high brick wall ran the width of the street between it and the house opposite, closing off the road from the open drop to the rails of the Metropolitan Line which surfaced here, briefly, before plunging once more into subterranean darkness.

These houses had been condemned two years before,

224

unfit even for restoration. But a preservation order was holding up their demolition, and they continued to be slowly shaken to pieces by the vibration from the passing trains. Another went by now, the sound of its passage transformed into the rumbling of electric animals kept behind the brick wall: dangerous, powerful, large.

The pavement trembled beneath Tess's feet as she stood staring at the door of the condemned house. Boarded up, like all the rest, it had a boy-sized hole at the bottom where two bits of wood had been pulled away – so tempting.

'Max! I saw you go in there, young man! Come out here this instant!'

But there was only the sound of the train, fading fast as it entered the tunnel, and then only silence and the steady drip of condensation from a broken gutter.

'Max! Max Leland! Come out here this instant!'

A rattle of grit, the creak of a board – something *was* beyond that boarded door. Something or someone.

Was it her son?

The prospect of entering that filthy, crumbling house was terrifying to her, but she had to do it. She had to *know*.

She took her hands from her pockets and went up the uneven path to the gap in the boards, bent down, and peered through. Faint streaks of light from the street lamps illuminated the hall beyond, and showed the shattered lower half of the stairway which led upward, to darkness.

Taking hold of one of the boards, she pulled hard, and nearly lost her footing. It hadn't been nailed shut at all, merely balanced there to provide the illusion of closure.

For someone, for some reason, the house was still alive.

She put down the board and crouched slightly to step through the opening. The house smelt oddly, as if work was going on here. What was it, that sour, penetrating odour?

The light from outside was very faint now, and she had neither torch nor matches to show the way. Twice she skidded on what felt like plastic bags, once she put a foot through a hole in the floor, cutting her shin and nearly losing a shoe.

There was a brief flicker of light from the door at the end of the hall. 'Max? Don't be afraid, love. It's Mummy – and I'm not angry. Please come out.'

'Ooohh, Max . . . it's only Mummy . . . and she's not angry. Noooooooooo . . .'

Tess froze in the doorway as she found herself facing a ring of pale faces, watery-eyed, grinning, wavering and rocking, the floor in front of them littered with plastic bags and rolled-up tubes of glue and cigarette butts and empty cider bottles and spoons and squares of foil and four or five disposable syringes.

None older than twelve, she thought in that first, shocked moment. Boys or girls, it was impossible to tell. And any one of them could have been Max.

But wasn't.

They giggled as she stared, and then the grins became feral, defensive, vicious. 'Piss off,' one of them, snarled. 'Piss off or we'll cut you.' When she didn't move, one of them, the largest and oldest, began to gather himself up.

'PISS OFF!' he shouted, balancing himself precariously and then stumbling towards her as his foot rolled on a bottle. Instinctively she caught him by the shoulders before he fell. His breath, foetid with decay and the acrid tang of solvents, whooshed into her face. She waited a moment, pushed him away, and spoke in a cold, hard voice.

'Have you seen a little boy in a red anorak. A little boy named Max?'

The boy looked at her blearily, caught unexpectedly by a question rather than the expected accusation. 'Go away,' he said, thickly.

She looked past him. 'Have any of you seen a little boy in a red anorak?'

They stared back at her, uncomprehending, uncaring, lost in their haze of glue and drink and whatever else they had been sold. Their clothes were cheap and worn, their faces thin and surrounded by matted tendrils of unwashed hair, and she did not blame them or dislike them or pity them or excuse them.

She just wanted her child.

'The police are searching the neighbourhood for my little boy,' she said, quietly. 'They will be here soon, I expect. They weren't far behind me.'

'Shit,' the oldest boy said.

There was a whining scramble as they all struggled to their feet and pushed past her, running down the hall and dropping to their knees to scuttle out of the door and into the street beyond.

Tess, knocked to the floor by their frantic passage, tried to get up and cried out at the sudden pain in her ankle. This room had obviously been the kitchen, and her foot had caught in a corner of the torn linoleum as she went down. The house suddenly shook with the passage of another train behind and below it. There was a brief faint flashing from the rear window, and in its light she saw a figure standing in the hall doorway.

Before she could get up, the figure moved forward and lifted a foot to press her down into the filth of the broken floor. The foot was between her shoulder blades, squeezing the breath out of her, forcing her face down into the plastic bags still reeking of glue. Just inches from her eye, the exposed needle of one of the used syringes glittered in the faint, treacherous light. High above her, a voice spoke.

'Time this was finished, Tess. Time for the game to end.'

THIRTY-ONE

IT WAS ARCHIE – OR KOBALSKI, they'd said his real name was. The fake Australian accent and slang were gone – as were the lovely manners he'd displayed at the Ritz.

He was big and strong and terrible, strong enough to hold her down with one foot while he lit a cigarette and enjoyed the spectacle of her squirming there.

She looked up over her shoulder and saw his face momentarily illuminated by the flickering flame of his lighter. The handsome features, once so warm and lively, were cold, and there was cruelty in his beautiful eyes.

'Now we can do this easy, babe, or we can do this tough.'

He lifted his foot from her back, and for a moment she thought she might get up and run, but it was only so he could kneel beside her. And there was no running away from those hands.

'Where's my son?' she demanded. 'What have you done with Max?'

'I haven't done anything with your damn kid. Maybe we'll deal with him later, after we've finished with you. After *I've* finished with you.' Suddenly his hands were in her hair, twisting it around his fingers, pulling her head back. She cried out with the sudden pain of it, her eyes filling with tears.

'Where's the money, babe? Where's the money your husband stole off us, hey? Got it stashed away good, have you? Keeping it a secret, biding your time waiting for that rainy day? That stupid old man didn't take it from the car, like I thought at first. And I couldn't find it at your place, so I figured you'd got really smart and maybe stashed it at that old house you were working on. I tried being nice, but

228

you don't fall for nice, do you? And I'm fed up with waiting around. So where is it, hey? In some safety deposit box somewhere? Yeah, that's it, isn't it? Not a bank account – the tax man might be nearly as interested as I am, right? No, a box. Or maybe you buried it in the garden, how about that?' He jerked her head back even further, and she heard the sudden, horrifying click of a flick-knife opening. 'Did you bury it in the garden, sweetheart?'

Because he'd pulled her head so far back her throat was tight, and the words could barely crawl out. 'There's no money. Roger wouldn't steal money from anyone.'

'That's what you think. He stole it from my main man, and my main man doesn't like getting stolen from, on principle. Leaves a nasty taste, makes him look a little foolish. Makes him mad. And when he gets mad, he gets even. *Capice?*'

'I don't have any money. I don't know what you're talking about,' she gasped in a strangled voice. The cold edge of the knife was under her ear, but after a moment of staring down at her he took it away and laid it down on the floor. Then he rolled her over onto her back, half across his knees.

Tess screamed at the half-seen expression on his face – greed and anger and lust combined to twist his handsome features into a demonic mask – and then her scream was cut off by the pressure of his cold, wet mouth over hers. He tasted of garlic and stale whisky and cigarettes, and she twisted her head away to scream again.

It was a mistake.

His snaking hand left her body and returned with the knife.

He drew the razor-edged blade down the side of her neck – she could feel the sting of air on the thin wound – and then dug the tip of it into the cleft between her breasts.

'Like I said, it can be easy or difficult, sweetheart. If I don't get the money back, my main man is going to think I can't do my job right. But I can do it – when I'm not interfered with. "No violence," he said.' He mimicked a voice she thought she recognized. ' "Don't hurt her," he said. Pigwash. I handle assignments the way *I* want to, not anyone else. What I start, I finish, you understand? I have a reputation to maintain. I lay off one, maybe they think I'm going to lay off the next one, or the next. Or that I can be bought off, maybe. That's no good for business. No good for me. I have an investment in myself, you might say.' Though he kept the knife pointed towards her throat, held lightly in his fingertips, he rubbed the palm of his hand over her breasts, lingering over the nipples, pressing down, and all the while breathing into her face. Another underground train rumbled past, the faint flickering light from its windows showing the white of his teeth, the strong lines of his nose and jaw. Oh, the betraying perfection of those handsome features behind which lurked a cruel and greedy man. 'Mmmmm,' he said. 'Nice little knockers, sweetheart. What else have you got to offer a hungry man?' He laid the knife between her breasts and his hand slid down her body until it reached the hem of her skirt, and began to slide upwards again, beneath it.

'You obviously don't have a very good memory.'

A voice, hard and harsh, came from the hall.

At the sound Kobalski jerked around, caught by surprise. The knife slid onto the floor, and his hand loosened in her hair. 'I remember what I want to remember,' he snarled. 'And I remember we have some unfinished business.'

'Then let's get it sorted out, shall we? You can deal with her later.'

Kobalski pushed Tess off his knee and got slowly to his feet, squinting into the darkness of the hall. He bent down and snatched up the knife, held it blade out towards the shadow in the doorway. 'Right,' he said.

As he moved forward the man in the hall stepped back into the darker shadows. 'I think we should talk about the money first.'

'Oh, yeah? You have it?'

'I know where it is. I found the hiding place you were too stupid to find. I can put my hands on it anytime I like.'

They moved down the hall, the newcomer backing

230

away, Kobalski coming after, drawn inexorably by the lure of the money. Drawn away from Tess. She lay there, unbelieving, her mind refusing to accept what it heard. It wasn't true. It couldn't be true. But she knew the voice so well, had heard it in the dark before, had heard it in the light, had heard it and been grateful,

Fool.

The man in the hall was John Soame.

She got up as quietly as she could and looked around her. The door from the kitchen to the rear of the house was no more than a black gap in the wall, covered by a couple of loose boards. She edged over to it and quickly ducked under the lower one, stumbling down a stone step into the pitch-black yard beyond. Her ankle stabbed pain up into her leg, and she gasped with the shock of it. It was weak and wobbly, but it did not give way. She nearly did, the pain was so great. But she must not give way, she must *get* away.

There was still Max.

He wasn't here, so Kobalski had taken him somewhere else. She *knew* she could find him – if she could just get away.

She couldn't see the fog, but she could feel it against her face, cool and clammy. Overhead the lights of the city diffused into it a pale grey glow, tinged with orange from one side of the sky to the other. A glow that gave no light, but only absorbed it, so that here, on the ground, she was blind. In the darkness her stumbling feet encountered a bottle which skittered away and smashed against something metallic.

'Hey!' came a shout from the house behind her. 'She's out!' and she could hear Kobalski cursing as he kicked away the boards over the door.

She ran down the littered, overgrown yard, stumbling and lurching as she prayed for escape. But there was no escape – and she realized why the glue-sniffing children had chosen to risk running straight into the arms of the police rather than escape from the house this way.

The yard was enclosed on all three sides by a brick wall, its surface slimy and cold under her scrabbling fingers. It

231

was very high on either side, but against the sky she could see that the rear wall had tumbled down in one place. It would have to be there, she had no other alternative. She could hear Kobalski coming down the yard towards her, closer and closer.

Desperately she climbed up the wall, sticking her fingers and toes into the chinks left by fallen or broken bricks, trying to reach the top, planning to go over into the next yard and get away. As she reached the top and swung a leg over, another Tube train rumbled past, shaking the ground, the wall, and – seemingly – the whole world. There *was* no other yard on the far side of the wall.

Just a straight drop to the Metropolitan Line.

And its electrified rails.

As she hesitated, she felt Kobalski's hand clutching at her legs, and realized that she, like the wall itself, was outlined clearly against the oddly pale fog-lit night sky. There was no real choice, no other way.

She kicked out at him, felt her toe connect with what she hoped was his head, heard him yell, and then swung herself over the wall. For a moment she hung there, a moment that was as close to eternity as she had ever known. Then she let go.

And dropped to the tracks below.

THIRTY-TWO

TESS LAY PERFECTLY STILL WHERE she had fallen.

She'd been stunned for a moment, but now her mind was clear – terribly clear. She sensed, but could not see, the electrified underground rails beside her. She could smell the acrid presence of high voltage, rubber buffers, oil. Lifting her eyes she saw a long narrow strip of sky high above her – the diffuse luminous orangey glow of the city under the fog. Beneath her, dirt and grit pushed a thousand points into her skin, penetrating even the heavy wool of her skirt.

She was afraid to move for fear of touching the live rail. That was certain death.

Gently she flexed her arms and legs and neck, testing to see if pain shouted the news of broken bones, torn muscles. No. She was bruised, but aside from the throb of her previously twisted ankle, she seemed whole enough. Despair had made her go limp as she fell through what had seemed like miles of space – as if the ground, seeing her descent, had pulled away to avoid the impact.

Overhead, where the wall to which she had clung edged the sky, she could see the outline of a head – Kobalski had reached the top and was peering down into the cutting. She could hear shouting, but the words were not clear because of the noise from the approaching train.

The approaching train.

Her stomach lurched and her heart seemed to go into suspended animation. A train was coming and she was lying within inches of the rail. What would happen? Would she be sucked beneath it? Worst of all, would the electricity in the rails arc to her body and burn her to death as she lay there, helpless?

The rumbling grew louder, filling the long narrow declivity, growing, swelling. There was a screech of metal on metal as the wheels scraped the rails. The ground beneath her shook and trembled as if it were as terrified by the approaching monster as she. Suddenly light came, the light of the train bursting from the tunnel, emerging one-eyed from its lair, bearing down on her.

She screamed but could not hear herself at all, curled back against the filthy wall, a small terrified animal transfixed by the light. Beneath the dumbfounding roar of the train, echoed and amplified by the enclosing walls, she could hear the crackle from the thousands of volts of electricity that propelled it, felt the wind of its passage sucking grit and paper and discarded rubbish into a whirlwind that rose and surrounded her. She screamed again as the train thundered past. She knew she screamed only because her mouth stretched and her breath was expelled and there was a tearing in her throat – but she heard only the deafening clack and clatter and thunder of the train itself.

And then it was gone.

Disbelievingly, she lay there, her breath coming painfully from her constricted chest, her hearing numbed by the explosion of sound that was even now diminishing as the train disappeared into the far tunnel, the last of the lights from the coaches flickering against the sooty walls.

Darkness came again.

Tess began to sob, great wracking sobs of relief. But that relief was tempered by the realization that this was not the end, that more trains would come, and that she could be – would be – battered again and again by the maelstrom of noise and wind. She had survived one onslaught, the thought of others inevitably coming was almost impossible to bear.

The tube trains stopped during the night, didn't they? Maintenance crews came along, then, so the electricity in the rails would be switched off, eventually.

She clung to the thought, even as the ground again began to shake beneath her and once more the distant rumbling began. From behind her, this time. The last train had gone by on the far side – this one would probably come closer for it was travelling the other way.

'Oh, God, please help me,' she sobbed, and again curled against the wall as the light burst forth from the tunnel and noise became a pounding ram of force that would surely crush her or tear her apart.

But it didn't.

This train also passed by on the far side.

Breathless, grateful, she lay there and tried to sort out her impressions. She had closed her eyes each time the trains had burst out of their respective tunnels. There were tracks next to her, she had glimpsed them momentarily before she blindly cringed away. Why weren't the trains using them?

Someone was shouting from above. She paid no attention. Kobalski, John Soame – they had nothing to do with her now. Whatever danger they represented paled in comparison to the danger only inches from her.

After a few minutes the ground began to vibrate once more, and again there came the distant mutter and rhythmic pulse of an approaching train. She was ready, she could bear it, she would keep her eyes open this time.

At the last minute she lost her nerve, and her eyes closed involuntarily against the wind and the spinning grit and rubbish. But she had seen enough. The tracks next to her were overgrown and barricaded at the tunnel's mouth. They were not being used. She could move.

Maybe.

Just because they weren't being used was no guarantee that electricity still didn't pulse through them when the trains passed on the far side, did it? Wasn't there something in electricity about completing a circuit? Isn't that why lightning didn't hurt you if you were earthed – whatever being earthed entailed. Not for the first time, she cursed her ignorance of the way things worked. She knew nothing about the underground system or how it functioned – she only knew how to get from one station to another. To touch the wrong rail – the centre rail? – was certain death, she knew. On the other hand, she knew that she had read of people falling beneath the trains and surviving – or was that simply in the stations where there was a deep channel beneath the rails?

At any rate, it was simply a matter of staying where she was until the trains stopped, and then perhaps a maintenance crew would come along and —

Something touched her face. She screamed and flailed out wildly with her hands. Was it an insect? A bat?

After a moment she saw it against the sky and realized it was a rope. A rope! Lowered down to her – was this salvation? She struggled to her knees and looked up.

'Come on, sweetheart, grab on and we'll pull you up,' came Kobalski's voice, sweet again with lies. 'You don't want to get electrocuted down there, do you? We won't hurt you, I promise. I only want the money, honey.' He chuckled, he actually chuckled, and the sound whispered back and forth in the small canyon of the cutting, reverberating between the walls in a mockery of the thunder that had gone before.

She waited for John Soame to add his treacherous voice to this less than tempting lure. But he was silent, perhaps realizing she would not trust him any more than she would trust Kobalski, who was apparently under the impression that she was stupid enough to climb back up to him.

She sat back down, ignoring the rope that dangled before her. Then it began to jerk about wildly: did he think that would increase the temptation? She looked up, preparing to tell him what he could do with his damned rope, and saw he was already doing something with it.

He was climbing down to her.

Perhaps to make certain she fell in front of the next train.

'Oh, God — ' That was twice she had invoked the deity, and twice she had been disappointed. She was sure there was one, but He seemed to be looking elsewhere at the moment. She struggled to her feet, gasped at the pain from her ankle which she had momentarily forgotten, and began to edge away down the wall.

'No! No!' she yelled. She saw the figure on the rope turn towards her, spinning awkwardly against the sky, searching the dark shadows for her and stiffening angrily when he realized she had moved away.

To what?

She didn't know, she didn't care. Sheer terror robbed her of reason, gave strength to her legs, and drove her before it. Mindless and blind, she ran along the wall, squeezed past the barrier, and went into the black mouth of the tunnel, where even the faint luminosity of the night sky could not reach.

In the distance, the fresh thunder of an approaching train began to mutter.

THIRTY-THREE

THE NOISE IN THE BRICK-WALLED cutting had been bad enough, but the crescendo of the passing train within the tunnel was like a fist to her head and a hammer to her body. Tess turned and pressed her face against the grimy wall and felt her skirt whip around her legs as the train went by.

Out of the corner of her eye she saw the passengers in the coaches, peacefully reading their evening papers or staring blankly at the advertisements that ran in a line above the windows, oblivious to her existence or her terror. Some were even chatting, hanging from the straps and exchanging polite but weary evening smiles.

It was the crackle of the electricity that was the worst – and the strange metallic smell it left in the air. The space within the tunnel was even more restricted than it had been in the cutting, although this was still a double tunnel. There was no shoulder of ground, here. Just a ledge, barely walkable. The curved walls seemed to press her over as her feet edged along.

For a while there was silence, blessed moments of relief. She didn't know how long it would last, but she wanted to make the most of it. She could hear her own breath, panting, and a low moaning whimper that seemed to originate in her throat – a throat already sore from screaming.

And someone else was in the tunnel, too. Scraping sounds overlapped her own, more than echoes. So Kobalski had followed her in. He was intent on her destruction, one way or another.

Doggedly she kept on, trying to remember how long a

run it was by train between stations. Surely she'd come this way a hundred times over the past years? But which station to which station it was she didn't know, because as she'd wandered the streets looking for Max she hadn't kept track of distance or direction. She could have gone in a circle for all she knew – where were those derelict houses? She'd only seen them from the car when Roger was driving the back way to avoid a jam.

It couldn't be far, she thought. This is still London, not the suburbs. Not more than two minutes between stations here, surely? Unless I'm under the park. The wall curved under her outstretched hands, seemed to go on and on and on.

Now she could see signal lights ahead. Didn't that mean a station was near? Or was it a junction? She moved along, then paused beneath them to catch her breath. They shed red illumination on her face, casting her eye sockets into darkness, turning her into a desperate masked creature of the forever night, crawling beneath the earth.

Beside the signal lights there was a small niche in the wall. On the floor lay some tools, discarded or left deliberately for the next man or the next job. She bent down and ran her fingers over them. She grasped what felt like a pipe or a wrench. It was heavy, about a foot long. At least she had something to defend herself with now. She could wait until he came along and —

But he can see me here, because of the lights, she thought, and moved on.

About twenty feet past the lights and around a last, sharp bend, she came to a place where the rails divided. A faint light came from a grimy light bulb set high in the tunnel roof, showing her two ways to go. Obviously the left hand tracks would eventually lead to a station, but at what cost? It was a narrow tunnel, holding only one track – a live track – with no more than inches between the wall and the sides of the racing trains.

There hadn't been a train for some time. Odd, considering this was the rush hour. Looking back she could see that the signals were still red. If she chose the narrow tunnel she might make it to the next station before

239

a train came. Or she might try to go too fast, and fall onto the live rail. Or a train might come and smear her along the wall, crushing her like an insect.

The right-hand tunnel only offered blackness, but safety from the terrible voltage of the live rail, and perhaps from Kobalski, too. What else it might offer she would not think about.

She went right.

This tunnel was wider, with a margin of cinder track beside the rails. And there was no smell of electricity here, either. Perhaps only because the circuit was not complete. One touch and she could become the last arc. She kept on, blindly, holding her hands out in front of her, keeping her shoulder against the wall so as not to stray onto the rails. The ground seemed to slope upward, slightly. After what seemed like an eternity of slow, groping progress, she sensed an open space ahead. Perhaps through some change in the quality of her own breathing and the sound of her shuffling footsteps? A draught of fresh air? Was it yet another junction? She knew there was an absolute maze of tunnels and junctions beneath London streets of which ordinary people like herself knew little. Like the sewers and the conduits for electricity and phone cables, it was a secret and hidden world.

She began to move along more quickly, hoping for another niche in the wall in which she could rest or hide. Instead, her groping hand encountered what felt like the edge of the wall. She could thrust her arm all the way back and still she did not encounter anything but space.

It was a platform!

With some difficulty, she climbed up and felt her way onto the flat space. She moved forward until she ran smack into another wall. Splaying out her hands, she felt the cold shininess of tiles, some missing, and then stepped to the side and barked her shins against a rough bench, onto which she sank. It was a station!

But there were no bright lights, no gaudy advertisements, no crowds of people impatiently waiting. Nothing. It was deserted, abandoned. She sat there, panting, gathering herself together. She ran a hand down

240

her leg and encountered a large swelling – the ankle had bandaged itself. She could hardly flex it, but the pain had diminished a little.

Her breath was coming in hiccups and sobs now. Had she been seen under the faint light at the junction? Had Kobalski followed her into the blackness or not? There was no way of knowing, but she had come to expect the worst. God still seemed to be looking the other way.

She couldn't risk it, couldn't stay where she was. She had to hide or – better still – find a way out of here and into the open air.

She forced herself to her feet and, arms outstretched as before, began to work her way along the old platform. She could still see nothing, and the air was dead and still. Claustrophobia, which sheer terror had kept at bay while in the tunnel, now began to press in on her.

Her groping hands suddenly went forward into space, and she nearly fell to her knees again.

A way out?

She moved forward, feeling ahead of her with her good foot, and almost immediately banged into another wall. Right or left? She tried both and realized she was in a pedestrian tunnel that turned after leaving the platform and led – where?

To some stairs, she discovered, after falling painfully up the first three. Pressing her back against the handrail that was fastened to the wall, she started to edge up the stairs one at a time. They were wooden, and creaked alarmingly under her weight. For all she knew, the staircase was incomplete. For all she knew, she could fall through on the next step. Or the next. Or the next.

She continued to climb, she had to climb, there was no other option. From below her she saw, reflected in the dusty tiles, a brief flicker of light. Kobalski and his damned cigarette lighter. The light disappeared. He wasn't wasting it – just giving himself brief illumination now and again.

And he was still coming after her.

Tess continued to climb, a step at a time, until she reached the top. She sensed a great space ahead of her, and began to move through it, arms outstretched, testing each

241

step before she transferred her weight to it.

By the time Kobalski reached the top of the staircase behind her, she was in the middle of what – in the flare of his lighter – seemed to be the booking hall. She froze where she stood, arms out as if she was preparing to fly, her tear-filled eyes starred by the reflection.

'Well, hello there,' he said. He sounded quite cheerful.

'Stay away from me,' Tess croaked, raising the metal bar she'd found in the tunnel. 'Just stay away.'

'My goodness, you scare me half to death,' Kobalski said, and smiled. He came towards her, holding his lighter at shoulder level. The light reached out faint fingers all around, and Tess could see that the ticket booths were shrouded in cobwebs and dust, and the walls contained shreds of old advertisements, half torn away and faded. One said 'Careless Talk Costs Lives' – telling her when the station was closed.

And possibly why.

She started to back away, glancing over her shoulder, prepared to see a yawning gap of bomb damage, or some fallen timbers. But the way was clear, only a rusting folding gate drawn across a solid wall of wood. Station closed. What lay beyond the gate and the boarding she could only guess at. She didn't remember seeing a deserted station anywhere in the streets of the area. Perhaps it had been bombed. Perhaps there was an entire building beyond the boards.

Her tomb was going to be an impressive one.

When, one day, they re-entered this place, what would they think when they found her body lying here – or even, by then, her skeleton? Would they think she was an ancient war casualty? Would she haunt the hall, wandering forever down the tunnels, searching for a way out, for a way to her son?

'Where's Max?' she demanded, hoarsely.

'How the hell would I know?' he asked.

'Didn't you kidnap him?'

'Hell, no. But it would have been a good idea, come to think of it. You'd have handed over the money, then, wouldn't you?'

242

'If she had it – which she doesn't,' said John Soame, emerging at the top of the stairs behind Kobalski. 'I told you that before. She never had it.'

Kobalski whirled so quickly at the sound of John's voice that the lighter went out, and he had to flick it into life again. As he did, she saw him reach into his pocket.

'He's got a knife!' she shouted. But then, John knew that, didn't he? Why on earth had she bothered to warn him?

'Yes, I know he has. And I have a gun.' He moved a hand inside his jacket pocket, extending it as if there were a pistol inside. Kobalski sneered at such a pathetic subterfuge.

'Oh, wow,' he drawled. 'A two-finger thirty-eight. Why shucks, you can't hardly get them no more.' His tone was bored – he'd seen it all before. 'I thought you'd run for it,' he said. 'Thought you'd turned tail. Persistent bastard, aren't you? Well, you can't pretend you have anything to offer me any more, because I know you haven't.' Flicking his knife open in one movement, he thrust the naked blade towards Soame. It was a mistake.

The sudden movement casused him to slide on the gritty surface, and he dropped the lighter. It cracked onto the marble floor and lay there, its fluid flooding out and burning brightly for a moment before flickering out.

Darkness again.

There was a sharp intake of breath, a scuttle of steps, a grunt, a moan, and then the noise of struggle. Tess backed away, afraid to strike out in the dark, although she still held the metal pipe. She kept backing until she hit the wall, and then just stood there, helplessly.

The sounds, the terrible animal sounds, seemed to recede from her, and then there was a sudden shout and a crash of splintering, rotten boards. They had broken through the stairway and fallen, locked together, to the platform below.

Tess covered her face with her hands.

And then there came a new sound.

A high, thin whistle.

Suddenly there was light. Faint and pale yellow, two of

243

the three globes in an overhead fixture came to life, throwing barely adequate illumination onto the vast, dusty hall. They brightened for a moment, and then one flickered and popped out, leaving only one to shed its light, creating more shadows than sense in the big space.

At the same time there was a loud noise and more light poured in – this time from a slowly widening gap in the boarding beyond the metal gate. Men stood there, silhouetted in a bright light that scalded Tess's eyes. She could see them moving, peering through. Then she heard Abbott's voice. He sounded almost bored – certainly annoyed.

'All right, that's enough. I am a police officer and I am armed.' He stood to one side while a man in a London Transport uniform unlocked the gate. With a protesting shriek of rusty metal they pushed the gate aside. Policemen poured in, and stood staring around them.

'They're down there,' Tess shouted, pointing.

A torch beam swung around and revealed her pressed against the frame of a torn advertisement for Cadbury's chocolate. 'Good God,' said Tim Nightingale.

She was never to know how she looked standing there – face filthy with soot and grime, clothes torn, legs bleeding through ripped tights, white streaks of tears dividing her face like river channels, hair strung with cobwebs, eyes wild.

'Are you all right?' Nightingale asked, gruffly, coming over to her, while other men went over to the stairway and peered down. She leapt forward. 'Make him tell you where he's got Max!' she screamed. 'Get him, make him tell — ' She was hammering on his chest, desperately. What if Kobalski was unconscious? Hurt? Dead? He'd never speak, then. 'I'll do it. Let me do it. Let me hurt him, let me kill him, make him tell me, make him — '

'Mrs Leland!' He grabbed her arms, shook her. 'It's all right. We've got the boy – he's quite safe.'

She cried out with the sudden relief and felt the floor giving way – was she, too, to fall into darkness? But Nightingale was there, holding her up with one strong arm, helping her over to a bench, saying encouraging,

peaceful things until the vast dust-fogged hall ceased spinning and humming around her. Some of the men by the
broken stairway had edged forward, clinging to the handrail and one another, tentatively descending via the surviving edges of the stairs.

'Is Max all right?' Her throat was so raw from screaming
that when she tried normal tones they were no more than a
croak.

'He's fine.'

'Where — ' she began to ask, but then the men who had
gone down the stairway re-appeared, hauling Kobalski and
John Soame with them. As she watched she saw John hold
out a bleeding arm while one of the officers tied a hand-
kerchief around it. He looked across the man's shoulder at
Tess.

And she looked at him.

There was a sudden burst of voices from the direction of
the rusty gate, and Tess turned to see Adrian Brevitt being
led through the gap in the boarding. He stood there staring
at her. From beyond him there came the sound of traffic –
just ordinary street traffic. So there was a street out there,
after all, and she hadn't climbed from the tunnels merely to
find herself entombed beneath a pile of concrete.

Then Richard pushed past Adrian and the man in the
London Transport uniform. He came straight over to Tess,
put his arm around her and tipped her face up. 'Are you all
right? Did he hurt you?'

'I'm fine, Richard.'

'Christ, you're bleeding,' he said, and produced a hand-
kerchief which he used to wipe the long, thin cut that was
oozing blood into her collar. She had forgotten that – it
seemed to have happened many years before. 'And your
legs — ' he bent to wipe those, too, and saw her swollen
ankle. 'Oh, Tess,' he said. 'My dear.'

Adrian came across, too, and gazed down at them. 'All
this is not very nice, is it?' he said, in a strange and sorrowful
voice. 'So – unnecessary.'

There was a snort of derision, and they all turned to see
that Detective Constable Murray had moved to the centre
of the hall, and was holding Kobalski's arm in an iron grip.

'All she had to do was tell me where the money was,' Kobalski said to him, in a perfectly reasonable tone.

Abbott went over and stood next to the handsome American, whose good looks were not lessened by the dirt on his face nor the fact that his hair was tumbled over his forehead. If anything, he looked more attractive than ever, Tess thought. Only the anger in his eyes spoiled things. That, and the cruel twist of his mouth.

It did not seem at all strange to her that she could think that he was attractive, even now. All the men around her seemed frozen in a tableau so that she could examine them one by one, as if she were suspended in a bubble of time. All the men in her life. Richard, so solicitous, so protective, his good square face earnestly gazing down at her. Adrian, elegant and impeccable, but still with that odd and distant expression in his eyes. John Soame, dirty and dishevelled, watching her intently, his narrow face scratched and bruised, his expression strained.

Detective Chief Superintendent Abbott, tall and self-contained. Detective Sergeant Nightingale, who had believed her when no-one else had. Detective Constable Murray, and the other detectives who had been at the house. Even the London Transport man looked familiar, standing there in his uniform, twisting the keys in his hands, gazing around the empty booking hall making a mesmerized inventory.

And Roger, who was not there, but whom she could see clearly now in her mind's eye, the way he'd looked when he'd left on that last, terrible morning. His dear, familiar face had been haunted, his natural ebullience dulled – as if he'd been invisibly bruised, and was hurting inside. 'Don't worry, Tess,' he'd said. 'It's a bit of a mess, but at least I've decided what to do about it. I'll sort it all out.'

But he'd never said what it was.

And he hadn't lived to sort it all out, either.

She'd been left to pay the bills.

All the bills.

Abbott spoke to Kobalski. 'Perhaps you'd like to make things easier for yourself now,' he suggested. 'Perhaps you'd like to bring someone with you for company when we

246

take you to the Yard. Your local contact, for instance?'

'Yeah, sure, why not?' Kobalski agreed. 'Misery always loves company – not that I intend to be miserable for very long.' He walked forward, Nightingale coming with him on one side, Murray on the other. As he moved, Kobalski spoke with a kind of resigned disgust. 'My main man warned me about you and your damned English caution. Always interfering. Always making me slow down, back off. You should have let me do the job right from the beginning,' he sneered. 'We could have finished it long ago, if you'd let me do it right.'

And Nightingale's hand closed on Richard Hendricks's arm.

THIRTY-FOUR

ADRIAN BREVITT SAT DOWN BESIDE Tess and rested his chin on his silver-headed cane. 'One should have known,' he murmured. 'He had absolutely no taste. And as for his clothes — ' He shuddered, delicately.

'I can't believe it,' Tess whispered, shivering.

'I can,' Abbott said quietly. 'Richard Hendricks is the kind of man who is always right, in his own eyes. When that kind of man is crossed, he is very dangerous indeed, because every argument is a threat to his ego and his self-image. We spent most of this morning with the Fraud Squad, going over and verifying information Tim had got from . . . somewhere.' He glanced over at Nightingale, who flushed and managed to look both proud and sad.

Abbott went on. 'We were pretty certain Hendricks was behind the trouble, but we didn't know how he fitted in, and how far back it had begun. At first we assumed it was just the accident – that perhaps he'd been driving the car that old Ivor Peters thought was chasing your husband, and that Max could identify him — '

'Where *is* Max?' Tess demanded. 'You said he was all right, but where is he? I want to see him!'

'You might better ask where *was* he,' Adrian said. 'All the time we were searching for the little devil, he was sitting in Hendricks' outer office, waiting to see him. That young curate drove him over, apparently under the impression that you knew all about it. Hendricks' secretary finally rang through because she wanted to go home and didn't want to leave Max sitting there alone. Sergeant Nightingale went for him in a police car – I expect riding in that made his day.'

248

'He went to see Richard? But why?'

'To return the money, in a manner of speaking,' Nightingale told her. 'You see, he had it all along. His father had given it to him.'

'Three hundred thousand pounds,' Adrian murmured.

Tess stared at them, aghast. 'Where did Roger get three hundred thousand pounds, for goodness' sake?' Her head was spinning again, and it had nothing to do with the concussion, or the terrible flight through the darkness of the tunnels below. 'Are you telling me that Roger *did* steal some money? That he *was* involved in drugs?'

Abbott shook his head. 'Not in the way you're thinking. I'm sorry if this upsets you — '

'I think I'm beyond being upset,' Tess said, weakly.

'Yes, I suppose you are. Well, I had a word with the pathologist – and it's quite likely that your husband didn't die instantly in that crash. He and the boy were trapped there together for perhaps ten minutes or so before the ambulance came. He must have realized he was dying. He managed to tell Max something about what he had done – although it was probably pretty incoherent – but before he could tell him what to *do* about it, he died.'

'Oh, Lord.' Tess felt as if she had been stabbed, the pain in her chest was so great. 'My poor Max. No wonder he had nightmares,' she said. 'But why didn't he say something? Why didn't he ask *me* about it?'

'Your husband may have told him not to tell you. We didn't question the boy closely, there wasn't time, so you may learn more eventually. But it's obvious that he was upset and confused about it all. It was quite a dilemma for a youngster. And then he became ill. That meant he had a perfect excuse to delay doing anything, but the delay also made the burden of guilt heavier. The time went on – and so did those nightmares. Max knew that by rights the money was Hendricks's, but he didn't *like* Hendricks. He may even have blamed him for his father's death. So he didn't *want* to give it back. And, of course, he didn't know anything about what you were going through, did he?'

'No, I didn't want to frighten or worry him,' Tess said, slowly. Then the enormity of it hit her. 'But how could

249

Max have had all that money? I mean, that much would be very bulky, wouldn't it? I've cleaned his room dozens of times since Roger died, and there was no money there. And Kobalski didn't find it, either.' She remembered something and turned to John Soame. 'You told Kobalski *you* knew where it was.'

He didn't look at her. 'I was bluffing,' he said, dully. 'Trying to buy time.'

An ambulance siren sounded in the distance, muffled by the fog, coming closer. Some blood was still trickling down John's arm and splashing onto the marble floor by his feet, combining with the dust to make small, muddy crimson puddles. She could feel the warmth of him beside her, and was ashamed. She had been so wrong, so quick to assume he was associated with Kobalski when all along he had been trying to protect her. The blood he was shedding, the struggles he'd had, the time he'd lost from his work, all of it was because of her, and when the final moment had come, she had not trusted him.

'Oh, Max has told me where it was,' Nightingale said. 'I talked to him in the car on the way back to the house. I have a couple of younger brothers of my own.' He grinned. 'You might not have seen it, but it was in his room all the time.'

'But where?'

'In his stamp album.' Nightingale smiled at their astonishment, enjoying the moment. Then his face saddened, because he knew he had to tell her the rest, and it wasn't easy. It was never easy to tell someone that they had been deceived by a person they trusted, in whatever way, and for whatever reason.

He took a deep breath. 'You see, for quite a while your husband and his partner were involved in a little more than public relations, I'm afraid. Under cover of servicing their actual clients they'd been running a nice little sideline in smuggling stolen or proscribed works of art or even occasionally transferring money for some very questionable clients on their "private" list. I think your husband did it for fun, but Hendricks was always interested in profits. There came a day – perhaps inevitably, considering the kind of people they were dealing with – when Hendricks was shown there would be even *more* profit in drugs. Hendricks was willing, but there your husband drew the line. Little tricks to cheat the taxman or Customs were one thing – sort of glamorous, I suppose – but drugs were something else again.'

'Roger would *never* have touched drugs,' Tess said.

'Your husband went to France just before he died, didn't he?'

'Yes, that's right. Marseilles.'

'It would be. Hendricks probably gave him money to make a "purchase",' Abbott said. 'The contact had been pre-arranged, but when your husband realized it was to be drugs he was to carry, and not negotiable bonds or some work of art, he couldn't bring himself to do it. He never made the meeting. There he was in Marseilles with all this money. He was furious with Hendricks, and worried about being implicated in some way because of it, so he bought something else instead. Something that would look quite innocuous if he was stopped at Customs at either end.'

'What?'

'A set of stamps. Not so much to look at – just very, very rare. When he got back, he slipped them into Max's stamp album. And when Max saw them, he loved them. That *also* made it difficult for him to turn them over to Hendricks. But in the end, seeing the house torn apart and, most importantly, seeing you hurt, was more terrible to him than losing any stamps, however rare and wonderful. So he decided to give them back to Hendricks, as his father had told him to do. He thought the trouble would stop then.'

'Did Richard . . . kill Roger?' She was almost afraid to ask.

'We don't think so,' DC Murray said. He had returned from handing the prisoners over. 'Anyway, it would be hard to prove, with Ivor Peters dead.'

Abbott became reflective. 'It *might* have been a genuine accident – Peters could have been totally wrong about the intentions of the following driver – it could have been anyone in a hurry who didn't want to get "involved". Just

251

one of those terrible things that happen to the very people who least expect it. And it came at the worst possible time, because it left you facing a great deal of unfinished business.'

'When Roger kissed me goodbye he said he was going to clear up "the mess",' Tess said, sadly. 'I didn't know what he meant, but I saw he had come to some kind of decision about something that had been worrying him.'

'Well, for what it's worth, I tend to trust Ivor Peters' instinct,' Nightingale said. 'I always did. I think it *was* Kobalski driving the chase car, and Kobalski who frightened Peters sufficiently to precipitate a heart attack.'

Tess remembered something. 'He said something about thinking the old man had taken the money.'

Nightingale allowed himself a glance of satisfaction at Abbott, who raised an eyebrow but said nothing. 'Perhaps the car hire clerk will recognize him,' Nightingale said.

Abbott shook his head. 'It won't make any difference,' he said. 'Kobalski will simply say he never intended to kill your husband, just frighten him into handing over the money. And it could be true, because it was early in the game, after all. We could never prove otherwise.'

'And Richard hired him?'

'Not exactly,' Abbott said.

'But Kobalski — '

'Kobalski was wished on Hendricks by the American syndicate, he didn't have much choice about it.'

'He said something about "a main man".'

'Yes. You see, Hendricks never suspected your husband had done anything with the money except what he had been *told* to do – he assumed he'd made the buy and passed on the goods – until the Marseilles dealer got in touch with him a few days after Roger's death and asked him if he was still interested in the shipment. That was the moment Hendricks realized your husband had stolen the money. By then, the client knew it, too. At first they assumed Roger had either given the money to you or hidden it at home, hence the break-in during the funeral. When nothing was found, Hendricks was told to get close to you.'

252

'And that's why he was so attentive,' Adrian put in. 'Not that you're not worth pursuing, my dear, but he had ulterior motives beyond the obvious, I'm afraid.' He patted her hand in a fatherly fashion.

As he spoke, the ambulance drew up outside, they could hear the distinctive throb of the engine, and then the ambulancemen came through the gate.

'Here,' Abbott called, gesturing them over and indicating John Soame's bleeding arm. One of them ripped the sleeve open and got to work.

'Did Hendricks ever hear about your son's nightmares?' Abbott asked Tess.

She nodded. 'He actually witnessed one, in the hospital, when Max was delirious.'

'Mmmm. I'm afraid that may be what first made him think that *Max* knew something about the money, rather than you, and that there was still a chance he could get it back. But he couldn't get at Max in the hospital, and once Max came home he was never alone. You and Mr Soame and that housekeeper of yours saw to that.'

Nightingale spoke. 'Kobalski had tried the phone calls and the break-ins to frighten you. They didn't work, and now Mr Soame was in the way, too. Hendricks tried to turn you against him, but that didn't work either. So, Archie McMurdo was invented.'

'But why?'

'At first, to charm you. But you weren't having any. So he tried kicking up a fuss, to make you lose your job and perhaps either start spending the money or turn to Hendricks. I think Hendricks is genuinely fond of you, Mrs Leland, and insisted that Kobalski go gently.'

'I suppose I should be grateful for that,' Tess said.

'Yes. But there was increasing pressure on Kobalski from the "client" to get the job done.'

'I don't know why Hendricks just didn't pay the client back out of the insurance money,' John Soame put in. 'Or from his own funds, if he's so well-off.'

Abbott shook his head. 'I don't know if you know much about organized crime, but there was a lot more than just money involved here. It wasn't the money, it was the

253

getting back of the money that was so important. The big men don't like to be seen as soft, and they don't like to be made fools of. What they do like is revenge, and making their position clear. That's why, whenever Hendricks was out of town, Kobalski got a little rougher. He was under pressure, too, and eventually he stopped listening to Hendricks.'

Tess turned to Adrian. 'You seemed to know "Archie" was a phoney.'

'Oh, I did,' Adrian agreed. 'But *only* after I'd flown to Italy and tracked down Dolly McMurdo herself. When I saw what you had done at the mansion I knew there was nothing wrong with your work or your ideas, so there had to be something wrong with *him*. When I finally found her in her little "hideaway" – my God, Tess, you should have seen the frescoes in that place – she told me flatly that she had no nephew named Archie or anything else. I came back all full of my news, only to find it was old news.' He sighed. 'I felt quite miffed when you all turned on me.'

'And promptly went into a sulk,' John said, wincing as the ambulanceman bound his wound.

'I am a sensitive creature,' Adrian said, but his eyes were twinkling as he spoke.

Abbott wanted to finish this now. 'Time was passing. Kobalski was waiting for Hendricks when he came back this morning. When Hendricks learned Max had gone missing, Kobalski leaned on him. Hendricks was frightened – he had begun to realize the kind of people he'd so lightly taken on as "clients", and that they had no compunction about killing even useful people if they wanted to make a point. Fear for his own safety finally overcame his better judgement, as well as any finer feelings he might have had about you and the boy. When he came over, he knew Kobalski was watching outside, waiting for a chance to get you out of the way.'

'And I gave it to him,' Tess said, contritely. 'By leaving the house and going out to look for Max myself.'

'Come on, in you get,' the ambulanceman said, taking hold of John Soame's good arm. Soame staggered slightly as he got up, and they supported him out of the hall and through the gate to the waiting ambulance.

Adrian looked at Tess, who was staring at the floor. 'He followed you,' he said, softly. 'He knew you wanted to look for Max, but he didn't want you to be alone.'

Nightingale cleared his throat. 'Soame saw Kobalski go into the house after you, and managed to ring us from a box on the corner. We told him to just watch and wait, but he went in. When you went over the wall Kobalski knocked him out and went after you. As soon as he came to he went after Kobalski, even though he knew the man was a killer. He was over the wall by the time we arrived – he wouldn't wait – so all we could do was contact London Transport and get them to turn off the power. After that it was just a matter of covering all the stations to which you had access – including this one.'

Tess looked at them, and then towards the gate.

'Go on, Tess. Mrs Grimble and I will look after Max,' Adrian said, encouragingly. 'And you *should* have that ankle strapped.'

Tess stood up.

The ambulance doors banged shut and the vehicle swayed as the driver got in and engaged gears to drive away. John Soame opened his eyes when Tess sat down beside him. 'What about Max?' he asked.

'Mrs Grimble will feed him bangers and mash and Adrian will tell him all about what he missed.' She cleared her throat awkwardly. 'Thanks for saving my life, by the way.'

He shrugged, his half-moon smile curling up in his pale face. 'Thanks for saving mine,' he said.

'I don't know what you mean.'

'Oh . . . it's hard to explain. You see, last spring I had a nervous breakdown.'

'Yes, I know.'

'Oh?' He seemed surprised, but not embarrassed. 'Well, it happens to a lot of people, I guess. They got me functioning again – I could walk and talk just like a real person.' He smiled wryly. 'But I simply felt dead inside. I couldn't seem to care about anything or anyone. I hoped coming to London, a change of work and scene, might help. At first it didn't make a bit of difference. And then Adrian suggested our "arrangement".' He managed another smile. 'I won't say it's been *relaxing*, exactly, but it has stopped me thinking only about myself. And I don't think I've felt so alive for years. You did that. You and Max.'

'And the beautiful Julia?' Tess asked before she could stop herself.

He looked at her in surprise. 'What's my niece got to do with it?'

She stared back. 'Julia's your *niece*?'

'Yes, of course. My ex-wife wasn't Adrian's only sister, you know, and they're all pretty overwhelming. Is it any wonder he turned out the way he has? Julia is not only my niece, she is a very intelligent girl who is reading medicine at Barts, and whose parents have several other children to support. I'm helping to finance her – hence my present extreme poverty – and in return she's helping me do my research. What did you *think* she — ' He paused. 'Oh, I see.'

'Well, she *was* wearing your dressing-gown.'

He nodded. 'Yes, she was. And it was raining that night, if you recall. She had got her clothes soaked by a passing taxi and was drying them in front of my gas fire. You ran off before I could introduce you.' He sighed. 'She's just broken up with her boyfriend – I'd been hearing all the gory details of a broken heart. Poor girl can't move into her new place until the end of the week. She'll have to stay with us until then.' He started to put his good arm around her, then paused.

'You *did* call me "darling" that night, didn't you?' he asked, warily.

'Yes, I'm afraid I did.'

He looked relieved. 'That's all right, then,' he said. He pulled her close, bent his head to kiss her, then slid slowly off the seat in a dead faint instead.

The ambulanceman, who had been listening and watching with great interest, stared down at him and sighed. 'I was expecting that,' he said, resignedly. 'These intellectual types are all alike, aren't they?'

Tess smiled as she knelt to help him lift John onto the stretcher. 'Not quite,' she said. 'Not quite.'

THIRTY-FIVE

NIGHTINGALE STOOD ON THE PAVEMENT, watching the ambulance pull away. People were still pausing to stare, clotting on either side of the precipitately revealed Tube station. A few ignored the broken boards and thick dust, and were trying to buy tickets. Accustomed to stations that were vandalized, dilapidated, or in the throes of renovation, they assumed this was a functioning station, and did not like being told to move on. The man from London Transport looked on the verge of either strike action or a magnificent tantrum.

The fog was still with them, now visible only in lamplight and headlight beams, and Nightingale could feel the damp cold penetrating his jacket. 'Move these people on, will you?' he asked one of the uniformed officers. 'That poor sod from London Transport is going under for the third time. And get somebody to call 55 Broadway, they'll need to send a crew to board up the place again.'

'Yes, sir,' the constable said, and moved off to do the usual six things at once.

Abbott joined him, looking amused. 'We located Carter. He *is* a curate at St Winifred's. Or was. When we found him he was in bed with the vicar's wife, the vicar being out at his regular Monday karate class. So much for the worry that Carter was some kind of paedophile. I tell you, Tim, the Church is not what it was.'

'No,' Tim agreed.

'And we could have discounted Walter Briggs from three o'clock yesterday afternoon. He's been in the Hampstead lock-up since then, taken there after some kind of domestic punch-up with his son concerning a bottle of ten-year-old brandy that had been reserved for some important guests.'

'Thus we spread our largesse throughout the population,' Tim said. 'Bringing joy into every life we touch.'

Abbott ignored the sarcastic tone. 'Well, clearing this Leland thing up ought to look good on your record,' he said.

'I wonder,' Tim said. 'They aren't going to like the expense sheet – getting London Transport to turn off the juice on the Underground line, then having to send in extra men to handle the traffic jams as people poured out looking for buses, ripping open this place, mounting a search for the boy – they'll go raving mad.' He sighed. 'And all because one old cop was curious about one man who died too soon.'

Abbott looked at him. 'Everybody dies too soon,' he said, gently.

'Yes. But if Roger Leland had lived even a day longer, it would all have been different. I like to think he'd decided to come to us.'

'He might have come up with some other scheme,' Abbott said. 'Something not quite so noble.'

'I prefer my version. We do know that, at the last minute, he did his best. I hope the boy eventually realizes that.' He shook his head. 'Funny, the way Max hung on to those stamps. He showed them to me when we got back to the house. Very boring, not even attractive pictures on them. And worth all that money. Disgusting, really.'

'You mean, when you think of all the starving children in India?' Abbott asked, trying to raise a smile.

'Something like that.'

Abbott looked at him, recognizing the tone of voice, the slump of the shoulders, the emptiness. It always happened, every time, to everyone, at the end of the long, long run. There was nothing anybody could do, except ride it out. 'Go home,' he said, quietly, wishing it didn't sound so banal. 'Put your feet up, have a drink, let it all go. Just let it run out the ends of your fingers, Tim. It's the only way.'

259

But Nightingale didn't answer, and Abbott knew there was nothing he could do for him now.

Maybe later.

Maybe tomorrow.

But not now.

Tim stood looking at the grimy street and the passing people. There weren't that many now – it was past the rush hour – but they looked whey-faced and weary. Their feet made a sullen, shuffling sound on the pavement. Their eyes were down, their expressions blank.

He felt the weight of the crowd, and it crushed him.

You don't see me, he thought. You don't want to see me. I only come bringing trouble, after all. I walk through people's lives and out the other side, trailing disaster. I picked up a thread of Ivor Peters' life because I thought it would be exciting, because I thought I was doing the right thing. How many people are destroyed each day by someone like me, trying to do the right thing? And what difference did I make, in the end? Five years from now, none of them will remember my name.

Abbott will go home to his hills.

Chief Inspector Spry will come back and growl at everyone for a few years, then retire, glad to be out of it.

Murray will make sergeant.

Hendricks will soon be running whatever gaol he lands up in.

Kobalski will get a smart lawyer and probably be deported.

Sherry will marry her stockbroker.

Tess Leland will marry Professor Soame.

Maybe Max will even grow up to be prime minister.

After a brief interlude, they will all continue as before.

I won't have changed them.

But they will have changed me, because I can't turn them out. They stay within me, because I can't forget. And gradually I will be so full of them that there will be no room for me.

He looked at Abbott, now deploying the uniformed men to various tasks, clearing up the mess, tidying up the details, probably already planning the report he'd write

260

tomorrow. He looked so calm, so controlled, so damned *able*. How do you get through it? he wondered. You're standing there, scratching your ear, looking up the street, listening to Murray telling a joke and you're smiling. How did you learn to pretend it doesn't matter? Where do I sign up for the course?

Because there will be other cases, other victims, other villains. The city breeds them, and it is breeding them into me, too. Any one of these people walking by me now could be part of my next case. What will I be like when I've absorbed all the pain and the anger and the sorrow and the evil this city can create? Do I really want to be that man?

He glanced at his reflection in the darkened window of a nearby chemist. His shadowy self looked attenuated, hollow, and misshapen.

He turned away.

OFFICE POLICY IN BRITAIN:
A REVIEW

OFFICE POLICY
IN BRITAIN:
A REVIEW

GERALD MANNERS

Professor of Geography, University College London

and

DIANA MORRIS

Associate Research Fellow, University College London

Manners, Gerald
    Office policy in Britain : a review.
    1. Offices——Location——Government policy
    ——Great Britain——History
    I. Title   II. Morris, Diana
    338.6'042   HF5547.25

    ISBN 0-86094-212-0

Published by: Geo Books
              Regency House
              34 Duke Street
              Norwich
              NR3 3AP, UK

Printed in Great Britain by J. W. Arrowsmith Ltd. Bristol.

Contents

v

FUTURE.

LIST OF TABLES

LIST OF FIGURES

1

Introduction

Nineteen-sixty-three saw the inauguration of the first attempt
by central government in Britain to influence the location of
employment in private offices. Previously, Whitehall had confined its attention to a periodic review of the location of
Civil Service activities and employment. Local authorities,
through the process of land use planning, had controlled the
siting of office buildings, and hence influenced the geographical distribution of office work and office jobs. With the
creation of the Location of Offices Bureau, however, central
government for the first time gave a public agency directly
under its control the task of persuading the business community
that at least some of its office activities could advantageously
be located in places other than those which were its first and
instinctive choice.

   The decision of a Conservative Government to intervene in
the process of office location in this way flowed from the
development over the previous decade of an influential body of
opinion which believed that office jobs were multiplying in the
centre of London at a fast rate; that the commuters working in
them were imposing an unnecessary strain upon the transport
system of the capital by compounding an already severe problem
of traffic congestion; and that office activities could be
diverted to other locations to the advantage of not only
individual employees, and the firms employing them, but also to
the community as a whole. The Government's initiative was paralleled by other physical planning decisions relating *inter alia*
to green belt and new town policies, all of which were designed
to improve the overall living environment of the metropolis and
the rest of South East England. The establishment of the
Location of Offices Bureau was soon followed by further Government measures to influence the geography of office employment.
Amongst these was the decision to impose a temporary 'ban' upon
further office development in the capital in 1964 and the
introduction of Office Development Permits (ODPs) in the

1

following year.

In 1979, the new Conservative Government decided to abolish the Location of Offices Bureau (LOB). For some 15 years it had provided a great deal of valuable assistance to many in the business community; it had powerfully advocated, through advertising and personal contacts, the advantages of office dispersal from London; and it had encouraged much empirical research into many office location issues. The Government nevertheless took the view that it was no longer necessary for a public agency to continue to influence the geography of office employment. The LOB's role had in fact been officially changed as recently as 1977, in response to the previous Labour Government's perceptions of the inner city 'problem' and of the contribution that existing public agencies might make to its solution. The LOB's demise was in consequence regretted by many who, only some two years earlier and after much careful consideration, had seen a continuing and important role for such a body - although in the holocaust that swept away so many other 'quangos' at this time its closure did not come as a complete surprise.

At around the same time, the Government began to dismantle much of the associated apparatus of intervention in the location of office buildings and jobs, in particular abolishing the system of ODP's and setting aside the existing arrangements for regional strategic planning. A situation emerged, therefore, which was not altogether dissimilar from the circumstances prevailing 20 years earlier. By 1980 it was, in essence, only the local authorities (and central government on appeal) who, through the normal procedures of town and country planning, exerted a public influence over the location of office activities: no formal national strategic office location policy remained.

During the 16 years of active central government intervention in the location of office buildings and work, it was of course the very much more powerful influences of the market which dominated the processes of geographical change in the office sector of the economy. Shortly after the establishment of the Location of Offices Bureau, the office boom of the late 1950s and early 1960s, which was very much focussed upon Central London, began to peter out. For a time the supply of office space appeared to have caught up with demand, and trends in rents suggested a need for the consolidation and modernisation of the country's office stock rather than its further increase. By the late 1960s, however, the continued growth of office employment coupled with steadily rising standards in office working conditions, particularly the increasing amount of space allocated on average to each office employee, meant that demand once again began to outstrip supply. Rents began to move upwards in real terms, and the second post-war office boom gathered pace. Once again it was centred upon London.

Office completions from this speculative boom paralleled (and given the lags in the development cycle extended a year or two beyond) the exceptional burst of national and international economic activity which occurred in the early 1970s before the 1973-1974 oil crisis. The subsequent recession, however, and the associated collapse of rental values, brought this phase of development activity to an end. The mild economic recovery of the mid-1970s caused the market to turn round once again. Rents firmed in nominal, if not real, terms and property speculation looked increasingly attractive. The planning and then the construction of more office buildings began to gather pace once again - to produce a third post-war London office boom. Completions from this phase of development began to come on to the market in the early 1980s. This was a time when both the country and the world were suffering from a renewed, and indeed a particularly severe, economic recession, and when the growth of employment in office activities as a whole was at a virtual standstill. In consequence some observers began to take the view that at least part of this new office space represented a costly and unnecessary oversupply of accommodation.

The 1960s and 1970s also saw, quite independent of government policy, the growth of a substantial volume and range of office work away from the traditional centres of activity in the City and the West End. First, in the suburbs of London; then, in the smaller towns in the South East; later still, in some of the medium-sized and environmentally attractive towns and cities of Southern England; and finally, in the larger provincial centres of the Midlands, new locations began to win the attention of both developers and office employers alike. Shifts in personal and corporate perceptions of what were profitable and attractive locations bore heavily upon the changing geography of the country's office work. Sometimes the views of 'the industry' were closely in line with government preferences. At other times, however, the ambitions and the decisions of office developers and users were considerably at odds with those of the government.

The interrelationship between these 'market forces' and the operation of a public office location policy is the focus of the present study. In particular, the authors have sought to measure the effectiveness of central government's attempts to shape the location of office work, noting its achievements and acknowledging its failures. With government ambitions and market forces at times working in the same direction, however, no precise calculus can be made of the achievements, the benefits and the costs of public policy. What might have happened in the absence of government intervention simply cannot be defined with accuracy. Nevertheless, the possibility of renewed policy intervention in the location of private office activities in the future requires that at least some attempt should be made to learn from past experience. In the context of a wider public debate about the evolution and planning of the country's large metropolitan areas, and the continuing and possibly growing

3

disparity of employment opportunities in the different regions of Britain, there can be no doubt that office location policies will be on the political agenda once again in the near or more distant future, and **possibly** sooner rather than later. The lessons of the past should not be ignored.

This study begins with a survey of events leading up to central government's policy initiatives of the early 1960s (Chapter 2). It then reviews the policy objectives and the instruments of intervention in the 1960s and 1970s, concentrating upon the various attempts to influence the location of private sector office activities and referring only briefly to the several government programmes concerned with relocating civil servants and Civil Service work (Chapter 3). The study next examines policy experience in London in an era of employment expansion and generally quickening decentralisation (Chapter 4). Turning to the destinations of office movement and the growth of office activities in the provinces (Chapter 5), it then focusses upon the emerging new geography of office employment in Britain, attempting *inter alia* to assess the degree to which policy has helped to shape it. The collapse of policy in the late 1970s is discussed next (Chapter 6) and the evidence of these historical reviews drawn together to summarise the lessons of policy intervention in the 1960s and 1970s (Chapter 7). Finally, after briefly reviewing the evidence available on the most recent and prospective trends in the scale and location of office activities, the study concludes with some reflections on the challenges and dilemmas facing policy makers in the future (Chapter 8).

Gerald Manners served as a Member of the Location of Offices Bureau from 1970 - 1979. Diana Morris was Research Officer at the Bureau from 1973 - 1979. The authors acknowledge with thanks the financial assistance of the Economic and Social Research Council in the preparation of this study.

2

Offices in London:
early problems and responses

THE GROWTH OF OFFICE EMPLOYMENT

As in all advanced industrial economies, the last 50 years has
seen the steady growth of office activities in Britain. It was
not until after World War II, however, that they became a
significant component in the country's employment structure.
During the inter-censal period 1951-1961, for example, when
total employment in England and Wales increased by around 7%,
the number of workers in office occupations grew by some 40%.
This was an increase of over 1 million jobs, making the office
workforce at the beginning of the 1960s as large as 4.4 million.
Consequent upon this growth, office workers accounted for about
19% of all employment in England and Wales in 1961, compared
with only 15% a decade earlier (Table 1).

    This expansion of office activities was the result of
three differing but not unrelated trends commonly associated
with the emergence of an 'advanced industrial', and then a 'post-
industrial', economy (1). First, certain service activities
whose labour forces are composed of a high proportion of office
workers, activities such as insurance, banking and certain
professional services, grew significantly as a consequence of
rising industrial and consumer demand. Second, the growing
importance of government led to the recruitment of more civil
servants and, in the educational and health services especially,
an increasing number of administrators. Third, there was a
shift away from manual to non-manual jobs in other sectors of
the economy. In manufacturing, this was brought about partly
by improvements in the productivity of manual labour; it was
also the result of the growing complexity of production processes and the tendency towards a greater sophistication in
business organisation and management. Post-war manufacturing
activity, therefore, rapidly increased its employment of
administrative, technical, professional and clerical workers.
They were engaged in the organisation of production and

5

Table 1. Total employment and office employment in England and
Wales, Greater London, Central Area and the City of
London, 1951, 1961 and 1971

	1951		1961		1971	
	'000s	%	'000s	%	'000s	%
England & Wales						
total	19 940	100	20 913	100	21 587	100
office	3 237	15.9	4 491	20.7	5 440	25.2
Greater London*						
total	4 288	100	4 383	100	3 940	100
office	-	-	1 404	32.0	1 527	38.8
Central Area						
total	1 345	100	1 400	100	1 253	100
office	-	-	754	54.4	732	59.9
City of London						
total	338	100	391	100	341	100
office	211	62.0	264	68.0	255	74.7

* 1951 data for the London conurbation

- Data not available owing to changes in boundaries or the nature of
census returns

Source: Greater London Council (1969), *Greater London Development Plan,
Report of Studies*. London: GLC. Greater London Council (1981),
Evidence to the Coin Street No.2 Inquiry, mimeo.

distribution, in marketing, and in research and development.
It is significant that whilst a substantial proportion - about
60% - of the overall increase in office employment in England
and Wales in the 1950s was in the service sector, some 90% of
the total net expansion of the workforce in manufacturing during
that period was accounted for by the growth of office occupations.

In the context of a national expansion of office employment,
it was not surprising that London in general, and particularly
Central London (Figure 1), should have experienced an outstand-

Figure 1. Greater London, showing the Central Area

ing scale and rate of growth during this period. For long the City and the West End had been the locus for the concentration of a wide range of Britain's office activities. As one central government report put it:

> Central London holds highly specialised and closely interwoven networks of commercial, financial and professional activities. Firms engaged in similar, related or complementary functions are clustered in particular locations. Central banking, insurance, stock-broking, accountancy and legal services are concentrated in the central and northern parts of the City with some in High Holborn. Commercial trading and transport services, together with the commodity markets and import/export services are in the eastern parts of the City. The clothing trade and firms specialising in business services such as advertising, public relations, and management consultancy are in the West End. Architects, consulting engineers and many professional associations are in Victoria/Belgravia; printing and publishing in Fleet Street and Long Acre. These locations may be rooted in history, but the concentration in tight clusters persisting over many years indicates an economic advantage in being near other decision-makers, to have access to a wide range of associated services and expertise, and to minimise the time and costs of communications (2).

The precise nature and magnitude of London's office employment growth in the 1950s remains difficult to establish. The lack of generally available occupational data based upon workplace (as opposed to residence), as well as boundary changes, make it impossible to reconstruct the shifts that were occurring in the economic structure of the capital at that time. Nevertheless, the generality of the situation is quite clear. Developments in the predominantly office-based Insurance, Banking and Finance (IBF) industries, (as defined in the Standard Industrial Classification) which are recorded separately in census data, highlight a major element in the story. In England and Wales, employment in the IBF industries grew by 32% between 1951 and 1961. In Greater London the rate of increase was somewhat slower, some 26%. But because the London conurbation accounted for more than 46% of IBF employment in England and Wales in 1951, this lower rate of growth nevertheless added some 50 000 jobs to employment in the capital. Whilst London's share of certain types of office-based activities was clearly beginning to show signs of decline during the 1950s, the national growth trend nevertheless generated a substantial absolute increase of jobs within the conurbation, and especially in its centre.

The overall level of employment in Central London increased by some 55 000 during the period 1951-1961 (3). The proportion of this growth that was accounted for by office activities is impossible to determine, since workplace data on the occupations of persons in employment in 1961 is only available for a newly defined Central Area (4). It is highly likely that the increase in office jobs was in excess of the total net increase in employment, masking a decline in other activities, particularly

in manufacturing. This was certainly the case in the City of
London. The boundaries of the City were left unchanged by the
London Government Act of 1963 and in consequence trends in
office employment there between 1951 and 1961 can be analysed
in some detail. They provide some very useful clues about the
development of the Central London economy overall.

Office employment in the City increased by about 20%
between 1951 and 1961 (5). This rate of growth was only about
two-thirds that of the equivalent national figure. Nevertheless,
it resulted in an increase of around 45 000 office workers, to
bring total office employment in the 'square mile' up to
264 000. In fact, the City with its favourable office-dominated
employment structure - 65% of all employment in 1951 - generated
over 4% of the total employment growth of England and Wales in
the 1950s. This was from a base of less than 2% of the country's
employment in 1951, and despite its declining share of national
office jobs. The expansion of the City's workforce at this
time owes much to the general increase in the number of IBF
workers. In 1951 nearly 40% (85 000) of the City's office
workers were engaged in these activities. The national growth
of office employment in this sector was over one-third during
the subsequent decade. It is not surprising, therefore, that
27 500 extra office workers in IBF were added to the City's
employment by 1961, representing over 60% of the City's net
increase in total office employment during the decade.

How far the whole of Central London's office activities
reflected the City's experience is open to debate. Had office
employment in the other five central boroughs grown at the rate
of that in the City, office jobs in Central London as a whole
would have expanded by some 120 000. Since the fast-growing
IBF sector was heavily concentrated in the City, however, that
is unlikely to have been the case - particularly since there is
no evidence that the growth of other Central London office
activities, such as the headquarter functions of manufacturing
industry and central government employment, occurred on anything
like the same scale.

Despite the inadequacies of data, however, it is abundantly
clear that Central London as a whole, with an employment
structure heavily oriented towards office-dominated activities,
experienced a considerable growth of office jobs in the 1950s
at a time when that sector of the economy was expanding strongly
in the country as a whole. In the City as least, however, it
has to be added that many aspects of office employment were
either growing at a slower rate, or declining at a faster pace,
than they were throughout England and Wales as a whole. Therefore, although significant absolute increases in office jobs
occurred in Central London between 1950 and 1960 it is important to acknowledge that its office sector was in relative
decline *vis a vis* other parts of Greater London and the country
at large. The activities of the office development industry
confirm this.

In the 1950s the greater part of new office space built in London was for rent rather than for the use of its owners. Marriott (6) suggests 50%, but this figure probably refers to the total stock of office accommodation in London rather than new developments for which the share of owner-occupation was probably very much lower. The expansion of office activities in Central London, therefore, came to be heavily dependent upon the activities of the office development industry and at this time especially upon certain key personalities within it (7). Developers responded actively to the demand for extra office space in the capital. Particularly was this the case in the City where the scope for the redevelopment of bombed sites at this time was considerable. Some 6 million square feet of office space, out of a pre-war total of just under 38 million square feet, had been destroyed between 1939 and 1945. By 1951 the City had granted planning permission for the construction of some 4.8 million square feet of new space and by 1961 the total stock had increased to 43 million square feet. In Central London as a whole, with around 78 million square feet of office floorspace in 1948, an additional 46 million square feet of new office space was built in the following 14 years; offset by 8 million square feet of demolitions, this meant that just under 115 million square feet was available by 1962 (8).

Towards the end of the 1950s and in the early 1960s, however, office developers began to turn their attention to London sites outside the Central Area. They were led, Marriott argues, by the example of decentralised offices commissioned by companies already seeking an escape from the "spiralling cost of land and rising rents in central London" (9), and they were soon offering accommodation in such places as Hammersmith and Ealing, Wembley and Finchley. The County of Middlesex, for example, gave planning permission for some 9 million square feet of offices in the period 1956-1960, a figure that can be compared with a total of 17 million square feet granted in the Central Area of London during the same period. Later, Croydon began an aggressive programme of attracting office development and, by 1964, 2.75 million square feet was either built or under construction in its central area. Already in the early 1960s, therefore, there were visual signs that the "office boom" was beginning to spread outwards towards the periphery of London, while the amount of office space "in the pipeline" in Central London (as measured by outstanding planning permissions) was beginning to tail off (10).

In sum, the changing nature of the British economy in the 1950s generated growth in demands for services and activities which London in general and Central London in particular were well suited to satisfy. Both responded vigorously through the expansion and adaptation of their activities and their work-force, and through the redevelopment of their buildings. Employment and floorspace data together confirm, however, that this growth of office activities was geographically dynamic, and that new locations for office work outside the Central Area were being sought and found by the industry. The emerging Central London "office problem", therefore, must be seen as a

10

consequence of a continuing and, in retrospect, modest expansion
of an existing concentration of activities there, rather than a
growing localisation of the country's dynamic and expanding
office industries at the heart of the capital.

GROWING DISQUIET

Towards the end of the 1950s, the growth of office jobs in the
London area, as evidenced by the expansion of office space and
increasing congestion on the transport system, became a matter
of mounting public concern. To some, the growth was unquestion-
ably excessive.

     Local authorities, for example, reacted strongly to the
changes in the structure of London's economy, and especially to
the increasing dominance of office employment in the activities of the Central Area and the concomitant decline in
the resident population there. In 1951 the *Administrative
County of London Development Plan* (1) proposed, as one of its
objectives, that "the amount of employment in commerce and
other non-manufacturing activities in the Central Area should
be limited and where possible reduced". The solution to the
perceived problems of metropolitan growth and congestion at the
time, however, was in general framed in terms of the need to
promote the decentralisation of manufacturing industry rather
than offices, while land use planning problems were seen to
stem primarily from the "non-conforming" location of factories
and workshops. Such an emphasis within planning thought was
very much in line with the earlier 1944 Abercrombie *Plan for
Greater London* (12) - with its preference for a stable
population in the capital and the planned decentralisation of
"overspill", people and their manufacturing jobs, to free-
standing new towns beyond the Metropolitan Green Belt - and
with the classic 1940 Barlow report on the *Distribution of
Industrial Population* (13). This long-standing neglect of the
office-based component of employment in geographical and
planning debate makes the post-war failure of London planners
to anticipate a growing demand for the development and redevelopment of office space less surprising. At the time that the
Administrative County of London Development Plan was written,
for example, the analysis of future office space demands was
such that planning permission was sanctioned for only 1.7
million square feet of office space in new buildings, rebuildings
and extensions in the Central Area. With the abolition of the
development charge in 1953 and the lifting of building controls
in 1954, this was raised in 1955 to 5.9 million square feet.
By this time, clearly, an 'office boom' was under way.

     In addition to this fundamental failure to recognise and
react to changes in the economy of Central London, there were
other reasons why an increase in the amount of office floorspace
was allowed in the capital despite the original projections and
intentions of the planners. The powers of the London County

11

Council (LCC) to control office development in the Central Area were circumscribed by two factors in particular. Firstly, the plot ratios for office development in various parts of the Central Area as set out in the 1951 Development Plan had been determined on the basis of two propositions: the expectation that the demand for new offices would be such that by no means all potential sites would be developed and the belief that individual sites would not in general be developed to the maximum extent possible. The LCC, in 1957, reviewing the operation of the plot ratio control since 1948, commented that "although plot ratios were stated to be maxima, in practice they have come to be regarded as minima" (14).

Secondly, the powers of the LCC to react to the burgeoning demands for more office space were severely constrained by pre-existing development rights. With reference to plot ratios, for example, consents granted prior to the introduction of plot ratio controls and therefore under older and more flexible standards could not be withdrawn. These developments to some degree set the pattern for rebuilding in Central London and helped to create the situation noted earlier where plot ratios came to be regarded as minimum standards. In addition, many residential properties, particularly in Mayfair, were occupied as offices during and after the war. Although it was the local council's policy to ensure that many of these premises eventually reverted to residential use in order to maintain the varied character of Central London, attempts to enforce that policy met with considerable opposition. As individual cases were reviewed, occupiers were often able to argue successfully that the accommodation was not amenable to adaptation for modern housing.

One of the most important circumscriptions to the LCC's powers to control the expansion of office space, however, was the existence of certain rights to extend existing office buildings. The history of the role played by these Third Schedule Rights, as they were known, in the development of Central London office space is a cautionary tale of the dangers of *ad hoc* and incremental legislation. When, under the Town and Country Planning Act of 1947, development rights were effectively nationalised and a charge was thus to be levied on all land use 'improvements', certain types of minor development were established as being exempt from this development charge. These included generally the right to build minor extensions on to existing uses and specifically to add 10% to the cubic capacity of any building which had been erected prior to the 1947 Act coming into force. Any local authority wishing to revoke these Third Schedule Rights was initially required to compensate potential developers for any abortive expenditure incurred, such as architects' and solicitors' fees. But when the Conservative Government in 1954 amended the financial provisions of the 1947 Act, abolishing the development charge and thereby returning the profits from development to the owners of property with planning permission, compensation for

12

revoked Third Schedule Rights became payable at the full development value. Furthermore, the 1954 Act extended these rights to all buildings, not just those in existence before the "appointed day" (1st July, 1948) of the 1947 Act. With new architectural design and building methods, it was possible for developers - whilst adding only the allowable 10% to the cubic capacity of an existing building - in fact to achieve an increase in floorspace "of the order of 40% in some cases" (15).

Towards the end of the 1950s, when the availability of war-damaged sites for development was becoming exhausted, developers turned their attention increasingly to the opportunities provided for the redevelopment of old office buildings. The local authorities were powerless to prevent such redevelopment unless they were prepared to pay huge sums in compensation for the revocation of Third Schedule Rights. Marriott (16) quotes the case of the New Scotland Yard building as an example of the scale of financial resources that would have been required if the LCC had sought to pursue a policy of strict control over the development of office floorspace. By adding only 10% to the cubic capacity of four linked Victorian buildings, a plot ratio of 7:1 was achieved, which was twice the maximum permitted by the LCC on new office sites in that area. Although the case was never tested in the courts, the LCC was advised that it might be liable to buy the scheme from the developer at its full value on completion of £15 million; if it had then promoted a scheme which was within its own plot ratio standards the cost to the authority, and hence to the taxpayer, for adhering to its policies in respect of that one building alone would have been of the order of £7.5 million.

In its 1957 *Plan to Combat Congestion in London* (17), the LCC expressed publicly its fears that office development in the centre was beginning to pose real problems. The plan pointed in particular to the dangers of "congestion", both on the public transport network and on the roads, and the threats to the character and variety of Central London that stemmed from the growth of office employment there. The plan proposed a reduction in the areas where high plot ratios for office buildings were to be permitted, a policy of encouraging mixed developments to include both office and residential uses, and a decision to exhort other local authorities in the metropolis to promote office development at locations nearer to where the office work-force lived (these residences were, of course, at increasing distances from Central London). This package of policies was later confirmed in the 1960 *Review of the London Development Plan* (18). That document nevertheless acknowledged that much of the development that had taken place during the latter part of the previous decade had been substantially the result of a pent-up demand for the replacement of outdated and war-damaged buildings during the earlier period of building restrictions, rather than a net addition to the capital's stock of office buildings.

The theme of journey-to-work problems and of traffic congestion caused by the growth of Central London was echoed by

13

the transport authorities. Between 1952 and 1962, an extra
134 000 passengers were entering the Central Area during the
morning rush hours, with increases on all modes of transport
other than buses and pedal cycles. Increasingly, crowded
surface and underground trains, especially during the morning
and evening rush hours, were causing mounting press and public
complaints. In the absence of substantial subsidies, however,
the costs of investing further to improve the public transport
system - let alone to extend it - were greater than could be
justified by acceptable levels of fares. At the same time, it
had become apparent by the early 1960s that the main cause of
traffic congestion was not the increasing demands being made on
public road transport facilities, but the persistent growth in
the use of the private car. While the total number of public
transport passengers reached a peak in 1962 (19), those travelling by car continued to increase throughout and beyond that
decade. Indeed, London Transport argued that much of the steady
decline in the use of bus services was in fact the result of
road congestion, caused by the growing use of private cars for
the journey-to-work to offices in Central London.

In addition to the concerns of London's statutory planning
agencies, anxiety was also increasingly being expressed about
the apparent rise of office employment in the capital by several
independent but nevertheless influential observers. At the
British Association meeting in 1959, for example, Geoffrey
Powell (20), a planning official at the Ministry of Housing and
Local Government, questioned the Abercrombie assumption that the
population and activities of the London conurbation could be
largely contained within the existing built-up area, together
with the first generation of new towns located beyond the
Metropolitan Green Belt. He argued for a South East regional
strategy that would manage and steer the geographical distribution of an inevitable rise in both manufacturing and office
employment in the London city-region - partly in order to make
adequate provision for accommodation and work, and partly to
prevent the eventual collapse of green belt policy.

Probably the most influential body of the independent
observers, however, was the Town and Country Planning Association
(TCPA). Having organised a conference in 1958 to "explore the
possibilities of office decentralisation", a special study group
was set up to investigate "the effect of growth of office employment, particularly in Central London, on congestion in the
Greater London area, and the extent to which decentralisation
is a practical solution". Eventually, in 1962, *The Paper
Metropolis* (21) was published to report the findings of the study
group. It assumed at the outset that some 15 000 office jobs
had been created in Central London each year during the previous
decade, and pointed to the adverse journey-to-work consequences
of the divergent trends in the location of homes and of jobs.
In addition, the findings of a survey of some 60 decentralised
office firms, indicating the economic and social advantages of
dispersal, were enthusiastically detailed. On the basis of the

study group's findings, therefore, recommendations were made by the TCPA to government on the policy options available for dealing with the office "congestion" problem. The tone was one of urgency, seeking to impress upon Ministers the need for prompt action if a planning crisis was to be averted. At the root of their concern - it should be stressed - were their perceptions of the rates of expansion both in office space and in office jobs in Central London.

Central government's direct intervention in the sphere of office development and employment during the 1950s had been confined simply to the amendment of local planning policies towards offices as expressed in statutory land use plans. For example, the Minister for Housing and Local Government, in approving the London development plan in 1955 returned some 380 acres of land allocated to industrial and office development to residential use; he also inserted a policy statement to ensure that in the 'central zone' residential premises with temporary consents for office purposes should revert to their former use. In approving plans for Outer London, the Minister requested the local authorities to make provision for new offices in their areas in order to facilitate the policy of controlling office development in Central London. More enterprisingly, the Minister of Housing and Local Government in 1960, Henry Brooke, wrote a letter to 200 firms in Central London exhorting them to decentralise office employment. However, unlike policies directed towards the location of manufacturing industry, there was no central government intervention in the process of office development through the mechanism of floorspace controls.

Office employment, moreover, still lacked a place in spatial development policies at the inter-regional scale. Towards the end of the 1950s, with the economy moving into temporary recession, there was a renewed interest by government in the national distribution of employment and the possibilities of relieving the problems of those areas with persistently high levels of unemployment. Yet the policies of the Board of Trade continued to be directed towards the redistribution of manufacturing industry. They ignored office employment. In 1959, when the Local Employment Bill was being discussed in the House of Commons, it was suggested by Douglas Jay, later to become President of the Board of Trade, that there should be "just as tight a control over office development as over factory development" (22). In the contemporary preoccupation with the role that manufacturing industry might play in regional policy, however, the suggestion was not immediately taken up. In consequence central government remained essentially a by-stander as office employment grew in the London region generally and as the problems of congestion in the Central Area, in particular, steadily worsened. It was an apparent indifference which, as will be seen later, did not last for long.

15

Although the Macmillan Government did not consider it necessary
to take a view on the growth and the location of office employment in the context of their response to the recession of the
late 1950s and the enactment of the Local Employment Act 1960,
there were clear signs at the turn of the decade that the increase in office jobs and the burgeoning of office space in
Central London were beginning to cause serious Ministerial
concern. The only data on employment growth that was available
at that time (until the 1961 Census data were published in 1966)
were Ministry of Labour estimates. These estimates suggested -
erroneously, as it later transpired - that total employment in
Central London had risen by some 150 000 jobs between 1951 and
1961. Most of these extra jobs, it was assumed, were in offices.
It was against this estimate that the TCPA developed its arguments about the need to constrain the rapid growth of Central
London office employment, corroborated as it apparently was by
increases in commuting figures and the visible growth of office
floorspace. The Standing Conference on London Regional Planning
(23) calculated that, at the end of 1962, existing commitments
(in outstanding planning permissions, in zonings in the development plan and in Third Schedule liabilities) could add an extra
171 500 office jobs to the Central London workforce, (although
it was admitted that the actual increase was more likely to be
of the order of 125 000, allowing for density changes and for
permissions not being taken up). On this evidence, the case for
restrictions on development appeared overwhelming.

The planning consequences of such a scale of office employment growth were in fact most clearly set out in the Government's
White Paper on *London - Employment: Housing: Land* (24), which
appeared in 1963 and substantially reiterated the TCPA's earlier
understanding of the scale of office growth in Central London
and expectation that it would continue. Coupled with the trend
towards more dispersed patterns of residential location, the
transport consequences of this growth were already judged to be
burdensome. Prospectively they would be unmanageable. It was
argued that the additional office employees required to staff a
further expansion of office activities in Central London could
only be housed at increasing distances from the City and the
West End, and in areas served by the suburban railway lines.
Even allowing for improvements, the capacity of these lines
would quickly become "exhausted if the present rate of increase
in employment in Central London continues" (25).

Such (strictly) planning arguments for controlling the
further expansion of office floorspace in Central London were
reinforced by the growing public concern over the 'changing
face' of Central London. The destruction of Victorian theatres
and office buildings to make way for redevelopment provoked
emotionally hostile reactions to many of the modern office
buildings. Moreover, the architectural quality of at least
some of the new developments which replaced older buildings was
open to question - while those which met with professional

16

acclaim were often disliked by the general public. These
attitudes enhanced the political acceptability of any attempt
to restrict further office construction.

Although there appeared to be widespread support for a
policy of diverting growth away from Central London, opinions
varied on the best means of achieving that end. The TCPA's
recommendations (26) to the Minister for Housing and Local
Government suggested that strict control over office development
in Central London should be combined with encouraging office
development both in suburban locations and in a number of
selected centres beyond the Greater London conurbation. While
rejecting as impracticable both floorspace controls (the use,
that is, of office development certificates comparable to the
Industrial Development Certificates already in use to restrain
manufacturing expansion in the region) and a standstill on new
office building, the TCPA concluded that the Paris system of
levying varying levels of tax on office development in different
zones merited 'close examination'. They also argued that Third
Schedule Rights should be rescinded and that other forms of
control such as a payroll tax should be investigated.

A major gulf existed, however, between the perceptions of
reality, as seen by most observers in the late 1950s, and the
evolution of events as they can now be interpreted. The central
divergence concerned the scale of the growth of office employment in Central London. As was pointed out earlier in this
chapter, even now there is no hard evidence on the pace of
growth of office employment *per se* in Central London during the
1950s. What is known, however, is that total employment in
Central London was growing, not at the rate of 15 000 jobs per
year - the estimate on which pressures for an office policy were
substantially based - but at rather less than 6 000 jobs per
year. The evidence indicating this significantly slower rate
of growth did not appear until 1966 when the employment tabu-
lations of the 1961 Census became available. Moreover, the
Census revealed that the bulk of employment growth in the South
East had taken place not, as had been previously assumed,
within Greater London but in the rest of the South East region.
The Standing Conference on London and South East Regional
Planning commented in 1966 that:

> the dynamic of the Conference area's economy appears to be very
> different from what has been thought hitherto... Had this Census
> data been available when the (1964) *South East Study* was prepared,
> significantly different conclusions about the trends in the region
> and the proposals to meet them might have been made (27).

How had these earlier erroneous conclusions been arrived
at? In the absence of Census data, planning authorities had
perforce to rely upon estimates derived from Ministry of Labour
data, themselves based on the numbers of insurance cards
exchanged in different areas. It is unclear why this method
should so seriously have over-estimated employment growth in
London during the 1950s. Partial explanations may be found in

17

the inclusion of all part-year employees in the Ministry's data
and the statistical 'allocation' of the dispersed employees of
many firms to central workplaces where for administrative
reasons their cards were exchanged. Data for Central London,
with its relatively high labour turnover and its concentration
of head office activities, are likely to be singularly suscep-
tible to these problems.

As has been seen, however, the overestimates of employment
growth produced by the data from the Ministry of Labour were
apparently corroborated by other evidence. In particular, the
high level of office development activity in Central London
visually reinforced the impression of rapid employment growth.
Unfortunately, the monitoring of floorspace changes and their
effects upon employment was far from adequate. In their
Review of the London Development Plan in 1960, the LCC confessed
that it had "not been possible to compile records of office
floorspace lost through change of use or demolition of old
premises" (28). Thus, no data on the net growth in office floorspace were available. More importantly, perhaps, trends in the
numbers of office workers housed in new developments were not
investigated. As a result, an important consideration in assessing the employment-generating effects of floorspace growth -
that of the increasing floorspace/worker ratios resulting from
improving space standards for all workers and from the relative
shift towards higher-level office occupations - was not taken
into account.

The assumption of rapid growth in the number of Central
London jobs was further reinforced by the steady increase,
mentioned earlier, of 150 000 peak-hour commuters during the
period 1952-1962 (29). It was assumed that this phenomenon was
the result of an extension of Central London's labour catchment
area caused wholly by an increased demand for labour, and therefore that it reflected a net increase in the level of employment
there. In the light of subsequent information, however, it
became apparent that two other factors, simultaneously widening
the catchment area for Central London's labour force and thus
adding to the commuting population, had been ignored. First,
during the period 1951-1961 Inner London, despite an increase
in activity rates, lost 32 626 resident employees as a result
of population decentralisation. In such a circumstance, even
a stable level of employment with an unchanging occupational
structure would have led to high commuting levels. Second, the
greater propensity for office workers to live in Outer London
and beyond meant that even a stable total employment in the
conurbation, encompassing a shift from manual to non-manual
activities, would in isolation have also caused commuting to
increase.

All three available sets of information relating to London's
employment planning problems - those on the number of jobs, on
the creation of new floorspace and on journeys-to-work conspired
to indicate an increasing concentration of jobs in Central London,
particularly in offices. Two questions naturally follow. First,

18

did the false assumptions about the magnitude of employment growth eventually lead to the adoption of inappropriate policies towards the office sector in Central London? Second, if indeed a legitimate basis for public concern did exist, why did the market itself not provide adequate signals of land and space scarcity and the costs of congestion which would have set in train appropriate adjustments?

With regard to the second question, it could be argued that, if the problems of congestion in Central London were becoming ever-more severe, market forces would in time have ensured that it was brought to a halt and even reversed. Labour shortages, for example, would have begun to force up the costs to employers who would also have had to compensate employees for journey-to-work difficulties. At the same time, the pressures on office space would have led to escalating rents. Firms would have moved out of the centre until equilibrium in the Central London labour and office space markets was substantially restored. Although this natural dispersal was to some degree already operating, its scale was relatively modest. It is estimated that around 1000 jobs per annum were being decentralised from the Central Area at the end of the 1950s (compared with around 12 000-15 000 per annum at the height of decentralisation in the mid-1970s). A number of reasons might be suggested for this early reluctance of firms to decentralise.

First, at the time, the majority of Central London firms were small, and if they needed to maintain a presence there they would have found it impracticable to split their organisations. Later, with the growth of office firms in the capital and the processes of consolidation and merger, partial decentralisation became a realistic proposition. Second, in the late 1950s, the increasing problem of labour shortages was to some degree temporarily alleviated by the employment of a greater number of female workers, made possible by the decline of manufacturing activities in London and increasing female labour force partipation. Third, it has also to be recognised that the absolute differential between the costs of operating offices in Central London and suburban locations remained quite modest in the late 1950s and early 1960s. Geographical variations in both rents and the costs of labour (which made up a much larger share of total office operating costs) were small (30), so that in this respect market forces and prices were not yet reflecting the true cost of congestion. Later, during the mid and late 1960s, although the relative position of Central Area and suburban costs remained broadly similar, the absolute differentials became progressively greater and thus constituted a stengthening 'push factor' in decentralisation. At the beginning of the 1960s, however, the practicability of decentralisation was relatively restricted by the limited availability of office space outside the Central Area, whilst the feasibility of operating from a non-central location had hardly been demonstrated for activities in financial and professional services which made up the core of Central London office activities. Most of the

19

early decentralisers, it should be noted, were offices in the manufacturing sector. For all these reasons, planning authorities - both central and local - could be justified in their conclusions that market forces alone were insufficient to effect an immediate response to a perceived crisis in the development of Central London and that public intervention was required to speed up the process of market adjustment.

Returning to the fact that false assumptions were made about the scale of office employment growth in Central London during the 1950s, it might be argued that pressure for the restriction of office development and the decentralisation of office employment would have been substantially weaker had the actual and really rather modest growth in office jobs there been appreciated. However, this is not necessarily the case. By 1960, a number of problems were mounting both in London and what is now called the Outer Metropolitan Area (OMA) which suggested the need for at least some public supervision of the changing pattern of office location in the city-region. These problems stemmed in particular from the management of transport and land use change.

The growing specialisation of Central London's economy upon office activities, for example, posed obvious difficulties for planning the development of the capital's transport system. The increasingly dispersed residential pattern of office workers was partly responsible for these problems. But the rising incomes and the growing access of the workforce to private motor transport were also to blame. Marriott (31) argued that the answer to the journey-to-work difficulties was both "a radical improvement in roads and railways" and policies "to increase greatly (the amount of) residential accommodation near the Central Area", rather than solutions based upon a decentralisation strategy. To these suggested policies could be added measures to control the use of the private car as a means of travel to work in Central London. Yet, while the possibility of a substantially increased investment in transport infrastructure was regularly and seriously considered, it was equally regularly rejected (as, for example, in the 1963 White Paper) as being too expensive. The Barbican scheme was a gesture in the direction of providing and encouraging more residential accommodation in and near the centre; but it was not followed up with more substantial plans. Measures to ration or price private car transport in ways that might discourage its use for commuting were always relatively tentative and inevitably had only modest results.

Setting aside the various arguments for and against attempting to control the overall level of office development in the capital, it is clear that the general problem of road traffic congestion might have been ameliorated by office siting policies that steered new developments towards some of the principal nodes in the public transport network. It was not until considerably later, however, when much of the demand for Central London office space had been satisfied elsewhere within the Central Area, that the development of space adjacent to the main line termini was (first) permitted and (later) encouraged.

20

As far as land use planning in the City and Westminster was concerned, the growth of office employment, coupled as it was with rising floorspace standards, necessarily implied an encroachment of office activities on other users of Central London land. Conventional economic analysis would suggest that such an emerging pattern of land uses merely reflected the most efficient use of resources in the short-term. However, one of the declared aims of Central London planning was to preserve as much as possible of the varied character and activities there. It was proving to be a losing battle. Residential accommodation in and around the Central Area was steadily being squeezed out by competing land uses, especially offices. This in turn adversely affected the local labour market and, for example, in the early 1960s was clearly exacerbating staff shortages in many public services, including transport. More-over, the longer-term consequences of allowing Central London to become an area given over largely to a single land use, whose importance to developments in the national economy might possibly diminish over time, were legitimate causes for concern.

Thus, the realities of London's development as an office centre demanded some form of public intervention. The question is whether a different policy response would have emerged had contemporary analyses recognised that London's 'office problem' stemmed largely from the widening of the labour catchment area for a modestly increasing number of office activities in Central London, rather than from a rapid rate of past, current and prospective expansion of office employment. What measures would have been necessary to deal with London's journey-to-work problems? Two alternative sets of policies may be proposed, the first designed to alleviate the problems associated with accommodating the existing level of office jobs in Central London and the second seeking to reduce that level. The first set of policies would have involved, as has been suggested, major new investments in the public transport system, coupled with effective controls over the use of private cars and a programme of residential development and rehabilitation in and around Central London. The second alternative package of policies - designed to reduce office employment - would have inevitably included controls over the construction of additional office space, plus measures to reduce the existing number of office jobs (such as a payroll tax), positive encouragement for firms to decentralise and action to ensure that vacated space was not occupied by office users.

Whether either package of policies would have been pursued had a more accurate understanding of the problem been developed, must remain open to speculation. Certainly the tenor of the 1963 White Paper would suggest that measures which were either costly or directly infringed private rights, whether of motorists or office employees, would have been ruled out on political grounds. But the contemporary analysis of the problem shifted the focus of concern away from the need to deal with existing transport planning problems, which would not be eradicated by a marginal reduction in the number of jobs in Central London, to a desire to stem any further growth in the level of employment there. Thus, the decentralisation alternative (albeit a weakened version, as will be seen) was the preferred solution.

The adoption of the decentralisation option had the added attraction of appearing to be a response to the inter-regional consequences of the growth of office employment in Central London. In the 1950s and the early part of the 1960s, the overall buoyancy of the South East office economy was attracting many migrants from other regions. For example, during the period 1961-1966, 37 000 of the 41 000 economically active in-migrants were office workers. There were, in consequence, strong arguments on regional development and inter-regional equity grounds that the growth of office activities in the London region should if possible be restrained and diverted elsewhere to help improve the impoverished occupational structure and the longer-term growth prospects of the peripheral regions. Indeed, the possibility of longer distance office dispersal was in fact alluded to in the 1963 White Papers on both London (32) and the North East (33); the former argued that "Regions with unemployment should benefit from the diversion of some of this (London's office) employment".

Thus, while the 'problems' of the London region alone might have been solved by policies relating to improved transport provision and the location of residential development, the dual aims of intra-regional and inter-regional planning could only have been jointly met by the deliberate diversion of some office employment from Central London. Unfortunately, as will be seen later, by the time that public policy began to respond to the growth of office activities and such a strategy had been adopted, Central London's office employment was beginning to stabilise and the first post-war office property boom had begun to falter. Market circumstances were changing.

REFERENCES AND NOTES

1. D. Bell (1974), *The Coming of Post-Industrial Society*. London: Heinemann.

2. Department of the Environment (1976), *Office Location Review*. London: DOE, para 2.15.

3. Defined as the boroughs of City, Westminster, Holborn, Finsbury, St. Pancras and St. Marylebone.

4. Some 750 000 workers were employed in the Central Area in 1961, whereas the more narrowly defined Central Boroughs had, in 1951, an office workforce of 612 000.

5. Data in this paragraph are based upon the analysis of the Economists Advisory Group (1971), *An Economic Study of the City of London*. London: Allen and Unwin. They used a

slightly different definition of office employment from that used earlier and in Table 1.

6. O. Marriott (1967), *The Property Boom*. London: Pan, p.210.

7. *ibid.*, passim.

8. Minister of Housing and Local Government (1963), *London - Employment: Housing: Land,* Cmnd. 1952. London: HMSO, p.14.

9. O. Marriott, *op cit.*, p.208.

10. *ibid.*, p.199.

11. London County Council (1951), *Administrative County of London Plan 1951, Analysis*. London: LCC, para 495.

12. P. Abercrombie (1944), *Greater London Plan*. London: HMSO.

13. Royal Commission on the Distribution of Industrial Population (1940), (Chairman: Sir M. Barlow), Cmnd. 6153. London: HMSO.

14. London County Council (1957), *Plan to Combat Congestion in Central London*. London: LCC, p.16.

15. Minister of Housing and Local Government (1963), *op cit.*, p.5 and p.15.

16. O. Marriott (1967), *op cit.*, p.199.

17. London County Council (1957), *op cit.*, pp.5-9.

18. London County Council (1960), *Review of the London Development Plan*. London: LCC.

19. Greater London Council (1969), *Greater London Development Plan, Report of Studies*. London: GLC, p.178, passim.

20. A.G. Powell (1960), "The recent development of Greater London", *Advancement of Science,* May, pp.76-86.

21. Town and Country Planning Association (1962), *The Paper Metropolis*. London: TCPA.

22. D. Jay in *Hansard*, 9th November, 1959, London: HMSO, p.141.

23. Standing Conference on London Regional Planning (1964), *Office Employment in the Conference Area,* LRP 279. London: SCLRP.

24. Minister of Housing and Local Government (1963), *op cit.*

25. *ibid.*, para.15.

26. Town and Country Planning Association (1962), *op cit.*

27. Standing Conference on London and South East Regional
    Planning (1966), *Population and Employment in the
    Conference Area,* LRP 721. London: SCLSERP.

28. London County Council (1960), *op cit.*   .

30. Town and Country Planning Association (1958), *Office
    location in the London Region,* Report of a Conference,
    mimeo.

31. O. Marriott, *op cit.,* p.215.

32. Minister of Housing and Local Government (1963), *op cit.*

33. Secretary of State for Industry, Trade and Regional
    Development (1963), *The North East,* Cmnd. 2206.
    London: HMSO.

3

A national office policy for
the 1960s and early 1970s

THE EMERGENCE OF A POLICY, 1960-1963

By the beginning of the 1960s, as was noted in the previous
chapter, a considerable body of opinion was demanding action to
control and even to direct the location of office development
and employment. This attitude formed part of a wider concern
over the inadequacies of the arrangements for the planning of
the London region. During the previous decade it had become
increasingly clear that the Ministry Memorandum of 1947 (1),
based on the Abercrombie proposals and continuing to be the
only central government directive on the planning of the region,
no longer provided an appropriate framework. Although the
Town Planning Institute as early as 1956 had pointed to the
"lack of any machinery in which to effect the coordination of
development in the region" (2), no action to rectify the situation had been taken. In 1959, however, the Surrey County
Council - under increasing pressure to allow further housing
development in particular, and having experienced during the
previous five years a population increase of the order of
60 000 persons (including some 27 000 in its green belt) - took
the initiative. It asked the LCC to convene a conference of all
the planning authorities in London and the Home Counties "in
order to consider how far the growth of employment in the region
could in fact be restrained, or alternatively what consequential
development plan provisions should be made" (3). Although
agreement on setting up such a conference had been reached by
late 1960, its establishment was delayed by the appointment of
a Royal Commission on Local Government in Greater London (4)
whose recommendations eventually led to the replacement of the
LCC by the GLC administering a more extensive area. It was
soon recognised, however, that whatever administrative arrangements might eventually emerge for the planning of the London
conurbation and region, certain employment, housing and land
use issues could not properly be resolved within one authority's

25

boundaries. The Standing Conference on London Regional Planning was therefore established in 1962.

Through the Conference, local authorities expressed collective concern about the continuing growth of office employment in the region. The LCC, in its 1957 *Plan to Combat Congestion in Central London,* as well as amending its office zoning arrangements in an attempt to restrict the further growth of office space, had advocated a policy of decentralisation to areas beyond its boundaries. To this end the LCC had produced propaganda which exhorted firms to disperse from the Central Area. It pointed to the development opportunities available generally in the Home Counties, as well as the New and Expanded Towns, and quoted various 'success stories' (5). Yet by the early 1960s the willingness of those surrounding counties to cooperate in an office decentralisation strategy was beginning to disappear. Middlesex and Essex, as well as Surrey, criticised the *First Review of the London Development Plan* on the grounds that its provisions failed to control adequately the expansion of Central London's office activities. The shire authorities objected to the fact that, without strict control at the centre, the provision of office accommodation within their administrative areas to house Central London decentralisers was merely adding to the volume of office employment in the region. It therefore became apparent that the relief of London's planning problems via a policy of office dispersal could no longer solely rely upon cooperation between the LCC and the Home Counties but required regional or indeed central guidance. Thus, an appreciation of the interdependence of employment problems throughout the whole of the South East, and the need to draw up strategies covering the constituent administrative units gained increasing currency.

This recognition of the desirability of a regional planning policy was symbolised by the initiation in 1962 of the *South East Study* (6) by the Ministry of Housing and Local Government. It was part of a wider awareness of the inadequacies of the planning attitudes and institutions which had developed once the preoccupations with post-war reconstruction waned. New thinking about urban planning, for example, was increasingly being aired. In particular, the growing conflicts between the expansion of road transport, both private and commercial, and existing urban structures were exposed and examined in the Buchanan report on *Traffic in Towns* (7). Not only did that report suggest the need for radical departures in the planning of urban form but also, in the Preface of its Steering Group, the advantages of innovative administrative arrangements including a fuller exploitation of Development Corporation arrangements to override the inadequacies of existing modes of local administration.

Moreover, at the national level, it became apparent that the British economy, after enjoying the advantages of an early return to peace-time production in the immediate post-war period, was experiencing a somewhat slower rate of growth than its

Western European neighbours. Recognition of this emerging
problem and of the failure of relatively *laissez-faire* policies
led to the establishment of the National Economic Development
Council in 1962. The first task of the Council was to examine
the possibility of achieving faster economic growth and the
obstacles in its path. The Council reported that one of the
means by which such an objective might be attained, whilst
avoiding the dangers of 'wage push' inflation and further
'congestion' which might arise from continued and unchecked
development in the South East, was to encourage the use of
labour reserves that existed in the peripheral regions of the
country where structural maladjustments had left a legacy of
relatively high levels of unemployment and low activity rates.
It was thought that a strengthening of regional policies could
make a significant contribution to national employment and
economic growth (8). Thus the political pressures to reduce
regional inequalities were reinforced by arguments about
national economic efficiency.

Such a new attitude to the spatial structure of the
British economy, and the willingness generally to consider more
'dirigiste' policies than had prevailed during the 1950s, was
paralleled by a growing concern with regional issues throughout
many of the unitary states of Western Europe. In France, for
example, a Committee of Regional Plans had been established in
1958 to coordinate the preparation of separate economic and
social development plans for each region, and in 1962 the
process of 'regionalisation' of the Fourth National Plan was
begun with the introduction of regional sections - *tranches
operatoires*.

At the beginning of the 1960s, therefore, it was widely
accepted that, firstly, as far as the physical planning of the
South East was concerned, and particularly with regard to
employment issues, the existing arrangements consisting of
uncoordinated local policies were no longer appropriate; and
secondly that the overall performance of the British economy
might be improved by more concerted public attempts to facili-
tate the adaptation of the country's spatial structure,
especially by reducing regional levels of unemployment. This
new climate of opinion paved the way for the introduction of
measures to influence the distribution of office employment,
initially by the Conservative Government in 1963 and later,
more forcibly, by the new Labour Administration in 1964.

OFFICE POLICY FOR LONDON AND THE SOUTH EAST

In 1963 the Conservative Government responded to the pressures
for a greater central influence upon the planning policies for
the London region in the White Paper entitled *London - Employment:
Housing: Land* (9). As was noted in the previous chapter, it
substantially endorsed the TCPA's analysis of the office

27

problems of the capital that had been outlined in *The Paper Metropolis,* and recognised the increasing pressure being placed upon the region's housing and transport system by the continuing growth of office employment in the Central Area. The policy proposals adopted in the White Paper, however, were a considerably weakened version of the TCPA's recommendations.

With regard to the methods available to control office development, the Government had examined the possibility of introducing a system of licences for the construction of new office buildings, somewhat akin to the Industrial Development Certificates that were used to influence the geography of new manufacturing plant. It accepted the objection raised by the TCPA, however, that the system would be difficult to implement both effectively and fairly because office developments, unlike much industrial floorspace, were often built speculatively and occupied by a number of different firms, both simultaneously and consecutively. The TCPA had recommended instead that new financial measures to control office development and employment should be investigated. It offered for consideration both a payroll tax and a levy on office development, which might vary from area to area according to the degree of 'congestion'. Such measures had been adopted in the Paris region a few years earlier.

These proposals were, however, ignored in the White Paper. Instead, the goverment decided to rely only upon amending Third Schedule Rights as they applied to office development. They reduced the tolerance limits on rebuilding from 10% of cubic capacity to 10% of the floorspace for office buildings erected before the Town and Country Planning Act 1947 came into force, and they removed altogether the right to enlarge buildings constructed after that date. According to the LCC, this measure had the effect of reducing their commitments to further office development by some 10 million square feet. The LCC nevertheless criticised the proposals of the White Paper on the grounds that, had the extension to existing use rights as embodied in the Third Schedule been abolished entirely, 17 million square feet of potential office floorspace would have been removed from its commitments (10).

The TCPA had argued that one of the benefits of a levy on Central London employers, such as payroll tax or special local authority rates, would be to "drive home to office employers the advantages of decentralisation" (11). In the strategy adopted by the Government, however, this latter objective was to be achieved by persuasion rather than financial sanction. To this end the Location of Offices Bureau was to be set up by the Minister for Housing and Local Government. The LOB, duly established by Order in Council in April 1963, was given the specific task of encouraging "the decentralisation of office employment from congested areas in Central London to suitable centres elsewhere" (12). Its functions were to include the promotion of publicity and research, and the provision of information. The LOB was established on the assumption that

there were imperfections in the markets that influenced the
location of office space and office employment. It was
believed that once businessmen were made aware of the true
facts about the private costs of maintaining an office in
Central London, compared with those in alternative locations,
they would decentralise some or all of their activities from
the metropolitan core. To appeal to its potential clientele
the LOB was to adopt more of a business approach to relocation
than was traditional among government agencies. The Chairman
and the Members of the Bureau were initially drawn from the
business community and, although the original nucleus of full-
time jobs were filled by seconded civil servants, the agency
was given permission to recruit its own staff.

The objective of the White Paper was in part to secure a
reduction in or a stabilisation of the level of employment in
Central London. There was little overt concern about the
benefits which might accrue to those areas which received
decentralised employment, or how these benefits might be
distributed. Some discussion of the types of destination which
might attract dispersed office activities was nevertheless
noted in the White Paper with suburban centres in London, the
New Towns and the larger urban centres of the south of England
(such as Reading and Norwich), as well as the peripheral regions,
being mentioned. It was suggested that at some later stage,
following discussions with local authorities, a list of preferred
locations would be drawn up. The central strategy on office
employment that was formally initiated by the White Paper itself,
however, simply sought to encourage the dispersal of private
sector office employment away from Central London regardless of
distance or direction, through the activities of the Location
of Offices Bureau. It was assumed that the destination of
office movement would be properly determined by the preferences
of the firms concerned, within of course the constraints set by
the land use planning policies of the receiving local authorities.

In tandem with this policy towards private sector office
employment, Civil Service work was also to be encouraged to
disperse. The White Paper announced a review of the location
of government work, to be undertaken by Sir Gilbert Flemming.
He reported later in 1963 and the Government adopted his
recommendation to disperse some 18 000 jobs. Of this total,
10 500 jobs would 'for practical reasons' remain either on the
periphery of the London area or within two hours' travelling
time of Central London. Some 7 500 jobs in the Post Office
Savings Bank were to be dispersed further afield (eventually the
move took place to Durham). According to the Chancellor of the
Exchequer's statement at that time, the Flemming recommendations
would bring the number of government headquarters staff located
outside Central London to just under 50% - some 60 000 out of a
total of 133 000 (13).

The need for employment dispersal was reiterated in the
South East Study. Published in 1964, it was based upon the
expectation of a substantial growth of population both in the

29

country as a whole and in its largest region (14). The Study
reached the conclusion that, without determined intervention,
London's employment - and particularly its office employment -
would continue to grow. Hence, "a big change in the economic
balance within the South East is needed to moderate the dominance
of London and to get a more even distribution of growth (15).
To this end a stategy was proposed which sought to build up
major alternative centres of population and employment
in the region, including the development of new cities such as
Southampton/Portsmouth and the expansion of a host of other
towns. Other than urging the general need for dispersal,
however, the Study's conclusions with specific regard to the
location of office employment were vague. The suitability of
some of the proposed major growth centres for office employment
was briefly demonstrated. At the same time it was recognised
that many of the region's smaller towns on the south coast and
in the Metropolitan Green Belt could also accommodate a
"moderate growth of office employment". It was simultaneously
acknowledged that many firms for sound business reasons would
need to remain on the periphery of the London conurbation. Thus,
although the physical planning strategy advocated in the Study
was one of concentrated dispersal, no such recommendations were
made with respect to office employment.

The Conservative Government's *South East Study* was super-
seded by the *Strategy for the South East,* hastily prepared in
1967 by the newly-established South East Economic Planning
Council (16). In its suggested provisions for accommodating
further urban growth in the region, the Strategy proposed several
major growth points in South Hampshire and in the Ashford and
Bletchley areas. It also suggested the encouragement of
'counter-magnets' (to London) outside the region at Swindon,
Northampton and Ipswich. The Strategy thus argued for a rather
more concentrated pattern of decentralised office employment
than that advocated in the 1964 Study, and placed particular
emphasis upon the need to steer such employment into the larger
growth centres in order to ensure their viability and 'self-
sufficiency'. Nevertheless, it was again advocated that the
prime aim of office location policy should be to reduce the
scale of office employment in Central London, and that provision
should be made for a multiplicity of relatively small office
developments in many alternative locations. In contrast to
earlier thinking, however, the 1967 Strategy argued that the
accommodation of office employment over and above existing
commitments in many of the London suburbs was undesirable, since
the outer suburbs in particular were "already experiencing
traffic pressures and congestion" (17).

The early and mid-1960s, therefore, saw the principle of
office decentralisation - both for the private and for the
public sectors of the economy - established as part of central
government policy towards the spatial development of the South
East. Subsequent plans for the region (18) also assumed the
wisdom of that policy but, rather than offering locationally
specific proposals for accommodating office dispersal, they

provided no more than a broad and flexible spatial framework within which decentralisation might be encouraged and accommodated. Only in the 1967 Strategy, and assisted as will be seen later by the introduction of central government floorspace controls, was it suggested that large scale office developments should be concentrated in the (proposed) major growth centres. Despite this new concern with the destinations of office moves, the overriding aim of government policy thinking continued to be the control of office employment growth in Central London.

OFFICES AND REGIONAL POLICY

As has been seen, the Central London office 'problem' was the initial spur to, and the focus of, central government intervention in the location of office activities. Even though mention was made in the 1963 White Paper of the contribution that office employment might make to "regions with unemployment", the policies adopted were framed very much in terms of metropolitan planning issues. Nevertheless, around this time a new understanding of the complex employment problems of the country's peripheral regions was beginning to emerge.

The 1961 Toothill report on the Scottish economy (19) had discussed the need for employment diversification to replace declining basic industries with new science-based manufacturing activities such as electronics. No consideration was given, however, to the role that the office or service employment might potentially play in the revitalisation of the Scottish economy. By 1963, in contrast, attitudes had significantly changed. The Government's White Paper on *The North East* (20) published in that year recognised the desirability of developing in the region a "wider range of trade and commerce" which would provide "a better balance of employment" there. Nevertheless, the Conservative Government's formal policy towards the location of office employment contained no special provisions for promoting inter-regional office mobility, other than the incentives available in the areas of high unemployment for any manufacturing business wishing to build its own premises, including ancilliary offices. Potential reception areas for office activities outside the South East had, of course, to compete for decentralised office employment with locations nearer to London, and by virtue of their proximity to the hub of the country's office activities in Central London the latter were generally more attractive.

With the election to office in October 1964 of a Labour Government, new directions in office location policy began to emerge. The Labour Party was generally "much more committed to economic planning in all its forms than the Conservatives had been" (21). One of its first actions was to set up, under the newly-created Department of Economic Affairs (DEA), an institutional framework for regional planning which included the

Regional Economic Planning Boards and Councils (22). As well as assuming overall responsibility for regional policies, the DEA developed an interest in regional office problems, a potential policy area that was outside the traditional spheres of influence of existing Departments of State. During the next four years the DEA undertook and commissioned a number of studies to explore the nature of office employment "in the regions", encouraged the LOB to do the same (23), and sought to assess the scope for office development outside the South East and the suitability of various provincial cities as reception centres for mobile office jobs.

George Brown, the Secretary of State for Economic Affairs, was also the architect of the Labour Government's first legislative initiative in the field of office location policy. On 4th November, 1964 a statement was issued on new measures "to control the growth of offices in South East England, especially London" (24). The new measures imposed upon prospective office developers a requirement to obtain from central government an Office Development Permit (ODP), in addition to normal planning permission, for all developments over 2 500 square feet in the London Metropolitan Region (broadly the GLC area and the current Outer Metropolitan Area). The new control was to be applied particularly strictly in the GLC area, and unless a contract to build had been entered into by midnight on 4th November - known to some as 'the night of the long pens' because of the number of contracts which were hastily signed (25) - even developments which had already received planning permission were required to have a permit. A virtual standstill on office development in London was thereby envisaged.

This move towards a stricter control of office development in the London area was clearly in keeping with the Government's desire to promote the movement of offices "right outside the South East". Yet it would appear that the urgency with which it was introduced was related to matters unconnected to planning concerns. The Crossman Diaries subsequently indicated that the statement formed part of an attempt by the Government to demonstrate that it was prepared to act decisively in a worsening economic situation by diverting resources away from what it regarded as 'non-productive' activities, such as office development, to more productive ones. The proposals found favour with Crossman himself because, as Minister of Housing and Local Government, he believed that they could only serve to release construction workers for a new and enlarged housing programme (26).

The ODP system was formalised in the Control of Office and Industrial Development Act 1965 which gave the Board of Trade both the immediate power to administer it and the longer-term opportunity to apply it to any other part of Britain. Under this latter provision ODP control was in fact extended, by the summer of 1966, to cover the whole of the South East, the West Midlands, East Anglia and the East Midlands, to conform with

32

more general changes in regional policies, including the setting up of region-spanning Development Areas following the Industrial Development Act 1966. Thus, office development became, like its manufacturing counterpart, the subject of a negative floorspace control for the purpose of diverting mobile employment away from the prosperous regions of the country - especially the South East - to the peripheral and 'problem' regions. This phase of office location policy with its distinctively regional flavour continued until 1969, albeit with the raising of the floorspace threshold to 10 000 square feet for the control areas outside London. With the transfer in 1969 of ODP administration from the Board of Trade to the Ministry of Housing and Local Government, and then the removal of the controls from all but the South East region in 1970, this period of office location policy was brought to a somewhat early end. Subsequently the declared objective of the Ministry in administering the control was to further the objectives of spatial planning in the South East.

The regional dimension of policy towards the private office sector in the late 1960s, therefore, consisted of a negative control over the construction of new office floorspace which was grafted onto a pre-existing policy of exhortation that sought to promote office decentralisation from Central London, a measure devised largely for metropolitan or intra-regional planning ends. Indeed, the ODP control itself was used initially as a tool of metropolitan planning in that it applied only to the London area and the West Midlands conurbation. This confusion of policy aims was reflected in the variety of agencies involved in office location matters - the Ministry of Housing and Local Government with its responsibility for LOB during most of the period: LOB itself; the Board of Trade administering ODPs (and for a short period in the late 1960s assuming control over LOB); and the DEA, attempting to devise a rational frame-work and realistic objectives for an inter-regional office location policy. Meanwhile, policy towards the location of public office employment continued to transfer Civil Service jobs into the Assisted Areas in increasing numbers.

OFFICE LOCATION POLICY IN CONTEXT

The increasing government concern with the location of office activities, as noted earlier in this chapter, was part of a trend towards a more 'managerial' approach to the spatial structure of the British economy. It flowed in particular from a desire to challenge the persistence of regional inequalities despite the country's generally rising level of prosperity. In a number of ways, however, concern about the location of office employment, both between and within regions, departed from the mainstream of attitudes towards economic development. In Britain as a whole, office activities were regarded as being non-exporters. In consequence they were discriminated against during the latter part of the 1960s when a Selective Employment

Tax was imposed on service activities. In the Assisted Regions, this discrimination was amplified by the denial of the Regional Employment Premium to the service industries. Indeed, incentives for investment in the Assisted Areas were designed specifically to influence manufacturing activities in that they consisted of subsidies for capital investment, in the form of buildings, plant and machinery, and were largely irrelevant to the office sector of the economy.

These underlying attitudes towards the role of office employment were also prevalent in the South East. Many local authorities that were the early recipients of decentralising firms questioned the desirability of encouraging further office employment within their areas, seeing it as their duty to encourage more 'productive' employment. In many centres of planned dispersal, the emphasis still lay on the attraction and accommodation of manufacturing industry. Housing for key workers in the London ring of New Towns was generally provided only for relocating industrial firms. In other areas, office development was often regarded more as a necessary evil than as a welcome source of employment growth and local income.

These attitudes reflect the fact that the attempts to control and direct office employment in Britain arose primarily from a concern about the planning problems that its apparent growth implied for the traditional functioning of Central London in particular and the London region in general. They did not stem from a recognition of the problems associated with the under-provision of such employment elsewhere. Increasingly, therefore, the interaction of these somewhat antipathetic attitudes towards the growth of office employment, and the use of ODP controls to encourage inter-regional relocation, reduced the opportunities for the intra-regional redistribution of employment and population in the South East. A major obstacle was thereby placed in the path of the Government's declared policy of encouraging dispersal from Central London.

THE GROWTH OF OFFICE ACTIVITIES IN THE 1960s AND EARLY 1970s

Before assessing the impact of government office policies, it is necessary to examine with some care the changing employment and industry context within which those policies came to operate. Because of both definitional and data problems, that task is somewhat complex.

There are at least two possible ways of defining what is meant by 'office employment'. It can be defined as either a group of occupations which can be broadly classified as information processing (or office jobs), or it can be defined as those activities which take place in office buildings. Neither definition is watertight. The selection of a generally-agreed list of office occupations has not been arrived at without some reference to the types of activities which are carried out in

office buildings. Similarly, office buildings as such are defined not just by their physical attributes, but by the nature
of the activities contained within them, that is, whether these
activities generally belong to the list of agreed office occupations. Nevertheless, the two concepts of office employment are
by no means coterminous. Office workers, as defined by their
occupations, are housed in factories, shops, hospitals and educational institutions. Office buildings, on the other hand,
house workers who fulfil non-office functions, for example,
caretakers, catering staff and cleaners.

Because of its prime initial concern with the problems of
Central London, where the bulk of office employment is housed
in office buildings, policy tended to ignore the distinction
between the occupational and land use definition of this employment. Its tactics sought to manipulate the location of new
office buildings and of the enterprises that employed labour in
those buildings. By doing so it was assumed to be influencing
the spatial distribution of all but an insignificant amount of
office jobs. Although policy makers chose to disregard these
distinctions because of data inadequacies, it is
impossible to do so when attempting to describe and interpret
the employment and industry context within which the policy
operated.

Two different sets of government data relating to office
activities are available. Firstly, data on office occupations
form part of the information collected by the Census of
Population taken at periodic intervals; and secondly, statistics
on the amount of occupied office floorspace throughout the
country are assembled by the Department of the Environment from
records compiled by the Valuation Office of the Inland Revenue
for rating purposes. The first set of data relates, therefore,
to the occupational definition of office employment; the second
supplies information on the amount of space occupied by the land
use based definition of office employment, but it provides no
estimate of the employment that is housed in that space.

Office occupations

In analysing the Census data for the 1960s, it is judicious to
bear in mind some of the problems surrounding the use of the
available data. Firstly, difficulties arise from the choice of
Census years. Since office employment in manufacturing industry,
"is in the nature of an overhead", it is less subject to cyclical
variations in the level of economic activity than is manual
employment (27). Thus the taking of the Census in 1971, a year
of recession, may have tended to overestimate the importance of
the office sector in relation to other forms of employment.
While this problem may be of considerable significance in trend
assessment and prediction, it is of less importance when describ-
ing changes in the level and structure of office employment in
isolation. A second difficulty arises from the fact that Census
data are derived from 'self-completion' questionnaires. It is
entirely possible that this method of data collection will bias
the information towards higher-order occupations such as managerial jobs and thus inflate the apparent level of office

employment. Moreover, the introduction of an incomes policy during the 1960s may have led to a spurious regrading of jobs to circumvent the legislation, which would again have distorted upwards the apparent occupational structure and suggested a greater number of managerial jobs than actually existed at the time. It is impossible to estimate how far these factors may have influenced apparent occupational trends during the 1960s; nevertheless, they must be borne in mind in the following analysis.

The 1960s saw a continuation of the early post-war trends. Office employment in England and Wales expanded rapidly both in absolute terms and also relative to other types of employment as a result of a general shift towards tertiary sector activities. This was evidenced by the growth of the office-based service sector, and by the expansion of office employment associated with manufacturing industry. According to Census returns, the number of office jobs in the economy as a whole expanded between 1961 and 1971 by around 22% (some 1 million). By 1971, office employment accounted for some 25% of the working population, compared with around 20% a decade earlier. There is, however, evidence of a deceleration in the rate of growth of office employment during the 1960s. The earlier half of the decade experienced a growth rate of 12%, but after 1966 the number of office jobs expanded by only 9%. Moreover, because of a rise in the proportion of part-time workers, the true growth in the demand for office labour was rather less than these figures suggest (28). Thus, the expansion of office employment in terms of full-time equivalents was only of the order of 7.5% in the late 1960s.

The trends outlined above refer to all office workers in both the public and the private sectors. During the 1960s, it should be noted, a considerable expansion took place in public services, particularly in education and in medical provision. This growth contributed significantly to the expansion in office employment. Private sector jobs in fact, plus those in the nationalised industries, grew rather more slowly than the aggregate data on office employment would suggest, and between 1966 and 1971 for example increased by 6.5% compared with 9% for office employment as a whole.

Significant changes in the composition of office employment took place during the 1960s. The bulk of office employment growth in the previous decade was accounted for by the expansion of clerical work. During the late 1960s, however, with the introduction of computers, clerical occupations grew by only 5%, compared with an expansion of managerial and professional jobs of some 20%. Thus in 1971 clerical workers accounted for 59% of the office workforce; in 1961 they had accounted for 64%.

As was noted earlier, these occupational trends towards a higher overall proportion of office workers reflected in part the growth of the office-based service sector. Marquand (29), in a study of the performance of the service sector in the 1960s and early 1970s, has shown that the fastest growing

service activities were mainly those which are office-based
such as Insurance, Banking and Finance and Professional and
Scientific Services. Employment in the physical services, such
as Transport and Communications and Distribution either
declined or remained static. The growth of these office services or quaternary activities was related both to changing
consumer demand and the greater sophistication of the needs of
the manufacturing sector. For example, the demand for banking
services expanded steadily throughout the 1960s as a growing
proportion of the population came to use bank accounts and as
the number of cheques that were cleared each year rose several-
fold. In parallel, employment in the clearing banks grew apace
from around 106 000 in 1959 to 177 000 in 1970. Business
services, such as advertising, market research and research and
development, similarly expanded in response to industrial demand.
British R & D expenditure, for example, grew from 1.8% of GNP
in 1955 to around 2.7% in 1967-1968. Employment in both activities grew by a significant amount during the 1960s - 68% and 51%
respectively.

As well as generating demands for externally produced
services, the manufacturing sector also began to employ more
office workers in a variety of activities. The occupational
structure of high technology industries in particular - industries such as Chemicals - became increasingly oriented towards
scientific and technical jobs. Between 1966 and 1971, this
industry had the highest growth rate of office employment of all
industrial groupings, including those in the service sector.
Technological developments in manufacturing processes were not
the sole cause of growth of office occupations, however.
Significant changes were taking place both in the structure of
British manufacturing industry as a whole and in the organisational structure of individual companies. Under increasing
international competition, considerable concentration took
place. In 1957, the top 150 companies held 50% of the assets
of quoted companies; by 1968 this proportion had climbed to 71%
(30). As these large companies expanded, partly by aquisition
and merger, they became increasingly diversified. With diversification came the need to adopt new organisational structures.
The problems of control over these large diversified corporations
in particular called for increased skills in management. This
more competitive environment required "corporate scanning
functions in order to continuously search for new profitable
ventures" (31). All these developments in manufacturing
industry - the growth of large corporations, diversification,
and the need for new product and market opportunities - led to
a higher proportion of office jobs than hitherto. It is not
surprising, therefore, that office employment in the manufacturing sector expanded by around 6% in the period 1966-1971,
whilst total employment in this sector declined by 3.4%.

Office floorspace

The statistics available on changes in office floorspace date
from 1964. Because they are collected as a result of the rating
process, they refer to rateable units or heriditaments.

These heriditaments are classified according to their 'major
use'. The commercial offices category, which is the focus of
attention here, includes all premises where the major use is
for normal 'commercial' purposes. Included in this category
are the offices of institutions and charities, banking establishments in office areas and also large 'head office' buildings of
all types of activity. The offices of central and local government are included only if the space is rented from the commercial sector. There are, however, three important exclusions
from the data; first, banks in shopping areas and similar
'shop-type' office premises of insurance firms, estate agents,
building societies and the like; second, the offices of public
utilities and transport undertakings, such as gas, electricity
and water supply, passenger and freight transport and the
National Coal Board; and, third, all offices which form an
ancillary part of another type of hereditament, for example,
shops, factories, warehouses, libraries and hospitals. Thus
the data provide only a broad estimate of the amount of space
in detatched office buildings. They offer no guidance on the
amount of space occupied by ancillary office workers.

Some general observations on national changes in the
amount of commercial office floorspace can be made at this point.
Between 1964 and 1967, about 25 million square feet were added
to the office stock, a 10% increase. This compares with an
increase of only 5% for all floorspace used for industrial, shop
and office purposes. In a later period, 1967-1974, which
encompassed the second office property boom, the rate of office
construction increased considerably, and an additional 107
million square feet of floorspace was built. This increase was
at an annual rate of about twice that experienced in the earlier
period. By 1974, commercial office floorspace accounted for
10.5% of total floorspace in all surveyed uses; this compares
with 8.2% in 1964 (32). The increasing rate of growth in office
floorspace at the end of the 1960s would appear to be contra-
dictory to the trends noted earlier with regard to office employment.

These apparently conflicting tendencies may, however, be
reconciled in two ways. Firstly, it is possible that an increasing proportion of office employment during the 1960s was being
housed in detached offices rather than ancillary space. This
suggestion is consistent with the growing scale of enterprises
noted earlier. Secondly, the accelerating expansion of higher
order office jobs in the late 1960s, with proportionately
greater demands for office space per worker may also have led
to a higher (detached) office floorspace/worker ratio overall.
Because of the lack of firm evidence on these two factors,
however, their individual contributions to a reconciliation of
the apparent contradictions between floorspace and employment
trends must remain a matter of speculation.

REFERENCES AND NOTES

1. Standing Conference on London Regional Planning (1962), *Events leading to the establishment of the Conference,* LRP 4. London: SCLRP.

2. *ibid.*

3. *ibid.*

4. Royal Commission on Local Government in Greater London (1960), (Chairman: Sir E. Herbert), London: HMSO.

5. London County Council (1958), *Offices on the Move.* London: LCC.

6. Ministry of Housing and Local Government (1964), *South East Study.* London: HMSO.

7. Ministry of Transport (1963), *Traffic in Towns.* London: HMSO.

8. National Economic Development Council (1963), *Conditions Favourable to Faster Growth.* London: HMSO.

9. Minister of Housing and Local Government (1963), *London - Employment: Housing: Land,* Cmnd. 1952. London: HMSO.

10. London County Council (1963), *Town Planning Committee, Report, 19th March.* London: LCC.

11. Town and Country Planning Association (1962). *The Paper Metropolis.* London: TCPA.

12. The Order in Council was made under Section 8 of the Town and Country Planning Act 1943.

13. The Flemming Review was reported to Parliament on 18th July, 1963.

14. Ministry of Housing and Local Government (1964), *op cit.,* p.7.

15. *ibid.,* p.52.

16. South East Economic Planning Council (1967), *South East Strategy.* London: HMSO.

17. *ibid.,* p.54.

18. South East Joint Planning Team (1970), *Strategic Plan for the South East,* London: HMSO.

19. Committee of Inquiry into the Scottish Economy (1961), (Chairman: J.N. Toothill), Edinburgh: Scottish Council.

20. Secretary of State for Industry, Trade and Regional Development (1963), *The North East,* Cmnd. 2206. London: HMSO.

21. G. McCrone (1969), *Regional Policy in Britain.* London: Allen and Unwin.

22. J.D. McCallum (1979), "The development of British regional policy" in: D. Maclennon & J.B. Parr (ed), *Regional Policy, Past Experience and New Directions.* Oxford: Martin Robertson.

23. M.V. Facey and G.B. Smith (1968), *Offices in a Regional Centre, a Study of Office Location in Leeds.* London: LOB. M.J. Croft (1969), *Offices in a Regional Centre, Follow-Up Studies on Infrastructure and Linkages.* London: LOB.

24. H.M. Government (1964), *Offices: A Statement.* London: HMSO.

25. O. Marriott (1967), *The Property Boom.* London: Pan.

26. R. Crossman (1975), *The Diaries of a Cabinet Minister,* Vol. 1. London: Hamish Hamilton and Jonathan Cape, p.37.

27. V.H. Woodward (1975), *Occupational Trends in Great Britain, 1961-1981.* Cambridge: Department of Applied Economics, Cambridge University.

28. On the rather crude assumption that two part-time workers equal one full-time worker.

29. J. Marquand (1979), *The Service Sector and Regional Policy in the United Kingdom,* CES Research Series No.29. London: CES.

30. Monopolies Commision (1970), *A Survey of Mergers, 1958-1969.* London: HMSO.

31. D. Channon (1973), *The Strategy and Structure of British Enterprise.* London: Macmillan.

32. Warehouses and local government offices excluded.

4

London office decentralisation
in the 1960s and 1970s

In earlier chapters, the growth and development of office
activities in London in the 1950s have been described. Subsequently the changes that were taking place in the economy as
a whole during the following decade and which favoured the
further expansion of office activities were outlined. This
chapter seeks to explore the impact of these macro-economic
changes on the economy of London in the context of general
metropolitan decentralisation - both of population and of
employment - during the 1960s and 1970s. It also examines the
development pressures that built up in Central London, and how
the rest of the capital came increasingly to share in the growth
of office activities.

LONDON'S OFFICE ECONOMY

Considerable difficulties arise in establishing with any
precision the impact of macro-economic changes on the level and
structure of office employment in London in the 1960s and early
1970s. As will be described later, both natural and policy-
induced employment dispersal took place during this period. Thus
the actual shifts which occurred represent the result of a
combination of forces - general economic change, the process of
locational adaptation and the effects of public policies. In
theory it should be possible to estimate the potential growth
of London's employment in response to macro-economic change
alone by reference to the rate of expansion that its particular
mix of economic activities experienced nationally. Such an
approach, however, requires industrial employment data that is
disaggregated to the level of homogeneous groups of activities
such as is not currently available, and in any case it denies
the possibility of industries behaving differently in different
locations. For example, part of the growth in finance activities during this period was accounted for by the prodigious

expansion of building societies. Clearly that growth,
arising as it did from the extension of the societies' branch
networks, benefitted London to a lesser extent than would be
supposed from its share of finance activities generally.
Despite these data problems, the most important tendencies in
the development of London's economic base can nevertheless be
established and it is to these that we next turn.

The changing structure of employment encompassing a shift
towards tertiary, especially office, activities throughout all
sectors of the national economy favoured London. By virtue of
its historic concentration of such activities (over 30% of all
office employment in England and Wales in 1961), it was particularly well placed to benefit in employment terms from these
developments. In general Greater London, and particularly
Central London, had higher proportions (30% and 46% respectively)
of 'growth services' than did England and Wales as a whole (22%)
(1). Certain activities such as Insurance, Banking and Finance
(IBF) which were growing fast nationally (by 43% between 1961
and 1971) were heavily represented in the London economy. IBF
accounted for some 35% of the City's total employment in 1966,
compared with only some 5% of employment nationally.

Within particular broad industry groupings there were certain
developments which favoured London. Within the IBF Order, for
example, international insurance and foreign banking, both
strongly concentrated in the City, grew substantially. The
number of foreign banks in London more than doubled after 1960,
and they employed over 10 000 people by 1973. The largest
single group was American. Some American banking activities
had been in London for over 50 years; but the majority began
arriving in London in the late 1960s, after the squeeze on the
American economy and the consequential growth of the Euro-dollar
market (2). All of the foreign banks were attracted to the
existing locus of financial activities in the City of London,
rather than to locations elsewhere in the country. There can
be little doubt that their arrival had significant, albeit
indirect, employment-creating effects in the City, especially
through the stimulation they gave to the expansion of international banking activities by Britain's own clearing and
merchant banks.

Developments outside the service sector were also increasing
the buoyancy of London as a centre of tertiary employment. The
growth of headquarters activities of manufacturing firms favoured
the London region. Westaway (3) found that in 1971-1972 London
housed the head offices of over one-half of the 1 000 largest
companies in the United Kingdom (as measured by turnover). Data
for changes in the distribution of such manufacturing headquarters are not available for the 1960s, but evidence for the
subsequent decade shows an increasing concentration of the
larger companies in London in particular (4). Such trends are
no accident. The growing complexity of industrial financing and
the increasing role of government in the regulation of industry

required that large industrial corporations kept intimate contacts with both City institutions and Whitehall. This is particularly true in the case of industries that were undergoing rapid change. For instance, during the 1960s many of the major oil companies were undertaking substantial decentralisation programmes for their administrative activities. With the discovery and exploitation of North Sea oil and gas, and hence the need to be in close touch with government to negotiate licences and taxation arrangements, however, this dispersal was brought to an end. In the 1970s the industry tended to consolidate its headquarters' office functions in Central London, particularly in the area of (a partly redeveloped) Victoria Street.

Although public sector office employment is not a central concern of the present study, its growth during the 1960s and early 1970s must not be forgotten. Office workers in national government service in Britain increased by some 22% during the period 1966-1971. This represented an absolute increase of nearly 150 000 jobs. Some of the expansion in national government services was housed in privately-built office blocks in London. In 1971, for example, nearly 14 million square feet of office floorspace were rented by government from private interests in the London area (5). The growth of the Civil Service, therefore, contributed to the overall level of demand for office space. In addition, the extra office labour requirements of government could only be satisfied at the expense of a tightening of the market for white-collar labour in London.

During the 1960s and early 1970s, therefore, London's economy was subject to two broad influences. First, there was this general growth in office employment. Second, there was the expansion of certain Central London private and public activities in particular. These influences served to emphasise the dominance of Central London as a focus of office employment, particularly of higher-order activities. At the same time, however, conflicting forces were operating in the realm of population distribution, to which we now turn.

THE DECENTRALISING CITY

The decentralisation of population within and from London was by no means a new phenomenon. The built-up area had been expanding continually, with the fastest rate of growth occurring at the periphery rather than at the centre. The creation of the Greater London Council and the redrawing of the county boundaries in 1964 was a clear recognition of this trend, which was of course physically constrained and shaped by the existence of the Metropolitan Green Belt. The planning crisis of London and the South East, as expounded in the 1963 White Paper, however, arose not from the decentralisation of population itself but from the fact that people were dispersing from London faster than were jobs.

The process of population dispersal accelerated during the 1960s, when London's urban core lost over 500 000 inhabitants compared with under 300 000 during the previous decade. At the same time both the metropolitan ring and the outer metropolitan ring each gained around 150 000 persons. The net result, however, was that the population of both the Standard Metropolitan Labour Area (SMLA) and the wider Metropolitan Economic Labour Area declined (6). The losses were the result of a high level of net outward migration from the city-region, rather than the result of natural decline. Indeed, the natural increase component of population change in the London SMLA during the 1960s was as much as 500 000 inhabitants.

This pattern of urban decentralisation was not peculiar to London. It was reflected in the evolution of most of the country's major conurbations during the 1960s. The trend was partly a result of planned dispersal under various overspill schemes; but even more important was the tendency for better-off people to flee the cities in search of space and more pleasant surroundings. Such a dispersal was of course facilitated and encouraged by the increasing levels of car ownership.

There are two main differences between the behaviour of the London conurbation and other British metropolitan areas at this time. Firstly, the scale of dispersal from London was far greater. London had the highest percentage decline in population of any SMLA, other than Rhondda, during the period 1961-1971. Secondly, the centre of London's core area, because of the growth of tertiary activities, remained unusually buoyant in employment terms, while the central business districts of the provincial conurbations were in noticeable decline.

During the 1960s, therefore, while the underlying trend in London's office economy was towards expansion as a result of the factors outlined earlier, London's labour force, particularly the more skilled office workers, were opting for residential locations further away from the centre of London and often at considerable distances from the Greater London Area. Two types of pressures on Central London employers built up as a consequence of these diverse trends. Firstly, the demand for office space in Central London began to outstrip supply, subject as it was to physical and planning constraints. Secondly, Central London employers had to bear the increasing costs of attracting office workers to travel from their dispersed homes to work in the Central Area. These 'push factors' on the location of London's office activities are explored in the next section, which is followed by an examination of the reactions to them of office employers, in terms of their locational behaviour.

PUSH FACTORS

Rents

Before discussing the relationship between growth in the demand
for Central London office space in the 1960s, the supply that
was available and the resulting changes in the levels of office
rents, it is necessary to examine another factor which contributed to the demand for space - the rising standards of office
floorspace use.

Although most commentators on the London office market
would agree that the increasing area of floorspace per worker
was of considerable importance in bolstering the demand for
office space, direct and quantifiable evidence on the subject
remains elusive. A divergence between trends in the growth of
office employment and those of occupied floorspace - with
occupied floorspace growing faster than employment - has however
been offered as an indication of such a tendency (7). With
declining levels of manufacturing and warehousing activity in
Central London, a partial explanation of this divergence of
trends must lie in the tendency noted earlier for high proportions of office workers to be housed in detached office space,
to which the available floorspace data refer. Nevertheless,
it would appear highly probable that floorspace/worker ratios
in London did increase during the 1960s. In part this increase
would have resulted from a general improvement in the standards
of office accommodation; in addition it would have been a
function of changes in the occupational structure of Central
London's office labour force. Within the context of a static
level of office employment overall in Central London during the
period 1966-1971, clerical occupations declined by 7% (33 000
jobs) while managerial jobs expanded by 14% (12 000). If one
assumes a differential of around 10 square feet per person
between the space allocations for managerial and clerical
grades (8), the shift to managerial jobs alone (and ignoring
shifts to other higher-order functions) would have added around
500 000 square feet to the demand for office space in Central
London during that period.

These office occupancy trends, combined with the generally
prosperous nature of the London economy, generated an increasingly buoyant demand for office space. This strong demand
meant that, although much development had taken place during
the late 1950s and the early 1960s, and some commentators had
even suggested the danger by the mid-1960s of there being a glut
of office space, rents in Central London grew steadily throughout the 1960s. In the City, for example, rent levels rose from
about £2.00 per square foot in 1962 to around £4.50 per square
foot in 1967 (£3.80 in 1962 prices) (9).

By the end of the 1960s the additional supply of office
space created during the first development boom of the 1950s and
early 1960s was beginning to run out. However, as has been seen,
demand particularly in the City was being intensified especially

45

by the influx of foreign banking activities at this time.
Delays in the response of the development industry - the
characteristic lag in the development cycle that has been docu-
mented by Barras (10) - together with the operation of ODP
policy meant that new supply was restricted. Prime rents in
the City in consequence rose sharply from £5.00 per square foot
in 1968 (£4.11 in 1962 prices) to £12.50 (£9.23) in 1970. This
was an increase in real terms of well over 100% in two years.
In the City, the prime influence on the London property
market, available space declined to 500 000 square feet, only
1% of the total stock. However, the first wave of developments
from the second office boom began to appear on the market in
that year. Rents began to stabilise, and by 1972 those in the
City were lower in real terms (£8.18) than they had been in
1970 (Table 2).

Table 2. Prime rents in the City of London and the West End*,
         1962-1980

                        (£ per square feet)

	City of London			West End	
	Nominal	Real		Nominal	Real
1962	2.00	2.00			
1963	n.a.	n.a.			
1964	2.75	2.60		no reliable data	
1965	3.00	2.74		available	
1966	4.00	3.50			
1967	4.50	3.80			
1968	5.00	4.11			
1969	8.50	6.58			
1970	12.50	9.23		4.00	2.96
1971	13.00	8.84		5.00	3.40
1972	13.00	8.18		7.00	4.40
1973	16.00	9.34		9.50	5.54
1974	22.00	11.47		12.00	6.26
1975	18.00	7.82		9.50	4.13
1976	12.00	4.23		8.00	2.82
1977	13.50	4.08		9.00	2.72
1978	15.00	4.12		n.a.	n.a.
1979	18.00	4.52		n.a.	n.a.
1980	22.00	4.68		n.a.	n.a.

*   West End figures refer to the Victoria area

Sources: Various estate agents, 1962-1969; Debenham, Tewson and Chinnocks,
         1970-1980

     The new space created during the boom of the early 1970s
was, unlike that built during the earlier one, largely the
result of the redevelopment of existing secondary office stock
(11). This meant that space was taken off the market in order
to achieve that redevelopment. Thus redevelopment, of itself,

46

reduced the overall supply of office space in the short-term.
At the same time there was an upturn both in the British and
the international economy which was reflected in a substantial
growth of activity and employment in the City's financial
sectors. This was the period, too, when the Heath Government's
'rush for growth' and the 'Barber boom' led to the burgeoning
of secondary banking activity. As the demand for office space
from both expanding domestic and overseas firms rose, it became
apparent that the increase in the rate of supply was insufficient
to meet the market's growing requirements. Indeed, the level
of development completions in the early 1970s was running at
only one-half that prevailing in the 1960s (400 000 square feet
per annum compared with 800 000 square feet).

As part of the Government's counter-inflationary measures
of 1972, a freeze on business rents was introduced. The freeze
initially served to discourage the marketing of office space
which had previously been rented (new space was exempt from the
control), and further constrained supply. Only later, as the
freeze became accepted as a semi-permanent measure, did the
office market adapt through the use of premia payable on the
signing of a lease. At the same time, it might be argued that
the tightness of the office market was to a degree self-re-
inforcing. Office occupiers who had surplus space, which under
other circumstances might have been marketed, retained that
space in the fear of not being able to obtain similar property
when the need arose. Indeed, the knowledge that supply was
running far short of demand produced a sort of 'Weimar inflation
psychology', with bargains been struck at a higher level than
contemporary market conditions necessitated, through fear that
any delay in acquiring space would result in even higher rent
levels having to be paid in the near future. Rental values rose
particularly rapidly during 1972 and 1973 such that by the
beginning of 1974 the price of prime office space in the City
of London had reached a peak of £22.00 per square foot (£11.47
in 1962 prices). This was by far the highest rent for office
space in any Western European city (12).

The tightness of the City property market began to be
reflected in rents throughout Central London. Previously,
trends in the West End market had tended to be determined
somewhat separately from those in the City. In the early 1970s,
however, with the redevelopment of Victoria Street to provide
prime space, and the growing willingness of international
companies (including banking organisations) to countenance non-
City locations, rents throughout Central London began to rise
in response to City trends. By 1974, rents had risen to £15.00
in Mayfair and to £12.00 in and around Victoria Street (13).

In order to comprehend the significance of these rental
values as 'push factors' in the process of office decentralisation, it is necessary to examine trends in rental values in
alternative locations. In 1964, when rents in Central London
were around £3.00, those outside the centre ranged from £1.00

47

in the suburbs to about £0.50 in such locations as Sheffield and Northampton. By 1974, with prime rents in the City at £22.00 per square foot, the range in decentralised locations was from £8.00 in Croydon to less than £1.50 outside the South East. Thus the absolute differential widened considerably during this period.

This discussion of trends in rental values in Central London has, of necessity, focussed on rents achieved for marketed space. These rental levels, however, directly affected only those office users who for one reason or another needed to acquire premises. Their impact was felt most immediately by firms wishing to expand, or those whose premises were subject to redevelopment and who were thus forced to seek new offices. Other existing occupiers were, of course, also subject to rental pressures via the rent review procedure. In the early post-war period, before the substantial rental growth performance of office property had been established, it was normal for rent reviews to be every 21 years. As rental values grew and property owners sought to claw back from tenants the increase in the market value of their premises, however, the rent review periods stipulated in new leases shrank. First, a 7-year review period was adopted; then in the 1970s 5-year reviews became the norm. In this way, during the period under review, the users of office space, other than owner occupiers, came to pay rents which were increasingly in line with open market values. Nevertheless, even office users who signed leases as late as the latter part of the 1960s faced substantial rent increases on review, as is illustrated in Figure 2.

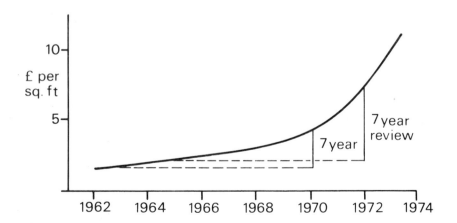

Figure 2. The effect of rising rentals on the magnitude of rent reviews, 1962-1974

Theoretically, owner occupiers were under the same cost
pressures as other users of Central London office space, since
the opportunity cost of occupying space was equivalent to its
market value. It was not until the early 1970s, however, that
many of them responded to that pressure. Then, with rapidly
rising rents and falling yields, capital values soared. It
thus became possible for many owner occupiers to finance the
construction of new, purpose-built, decentralised offices
substantially from the proceeds of the sale of their Central
London premises.

Although during this period the rise in Central London rents
was considerable, and so too was the growth in the absolute
differential with those elsewhere, many firms did not respond
to the incentive to relocate. This was because the cost and
availability of office space was only part of the total location
equation. A study of Central London firms in 1969 showed that
rent and heating together accounted for only 14% of the total
costs of operating a typical office (14). Thus, when other
factors, such as the need to remain in physical contact with
customers and suppliers, tied an office to a Central London
location, firms found it advantageous to continue bearing the
higher rental costs which were payable there.

Rates

In the 1969 survey of the operating costs of a typical Central
London office, it was found that local authority rates constituted an insignificant component of total costs - only 4%.
This remained substantially true until the rating revaluation
of 1973. In the City, for example, rates amounted to some 11%
of rent in 1970, or £1.42 per square foot (15). The fact that
the rating revaluation coincided with the period of peak rents
substantially altered the situation. As can be seen from
Table 3, rates increased to over 20% of the higher rent levels
prevailing in 1974 - to around £4.70 per square foot, an
increase of 125% in real terms.

In contrast to Central London, a later report by Debenham,
Tewson and Chinnocks shows that rates in other locations in
1974 ranged from £1.20 per square foot in the suburbs to around
£0.50 in the provinces. Even in Southampton, for example,
rates amounted to only £0.62 per square foot (16). Thus from
1973 onwards, but not before, rates became an important item in
the higher operating costs incurred by Central London firms.

Salaries

The tightness of the office labour market in London itself, the
growing residential preference for the Outer Metropolitan Area,
and thus the need for Central London employers to attract labour
from considerable distances have already been noted. By pushing
up wage levels in real terms in the 1960s and 1970s, each of
these features of the London labour market added to the growing
cost of operating an office in the centre.

Table 3. Prime office accommodation costs in the City of London,
1970-1980

	Rates/ sq.ft. / year	Open Market rent/sq.ft./ year	Rates as % of rent	Total Rate and rent/ sq.ft./year
	£	£	%	£
1970	1.40	12.50	11.4	13.90
1971	1.70	13.00	13.0	14.70
1972	1.90	13.00	14.7	14.90
1973	3.30	16.00	20.8	19.30
1974	4.70	22.00	21.1	26.70
1975	7.40	18.00	40.8	25.40
1976	8.20	12.00	68.7	20.20
1977	8.80	13.50	65.0	22.30
1978	8.80	15.00	58.7	23.80
1979	9.20	18.00	51.1	27.20
1980	11.20	22.00	50.9	33.20

Source: Debenham, Tewson and Chinnocks. *Office rents and rates 1973-81,*
DTC, London, 1981 and earlier years

Broadly speaking, and for the same quality of labour, the salary levels of professional, technical and managerial labour, for which a national market exists, were not significantly higher in London than elsewhere. Secretarial and clerical labour in London, on the other hand, attracted considerably higher wages than elsewhere. In 1966, while the average top-grade clerical weekly wage was £20.00 in the City, it was around £16.25 in locations in the rest of the South East, and as low as £14.00 in provincial cities (Table 4). The rate of increase in wage levels was by and large the same throughout the country in the period up to 1974. As a consequence, however, the absolute differentials widened considerably. As can be seen from Table 4, the difference between clerical wages in the City and in the rest of the South East increased from less than £4.00 in 1966 to around £6.00 in 1974. That between London and the provincial centres grew from £6.00 in 1966 to £8.00 (or even £11.00 in some cases) eight years later. The growth in these differentials was by no means spectacular bearing in mind an inflation rate of over 70% between 1966 and 1974. But they assume considerable importance when one considers that, according to the survey of office operating costs quoted earlier, staff costs accounted for over 70% of total costs.

More important than the differentials in direct staff costs, perhaps, were the higher indirect costs of employing staff in Central London as compared with elsewhere. Although quantitative evidence in this area is notoriously difficult to obtain, it is generally accepted that Central London employers suffered from higher rates of staff turnover and of absenteeism than did employers elsewhere. In addition, many Central London firms

Table 4. Top grade clerical salaries in selected locations,
          1964-1974

(£ per week)

	1964	1966	1968	1970	1972	1974
CENTRAL LONDON						
City	16.65	20.10	23.85	26.20	32.00	37.65
West End	15.10	20.10	22.50	23.75	30.28	39.17
GREATER LONDON						
Croydon	13.35	17.90	20.55	23.75	28.46	32.70
Romford	12.80	17.75	19.35	22.70	27.75	31.32
Wembley	14.00	16.90	18.35	20.35	27.85	33.58
SOUTH EAST TOWNS	13.00	16.25	17.65	20.65	24.07	31.63
ELSEWHERE						
Birmingham	11.80	14.55	14.80	19.80	25.53	28.13
Bristol	10.95	14.45	17.00	24.85	26.60	30.65
Cardiff	11.00	14.40	14.95	20.50	24.67	29.94
Glasgow	10.50	16.00	16.45	20.15	21.44	34.61
Leeds	12.60	15.60	13.90	16.95	23.84	29.80
Liverpool	12.75	14.85	16.50	18.65	26.01	28.42
Manchester	10.50	15.55	14.60	18.00	26.90	30.69
Newcastle	10.50	14.00	14.50	15.60	19.80	26.90
Nottingham	10.95	13.55	12.90	16.50	20.00	26.04
Sheffield	12.35	13.60	13.60	14.35	20.98	28.84

Source: Institute of Administrative Management, *Office Salaries Analysis*,
        IAM, Beckenham, 1975

were unable to maintain full staff complements by ordinary
recruitment methods and thus had to resort to the use of
temporary labour, incurring higher costs both directly and
indirectly. All these factors naturally led to losses in
efficiency and increased costs, including those of training
staff, for office employers. Many organisations which subsequently decentralised all or part of their activities from
Central London reported improvements in efficiency in their use
of labour and thus reductions in the indirect costs of staffing
their offices.

The higher staff outgoings in Central London combined with
the substantial differentials in the costs of office space,
both in rents and (later in the period) in rates, proved to be
a powerful incentive, for those firms for whom a Central London
location was not perceived as imperative, to avoid or minimise
the occupation of office space there. As a result, a substantial
amount of decentralisation took place both to locations within
Greater London and over greater distances. The characteristics
of this dispersal and its impact upon London - as the origin of
all moves and as the destination of a significant proportion of

them - is examined later. Since extensive use is made in this
study of the statistics on office movement collected by the
Location of Offices Bureau, it is important to describe precisely the nature of this evidence.

LOB DATA

LOB recorded details of the relocation activity of its clients.
These clients included organisations in the manufacturing and
the service sector, including nationalised industries and
public agencies (but not government departments), as well as
private firms who were considering the possibility of relocating
their office activities in accordance with LOB's terms of
reference. Those terms of reference, during the period 1963-
1977, restricted the LOB to giving advice primarily to organisations located in Central London who wished to move all or
part of their office activities elsewhere, either to the rest
of the Greater London or further afield. A small proportion of
the clients consisted of London organisations located outside
Central London who were considering locations beyond the boundaries of Greater London. Over time, as office activities became
more dispersed throughout Greater London, this proportion tended
to increase.

    The LOB's terms of reference did not preclude the provision
of assistance to employers of office labour which was not housed
- or to be housed - in detached office accommodation. But in
practice, because the services offered were very much geared to
occupiers of detached office space, the help that could be given
to such employers was limited. Thus, only a minority of clients
were considering the relocation of office jobs that were housed
in factory or warehouse premises. In this way, the LOB's data
refer to the activities of a biased sample of organisations
relocating office employment, as it is conventionally defined.

    The data on the characteristics of LOB moves were derived
from the responses to questionnaires completed immediately
after the move had taken place. The questionnaires included a
request for information on the number of office staff to be
employed when the premises were fully operational. The data so
derived therefore refer to the number of jobs housed in the new
location, which cannot be assumed to represent the number of
jobs removed from the origin of the move. Indeed, the net loss
of jobs at the origin could have been considerably lower for one
of several reasons.

    First, moves were often undertaken because a firm's exist-
ing functions in London were expanding. In the case of complete
moves, the number of jobs housed in the decentralised location
would normally be greater than that lost at the origin. Among
partial moves, it was quite often the case that the departments
remaining in London were allowed to expand to occupy existing
floorspace (although very often at higher space standards) so

52

that the net loss of jobs at the origin of the move amounted to
only a relatively minor proportion of the number of jobs dispersed. Second, partial moves sometimes involved the duplication of certain administrative functions, with the result that
the total number of jobs in London and in the decentralised
location exceeded the total employed before the move took place
- even after the expansion element is discounted. Third, new
locations were often sought by London firms to house new activities. Such moves represented a diversion of employment which
might otherwise have been located in Central London. As such,
their contribution to any loss of jobs at the firm's old
location was purely theoretical. Finally, a small proportion
of the total amount of recorded 'dispersal' consisted of
completely new activities, such as the creation of a new
company or the establishment of an overseas company in the
United Kingdom, which might have been located in Central London.
In the LOB data, such 'moves' were not allocated a London
origin, but they were classified as 'new branches'.

      Thus, the LOB data provide a measure of the diversion of
office employment from Central London rather than the actual
transfer of office jobs. In addition, it must be borne in mind
that the employment data were collected on the basis of a land
use classification of office jobs (that is, employment in
office buildings) and not on the conventional functional basis.
Although attempts were made to exclude them from the statistics,
a small number of non-office jobs, such as canteen and maintenance workers, were thus inevitably included in the LOB statistics.

      As well as compiling data on the decentralisation activity
of its clients, the LOB also recorded details of all the
approaches made to it by organisations considering dispersal,
together with the decisions of those clients who - after
weighing up the pros and cons of decentralisation - abandoned
the idea. In both cases the number of jobs recorded as being
involved was that quoted on a firm's initial approach to the
LOB.

                  THE LEVEL AND RATE OF DISPERSAL

The level of decentralisation from Central London prior to the
early 1960s is a matter of some speculation, although survey
results suggest that it was of the order of some 1 000 jobs each
year during the 1950s. After the establishment of LOB in 1963,
hard information became available on at least the minimum level
of dispersal that was taking place, both within and beyond
Greater London. Although it is impossible to establish with
certainty the proportion of total dispersal that was accounted
for by LOB moves, it was estimated at the beginning of the
1970s that they represented approximately one-half of all the
office decentralisation taking place (17). It was also

                              53

suggested that LOB-associated dispersal was not representative
of total dispersal, in that the moves undertaken by clients
tended to be biased towards larger, longer-distance moves. The
degree to which small and short-distance moves might be under-
represented must, therefore, be remembered when considering
dispersal within Greater London on the basis of LOB data.

There is, however, no reason to believe that the degree
and the nature of the coverage afforded by the LOB records
varied significantly over time. LOB data, therefore, provide
some measure of the changing scale of decentralisation. Taking
the period 1963-1977, from LOB's establishment to the last full
year of its operation under the original terms of reference,
some 145 000 jobs were decentralised in over 2 000 moves by the
LOB's clients. This represents an annual average of around
11 000 jobs (ignoring the first year of operation when only
185 jobs were moved). The yearly total, however, varied between
6 500 in 1964-1965 and 14 700 in 1973-1974. The level of movement gradually increased from the year of LOB's establishment
until 1968-1969. For two years thereafter, a relatively low
level of decentralisation took place coinciding both with a
downturn in the economic cycle and with a reduction in the
amount of office space available in the South East, a reduction
occasioned by the strictness with which ODP control was applied
in the mid-1960s. Subsequently, as ODP control in the South
East (outside Central London) was eased and rent levels in the
centre began to rise, the rate of decentralisation returned to
and surpassed the previous level. During the following five
years an average of over 12 500 jobs were being decentralised
annually, with a peak of nearly 15 000 jobs being involved in
relocations in 1973-1974. Three years later, with the economy
again in recession and with dramatic changes in the London
property market having resulted in a far greater availability
of office space, the level of dispersal fell back substantially.
Nevertheless, the total number of jobs moved during 1976-1977
was only just below the average for the whole period; it
included some particularly large moves that had been planned
under earlier and very different economic circumstances.

The total level of movement includes dispersal from
locations outside Central London. But if moves originating in
LOB's definition of the Central Area (18) are examined separately, the same temporal pattern emerges in terms of a late
1960s slump and a mid-1970s boom - despite the fact that the
level of decentralisation from the rest of Greater London
increased steadily over the period.

Throughout the years 1963-1977, some 127 000 jobs were
dispersed from Central London in over 1 700 moves. This total
represents over 15% of the office employment located in 1971 in
the slightly more widely defined Central Area of the Registrar
General. But Central London office employment fell only
marginally during the period 1966-1971, years during which
nearly 50 000 jobs were dispersed. Part of the explanation of

this apparent contradiction lies in the fact, suggested earli r
in the discussion of LOB statistics, that many of these seemingly 'dispersed' jobs were in fact new employment that had
been created by decentralising firms outside Central London.
As far as actual transfers of jobs are concerned, however, it
is clear that employment was being created in Central London as
fast as it was being dispersed. Hence, LOB's claim that its
activities could be regarded as simply 'bailing the boat' (19).
The replacement employment in the metropolitan centre was
created in part by the very organisations that were undertaking
dispersal programmes, but also by the birth and expansion of
other firms. The individual contribution of each of these two
processes to the maintenance of employment levels in Central
London is impossible to estimate. Information about the birth
and expansion of office firms is not available from official
statistics; nor are general survey data available. The growth
of the overseas banking sector, as noted earlier, is the only
well-documented example of such expansion.

REASONS FOR DECENTRALISATION

The suggestion that it was the expansion of firms involved in
decentralisation which was responsible (at least in part) for
the job replacement process that was taking place at least up
to 1971 is corroborated by the reasons for considering relocation given by firms to LOB executives. 'Expansion' accounted
for over 25% of the reasons mentioned by LOB clients. In
addition, since firms were questioned about their reasons for
contemplating decentralisation rather than simply a move within
the locality, it is possible that the quoted reason of 'economy'
- accounting for some 30% of all mentions - also refers to the
savings made by expanding firms as they accommodated their
increased number of employees in decentralised rather than
central locations. Particularly influenced by such considerations would be organisations whose activities were housed in
accommodation rented at historic prices but who would need to
acquire extra space at current rentals. The role of the high
level of rents in Central London as a spur to decentralisation
is underlined by the fact that while 'economy' accounted for
35% of the reasons quoted by Central London firms, it represented
only 22% of those mentioned by firms in the rest of the Greater
London Area. For these latter organisations, 'expansion' was
the single most important reason (36%)

Clearly, however, both economy and expansion are related
to accommodation problems. Together with another aspect of the
same set of difficulties, 'the expiry of leases', they accounted
for over 70% of all the reasons mentioned. These 'push factors'
were thus of paramount importance in London office relocation
decisions, while the advantages of decentralised locations -
especially easier staff recruitment and travel to work - appeared
to be of secondary importance.

Over time, expansion and economy remained at roughly the same level of relative importance until the mid-1970s when significant changes in the pattern of response among firms approaching the LOB occurred. In 1974-1975, 'expansion' accounted for only 15% of the quoted reasons. In that year, 'economy' assumed a much greater importance as a spur to decentralisation and was quoted by 50% of LOB's clients. It appears, therefore, that with the economy in recession and with the increased availability of premises in Central London, relatively few firms were expanding and those that were growing were able to find comparatively cheap premises within London. An interest in decentralisation, which had declined by over 30% from the high level of around 400 enquiries in each of the the two previous years, was being shown increasingly by those firms who, in the stringent economic conditions following the international oil crisis, needed to reduce their outgoings.

Little connection appears to exist between the reason for a move and the likelihood of a proposed relocation being translated into an actual move. The distribution of the different reasons for decentralisation quoted by those who actually moved broadly concurs with that for LOB clients as a whole. One exception is the greater importance of 'integration' as a reason for decentralisation among movers. This exception can be explained by the operation of three factors. Firstly, firms who were already functioning outside London were more likely to be receptive to the idea of dispersal. Secondly, such moves had clear organisational benefits in addition to the usual cost advantages. Thirdly, it is likely that LOB was approached by such firms to provide information at a fairly advanced stage in the decision making process when a commitment to integrate and relocate had already been taken.

Overall, an examination of the reasons offered by the clients of the LOB confirms the importance of the costs of London office space as the major rationale for dispersal. Since public policy, at both the central and local government levels, had restricted the supply of office space there, it can be regarded as having an indirect effect on the level of decentralisation. The Location of Offices Bureau by constantly publicising the relative costs of operating an office both in London and out-side must have amplified the locational response of London office employers to those indirect effects of public policy initiatives.

SIZE AND TYPE OF MOVE

The preponderance of the office moves recorded by LOB are small in size. Around two-thirds involved the dispersal of less than 50 jobs. Whether LOB movers were, as far as size is concerned, unrepresentative of Central London office establishments in general is difficult to establish since information on the size of Central London offices, as on so many of the characteristics

of London's office activities, is sparse. The only source of
such data is an analysis, presented by Goddard (20), of
statistics for 1967; these were collected in connection with
certain responsibilities and powers of local authorities under
the 1963 Offices, Shops and Railway Premises Act (OSRP). That
study found that 85% of Central London office establishments
employed 25 or fewer workers; by comparison, just over 50% of
LOB moves originating in Central London fell into that category.
This contrast would at first sight suggest that firms involved
in decentralisation were on average larger than Central London
office firms generally. The fact that LOB data refer to the
size of moves, whilst the OSRP data relate to the size of an
office establishment, however, makes such a comparison somewhat
less than straightforward.

     Particular problems are associated with the fact that the
LOB data include partial moves of organisations which may well
involve fewer jobs than are contained within a single Central
London office establishment. Moreover, LOB moves sometimes
involved the combined relocation of employment previously
housed in more than one establishment, and, as pointed out
earlier, they often included an element of employment expansion.
The number of jobs involved in a move, therefore, could be
greater than the number of jobs previously housed in the
establishment from which the move originated. The operation of
the first factor means that the data on LOB moves tends to
underestimate the size distribution of the establishments from
which they originated; the other two factors, on the other hand,
would have the opposite effect. Thus, the true size distribution
of establishments generating decentralisation is difficult to
ascertain. However, the contribution of partial moves to the
overall level of dispersal, accounting for some 39% of LOB
moves, makes it likely that decentralising firms tended to be
biased towards larger-sized firms in Central London.

     This conclusion seems reasonable. Small firms are less
able to split their functions and therefore must relocate as a
whole. Those needing to retain a presence in the Central London
area were thus reluctant to decentralise. This relationship
between the size of move and type of move is borne out by the
fact that over 60% of complete moves involved fewer than 25 jobs,
while less than 40% of partial moves fell into this category.
Thus, in terms of the number of actual jobs dispersed, large
partial moves made the greatest contribution to LOB-assisted
decentralisation; over 45% of the total were accounted for by
partial moves of 100 or more jobs.

INDUSTRIAL CLASSIFICATION OF MOVERS

Firms belonging to all industrial types were involved in office
dispersal, but some groups in particular contributed significantly to the total volume. The insurance industry, for example,
accounted for nearly 20% (31 753) of all jobs dispersed and 22%

of those relocated from Central London. The prominence of the insurance sector as a generator of decentralised office employ-ment stems in the main from the size of the individual moves made by this industry, with the average move involving over 120 jobs compared with an average of around 75 jobs for all Central London moves. But the size of the moves undertaken was not the only reason. The insurance industry was surpassed by only one other industrial grouping - the distributive trades - in terms of the number of individual dispersals which it carried out.

There are a number of factors explaining the high level of employment dispersal undertaken by the insurance industry. The location of the industry was traditionally biased towards London. Thus, as considerable expansion of their output and employment took place in the 1960s, insurance firms were faced with the office accommodation costs and problems that were described earlier. Because the industry was concentrated in the City, where costs and space shortages were greatest, its problems were particularly acute. However, a substantial proportion of headquarters' employment in insurance consisted of routine clerical work which, provided that the damage caused by splitting an organisation was outweighed by the savings on accommodation and labour costs, could be easily housed in decentralised locations. Moreover, the introduction of new computer systems often provided a suitable occasion for relocation activity. The insurance industry, therefore, as a result of its persistent growth and its historic headquarters' concentration within Central London, was subject to particularly strong economic pressures to relocate. Due to the nature of its office activities and its organisational structures, it was readily able to respond to these pressures through decentralis-ation. The high proportion of partial moves among the reloca-tions accomplished by insurance firms - some 70% compared with 42% for all Central London movers - confirms this picture of the industry's decentralisation behaviour.

The role of the insurance industry as a prime decentraliser is emphasised by the fact that it accounted for over twice as much of total office employment dispersal from London as it did for Central London office employment. By contrast, another City-based activity, banking, while comprising some 16% of office employment in Central London in 1968-1969, accounted for only 9% of the total number of jobs dispersed from the Central Area. This was in part due to the late start in the process of decentralisation made by the banking industry, delayed as it was in its response to the changing economics of location by the considerable reorganisation that took place as a result of its merger activities in the late 1960s. An analysis of the industrial breakdown of dispersal for the period up to 1972 shows that, at that time, the banking industry accounted for less than 4% of the jobs decentralised from Central London. After the early 1970s, however, all the major clearing banks undertook substantial relocation exercises spurred on by the continuing expansion of their services and employment in centralised banking activities. Thus the differing relocation

experiences of the insurance and banking industries underline
the importance of structural and organisational characteristics
of individual industries in determining their locational
behaviour.

During the 1960s and the early 1970s, other 'office'
industries - industries such as professional and scientific
services, business services, miscellaneous services and trades
associations - were all relatively under-represented among
decentralisers in terms of the amount of employment they dispersed. Some were certainly responsible for fewer moves than
might have been expected from the share of Central London
establishments for which they accounted in the latter part of
the 1960s. All four groups were, however, dominated by small
establishments that often provided local services to other
Central London organisations; they were therefore less likely
to be candidates for dispersal. Trade associations, although
sometimes more nationally oriented than other activities in
this broad group of services, were additionally constrained by
the need to be accessible to their membership and London was
often seen to be the most convenient location from that point
of view. The tendency of all these organisations to opt for
remaining within Central London is illustrated by the fact that
only 46% of the proposed decentralisations in this group of
industries actually materialised, compared with 54% for LOB
clients as a whole.

The nature of office employment in manufacturing companies
differs significantly from that in such 'office' industries as
insurance and business services. The production process of
insurance, for example, consists in itself of office activities;
and where these have consisted of largely routine clerical
activities, they have been prime candidates for dispersal. In
the manufacturing sector, however, office activities are biased
more towards higher-order jobs. They are concerned partly with
the internal management of the organisation, but also with
marketing and strategic functions, both of which require external
contacts. It is surprising therefore that, with this apparently
lower potential for decentralisation, a number of manufacturing
industry groups - and the engineering sector in particular -
accounted for a greater proportion of decentralisation than
their share of Central London employment would suggest. Part of
the explanation must lie in the nature of the markets that they
serve; these tend to be national by contrast with the sub-
regional markets of many service industries. Moreover, as the
production processes of the manufacturing sector have dispersed
from the London region (21), the rationale for maintaining a
Central London office has been eroded. Many manufacturing
organisations with strong international connections have been
able to satisfy their communications requirements at non-London
locations accessible to Heathrow Airport. But those organisations for which a Central London location is essential, with
its unique advantages of ready access both to higher-order
financial services and advice and to central government, were

reluctant to decentralise. Among these the most notable were the oil companies who (as we have noted), having effected some decentralisation programmes in the 1960s, shelved further relocation plans after the commencement of the commercial exploitation of North Sea because of their need for close contacts with both the financial institutions and central government. Other manufacturing organisations locked into the occupancy of freehold premises for which there was no ready market, whether because of their size, location or outdated facilities, were also slow to respond to the cost-differentials between London and elsewhere.

An overall analysis of the characteristics of organisations taking decentralisation decisions, and of the type and size of their moves, presents a rather complex picture. Nevertheless, three separate strands may be distinguished. First, there was the dispersal of the headquarters' offices of manufacturing organisations, partly as a response to the increased costs of operating in London but also, and perhaps more significantly in the longer-term, as a result of the flight of manufacturing activities themselves from the capital. Second, there was the complete relocation of small companies in the service sector. These companies could survive in a non-central location and were reacting to rising rents in Central London and the physical shortage of accommodation there. Third, there was the partial decentralisation of the relatively routine activities of larger firms, particularly those in the financial sector, and once again in response to the rising costs of operating in London. Especially relevant to these latter organisations were the costs associated with the difficulties of clerical staff recruitment and high levels of staff turnover. As time went on, and the relative ease and benefits of operating from decentralised locations became firmly established, and more widely known, such organisations also began to disperse other less routine functions, leaving the capital with only those activities directly linked to the Central London contact environment. In consequence, decentralisation contributed to a shift in the occupational structure of Central London office activities away from clerical work and towards administrative and professional occupations.

Thus, office dispersal was part of a process of adaptation in Central London's office economy, in response to the high level of space and labour demands there. Although some organisations were shielded from the exigencies of the market by freeholds and long leases, in general it was those activities which had least need for a Central London location that were dispersed. In this way, decentralisation broadly led to a more efficient use of Central London office space, that is 'efficient' defined in the conventional economic sense. However, the 'ability to pay' criterion on which such a 'need' for a Central London location was established meant that certain office activities whose market power was weak, but which derived certain benefits from locating there - activities such as charitable organisations - were also forced to disperse. In consequence the range and variety of Central London activities was reduced.

Moreover, the drift towards higher-order functions has in some ways confounded the problems that the decentralisation policy was intended to cure. Higher-level office staff generally live further away from the centre of London and rely more upon the use of the private car for commuting purposes.

As well as consolidating its role at the apex of the national office market during the 1960s and early 1970s, Central London simultaneously enhanced its status as an international office centre. Until the mid-1970s, London was a relatively expensive location internationally, with rents some two to 12 times higher than those in other Western European capitals. Nevertheless some overseas institutions were prepared to outbid other users of City office space in order to gain a foothold in the world's leading financial centre. After the Sterling crisis of the mid-1970s and the downturn in office rentals, London became relatively cheaper, particularly when other locational costs, including salaries, were taken into account (22). In consequence, some domestic firms were squeezed out of Central London by their inability to compete for office space with international office users. The process of dispersal, therefore, released space for the development, at the core of Central London's office economy, of a group of internationally competitive, higher-order office functions.

Office dispersal affected the various parts of the country differently. Its contrasting impacts can be explored through an analysis of the geographical pattern of decentralisation. To conclude this chapter, its consequences within Greater London are summarised. The discussion of the geography of decentralisation to places outside the Greater London Area is reserved for the next chapter.

OFFICE DISPERSAL WITHIN GREATER LONDON

As will be described and analysed in some detail later, the volume of office movement from Central London declined with increasing distance from the centre. Thus, a substantial proportion of the decentralisation which took place under LOB's auspices was to locations within the Greater London Area (Table 5). Places both in Inner and in Outer London received some 814 moves (37% of the total) and 51 544 jobs (32%). Moves to destinations within the Greater London Area were on average smaller than the generality of moves. This characteristic of dispersal within London was related to the preponderance (58%) of complete moves among these relocations which, as was seen earlier, were on average smaller than the other main category of relocation - partial moves. These relocations were undertaken by organisations anxious to escape the high costs of the Central Area, but reluctant to move away from the London environment.

Table 5. Decentralisation within Greater London by LOB clients, 1963-1979

DESTINATIONS

Borough	Moves	Jobs	Borough	Moves	Jobs
Barking	13	1654	Hounslow	52	4951
Barnet	40	1075	Islington*	10	187
Bexley	16	1267	Kensington and Chelsea*	6	112
Brent	54	3753	Kingston-upon-Thames	46	2565
Bromley	36	1624	Lambeth*	15	475
Camden*	16	261	Lewisham	10	917
Croydon	133	12 775	Merton	32	1450
Ealing	39	1102	Newham	18	1714
Enfield	23	1302	Redbridge	20	1120
Greenwich	11	943	Richmond-upon-Thames	46	1680
Hackney*	5	141	Southwark*	6	113
Hammersmith	21	1274	Sutton	30	2943
Haringey	8	113	Tower Hamlets*	4	170
Harrow	43	2913	Waltham Forest	9	406
Havering	12	673	Wandsworth	16	880
Hillingdon	23	989	Westminster*	-	-

(1 move of 2 jobs was to an unknown location in the NW sector)

TOTAL 814 moves 51 544 office jobs

* Excluding the parts of these boroughs that fall within central London.
  The definition of central London used here is rather wider than that
  defined for census purposes and consists of the postal districts
  EC1-4; E1; NW1; N1; WC1-2; W1; W2; W8; W11; SW1; SW3; SW7; SE1; SE11.

Source: LOB

Despite the high proportion of complete moves, partial moves of organisations accounted for over one-half of the total number of jobs dispersed within Greater London. Especially during the period before 1970, some quite substantial relocations of routine office functions took place within the London area. In this early phase of decentralisation, considerable savings on office space costs could be achieved by moving relatively short distances from the Central Area. Moreover, the early movers were able to tap the very considerable reserves of labour in the outer suburbs, including part-time female labour.

The geographical pattern of dispersal within London was by no means uniform (Figure 3). Over three-quarters of the total number of decentralised jobs were relocated to places in the North West and South West sectors of the capital, that is to locations with access to substantial numbers of office workers, in the direction of Heathrow Airport and towards the emerging axis of economic development in the Thames Valley. The North Eastern and South Eastern sectors, by contrast, fared badly.

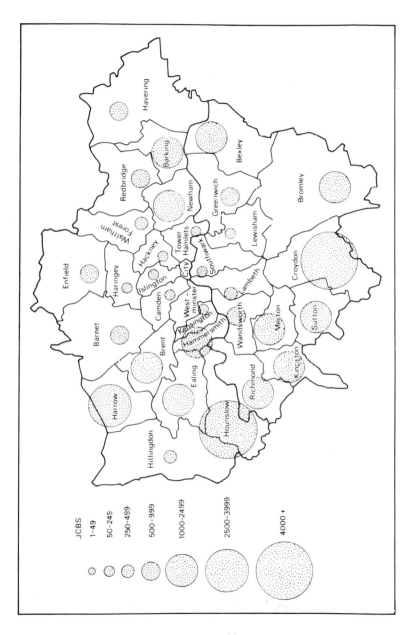

Figure 3. Office dispersal within Greater London, 1964-1979
Source: Location of Offices Bureau, records

JCBS
1-49
50-249
250-499
500-999
1000-2499
2500-3999
4000 +

This is surprising given the high level of dispersal from the City, and the tendency noted among other types of business organisations to undertake radial movement from their previous location (23). The absence of developed office centres in East London for much of the period during which this dispersal took place, and the relatively underdeveloped nature of the local office labour markets compared with those in West London, meant that eastward moving firms relocated further afield, beyond the GLC boundary to locations such as Basildon and Southend.

As well as exhibiting a distinct sectoral pattern, the distribution of decentralised employment within the Greater London Area favoured Outer London rather than Inner London. Some 82% of the moves and 86% of the jobs decentralised within the capital were to destinations in Outer London; and while only three of the 18 Outer London boroughs failed to attract more than 1 000 jobs, only two of the 14 Inner London boroughs (outside the Central Area) actually achieved that level. The reasons for the failure of Inner London to benefit substantially from the process of office dispersal have been explored by Damesick (24). In summary, he has concluded that most of Inner London was generally perceived by developers and occupiers alike to have too many of the disadvantages of a Central London location, including traffic congestion and journey-to-work problems, and too few of the benefits of a location in Outer London. Not least of these latter advantages was the local supply of suitable labour. Nearly 800 000 office workers were resident in the Outer Ring of London in 1971, compared with only one-half that number in the Inner Ring. Probably more important, however, was the wider range of amenities available to office workers in many of the Outer London centres.

Despite the poor overall performance of Inner London as a reception area for office decentralisation, one or two locations within the Inner Ring were in fact the destinations for significant numbers of relocated office jobs. Hammersmith and Newham, together attracting some 3 000 dispersed jobs, were among the most successful Inner London boroughs in attracting office employment. Each capitalised upon its rather distinctive locational attributes. Hammersmith had the advantage of being located on the favoured western axis, between Central London and Heathrow Airport; it also enjoyed sympathetic local planning attitudes towards office development, in contrast to the somewhat antipathetic attitudes towards office activities that for long characterised the majority of Inner London authorities. The area was popular throughout the whole period of dispersal, attracting *inter alia* several large head offices that employed a considerable proportion of professional and technical workers.

The key to Newham's, or more specifically Stratford's, early success lay in its location downstream from the City and the availability of office space through redevelopment in the 1960s. The area first attracted a number of transport-related activities squeezed out of the City by more competitive financial firms. In more recent years, with the redevelopment of Stratford town centre which created several large office blocks as well as new shopping facilities, it also afforded the opportunity - previously lacking in East London - for the relocation of parts of City financial institutions. Elsewhere in Inner London, only Lewisham (again with a redeveloped town centre providing space for an overseas bank), Wandsworth (mainly in Putney with its largely Outer London characteristics) and Greenwich attracted more than 500 jobs.

In Outer London, the overwhelming 'success' story was the phenomenal growth of Croydon. It attracted nearly 13 000 jobs, around one-quarter of all office employment recorded by LOB as relocating within Greater London. It was the entrepreneurial behaviour of the local authority, assembling sites and promoting development, that initiated - sometimes against considerable local opposition - the creation of this 'mini-Manhattan' in London's suburbs. Although, as noted in earlier chapters, substantial development had already taken place there by the early 1960s, between 1960 and 1970 occupied floorspace in the borough grew from less than 500 000 square feet to 4.3 million square feet. The existence of this concentration of office space, at relatively low rents, acted as a powerful counter-magnet to the attractions of Central London. Over time, the volume and the range of office activities locating there began to provide at least some of the external economies that formed the basis of Central London's success, and a number of office services sprang up to meet local demands (25).

A number of City institutions, including a variety of insurance firms and a merchant bank, as well as the head offices of several manufacturing companies, relocated in Croydon. The borough was also the focus for the dispersal of a significant proportion of consulting engineering firms that were forced by redevelopment out of their traditional location in the Victoria Street area. These latter activities, in particular, chose Croydon partly for its easy access to the former centre of the industry, but also because of its advantageous location on the same railway lines that carried staff into Victoria. Thus, decentralised firms were able to retain many key staff and maintain traditional contact patterns, as well as to recruit local labour. The bulk of the dispersal to Croydon took place in the 1960s and early 1970s. Over 97% of the total number of jobs relocated to Croydon had been moved by 1973-1974, a period which accounted for less than 60% of all the dispersal recorded by LOB. As Croydon reached saturation from the point of view of office employment - with both rents and salaries rising and staff shortages developing - in-movement virtually came to a standstill. Indeed, as firms faced rent reviews, dispersal from Croydon itself began to be considered.

Other areas in Outer London which were successful in attracting office jobs were all located in the South West or the North West sectors. In the cases of Kingston and Sutton - as with Croydon - office development was associated with town centre redevelopment, albeit on a considerably reduced scale.

65

Other favoured boroughs such as Hounslow, Harrow and Brent confirm the importance of a location on the western axis, although the latter two boroughs had the advantage of having encouraged the development of office space as the process of dispersal first began to gain momentum. Despite the strategy of the *Modified Greater London Development Plan* (26) which proposed the development of a limited number of major alternative office centres in Outer London, none of these areas came anywhere near to challenging the dominance of Croydon as a focus of office activity outside the Central Area.

One theme underlying this description of the pattern of employment dispersal within London is the importance of the availability of office space, particularly at times of general shortage. The construction of office buildings is, of course, largely in the hands of the development industry. The powers of central government and of local authorities are broadly negative. Thus, public policy has to operate through reactions to private development initiatives, rather than by taking positive measures to transform the geography of office space. Even those local authorities which sought to encourage development in large measure only responded to the locational preferences of firms as interpreted by the development industry. Croydon alone, in the late 1950s and early 1960s, can be regarded as having taken a positive initiative in development to the extent that it encouraged the creation of office space before the magnitude of the trend towards dispersal was firmly established.

The development industry, on the other hand, seeking to minimise risks, generally interpreted the preferences and needs of firms in a somewhat conservative fashion. This characteristic of the development industry arises partly as a result of the considerable time lags inherent in the development process. Trends in the locational preferences and the behaviour of firms may alter considerably over the period, often as long as five years, between the initiation of schemes and their completion. The result is that office space is not always available in the right places at the right time, and the opportunity for particular areas to capitalise on emerging locational trends is foregone. Thus, locations in East London, which were not the most popular places for office investment from the development industry's viewpoint, have been largely bypassed in the decentralisation process. Yet they might well have been acceptable destinations for office users had the office space been available in the early 1970s when a flight eastwards of some financial activities followed a rapid rise in City rents.

As well as underlying the pattern of dispersal, the availability of office space appears also to have affected the volume of movement within the Greater London Area compared to that favouring more distant locations. In the period up to 1972-1973, 45% of the jobs decentralised from Central London were relocated within Greater London. After that, ODP policy began seriously to affect the amount of office space available in the Greater London area. The amount of space 'complete and vacant' in Greater London was, according to ODP data, down to a low of 1 million square feet in 1973, compared with three times that level in 1969, while that recorded in LOB's property register (including space under construction) stood at 1.1 million square feet in January, 1974 compared with 1.6 million square feet in 1971 (the earliest data for which LOB statistics are available). In the years 1973/1976, as a consequence, only just over 20% of decentralising employment found destinations in Greater London. The dynamics and the geographical distribution of the increasing scale of longer distance dispersal is examined in the next chapter.

REFERENCES AND NOTES

1. D.R.W. Knight *et al*. (1977), *The Structure of Employment in Greater London, 1961-1981.* London: GLC, RM 501.

2. H. McRae and F. Cairncross (1973), *Capital City.* London: Methuen.

3. J. Westaway (1974), 'Contact potential and occupational structure of the British urban system, 1961-1966, an empirical study', *Regional Studies,* Vol.8, pp.57-73.

4. I.J. Smith and J.B. Goddard (1978), 'Changes in corporate control changes in the British urban system, 1972-1977', *Environment and Planning, A.* Vol.10, pp.1073-1084.

5. Chancellor of the Exchequer (1978). *Public Expenditure 1979/1980,* Cmnd. 6393. London: HMSO.

6. R. Drewitt, J.B. Goddard and N. Spence (1974-1975), *Urban Change in Britain, 1961-1971,* Working Papers, Department of Geography, London School of Economics. See also, R. Drewitt *et al*. 1975, 'Whats happening to British cities?, *Town and Country Planning,* Vol.43, pp.523-530; and Vol.44, 1st January, 1976, pp.14-24.

7. R. Barras (1981), 'The causes of the London office boom', in: R. Barras (ed) *London's Office Boom.* London: CES Ltd.

8. Figure based upon a survey by F.J. Langdon (1966), *Modern Offices. A User Survey for the Building Research Establishment.* London: HMSO.

9. Location of Office, Bureau Information Sheet (compiled from information provided by various estate agents and the Economists Advisory Group).

10. R. Barras (1979), *The Development Cycle in the City of London,* CES Research Series, No.36. London: CES.

11. *ibid.*

12. Debenham, Tewson and Chinnocks (1977), *Rents and Rates 1977.*
    London: DTC.

13. *ibid.*

14. J. Rhodes and A. Kan (1971), *Office Dispersal and Regional
    Policy.* Cambridge: Cambridge University Press, p.32.

15. Debenham, Tewson and Chinnocks (1977), *op cit.*

16. Debenham, Tewson and Chinnocks (1981), *Office Rent and
    Rates 1973-1979.* London: DTC.

17. R.K. Hall (1970), 'The vacated offices controversy',
    Journal of the Town Planning Institute, Vol.56, pp.298-300.

18. Broadly the area bounded by the main line termini, including
    the postal districts of EC14, E1, SE1, WC1 and 2, SW1, W1
    and 2, NW1 and N1. This was the definition used by LOB.

19. Location of Offices Bureau(1973), *Annual Report 1972/73.*
    London: LOB.

20. J.B. Goddard (1973), *Office Linkages and Location.* Oxford:
    Pergamon. *Progress in Planning,* Vol.1 (2).

21. D. Keeble (1980), "The South East", in: G. Manners *et al.*
    (ed), *Regional Development in Britain.* Chichester: Wiley,
    passim.

22. Economists Advisory Group (1980), *Factors Influencing the
    Location of Offices of Multi-National Enterprises in the
    UK,* Research Paper No.8. London: LOB.

23. D. Keeble (1968), "Industrial decentralisation and the
    metropolis: the North-West London case", *Transactions of
    the Institute of British Geographers,* Vol.44, pp.1-54.

24. P. Damesick (1979), "Offices and inner-urban regeneration",
    Area, Vol.11, pp.41-47.

25. P. Child (1971), *Office Development in Croydon: a Descriptive
    and Statistical Analysis,* Research Paper No.5. London: LOB.

26. Department of the Environment (1976), *Modified Greater
    London Development Plan.* London: GLC.

5

New locations for office activities
in the 1960s and 1970s

THE SPATIAL PATTERN OF DISPERSAL

As within the capital, the pattern of office dispersal outside
Greater London was strongly differentiated geographically
(Tables 6 and 7). In general, the overall level of office
decentralisation declined with distance from London, with
nearly 70% of the moves recorded by LOB taking place over
distances of less than 40 miles. However, the 30% of the
movers who opted for more distant locations provided some 40%
of the total number of jobs dispersed. Thus, longer distance
moves were clearly biased towards the larger relocations. This
is confirmed by an examination of a breakdown, by size of move,
of dispersals to particular regions and sub-regions. Over one-
quarter of the moves to the Outer South East and beyond involved
the relocation of 100 or more jobs, while only 16% of those
dispersed to the rest of Greater London and the Outer Metropolitan Area were of such a size (Figure 4).

Significant changes took place in the geographical distribution of office moves during the period for which LOB data are
available, that is from 1963-1979. In particular, the mid and
late 1970s saw a trend towards more longer distance dispersal.
After 1973, over 40% of the jobs relocated by LOB clients were
dispersed to places over 60 miles from Central London, compared
with less than 25% of the total during the earlier period.
Indeed, 1973-1979 accounted for some 56% of the total number of
jobs dispersed over such longer distances during the whole period.
A number of factors contributed to this development.

As office decentralisation gained momentum during the 1960s,
the opportunities for cost-saving relocation within a short
distance from Central London became increasingly limited. It
has already been noted that the supply of office space in
suburban locations began to dry up. This applied also to many
places in the Outer Metropolitan Area. The amount of space on

Table 6a. Regions to which LOB clients moved: firms, 1963-1979

	1963/64 - 1969/70		1970/71 - 1973/74		1974/75 - 31.8.79		TOTAL	
	No.	%	No.	%	No.	%	No.	%
SOUTH EAST	759	86.6	574	94.7	475	71.1	1808	81.4
GLA	423	48.3	245	36.1	146	21.9	814	36.6
OMA	254	29.0	247	36.4	233	34.9	734	33.0
OSE	82	9.3	82	12.1	96	14.4	260	11.7
EAST ANGLIA	16	1.8	11	1.6	27	4.0	54	2.4
EAST MIDLANDS	16	1.8	16	2.4	25	3.7	57	2.6
WEST MIDLANDS	9	1.0	10	1.5	27	4.0	46	2.1
SOUTH WEST	17	1.9	37	5.5	53	7.9	107	4.8
YORKSHIRE & HUMBERSIDE	12	1.4	6	0.9	12	1.8	30	1.4
NORTH WEST	26	3.0	10	1.5	22	3.3	58	2.6
NORTHERN	9	1.0	4	0.6	8	1.2	21	0.9
WALES	3	0.3	5	0.7	8	1.2	16	0.7
SCOTLAND	7	0.8	5	0.7	10	1.5	22	1.0
NORTHERN IRELAND	2	0.2	-	-	1	0.1	3	0.1
TOTAL	876	100.0	678	100.0	668	100.0	2222	100.0

Table 5b. Regions to which LOB clients moved: jobs, 1963-1979

	1963/64 - 1969/70		1970/71 - 1973/74		1974/75 - 31.8.79		TOTAL	
	No.	%	No.	%	No.	%	No.	%
SOUTH EAST	48991	78.5	36807	79.7	30964	60.1	116762	72.9
GLA	28515	45.7	13750	29.8	9279	18.0	51544	32.2
OMA	14653	23.5	14500	31.4	14864	28.3	44017	27.5
OSE	5823	9.3	8557	18.5	6821	13.2	21201	13.2
EAST ANGLIA	1126	1.8	1156	2.5	3324	6.4	5606	3.5
EAST MIDLANDS	2845	4.6	771	1.7	1551	3.0	5167	3.2
WEST MIDLANDS	148	0.2	241	0.5	1758	3.4	2147	1.3
SOUTH WEST	2789	4.5	5212	11.3	7288	14.1	15289	9.5
YORKSHIRE & HUMBERSIDE	3373	5.4	132	0.3	3004	5.8	6509	4.1
NORTH WEST	1641	2.6	1236	2.7	2391	4.6	5268	3.3
NORTHERN	1201	1.9	335	0.7	718	1.4	2254	1.4
WALES	73	0.1	135	0.3	241	0.5	449	0.3
SCOTLAND	166	0.3	154	0.3	304	0.6	624	0.4
NORTHERN IRELAND	21	0.0	-	-	4	-	25	0.0
TOTAL	62374	100.0	46179	100.0	51547	100.0	160100	100.0

Table 7. Destinations of office decentralisation from London
by LOB clients, 1963-31st August, 1979

	MOVES	JOBS		MOVES	JOBS
SOUTH EAST (excluding GLA)	990	65136			
Bedfordshire	29	1783			
Bedford	11	507	Leighton Buzzard	2	34
Biggleswade	1	11	Luton	9	594
Dunstable	4	433	Sandy	2	204
Berkshire	122	10114			
Aldermaston	1	180	Pangbourne	1	20
Ascot	4	133	Reading	38	3565
Bracknell	12	2773	Slough	19	1441
Cookham	1	63	Sunninghill	1	48
Hungerford	1	3	Windsor	16	525
Maidenhead	21	1035	Wokingham	4	61
Buckinghamshire	81	4044			
Amersham	7	225	Gerrards Cross	2	19
Aylesbury	14	1245	High Wycombe	20	778
Beaconsfield	3	54	Iver	2	27
Buckingham	2	14	Marlow	6	197
Burnham	3	26	Milton Keynes	14	1271
Chalfont St. Giles	1	6	Newport Pagnell	1	75
Chalfont St. Peter	1	5	Princes Risborough	1	40
Chesham	2	19	Wendover	1	23
			Wooburn Green	1	20
Essex	98	8126			
Basildon	4	79	Hadleigh	1	47
Benfleet	1	3	Halstead	1	5
Billericay	5	210	Harlow	12	1905
Braintree	1	20	Loughton	3	100
Brentwood	10	760	Rayleigh	3	52
Buckhurst Hill	3	44	Shenfield	2	88
Chelmsford	8	249	Southend	17	2661
Clacton-on-Sea	2	112	Stanford-le-Hope	1	11
Colchester	12	1043	Tilbury	2	48
Epping	2	52	Witham	4	482
Grays	2	90	Wickford	2	65
Hampshire	88	10928			
Aldershot	5	160	Bishops Waltham	1	40
Alton	4	89	Cosham	1	1080
Andover	8	431	Farnborough	8	1415
Basingstoke	23	4044	Fawley	1	70

	Moves	Jobs		Moves	Jobs
Fleet	1	20	Portsmouth	8	1258
Gosport	2	530	Southampton	17	937
Havant	1	3	Whitchurch	1	250
Liphook	1	62	Winchester	4	487
Petersfield	2	46			
Isle of Wight	1	4			
Hertfordshire	138	7144			
Baldock	2	33	Hitchin	8	223
Berkhamsted	3	181	Kings Langley	2	6
Bishops Stortford	5	320	Letchworth	2	77
Borehamwood	3	89	Potters Bar	16	702
Broxbourne	2	38	Rickmansworth	9	216
Buntingford	1	20	St. Albans	10	596
Bushey	1	84	Sawbridgeworth	1	10
Cheshunt	1	8	Stevenage	8	706
Chorleywood	2	22	Tring	2	19
Elstree	2	82	Waltham Cross	3	110
Harpenden	2	61	Ware	3	124
Hatfield	2	65	Watford	24	1681
Hemel Hempstead	12	1181	Welwyn Garden City	8	459
Hertford	4	31			
Kent	124	8232			
Ashford	8	746	Hollingbourne	1	7
Aylesford	1	13	Maidstone	11	465
Borough Green	4	439	Margate	1	9
Brands Hatch	1	5	Northfleet	2	40
Canterbury	5	639	Paddock Wood	3	40
Chatham	5	1183	Ramsgate	3	79
Dartford	3	339	Rochester	3	226
Dover	1	4	Sevenoaks	25	1051
East Peckham	1	11	Sittingbourne	2	80
Edenbridge	2	171	Strood	1	73
Folkestone	6	1115	Swanley	4	475
Gillingham	3	32	Tonbridge	8	423
Headcorn	1	5	Tunbridge Wells	19	562
Oxfordshire	37	834			
Abingdon	2	10	Oxford	13	169
Banbury	9	263	Thame	3	270
Bicester	1	5	Wallingford	2	42
Henley	7	75			
Surrey	177	7560			
Addlestone	1	7	Banstead	1	3
Ashford	3	37	Camberley	6	304

	Moves	Jobs		Moves	Jobs
Caterham	1	130	Leatherhead	10	331
Chertsey	2	49	Oxted	4	88
Cobham	1	3	Redhill	11	539
Dorking	11	583	Reigate	6	181
Egham	7	82	Shepperton	1	30
Epsom	8	233	Staines	8	473
Esher	2	42	Sunbury-on-Thames	6	308
Ewell	3	14	Thames Ditton	3	86
Farnham	5	188	Walton-on-Thames	8	204
Godalming	9	376	West Byfleet	6	400
Guildford	19	974	West Horsley	2	32
Haslemere	2	55	Weybridge	9	125
Horley	2	15	Woking	17	1208
Kingswood	2	400	Worcester Park	1	60
Sussex	95	3367			
Arundel	1	3	Gatwick	2	10
Bexhill	1	5	Goring	1	30
Billingshurst	2	36	Hastings	4	253
Bognor Regis	2	15	Haywards Heath	9	452
Brighton	15	982	Horsham	13	1643
Burgess Hill	2	521	Hove	5	254
Chichester	5	164	Lewes	1	20
Crawley	9	263	Littlehampton	1	11
Eastbourne	2	81	Newhaven	1	24
East Grinstead	7	466	Ticehurst	1	3
Frant	1	100	Worthing	10	1031
EAST ANGLIA	54	5606			
Bungay	1	8	Huntingdon	3	126
Bury St. Edmunds	5	217	Ipswich	6	1935
Cambridge	5	251	Kings Lynn	1	144
Claydon	1	30	Linton	1	10
Ely	1	3	Norwich	9	818
Eye	1	100	Peterborough	9	1685
Felixstowe	3	74	St. Neots	5	102
Haverhill	1	100	Walton (Nr. Thetford)	1	3
EAST MIDLANDS	57	5167			
Barlborough*	1	1	Lincoln	1	100
Clay Cross*	1	12	Loughborough	1	50
Corby	1	20	Lutterworth	1	51
Derby	2	1502	Market Harborough	1	10
Desborough	1	10	Melton Mowbray	1	6
Grantham	1	8	Northampton	12	1261
Hinckley	1	15	Nottingham	13	820
Irthlingborough	1	3	Sleaford	1	65
Kegworth	1	60	Sutton-in-Ashfield*	1	9
Kettering	4	247	Wellingborough	4	463
Leicester	7	454			

	Moves	Jobs		Moves	Jobs
WEST MIDLANDS	46	2147			
Birmingham	20	1346	Redditch	2	61
Burton-on-Trent	1	145	Rugby	6	184
Coventry	2	12	Shrewsbury	1	32
Hereford	2	44	Solihull	2	117
Kenilworth	3	45	Stourbridge	1	10
Leamington Spa	1	7	Telford	1	45
Ledbury	1	18	Warwick	1	1
Nuneaton	1	40	Worcester	1	40
SOUTH WEST	107	15289			
Amesbury	1	47	Mickleton	1	17
Barnstaple*	1	170	Pewsey	1	4
Bath	3	119	Plymouth*	2	66
Blandford Forum	1	10	Poole	9	1409
Bournemouth	5	1034	Salisbury	4	315
Bristol	24	3481	Stroud	1	24
Cheltenham	14	2735	Swindon	17	3939
Chippenham	1	200	Taunton	1	450
Cirencester	2	42	Totnes	1	6
Exeter	4	498	Warminster	1	25
Gillingham	1	21	Wells	1	2
Gloucester	8	657	Westbury	1	6
Melksham	1	10	Wimborne	1	2
YORKSHIRE & HUMBERSIDE*	30	6509			
Bradford	4	344	Pudsey	1	9
Dewsbury	1	20	Rotherham	3	505
Doncaster	1	800	Sheffield	5	2213
Harrogate	2	49	Thirsk	1	142
Hull	1	7	York	4	2255
Leeds	6	159	Huddersfield	1	6
NORTH WEST*	58	5268			
Alderley Edge	1	5	Manchester	15	633
Altrincham	4	45	Preston	1	40
Chester	1	70	Radcliffe (GM)	1	8
Chorlton-cum-Hardy	1	4	Runcorn	2	81
Congleton	1	6	St. Helens	2	64
Crewe	1	73	Skelmersdale	1	12
Heywood	1	80	Southport	1	80
Horwich	1	120	Stalybridge (GM)	1	14
Ince	1	250	Stockport (GM)	3	148
Knutsford	3	1687	Wilmslow	2	51
Liverpool	10	1073	Wirral	1	4
Lytham St. Annes	2	600	Wythenshawe	1	120

	Moves	Jobs		Moves	Jobs
NORTHERN*	21	2254			
Aycliffe	1	3	Sunderland	1	1000
Darlington	2	94	Teesside)	2	36
East Boldon (S. Tyneside)	1	2	Thornaby-on-Tees)		
Newcastle	10	784	Tynemouth	2	75
Penrith	1	10			
South Shields	1	250			
WALES*	16	449			
Bridgend	1	20	Newtown	1	14
Caerphilly	1	10	Pontypool	1	75
Cardiff	4	74	Swansea	2	33
Clydach	1	40	Treorchy	1	16
Crumlin	1	10	Wrexham	1	17
Newport	2	140			
SCOTLAND*	22	624			
Aberdeen	1	6	Glenrothes	1	15
Dundee	1	63	Inverness	1	15
Edinburgh	5	109	Peebles	1	85
Glasgow	9	276	Stirling	2	54
NORTHERN IRELAND*	3	25			
Belfast	1	4	Warrenpoint	1	7
Enniskillen	1	14			
Unknown (outside the GLA)	4	82			

TOTAL 1408 moves, 108556 office jobs

* Areas for expansion (156 moves, 15387 office jobs)

the market - that is, complete and vacant - in the metropolitan region outside the Greater London Area fell from 800 000 square feet in 1968 to 200 000 square feet in 1971, whereas it had been as high as 1.1 million square feet prior to the introduction of ODP controls in November 1964. The shortage of large units of space was particularly acute. This resulted partly from the fact that it was only developments of over 10 000 square feet that were subject to central government floorspace controls after 1969. Moreover, local authorities in popular decentral- ised locations, such as Surrey and Hertfordshire, who at this time were concerned about the impact of in-migrant office employment on their local labour markets and thus on housing demands, were prepared to countenance only small-scale develop- ments to meet so-called 'local needs'. Firms seeking large units of office space were unlikely therefore to be able to satisfy their accommodation requirements in these favoured areas.

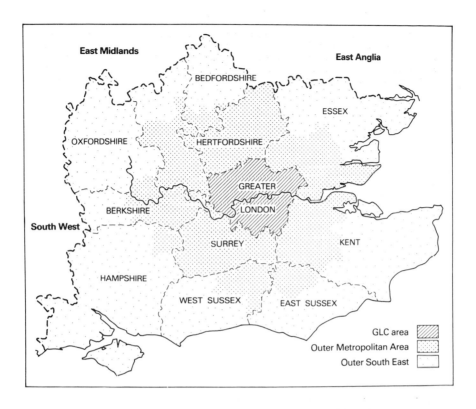

Figure 4.   The South East, showing major sub-divisions

As a result of the general shortage of office space and the continuing high demand for it, rents in locations near to London began to rise.   In Guildford and Slough, for example, rents reached levels of over £3.00 per square foot, whilst the general level of rents in the Outer South East and beyond was around £1.00 per square foot.   It thus became apparent that, even for those small firms which were able to find suitable accommodation, relocation to such places offered no long-term escape from the rent spirals characteristic of Central London.

The early 1970s saw the planning of a number of large moves, particularly in the financial sector but also among other organisations, such as manufacturing and construction companies. Not only were these firms constrained in their choice of locations by the restrictions on the supply of office space, imposed by both central and local government, but also by their need for labour.   Labour requirements influenced the decisions of these large movers in two ways.   Firstly, the magnitude of the recruitment needs of these companies meant that the new

location needed to be a large town, preferably located away
from the commuting belt around London. Secondly, the organisation needed to persuade key staff to transfer to the new location. It is unlikely that all such staff would be living
within the same sector of the London region; rather they would
have been attracted to work in Central London from all points
of the compass. Some key staff would probably therefore have
to move house in order to remain with the company after
relocation. A move from one part of the Outer Metropolitan
Area to another would not offer substantial benefits to such
staff in terms of reduced housing costs or improved housing
quality. Indeed, if staff were required to change their area
of residence from places to the east of London to those in a
westerly direction, they might incur significant additional net
costs. Thus, in order to retain key staff, companies needed
generally to choose a location at a greater distance from
London than that at which the majority of its key staff currently
lived. For large firms, therefore, the need both to recruit and
retain staff favoured relocation over considerable distances.

There appears to have been another influence at work in
the trend towards longer distance dispersal. This is the
'demonstration effect' of some earlier, pioneering moves. As
the fact of successful relocation became established, dispersal
gained greater acceptance among the business community. The
'move to the country' was publicised not only by LOB but also
by a variety of trade and professional journals which offered to
firms examples of relocation by organisations similar to themselves. Initially, firms erred on the side of caution in
selecting alternative locations to Central London. But some
large organisations, having established the practicality of
operating from a non-central location by effecting small-scale
suburban moves in the 1960s, became rather more adventurous
when considering larger scale relocation programmes in the 1970s.
Other organisations who had traditionally regarded themselves as
inextricably linked to the contact environment of Central London
were eventually persuaded by the demonstrable success of other
relocations that at least part of their activities might be
undertaken without detriment to their efficiency in non-central
locations.

These various factors - the restrictions on the supply of
office space, the labour needs of large organisations and the
growing acceptability of relocation as a business strategy -
led to an increased willingness of firms to contemplate more
distant locations. Nevertheless, those organisations which
needed to retain a presence in Central London and which were
not capable of being sub-divided into self-sufficient units were
constrained in their choice of location by distance from the
City or the West End. Quite commonly such firms, on their
approach to LOB, would express preferences for locations within
a certain time-distance from Central London - often one hour,
but certainly no further than would allow a return trip and a
lengthy business schedule within one working day. Over time,

transport improvements served to modify the relationship between distance and travel time. In particular, the construction of the M4 and the introduction of British Rail's 125 mph service brought locations such as Swindon and Bristol within very much easier reach of London. As will be seen later, such places benefitted substantially from decentralising employment. Thus, a combination of changing economics of relocation, modified perceptions on the part of the decision makers and transformed accessibilities brought about a trend towards longer-distance relocation, particularly amongst larger organisations undertaking partial moves.

Despite this discernible trend, however, over the whole period of LOB's activities it was mainly locations within the South East that benefitted from the process of office dispersal from Greater London. The Rest of the South East, comprising both the Outer Metropolitan Area and the Outer South East (Figure 4), accounted for some 60% of all the jobs relocated to places beyond the Greater London boundary, with some 40% being dispersed to the Outer Metropolitan Area alone. Of the 43 000 jobs relocated to places outside the South East region, the South West captured the lion's share - over 15 000 (35%). Four other regions attracted more than 5 000 jobs over the 16-year period - Yorkshire and Humberside (15%), East Anglia (13%), the North West and the East Midlands (each 12%). None of the country's other regions received more than 6% of the jobs dispersed beyond the South East. Apart from the South West, which appears to have been generally attractive to office movers, the regional pattern of dispersal reflected the destinations of a few large moves. These destinations will now be examined in some detail.

RECEPTION AREAS

Although a large number of locations shared in the process of office dispersal, a relative handful accounted for a large proportion of the total amount of employment relocated outside Greater London. Some 336 locations outside the Greater London Area were recorded by LOB as the destinations of moves. Of these, just 16 (5%) received 37% of the jobs dispersed. If moves beyond the South East are examined separately, the pattern of dispersal appears even more concentrated with 6% of the 146 reception locations attracting about one-half of all inter-regional movement. The pattern reflects the dominance of a few relocations by large organisations alluded to earlier.

At the end of the 1960s, Rhodes and Kan (1) undertook an examination of the types of destination to which LOB clients had moved. A list of the 'top 30' reception locations was drawn up and it was concluded that the most successful locations were long established towns mainly in the South East where "there was relatively little manufacturing activity but which had an

79

existing rather than a potential supply of office workers".
Rhodes and Kan in addition pointed to the fact that centres of
planned dispersal such as the New Towns had been no more
successful in attracting decentralising office employment than
these older towns. However, a similar examination of the moves
which had taken place up to the time of the LOB's closure
reveals that a somewhat different picture began to emerge in
the 1970s (Figure 5). Although some old established non-manufacturing towns such as Cheltenham, Southend and Horsham still
appear as important loci of decentralised offices, other types
of centre appear to have achieved equal or even greater
prominence. In particular, an analysis of the LOB records
reveals the dominance of a western axis of dispersal, with the
top 4 locations being Basingstoke, Swindon, Reading and Bristol;
each attracted more than 3 000 jobs (Table 8). Thus, in this later
period, the geographical distribution of dispersal became
characterised by certain directional features rather than being
dominated by a particular type of reception town.

Rhodes and Kan pointed to the relatively poor performance
of the London ring of New Towns in the 1960s. A subsequent
analysis confirms this fact. This group of towns have attracted
17% of the total number of jobs dispersed to the Outer Metropolitan Area, while accounting in 1971 for 12% of the urban
population of that sub-region (measured very crudely as the
total population in County Boroughs, Municipal Boroughs and
Urban Districts). A somewhat wider differential might have
been expected, given their role as centres of employment growth.
Their relatively poor performance must in part be attributed to
their initial and major expansion having coincided with an
earlier period of manufacturing dispersal. On the other hand,
newer centres of planned dispersal which failed to feature in
the Rhodes and Kan 'top 30', centres such as Peterborough and
Milton Keynes, did attract substantial numbers of office jobs
in the subsequent decade. So too did Bracknell, one of the
London's first generation New Towns, which benefitted from its
location on the favoured western axis.

Table 8. Towns ranked according to the numbers of jobs received
in moves by LOB clients

3000 +	2000 - 3000	1500 - 2000	1000 - 1500	1000 - 1500
Basingstoke	Bracknell	Ipswich	Slough	Aylesbury
Swindon	Cheltenham	Harlow	Farnborough	Woking
Reading	Southend	Knutsford	Poole	Chatham
Bristol	York	Peterborough	Birmingham	Hemel Hempstead
	Sheffield	Watford	Milton Keynes	Folkstone
		Horsham	Northampton	Cosham
		Derby	Portsmouth	Liverpool

Provincial centres also appear more frequently in the 1979
list than previously. York, Sheffield, Derby, Birmingham and
Liverpool, as well as Bristol, all attracted more than 1 000

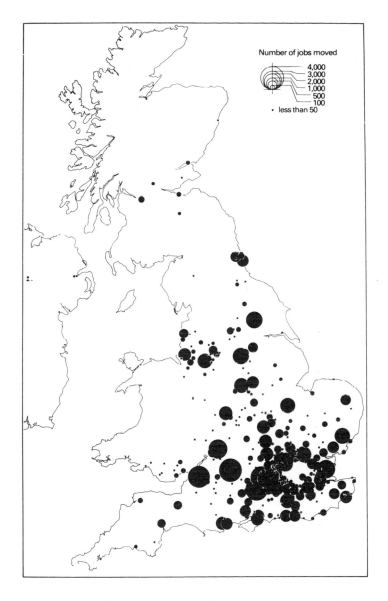

Figure 5.   Office dispersal beyond Greater London, 1964-1979

Source: Location of Offices Bureau, records

81

jobs. But the observation at the end of the 1960s that the most important provincial office centres of Manchester and West Yorkshire had failed to share in the process of receiving dispersed office activities to the extent that might have been expected remained true.

To sum up, therefore, three principal features characterise the destinations of office moves from London in the 1960s and 1970s. First, the predominance of moves into the western axis of development from London to Bristol. Second, the distinctive role of certain provincial centres, well connected to the national transport network, which became reception areas for individual large moves. Third, the relative importance of planned centres of dispersal on the fringe of and just beyond the south East region which played a key role in receiving decentralising firms; such places benefitted hugely from the ready availability of office space, consequent upon the generally sympathetic attitudes towards office development struck by both central and local government, and their planned population growth which ensured decentralised firms the continuation of an outstanding recruitment potential. While these features characterise the spatial pattern of concentrated dispersal, a host of other smaller centres also shared in the process of office dispersal.

OFFICE DISPERSAL AND REGIONAL POLICY

The list of the 'top 30' towns discussed earlier (Table 8) reveals that, although a few locations with the Assisted Areas (as they were defined in the 1970s and as they are shown in Figure 6) were the reception areas for significant numbers of jobs (both York and Sheffield, for example, attracted more than 2 000 jobs), in general the Assisted Areas were relatively unfavoured by the process of office dispersal from London. Over the period of LOB's activities from 1963-1979, fewer than 10% of all jobs dispersed (some 15 400 jobs) were involved in relocations to the Assisted Areas.

The poor performance of the Assisted Areas in attracting dispersed office employment was once again highlighted by the work of Rhodes and Kan in the early 1970s (2). After examining a number of case studies of moves, as well as the general economics of office relocation from London, Rhodes and Kan concluded that for the majority of London decentralisers a move to the Assisted Areas was not an economic proposition. Considerable savings in the cost of both office space and clerical labour might be achieved by moving to locations within 100 miles of London, but those savings could not be significantly increased by a longer distance move. Indeed, office rents in some of the provincial centres were higher than those demanded in some locations in the South East. In 1969, for example, rental data derived from LOB's property register showed that average office rents for new space were £1.28 per square foot in Sheffield, £1.15 in Edinburgh and Glasgow, but £1.00 in Chelmsford and Bedford and as little as £0.90 in Brighton.

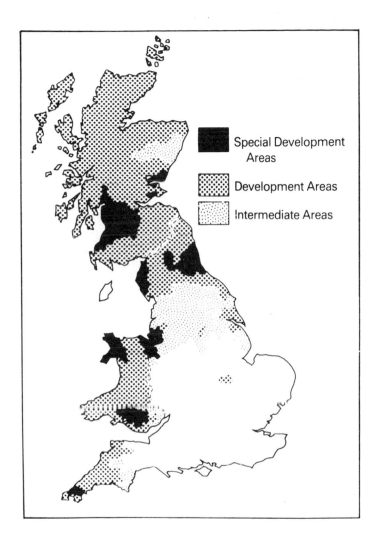

Figure 6. The Assisted Areas, 1974

    Longer distance relocations could, on the other hand, impose
additional costs. These were both of the transitional and of the
recurring type. Heavier transitional costs might be incurred
because more generous relocation allowances would be paid to key
staff in order to induce them to move long distances with the
firm. Additional recurring costs would generally result from
the larger communications expenses borne by organisations which
undertook partial moves from London and thus needed to maintain

contact between different parts of the organisation over long
distances. Rhodes and Kan argued that, in order to counterbalance these economic disadvantages, incentives specifically
designed for the service sector should be made available.
Eventually, in 1973, the Government responded to these arguments
when it introduced the Service Industries Incentive Scheme of
financial inducements.

Until 1973, only those office organisations who built their
own premises were able to take advantage of the incentives
available for relocation in the Assisted Areas based as they
were upon capital subsidies. The absence of any general
incentive for the vast majority of office organisations who
preferred to rent premises is illustrated by the idiosyncratic
nature of those LOB moves which did take place into the Assisted
Areas during the 'policy-free' period from 1963 to mid-1973 -
a total of 77 moves involving 8700 jobs.

These moves can be divided into five broad categories.
First, there was a set of partial moves, comprising some of the
office activities of manufacturing companies, to locations at or
near to their factories. Typical departments that were moved in
this category were accounts, purchasing, sales and regional
administration. Second, there were complete moves of factories
and warehouses and their associated offices out of London,
mainly because of expansion problems. Third, there were partial
office moves to existing regional or decentralised offices or
warehouses of the same company. Fourth, there were large partial
moves by nationalised industries, such as British Rail to York
and the National Coal Board to Doncaster. Finally, there were
new branch offices in provincial centres for London-based firms
that were intending to expand their regional activities and to
carry out work locally rather than in London.

All but the last category of move had some existing connection with the new office location and could not therefore be
regarded as making a genuinely free choice of location. The
last category of move reflects more an organisational shift than
a locational change. Thus, the types of move to the Assisted
Areas that were undertaken prior to the 1973 initiatives were
by no means typical of the bulk of office relocation exercises.
In particular, the first three categories of move would, unlike
most office relocations, have qualified for the government's
financial incentives that were then available because they would
have involved either the building or the conversion of premises.
Moreover, some of the companies undertaking these moves might
also have been able to reduce their Selective Employment Tax
liability by integrating their decentralised office functions
with their manufacturing activities.

It was this feature of office relocation to the Assisted
Areas - its responsiveness to the limited range of incentives
that then existed - that led to considerable optimism about the
likely impact of the more generally applicable Service Industries
Incentive Scheme when it was introduced. Its details are dis-

cussed in Chapter 6. Referring to the new incentives, the LOB *Annual Report for 1973/74* (3) asserted that:

> The Bureau warmly welcomed these encouragements to moves to these (Assisted) areas and believes that they will, in the long term, make an important contribution to regional distribution.

These hopes remained unfulfilled by the time that LOB was abolished in 1979. The performance of the Assisted Areas in attracting office employment proved to be only marginal during the mid and late 1970s. Some 7% of all jobs relocated during the period 1963-1973 were destined for the Assisted Areas. By 1979, the proportion had risen to only 10%.

The failure of the incentives radically to alter the geographical pattern of decentralisation from London must in part be due to the declining rate of movement from 1973 onwards. As has been seen, the year when incentives were introduced - 1973-1974 - marked the peak in the level of office dispersal from London. Moreover, the decisions leading to major moves in the subsequent two or three years would already have been taken by the time that the incentives were introduced. Further-more, it has been argued that the potential impact of the financial incentives package was limited because the level of inducements offered at the outset was insufficient to compensate for the communications costs of long distance dispersal when the value of executives' time devoted to travelling was taken into account. On the basis of their office location model and a very modest evaluation of managers' time Goddard and Pye (4) suggested that, in order to make Sheffield as attractive as Coventry as an office location for decentralising firms, the value of incentives would have needed to have been treble those of the mid-1970s. The same calculations would have implied a six-fold increase for Glasgow.

Whatever the reason, whether it be the overall decline in the level of movement or the initial inadequacy of the incentives and their failure to keep pace with inflation, it is certainly true that the destinations of very few of the moves recorded by LOB could be said to have been influenced by the availability of government grants. Nevertheless, during the 'post-policy period', that is between 1979 and 1983, a small number of large moves found their destinations in the Assisted Areas and the majority were aided moves (see Chapter 7). Two of the clearing banks set up major new headquarters establishments in Knutsford, in the North West region, and in Sheffield. A mail order company relocated a substantial component of its London activities in Sheffield. The Northern region was the recipient of relocations in the insurance and business services sectors and an engineering company decentralised part of its activities to Glasgow.

In many of these cases the rationale of the move - the desire to escape the clerical labour shortages of the London catchment area - dictated a long distance relocation. It was in the context of this type of movement that the Assisted Areas policy achieved what little success might be claimed. But it must be noted that during the 'regional policy period' from 1973-1979 over twice as many jobs were relocated to the non-Assisted Areas outside the South East - especially to places in the South West region - as found their destinations in the Special Development, Development and Intermediate Areas (see Table 6). Assisted Area incentives, therefore, clearly failed to divert a substantial proportion of the long distance office relocation that was taking place.

In the above discussion, the pre-regional policy and active regional policy periods have been treated in aggregate terms. Given that the whole period under review covers some 17 years, it might be expected that the data on movement to the Assisted Areas would reveal some temporal trends. Close examination of the regional tables, however, shows that the absolute and relative amounts of job dispersal to the Assisted Areas in any one year are determined by the random timing of a small number of large moves. Certainly the Assisted Areas do not appear to have benefitted, as has been suggested in the past, when the overall level of office movement was high. The peak year for movement, 1973-1974, saw a very small number of jobs (less than 500) being relocated to the Assisted Areas. Nor is the effect of incentives discernible when the data is analysed by individual year. The year in which the largest absolute number of jobs were dispersed to the Assisted Areas was 1968-1969, when over 3000 jobs (28%) were moved to such locations. This total was nearly matched in absolute terms by only one 'policy' year, 1974-1975, when the overall level of movement was greater and thus the relative performance of the Assisted Areas poorer. These facts suggest that the level of movement to the Assisted Areas may reflect a combination of the effects of the two main policy instruments - ODPs and financial incentives. The early peak coincides with the period when ODP controls had been in existence long enough to exert an important influence on the level of space availability in the South East and before the relaxation of the control. It must be stressed, however, that the erratic annual fluctuations in the level of office movement to the Assisted Areas render such interpretations hazardous.

REFERENCES AND NOTES

1. J. Rhodes and A. Kan (1971), *Office Dispersal and Regional Policy*. Cambridge: Cambridge University Press.

2. *ibid*.

3. LOB, Location of Offices Bureau (1974), *Annual Report 1973/74*. London: LOB, p. 16.

4. J.B. Goddard and R. Pye (1977), 'Telecommunications and office location', *Regional Studies*, Vol.11, pp.19-30.

6

Policy crisis and collapse,

1974-1980

A burst of economic activity in the early 1970s - exaggerated by
the Heath Government's 'rush for growth' in the context of an
unusually fast economic expansion throughout most of the developed world - triggered off a property boom. It affected the
London market especially, but had ramifications throughout the
whole country. By early 1975 average office rents in the City,
which had stood at less than £10 per square foot in 1969 had
risen to £20; new prime banking hall space had asking rents of
up to £35; and even suburban rents had increased to £8 in the
case of Croydon, for example. The consequential leaps in the
estimated worth of office properties afforded the launching
pad for an associated, and at times apparently frenzied, development boom. The scale and the speed of activity was undoubtedly
fuelled by the annual 25% increase in money supply during this
period, by the burgeoning of a secondary banking industry through
which an increasing share of property funds were raised and
allocated, and by many speculative transactions based upon the
dubious assumption that rents and property values would continue
to increase at the high rates of this exceptional period. As
a result of this boom, the stock of commercial offices in
Greater London rose from 127 million square feet in 1970 to
170 million square feet in 1978.

The boom came to an end in 1974-1975. Its speculative
excesses, however, were still very much in the public mind when
the Labour Government came into office in the Spring of 1974.
At their extreme they were epitomised by the events and emotions
that surrounded the construction, and the failure to let for a
decade, of a major 32 storey office block in the West End,
Centre Point. In fact, these events had encouraged the previous
Conservative Government to prepare legislation seeking to curb
developers in those aspects of speculation which appeared to
result in offices being kept deliberately empty. Predictably,
therefore, the new Secretary of State for the Environment sought

to press the point and to secure an appropriate (but in the
event unused) clause giving the Government such powers in Part
IV of the Community Land Act 1975. For this reason alone,
circumstances were ripe to demand a broad review of office
development and location policies.

Yet there were other reasons also. As early as 1972, the
Conservative Government had imposed a freeze on business rents.
With the passage of time pressures were inevitably mounting for
a review and relaxation of that policy. The incoming Secretary
of State for the Environment also had an early need to take
stock of existing office development procedures and policy if
for no other reason than the fact that the necessary enabling
legislation was due for renewal in 1977. More urgently, such a
stocktaking was necessary because a 'standstill' had been
imposed on all applications for office development in the South
East in 1973 by the Secretary of State's predecessor. This was
a measure that was inspired, not by office policy considerations,
but was part of the Government's response to the energy crisis
and a general shortage of resources and materials. The Conservative Government had slightly relaxed ODP policy with respect to
offices ancilliary to factories and to buildings where a change
of use to offices would involve minimal construction work. Although the new Secretary of State rather speedily granted further
exceptions in the case of railway station sites "if substantial
public benefit would accrue through developments on behalf of
public authorities", the new Government obviously needed to take
a view on the uses to which office floorspace controls might prospectively be put. Such a decision could hardly avoid a review
of its effectiveness over the previous ten years.

It was also the desire of the incoming Government generally
to stengthen inter-regional policies. The 1973 Service Industry
Incentive Scheme was still fresh on the statute book and it had
had no time to bear fruit. The effectiveness of the Scheme was,
therefore, unproven. Nevertheless, there was an instinctive
desire on the part of the Government to confirm and, if possible,
measure its merits alongside those of other incentives available
in the Assisted Areas, and to consider the implications of
further extensions to the areas within which the grants and
subsidies might be claimed. In addition, whilst the initial
outcome of the 1973 Hardman inquiry (into the possibility of yet
further changes in the location of the headquarters' functions
and posts of the Civil Service) had been for the Heath Government
to decide upon the further decentralisation of 31 000 jobs, with
one-third remaining within the South East and a little more than
one-half being transferred to the Assisted Areas, the 1974 Labour
Government immediately took a different view. Within months of
assuming office, it decided to pursue an alternative and more
radical Hardman solution by insisting that over 90% of the
decentralised posts should be relocated to places in the Assisted
Areas and that only a handful (some 850 posts) should remain in
the South East. It was following this decision that Glasgow
was allocated a substantial number of posts in the Ministry of
Overseas Development, that Merseyside (specifically, Bootle)

88

acquired some sections of the Home Office, that South Wales
increased its employment in the Ministry of Defence and that the
Property Services Agency moved to Teesside. Beside the moves
from London, other Civil Service posts in such relatively prosperous centres as Harrogate, Bath and Didcot were also moved
into the Assisted Areas at this time.

An equally urgent pressure for a review of office location
policies also came from within the South East region, including
interests in the Greater London Area. It should be recalled
that office policy had emerged within the physical planning
framework of the early 1960s when counties and county boroughs
were responsible for the preparation and implementation of local
development plans. In part it had been the failure of those
authorities to coordinate their activities and to reconcile
their sometimes divergent interests that persuaded central
government to initiate both a regional planning exercise (later
published as the 1964 *South East Study*) and an office location
policy involving the establishment of LOB and the introduction
of ODPs. Subsequently, however, the planning framework was
changed. First, with the creation of the GLC in 1964, and ten
years later with the reorganisation of local government throughout the rest of the country, a new spatial organisation for
planning was created. In parallel, and following the 1968
report of the Planning Advisory Group, a new statutory two-tier
arrangement for physical planning was established for the
resolution of broader 'strategic' issues through the preparation
of structure plans, whilst the districts and boroughs assumed
responsibility for local land use plans.

Superimposed upon these statutory functions was the advisory
regional planning system which by 1970 had produced a *Strategic
Plan for the South East*, a document which was subsequently
amended and approved by the Secretary of State for the Environment. This plan was the joint product of the local authorities'
own Standing Conference on London and South East Regional
Planning, the Regional Economic Planning Council, and the
Department of the Environment, whose task it was to ensure,
inter alia, that the county structure plans were in sympathy
with it. Given this new administrative structure and these new
planning arrangements, there was a growing expectation that the
elected local authorities could and would henceforth be left
increasingly to determine and oversee the evolution of land use
and economic development within the region, with a minimum
degree of Whitehall supervision and intervention. Thus, during
the second reading of the Town and Country Planning (Amendment)
Bill 1972, the Minister of Local Government and Planning argued
that:

> In the near future a balanced policy of office development for
> London and the region can best be brought about by the operation,
> principally by local planning authorities themselves of the new
> system of development planning.

In such an attitude lay an implicit challenge to the very existence of ODPs, and even to the traditional role of LOB.

This challenge to contemporary office policy was endorsed by officers and elected members of the GLC whose concern for the future economic health of the metropolitan area had become increasingly articulate after the publication of the *Greater London Development Plan* in 1969. The continuing fall in the population of the conurbation, the even faster decline in its manufacturing employment, the loss of jobs in wholesale and seaport activities and the first signs of a decline in the magnitude of even office employment within the tightly drawn and somewhat arbitrary defined Central Area, together suggested that some relaxation of central government's traditional constraints upon the adjustment and growth of the London economy (and particularly jobs in London) was overdue. By this time, market forces were strongly encouraging office and other activities to decentralise away from Central London; the loss of jobs in the surrounding collar of Victorian suburbs was not being followed by the speedy adaptation of land and buildings to alternative uses; and manufacturing sites even in the outer suburbs were no longer prized as once they had been. It was natural, therefore, that the whole programme of accelerating the decentralisation of population and employment away from the metropolis, which had been a key element in the Abercrombie *Plan for Greater London* and in all the subsequent regional studies and strategies of the 1960s and early 1970s, should be challenged.

It was particularly the inner areas of the conurbation for which the greatest concern was felt. Some financial assistance had been provided for them through the urban programme of the early 1970s, of course, and major investigations into the precise nature of their problems were launched in London, as well as in Birmingham and Liverpool, in 1972 (1). Only in the mid-1970s, however, did the generality of the inner areas become the focus of a major central government planning initiative which was eventually crowned with the Inner Urban Areas Act 1978. Simultaneously the government reduced its commitment to the existing programme of formal overspill and revised downward its population targets for several of the New Towns. The GLC, in the meantime, sought to remove any unnecessary planning policy inhibitions to beneficial structural economic change in the metropolis - inhibitions which included in their view the anti-London stance of LOB, especially that found in its advertising - and to wrest from central government the administration of the ODP floorspace control which the Council saw primarily as a tool for strategic rather than inter-regional planning.

Collectively, then, all these developments suggested the need for a major review of office location policy by central government. As part of a somewhat wider survey of the many issues surrounding the generality of commercial development, therefore, the Secretary of State for the Environment announced in July, 1974 his decision to commission the Office Location

Review (OLR). It reported two years later (2), by which time
the property boom of 1971-1974 had collapsed, the national
economy was in considerable distress, and the international
energy crisis and global recession had dramatically altered
economic prospects everywhere. Meanwhile, emotions about the
behaviour of the development industry during the property boom
had substantially subsided. Many property companies were in
fact in distress and a number had been forced into liquidation.
At least one of the immediate reasons for the policy review had
thus disappeared. All the other and in a sense more fundamental
reasons for a review - the mounting problems and employment needs
of the Assisted Areas, the crisis of the inner cities, and the
need to adjust central government policies to the new administrative and physical planning framework - remained high on the
political agenda. There also persisted a simple legislative
need to decide whether or not to renew central government's
powers with respect to ODPs, and whether or not (and when) to
abandon the freeze on business rents.

THE COLLAPSE OF THE OFFICE BOOM AND AFTER

The announcement of the Office Location Review in 1974 coincided
with the peak in Central London property values. As noted
earlier, prime rents at the beginning of 1974 had reached £22.00
per square foot in the City and £12.00 per square foot in the
West End (see Table 2). During the period in which the review
was undertaken, however, dramatic changes took place in the
property market, particularly that of Central London. These
changes arose from developments affecting both sides of the
demand and supply equation.

Several factors combined to significantly reduce demand
for City office space. Their repercussions were felt first
throughout Central London and eventually in the rest of the
country. The oil crisis of 1973 led to recession throughout
the industrialised world. It adversely affected the financial
services sector of the City in particular, since that sector
was heavily dependent upon demand from overseas countries. In
1973, for example, overseas business accounted for 65% of net
premiums in the insurance sector. Subsequently, and following
the collapse of the Stock Market and the need for the Bank of
England's 'lifeboat' operation to assist fringe banking activities, a major crisis of confidence spread throughout the City
as the whole British economy moved into prolonged recession.

Employment in the City declined in consequence. There were
mergers among activities connected with the Stock Exchange. In
the generally straitened circumstances, firms in a wide variety
of industries were forced to effect economies. At the same time,
however, many firms had already embarked upon decentralisation
programmes in response to the escalating rent levels of the
early 1970s and were rather slow to respond to the altered market
conditions. It was not until late 1974 that asking rents began

91

to fall back. Thus, the economic contraction at home and (especially) abroad, and the continuing dispersal of office employment away from Central London, led to a reduced demand for office space in the capital.

The downturn in demand led directly to an increase in the amount of office space available and on offer for renting. Firms whose employment was contracting and who were suffering from cash-flow problems began to market space that they did not immediately require, while those who were decentralising vacated space in the Central Area. A somewhat easier market was thus established through the increased supply of second-hand space. The excess of supply over demand was greatly exaggerated, however, by the marketing of new office space, the construction of which had been started during the development boom of the early 1970s. The significant rent rise of the period 1971-1973, together with a phase of easy money supply occasioned by the so-called 'Barber boom' and the relaxation of ODP controls, brought about a substantial increase in the rate of development activity. The amount of space under construction rose from about 1.5 million square feet in 1970 to over 6 million square feet at the end of 1975. But, as these dates suggest, due to the inevitable delays between the initiation and completion of office construction schemes, the new supply did not appear on the market until after demand had begun to fall off and used space had become available in increased quantities. In addition, developers recognising a continuing and deepening slump began to market space ahead of completion. This was in marked contrast to the earlier practice in a tight market when they tended to market space as late as possible in order to take advantage of steadily rising rents. The sellers' market of the early 1970s was thus reversed. Rents for prime space in the City fell to a low of £12.00 per square foot in 1976. This represented a decline of 63% in real terms from the peak in 1974.

The dramatic reversal of fortunes in the City office property market is well illustrated by the history of the relocation of the headquarters of the Wiggins Teape Company from the City to Basingstoke. The company was able in 1972 to dispose of the freehold of its 130 000 square foot City office building - Gateway House - for £27.7 million. With part of the proceeds of the sale, the company was able to finance the construction of an award-winning, purpose-built premises in Basingstoke. Indeed, in moving 850 jobs to Basingstoke the company was able to generate a capital surplus of some £18 million. Had Wiggins Teape attempted to undertake that same relocation exercise three years later, after rents had fallen and yields risen, the company would probably have realised little more than £10 million for the sale of its City headquarters, while the costs involved in construction and the move would have been substantially higher than in 1972. The costs of new, private commercial construction increased by 23% between 1974 and 1976.

Although the signs of the collapse of the property market
in the mid-1970s first became apparent in the City, the effects
soon spread to the whole of the country. The demand for office
space everywhere was adversely affected by the recession, and
in addition, of course, the combination of straitened economic
circumstances for many firms and the more ready availability
(and falling costs) of Central London space eventually reduced
the demand for office accommodation outside London by
decentralising firms. As in the capital itself, many developers
found themselves in a difficult situation. They had been
encouraged by a rising market to initiate developments financed
by heavy borrowing. Now caught between considerably higher
interest rates and weak demand, developers and other owners of
property were forced to reduce asking rents in the hope of
producing at least some income to service their debts. Indeed,
some new office properties were offered for sale rather than to
rent, thereby reflecting the dominance of short-term liquidity
problems over the returns from long-term rental growth in the
decision making of property companies.

These features of the property market generally began to
be reflected in asking rents in decentralised locations in 1976.
Even in relatively favoured places such as Bristol, rents fell
back in current prices as well as in real terms. The immediate
impact of these changes was to establish a buyers' (or renters')
market for office properties which persisted well into the late
1970s in most locations ouside Central London. Although in the
City and the West End there were signs of an upturn in demand
in 1977, it was at least 1978 before these were apparent elsewhere. Shortages of space then began to appear in some locations,
particularly on the western periphery of the London area. These
shortages arose because, while rental levels had fallen substantially, construction costs continued to rise with the result
that few potential developments offered any return. Thus, as
late as 1978 an *Economist* survey of property asserted that
"offices in many provincial centres still... have negative site
values" (3). It was not until rents appeared to be recovering
to levels which made development viable, then around a minimum
of £5 per square foot, that new construction commenced. With
three years or more between the initiation and completion of
most schemes, it was inevitable that shortages should occur
in particular places. Thus the property scene emerged from the
mid-1970s slump as somewhat maladjusted, with surpluses of space
in many parts of the country, but shortages in those locations
where demand was first to recover, such as in the Thames Valley.

The experience of the boom and slump during the 1970s had
some long-lasting effects on the property industry itself.
First of all, the early 1970s had been characterised by unreal-
istic optimism about the long-term worth of office property.
Demand, it was assumed, was almost infinite. So convinced were
investors of the attractions of office property that yields fell
to as little as 4% on some transactions at a time when general
interest rates were around the 7% level (4). Indeed, some
commentators on the property scene seemed to be suggesting that

rents followed capital values rather than the reverse. These attitudes were, of course, transformed by the experience of the mid-1970s. A rather over-cautious attitude towards development and investment took over. Many property companies were so shaken by the slump and so alarmed by the spectre of new taxes on development gains that they threatened to withdraw entirely from office development in Britain. In time, of course, a more realistic view of the prospective returns from well-chosen investments became generally established.

As well as affecting the attitudes of the industry, the slump also altered the shape of the property sector. The long-established companies with older patterns of investment were able to survive the slump. Many of the newer entrants to the industry, however, were forced into bankrupcy or were taken over, squeezed by high interest charges on borrowings raised to finance unlettable properties. More than 50 property companies that were publicly quoted in 1968 had disappeared by 1978, "either without trace or into the maw of larger companies" (5). Thus, the industry became more concentrated. In addition, developers who in the past had been anxious to retain a total interest in particular developments in order to derive maximum gains were now keen to share the risks of schemes with other funding institutions, such as pension funds and public authorities.

Thus, by the time that the *Office Location Review* was published, the property scene in Britain was undergoing a rapid and significant transformation. The demand for office space was sluggish; the property industry was extremely reluctant to become involved in anything other than prime development; the industry itself was more concentrated; and it had re-learnt the need, if not acquired the expertise, to assess more carefully the likely demand for potential developments.

THE CHANGING PHYSICAL PLANNING CONTEXT, 1974-1977

Attitudes towards office location policies in the mid-1970s were affected by the collapse of the property boom of the early 1970s, and in addition, they were shaped by the changing stance of both central and local government towards spatial planning objectives and practice. Altered economic and demographic circumstances in particular encouraged an almost continuous review of policies at several different scales between 1974 and 1977. Not least was this so in London and the South East. There, a retreat from the long-standing decentralisation philosophy of Abercrombie, and the emergence of policies designed to arrest the decline and facili-tate the adaptation of the inner areas of the capital, were gathering momentum.

It was in November 1974 that the Minister for Planning and Local Government announced a study to 'develop' the *Strategic Plan for the South East* (SPSE) (6). Whilst he remained satisfied with the general notion of promoting the designated major and medium growth areas in the Rest of the South East (ROSE), two factors in particular prompted the review. The first was the Registrar General's revised expectations about the future size of the region's population, which in 1968 had been forecast to rise some 3 million by 1991 but which was now expected to remain static at about 17 million. The second was the changed national economic climate, with its dismal expectation of a persistently slow rate of economic growth and a consequential need to revise downward many earlier ambitions with regard to the level of future public expenditure. A further development of significance came in the following year when, in the light of a report on the future of London's docklands, the Government indicated that an important objective of the Review of the *Strategic Plan for the South East* would be to ascertain the relative public costs of alternative patterns of urban development in different parts of the region, and in particular to establish the contrast between the costs of development in London and those in the ROSE.

The SPSE review (7), published late in 1976, confirmed the need to make provision for a substantial growth of population in ROSE - an extra 1.0-1.5 million by 1991. Moreover, continuing changes in household structure were recognised as likely to compound the requirement for many more dwellings there. These findings encouraged the Joint Planning Team, representing the Department of the Environment, the Standing Conference and the Economic Planning Council, to endorse earlier analyses and the established planning strategy for ROSE that had been proposed in the 1970 *Strategic Plan for the South East*. However, it was noted that since the main source of employment growth and mobility in ROSE was likely to be in the service industries and the office sector "stronger locational guidance of (their) movement and growth" would be required (8). It was implicitly assumed that this shift of emphasis would be reflected in the preparation and implementation of the county structure plans.

A more dramatic change of emphasis appeared in the Review with regard to the problems of Greater London. The capital's difficulties centred upon the rapid fall in its level of employment and the even faster decline in its population, in the rising levels of localised unemployment (especially in the inner boroughs) and in the narrowing of choices in its housing market. Although the Joint Planning Team was agnostic with regard to a 'preferred' or 'optimum' size of London's population and employment, it took the view that the recent pace of decline was improperly fast. It therefore made recommendations that were designed to ease the pace of population and employment change, including the adoption of measures that might encourage the longer-term development of service rather than manufacturing employment in the capital. To this end it advocated the abolition of ODPs. It also questioned whether the Location of Offices Bureau should contine its efforts to encourage businesses to move out of London and urged that the "terms of reference of the Bureau need to be reconsidered".

95

Meanwhile, within the metropolitan county, the GLC was struggling to assert its role as the structure plan authority and to ensure that a consistent set of attitudes towards the location of office development was being adopted by its constituent borough councils. The inherent difficulties of this task were multiplied by the growing economic and employment uncertainties facing the conurbation. Formally, in fact, the GLC was awaiting the response of the Secretary of State for the Environment to the Layfield Inquiry into the *Greater London Development Plan* (GLDP) (9). The Inquiry had broadly endorsed the GLDPs proposal for the concentration of further office development in "preferred locations", especially in the so-called Strategic Centres and Action Areas. It had, however, rejected two of the major planks of the GLC's employment policies, namely, the proposal to regulate the relationship between labour supply and demand within broad geographical sectors of London through the use of floorspace controls, and to reduce the rate at which employment was leaving London. The Inquiry had also encouraged the GLC to abandon the notion that its policies could and should seek to select for encouragement in London those activities which had a relatively high level of productivity there. With particular reference to the Central Area, the Inquiry team, which saw no virtue in the ODP system, firmly rejected any proposal to limit the growth of office floorspace through the application of quantitative controls, taking the view that there was little chance in the medium term of "an expansion of office development... of such a scale that it would significantly change the present position" (10). In addition, the Inquiry had concluded that any pressure to build in the centre of London "would be relieved by improving the desirability of the Growth Areas, or centres in the South East, and by the activities of bodies such as LOB" (11).

The Secretary of State for the Environment, in his (interim) Statement on the GLDP in October 1975 (12), in fact accepted the continuing relevance of policies that would assist decentralis-ation within and from London. Moreover, he rejected the advice of the Layfield Inquiry with reference to Central London, proposing that office development "should be encouraged to disperse to locations away from Central London" and that a "restrictive policy for development in Central London itself should continue" (13). Subsequently, therefore, when the Reasoned Statement of the modified GLDP by the Secretary of State appeared in 1976, only a shadow of the GLC's original proposals remained. Employment policy was highly generalised; office location policy simply took the form of a list of pre-ferred locations; and Central Area office policy was summarised in a single brief paragraph:

Some areas of Central London are more suitable for the development of offices than others. Accessibility is one of the principal considerations and the vicinities of the central London termini and other important traffic interchange points have advantages in this respect. The building and rebuilding of offices, like other forms of development, proceeds continually. The London Borough councils

having jurisdiction in Central London should take the opportunity
which it affords to guide new offices to the areas where such
development will be most advantageous (14).

The GLC itself, however, continued to believe that floorspace targets and controls were a necessary adjunct to other
forms of planning control. Despite the difficulties involved
in making labour supply and demand forecasts for different
geographical sectors of the capital, and despite the uncertain
future relationship between 'employment floorspace' as an
abstraction and the actual number of people employed in, say,
a particular 1.0 million square foot office block, the GLC
approved an office location policy in March 1975 which included
both types of forecast. Their associated policies sought,
inter alia, to continue with restraints upon further development
in the Outer West and Western sectors of the county, and to give
precedence and encouragement to development proposals in the
North East and South East boroughs. It was a policy based upon
the proposition that London could and would continue to make
a contribution to planned growth in the ROSE. It also assumed
that the constituent boroughs within the Greater London Area
would willingly assist with its implementation. Within months,
however, and in the wake of mounting concerns about the rising
level of unemployment in the capital, the GLC called for a
review of formal overspill policies (15). It also became
increasingly apparent that the details of its policies were not
always acceptable to the boroughs, and that the problems of
policy implementation were much more substantial than had
originally been imagined. Moreover, the policy made assumptions
about demographic changes and office employment growth which
were not always shared by the adjacent shire counties. Kent,
for example, took the view that the GLC's ambitions to encourage
the growth of office employment in the South East sector of the
Greater London Area were in conflict with their attempts to
stabilise the level of commuting into London and to encourage
office development in the South East sector of ROSE.

Not all the Home Counties were at this time in favour of
office development, of course. Throughout much of the OMA the
newly reorganised local authorities were pressing ahead with
their commitment not only to prepare structure plans but also
to satisfy a new-found need to provide for a high level of
'public participation' in the process. Having catered for the
brunt of London's formal and, even more important, informal
overspill over the previous 30 years, most of the county councils
surrounding Greater London were anxious to slow down the pace of
new housing construction and employment growth. Their policies
were, therefore, designed to place obstacles in the way of what
they regarded as non-essential office construction, and increasingly they came to attach the so-called 'local user' clause to
most of the planning permissions they gave. Through this
device it was hoped that only "offices serving the local
community" or "offices required as essential ancilliaries to
industry already established" in the locality would be allowed.

The logic of this policy rested on the presumptions that existing levels of commuting into London would persist (although the avowed aim of some of the plans was to reduce the level of commuting); that there was a general shortage of office workers in the OMA; and that a need existed to prevent a further substantial increase in the demand for office labour there in order that the pressures for additional housing land might be contained. The New Towns, of course, provided singular exceptions to these general planning objectives. However, a feeling was growing in many quarters that these policies in the OMA were denying significant benefits to both employers and employees there and in the South East generally. Certainly, the Location of Offices Bureau in its annual report of 1973 pointed to the restrictions upon office development in the OMA as an "impediment to decentralisation" and a challenge to the LOB's role.

THE OFFICE LOCATION REVIEW

The 1976 Office Location Review (OLR) thus took place against a background of changing market circumstances and shifting planning attitudes. Besides summarising experience in the several dimensions of office location policy since 1963, the OLR underlined the many changes that had occurred in the actual (and perceived) circumstances - both geographical and planning - since policies were first introduced. It noted, for example, that one of the principal reasons for introducing office floor-space controls by central government in 1964 was the view that without them:

> employment in London would continue to rise rapidly, putting
> unmanageable pressures on transport and on housing. These
> reasons no longer apply. Commuting into Central London has
> been falling steadily for a number of years. The anxiety now
> is about the flow of jobs and population out of London (16).

The OLR was conducted by the Urban Affairs and Commercial Property Directorate of the Department of the Environment, under the guidance of an inter-departmental Committee that represented the interests of the Department of Industry, the Department of Employment and the Treasury. The central but substantially unexplored assumption of the OLR, amongst others, was that an office location policy was desirable. The general case for intervention was only superficially and tangentially examined. Instead, the principal questions of the OLR concerned the past effectiveness of policy, the adjustments that might be made to it (especially the need to give office policy a more articulate and effective inter-regional dimension for the benefit of the Assisted Areas) and the most appropriate instruments that might be employed to achieve these ends. In particular, the experience of the Department of the Environment with ODP controls was subject to very careful review and the work of the Location of Offices Bureau was assessed.

98

The OLR was particularly critical of the ODP system. In the context of the changing planning arrangements of the South East, it questioned whether the control, which in the early 1970s had been used to further the objectives of the SPSE in the promotion of the designated growth areas, remained a useful tool for shaping the geography of employment. The OLR noted that: "With the trends now established... and the ability of the planning system to channel and regulate, it seems debatable whether other special measures are needed to this end". More fundamentally, however, the OLR raised doubts about the value of an instrument of policy which over time adversely affected both the supply of, and hence the market for, office space. It was accepted that ODPs, superimposed upon the workings of the normal planning system, had impaired the efficiency of the office market by compounding the delays facing the development industry as it responded to upswings in demand. Their use, in other words, had exaggerated the inherent instability of the market for office space - an instability that was reflected in the volatility of London office rents in both nominal and real terms. This was seen as too high a price to pay when other evidence indicated that the control had succeeded little in deflecting the demand for office space to other, policy preferred, locations. For example, 41 named-user ODP applications refused for London locations between 1965 and 1972 resulted in only six moves out of London, all to places in the South East. Therefore, whilst the ODP control was acknowledged as a means of identifying potential movers over longer distances, the OLR laid greater stress upon the rigidities and distortions that in practice it had introduced into the office market.

In contrast to its criticism of ODPs, the OLR took a very favourable view of the activities and the achievements of the Location of Offices Bureau. It noted that the LOB "provided an efficient and effective service at minimum cost to the Exchequer, and remained a suitable and economic vehicle for a propagandist and advisory role" in office location policy (18). It saw advantage in LOB making greater efforts on behalf of the Assisted Areas, although the difficulties involved in encouraging a swifter transfer of office activities there was fully recognised. Indeed, the view was taken that "the main gain in office jobs for the Assisted Areas will continue to come from 'indigenous' growth" (19).

Nevertheless, the OLR suggested that the advisory role of the LOB might valuably be revised to serve more directly the interests of inter-regional policy, and it canvassed the idea that its remit might be adjusted to encourage moves from anywhere in the South East to the Assisted Areas in particular. By chance, a few months earlier the Advisory Group on Commercial Property Development (the Pilcher Committee) had also endorsed, implicitly, the need for an agency (such as LOB) which would provide guidance to local authorities, especially those in the Assisted Areas, which were anxious to encourage office development. The Pilcher Committee noted that: "To enable them to

initiate effective development schemes, local authorities should
obtain specialist advice, particularly on demand and the requirements of occupants" (20). This advice needed to be grounded in
a full understanding of the office market as a whole, a virtue
that the LOB could legitimately claim to afford.

Following the OLR, the Government decided that ODP control,
rather than be abolished, should be relaxed. The exemption limit
was raised immediately from 10 000 to 15 000 square feet, and
then to 30 000 in the following year. At the latter figure the
control applied only to quite large office blocks capable of
housing perhaps 150 to 200 people. The publication of the OLR
was also followed by an announcement of improved regional
incentives for the service industries under Section 7 of the
Industry Act 1972. These were designed to "encourage the growth
of employment in service industries, including offices, in the
assisted areas".

The fixed grant for each employee moving with his or her
work to a location in an Assisted Area was nearly doubled to
£1500. An additional grant of £1000 in the Development Areas
and £1500 in the Special Development Areas became available for
each job created there. Rent relief grants for office premises
became available for periods ranging from three years in the
Intermediate Areas to seven years in localities with the highest
levels of unemployment. Although this scheme, administered by
the Department of Industry, pulled office employment nearer to
the centre stage of that Department's efforts to help the
Assisted Areas - which by this date had been extended to include
about 45% of the country's population (see Figure 6) - incentives
to manufacturing industry still continued to dominate both thinking and practice in inter-regional policy.

It was May 1977, however, before the Government was able to
announce during the Second Reading of the Control of Office
Development Bill its plans for the adaptation of the role of
LOB. By then the Secretary of State's commitment to assist the
process of adjustment and renewal in the country's inner urban
areas was becoming increasingly visible, and the purpose of
several policy initiatives at that time was to modify and re-
direct the activities of existing government agencies, LOB
included, to assist urban renewal and change. The new role that
was given to LOB, however, came to be substantially misunderstood.

A NEW ROLE FOR LOB

For 14 years LOB had been concerned with the promotion of, and
the provision of assistance to, office movement. Although its
publicity attracted most public attention, the mainspring of its
success had been the collection and collation of impartial and
current information which employers needed in order to consider
and plan a move properly. That information was provided on a

100

free and confidential basis. The LOB had operated from 1963
under a remit which was explicit about the origins of preferred
office movement - "from congested areas in central London".
But it was imprecise about the preferred destinations for office
movement - "to suitable centres elsewhere". Over time, however,
public concern came to be focussed upon the destinations of
office movement. In the early 1970s the growth areas of the
South East were singled out as desirable locations for the
reception of decentralising office firms, and the administration
of ODP policy was adapted to this end. In 1973, the first
Service Industry Incentives Scheme was introduced in the Assisted
Areas. Over the years, the LOB had tentatively adjusted its
activities and advice to take note of these political realities.
It drew the attention of its clients to intra-regional and
inter-regional policies and incentives, and to their implications
for the decentralising firm. The new Order in Council in 1977,
therefore, provided the Secretary of State for the Environment
with an opportunity not only to formalise this situation but
also to advance matters further.

Under a new general or strategic remit to promote "the
better distribution of office employment in England and Wales",
and in contrast to the LOB's initial objectives of 1963, the
Secretary of State was quite specific in 1977 about the preferred destinations of office movement but less precise about
its origins. For political reasons, he did not make it absolutely clear that Central London would continue to be the
principal source of such moves, even though this was implicit
in his statement to the House of Commons. However, he asked
LOB formally to promote the relocation of office activities into
the Assisted Areas. In addition, with the Abercrombie policy of
providing for conurbation overspill in New Towns simultaneously
curtailed, he instructed the LOB to encourage office movement
into the inner urban areas (21). This shift of emphasis, from
a straight-forward commitment to assist with the restraint of
office employment expansion in the metropolitan centre which
was increasingly subject to a natural tendency to disperse, to
a more general concern about the destination of office movement
and a more 'equitable' geography of office employment, posed the
LOB with a number of challenges. First, it was clear from the
outset that, whilst the LOB was expected to remain "a businessman's Bureau" and to continue to provide free and impartial
advice to its clients, the preferred destinations of office
movement as seen by government were determined by criteria of
social need and, often, by crude political influence. In contrast to its traditional role, therefore, LOB's new objectives
lacked the powerful and beneficial support of market forces.
They clearly required supporting actions - improved subventions
to encourage moves into the Assisted Areas, and a determined
application of a broad spectrum of inner urban area policies -
from both central and local government if they were ever to meet
with success. Such supporting actions, however, were matters
over which the LOB had no formal influence.

The instruction to promote and assist inter-regional office
mobility was, as has been noted, a policy tactic which the LOB

had tentatively espoused since its inception and especially
after 1973 - in cooperation with the Department of Industry
on such matters as advertising and promotion, and (where
appropriate) in its advice to its clients. The "inner urban
areas" remit, however, was entirely new. It presented the LOB
with the need to dispel a frustrating and persistent public
misunderstanding that this new objective involved a fundamental
reversal of office location policy, and that it was being asked
by the Government to 'stand on its head'. The misunderstanding
stemmed in part from the Secretary of State's phrase about 'the
promotion of office employment in inner urban areas, including
London'. Too readily was it assumed by politicians, journalists
and the general public alike that this would involve an attempt
to attract offices back into London (from elsewhere!), whereas
it was the Government's hope that the inner areas would be the
recipients of some of the continuing stream of office activities
decentralising from Central London, and possibly some indigeneous
office employment growth as well. But public impressions are sometimes difficult to alter.

Despite a substantial advertising campaign to put the
record straight and to ensure that a proper distinction was
being made in the public mind between Central and Inner London,
the misunderstanding dogged the LOB for the rest of its days.
It was an episode that demonstrated both the difficulties
involved in altering a simplistic public image of a planning
agency's objectives (such as had been deliberately cultivated
by the LOB since its inception), and the hazards involved in
building even relatively simple geographical notions into
public policy pronouncements. These matters are explored further
in Chapter 7.

The LOB was given a third role under the 1977 Order in
Council. This related to the broader national objective of
increasing the volume of inward investment for employment
generation, and it involved the LOB being asked to attract
foreign office activities to Britain - both to London and to
locations elsewhere in the country. Hitherto, the Department
of Industry, through its agency the Invest in Britain Bureau
(IBB), had been largely concerned with trying to attract
multinational manufacturing enterprises to this country, and it
had placed considerable emphasis in its activities upon the
availability of financial incentives in the Assisted Areas. The
1977 decision to give LOB an inward investment role was based
upon the view that, given the contrasting locational attributes
and information requirements of office activities, the task of
international promotion could be more effectively performed by
the LOB than by IBB. The view was also taken that any success
the LOB might achieve in attracting the regional headquarters
of multinational enterprises or branch offices of foreign service
industries to Britain would not necessarily conflict with its
role in domestic office policy. LOB would continue to advise
domestic firms in an impartial manner and in their best interests,
and would offer comparable advice to foreign firms. LOB would be
able to indicate impartially not only the advantages but also the

costs of movement to, and operation at, particular places, and it
would be able to draw the attention of its clients to both central
and local government policies as they might affect office costs,
performance and future expansion plans. Not only would it be in
a position to indicate international comparative costs about which
there appeared to be a good deal of misunderstanding, therefore,
but LOB would also be able to interpret dispassionately and with
some authority the costs and benefits of operations in different
parts of the country.

Hypothetically, some incoming firms might be best suited
with offices in the City or the West End. However, with
Central London remaining the principal source of intra-regional
and inter-regional domestic office mobility, and with the level
of office employment there tending to fall slightly, the
accommodation of more foreign banks, international oil companies,
business consultants, accountants, lawyers, international
agencies and the like was in fact increasingly acceptable. It
was also possible that some of the incoming firms might find it
advantageous to consider and adopt other locations, some a
considerable distance from London. After all, in the manufacturing sector over the previous 25 years inward investors had
shown a much readier willingness to take up locations in the
Assisted Areas than had domestic firms. In the case of office
activities, it was noteworthy that before 1977 American banks
had taken advantage of the lower costs and the office space
available in two Inner London locations - Lewisham and Stratford
- and in the process demonstrated one way in which the new
international role of LOB might valuably complement its domestic
activities.

The 1977 role of LOB, therfore, although it was not immediately understood in public debate, did provide a sound basis for
its continued existence as a propagandist, advisory and research
agency seeking to reconcile (at least in some measure) public
and private interests in the matter of office location. Barely
had its new tasks been announced and the Bureau begun to develop its
activities and research accordingly, however, when a major legal
difficulty required that it should mute its voice, lower its
profile and adjust its activities with regard to two aspects of
its new role.

POLICY COLLAPSE

Although the Secretary of State had been advised differently at
the time of his 1977 announcement, legal opinion by early 1978
was persuaded that the LOB's new international role was *ultra
vires*. This was substantially because the amending Order in
Council (like its predecessor) was based upon the 1943 Town and
Country Planning Act. This Act allowed the Minister, whose
powers subsequently came to be vested in the Secretary of State
for the Environment, to set up a commission "for the purpose of
assisting... in the exercise of his functions in relation to the
use and development of land in England and Wales, or any area

therein". It was judged, on reflection, that the attraction of foreign companies to Britain and especially the expenditure of funds overseas could not properly be justified within such legislation. The same legislative circumscription also meant that, strictly speaking, the LOB could not promote the growth of office activities in Scotland and Ulster. For some months the Whitehall bureaucracy pondered on the matter. The LOB was required to cease its international activities and a frustrating hiatus descended upon its affairs. The problem, it was eventually determined, could only be resolved by resort to new legislation, and the Government decided to pursue such a course. But before parliamentary time could be found a General Election was called. The Labour Government fell and a new Conservative Secretary of State was appointed.

The incoming Government was committed from the outset to public expenditure cuts and less intervention in the workings of the economy. It also took the view that many so-called "quangos" - quasi-autonomous non-governmental organisations - were unnecessary to the proper functioning of government, and LOB was amongst those whose utility was immediately questioned. Its considerable public visibility, as a result of its successful and memorable advertising over the years, left an exaggerated impression of the demands that it was making on public resources. Opposition to its activities continued to flow from many London interests. It was not surprising, therefore, that the new Secretary of State, within a few months of taking office, decided in September 1979 to wind up the activities of LOB. At the same time, he decided to abolish ODPs and to abandon any pretence that he espoused a national office location policy. The private sector, it was argued, could provide for office employers an equivalent to the advisory service of LOB, just as the private sector built offices on the ground. Private interests could also supply - through consultants, for example - any advice that was required by local authorities, and IBB could take over LOB's international role.

This was not an isolated development, of course. For several years before the change of government, inter-regional planning had become more tentative and less visible as the national economy remained depressed, as jobs in the manufacturing sector continued to contract, as anti-inflation policies were given a higher priority than those designed to increase employment, and as the perceived necessity to reduce public expenditure mounted. The Regional Employment Premium was withdrawn in 1978. As unemployment worsened throughout the whole country, national schemes such as the Temporary and Youth Employment Subsidies took precedence over additional expenditure on regional aid. The administration of Industrial Development Certificates, the thresholds for which were raised, became more relaxed as the volume of investment in manufacturing industry assumed an overwhelmingly greater importance than its location. Similarly, at the intra-regional scale, there was a marked weakening in the late 1970s of the earlier consensus about spatial development priorities.

104

The 1978 *Strategic Plan for the South East* (22), for example, lacked both an articulate time-scale and a precise geographical dimension, as the confidence and vision of the planning profession and the politicians together were found wanting. In essence, the debilitation of spatial planning at all scales stemmed from an inability of all concerned with public intervention and the planning process to adapt their ideas and policies to changing circumstances. Policy had evolved and matured in an era of economic growth and increasing wealth. Now it had to be cast within a fundamentally changed set of circumstances in which population, employment and economic growth were slow, circumstances which appeared likely to persist.

    As the crisis of confidence in planning heightened, and after the new Conservative Government had come into power, it was not surprising that the process of retreat from earlier planning intentions and styles should accelerate. Thus, from 1979 onwards, the amount of public expenditure in real terms spent on regional assistance was reduced, partly in fact as a result of a lower rate of take-up. The areas eligible for assistance were considerably narrowed and came to exclude nearly all the major provincial office centres. Earlier plans to move more Civil Service posts from London to the provinces were abandoned. The regional Economic Planning Councils in England and Wales were abolished, and central government's involvement in the development of regional strategies was effectively terminated. In this context, it was not surprising that LOB was closed down, that ODPs were abolished, and - but for some residual service industry incentives in the more narrowly defined Assisted Areas - an experiment in the locational guidance of office activities by central government was substantially brought to an end.

                        REFERENCE AND NOTES

1. Department of the Environment (1977), *Inner Area Studies: Liverpool, Birmingham, Lambeth*. London: HMSO.

2. Department of the Environment (1976), *Office Location Review*. London: DOE.

3. *Economist,* 10th June, 1978, "The new leviathans: property and financial institutions, a survey".

4. R. Barras (1979), "The returns from office development and investment", CES Research Series, No.35. London: CES.

5. M. Hanson, "Casualties and survivors", in: *A Review of the Property Market, 1968-1978,* to mark the tenth anniversary of *Estates Times,* 27th October, 1978.

6. South East Joint Planning Team (1970), *Strategic Plan for the South East*. London: HMSO.

7. South East Joint Planning Team (1976), *Strategy for the South East: 1976 Review*. London: HMSO.

8. South East Joint Planning Team (1976), *Development of the Strategic Plan for the South East: Interim Report*. London: DOE, p.71.

9. Department of the Environment (1973), *Greater London Development Plan: Report of the Panel of Inquiry,* 2 Vols. London: HMSO.

10. *ibid.,* p.115.

11. *ibid.,* p.117.

12. Secretary of State for the Environment (1975), *Greater London Development Plan: Statement,* London: GLC.

13. *ibid.,* p.2.

14. Secretary of State for the Environment (1976), *Modified Greater London Development Plan: Reasoned Statement,* London: HMSO, p.75.

15. Greater London Council (1975), *Planned Growth Outside London,* SPB 44. London: GLC.

16. Department of the Environment (1976), *op cit.,* para. 4.12.

17. *ibid.,* para. 4.14.

18. *ibid.,* para. 7.11.

19. *ibid.,* para. 7.9.

20. Property Advisory Group (1976), *Structure and Activity of the Development Industry,* (Chairman: Sir D. Pilcher). London: HMSO, para. 2.28.

21. Statutory Instrument No.1296 (1977), *Town and Country Planning, England and Wales. The Location of Offices Bureau (Amendment) Order.* London: HMSO.

22. Department of the Environment (1978), *Strategic Plan for the South East: Review, Government Statement,* London: HMSO.

7

Lessons from the
1960s and 1970s

Some of the achievements and recognisable benefits of office
location policies in the 1960s and 1970s have been given
tangential attention in earlier chapters. For example, it has
been claimed with reasonable confidence that the activities of
the Location of Offices Bureau made the market for office space
and office labour more transparent than might otherwise have
been the case. The LOB thereby encouraged more efficient location decisions by office users in general and London decentralisers in particular. It has also been made clear that public
policies to some degree shaped the geography of office
decentralisation, particularly to the benefit of certain planned
overspill communities in the South East and adjacent regions.
The transfer of Civil Service posts away from London undoubtedly
drew attention to the untapped white-collar labour reserves
available for office work in the Assisted Areas. As a
consequence of ODP policy, it has been argued that the London-
based development industry gave greater and earlier thought to
investment opportunities in provincial centres than might have
occurred in an unconstrained market.

At the same time, however, many of the failures of office
location policy cannot be denied. The very nature of the
metropolitan office 'problem', for example, was wrongly
diagnosed at the outset. Local authority policies in the inner
areas of Greater London were generally unsympathetic to office
development in the 1970s and undoubtedly frustrated some - and
possibly many - opportunities for beneficial redevelopment,
increased rateable values and more local jobs. Together,
the application of the Department of the Environment's
floorspace controls and the attitudes of local authorities
limited the availability of space and inflated the price of
accommodation in the Outer Metropolitan Area (OMA) of the South
East, to the detriment of many productive activities in that
zone. The Assisted Areas policy, as it was directed towards
private sector office activities, was both too late and too

timid to leave a significant imprint upon the map of office employment.

These contrasting observations concerning the achievements of office policies demand fuller elaboration. A major hurdle in policy evaluation, however, is the frailty of any judgement about what might have happened to the geography of office activities in the absence of government intervention. Insights gained from other countries such as the United States, in which there have been no comparable attempts at intervention, are useful only to the extent that they expose more vividly the spatial dynamics of market forces in a technologically advanced and urban society. They also reveal the contrasting geographical characteristics of office activities in metropolitan areas of different size and age, and with different commitments to the retention of public transport in the journey-to-work (1). Comparisons with experience in other Western European countries, and in particular those which have attempted to shape the location of their office stock and work through spatial inducements and controls - most notably France - afford yet another set of yardsticks by which to judge British experience (2). But international contrasts in the institutional and legal context of office development, in the historic patterns of metropolitan land uses and in the social geography of cities, together deny the possibility of reaching anything other than highly generalised conclusions. Certainly, they do not afford an opportunity to develop precise models to indicate what might have happened in Britain in the absence of policy, or how successful the achievements of policy might properly be claimed to be. These difficulties acknowledged, the lessons of intervention in Britain can nevertheless be usefully considered under three broad headings: these are the objectives, the instruments and the management of policy.

THE OBJECTIVES OF POLICY

In common with other aspects of spatial policy in the years after 1945, public intervention in the location of office activities was framed within a set of vague, often negative and to a degree vacillating objectives. The specification of the spatial policy goals, and the approximate time-scale over which the policy might need to be pursued in order to achieve its objectives, were persistently avoided. Thus, with reference to Greater London, policy makers sought to restrain the growth of office activities in the Central Area, but they took no view on how long the restraints should be applied, what to do once growth had been checked, or what activities might best be retained there indefinately. In addition, little thought was given to the question of where activities denied or attracted away from a Central London location might best be pursued. In the *Greater London Development Plan* (GLDP), of course, the Greater London Council paid lip service to the notion of strategic office centres; but, lacking both the necessary

108

executive powers and the financial muscle, the GLC was never
really in a position to implement its policy either directly or
through the London boroughs. Only in the decision of the (former
County) Borough of Croydon to encourage the development of a major
office complex there, and at a later stage the land assembly and
other initiatives taken by the Borough of Hammersmith and Fulham
that were designed to capitalise on an inherently attractive
location midway between the West End and Heathrow Airport, is
there some evidence of the positive impact that public policies
can have upon the changing pattern of office activities. Yet
these particular examples, it should be noted, were essentially
local initiatives and not part of a strategic plan.

Throughout the rest of the South East, office policy was
equally barren of consistent spatial goals. In the 1960s, the
ROSE was seen as a logical reception area for some of the office
activities moving out of London. The sub-region's ability to
receive office employment, however, was severely limited by
established policies of local development restraint and ODP
controls. Following the publication of the *Strategic Plan for
the South East* (SPSE) in 1970, the Department of the Environment began to give (ODP) preference to proposed office developments in the New and Expanded Towns, and in the major and medium
growth areas. For a few years, therefore, although it was not
widely publicised, a policy that was to some degree destination-
specific was administered in the region. However, it was a
policy which lacked any clear notion of the amount of new office
space and jobs that might be steered into those locations over
any particular time-period, and one that did not always have the
full support of the local planning authorities. Many of the
latter looked with grave suspicion upon any prospect of employment and population growth. Within only a few years, of course,
this policy was overtaken by the collapse of the property boom
of the early 1970s, by the consequential reluctance of the
development industry to embark upon new projects, by the growing
disquiet about the desirability of ODP policies, and by central
government's reduced commitment to the policy of formal overspill.

At the inter-regional scale, as has been noted, policy
continuously lacked any sense of spatial preferences. Even when
inducements were made available for the movement of office jobs
into the Assisted Areas after 1973, the map designed to serve
policy objectives concerning the location of manufacturing
employment was adopted unchanged for office policy purposes.
Despite the arguments of several academic researchers (3), calls
for the concentration of assistance upon only a few major cities
were ignored. Thus, an idea which had been canvassed as long
ago as the early days of the Department of Economic Affairs in
order to prevent too wide a geographical dispersal of office
activities was rejected. Even in the relocation of Civil Service
posts, the government appeared to respond more decisively to the
strength of local political influence than it did to the logic
of a policy which might have encouraged the emergence of a
limited number of major provincial office centres, in each of
which significant economic and social externalities for office

activities might have emerged and thereby stimulated further
employment growth.

It could be argued that the general lack of declared
spatial goals in office policy at all scales was a function
of an undeclared preference for a substantially dispersed
pattern of activities. There can be no doubt, however, that
such a preference in Greater London and the South East
especially would have been quite contrary to public transport
policies, to the extent that it would inevitably be associated
with growth in the use of private cars in the journey-to-work.
In the Assisted Areas, the same tendency to dispersal meant
additionally that even in the largest centres such as Manchester
and Leeds a relatively poor information environment (and hence
relatively few attractions to higher-order office functions)
persisted. It must be assumed, therefore, that the failure of
government to endow office policy with clear spatial goals could
not have stemmed from a covert desire to encourage a dispersed
pattern of activities.

Many factors undoubtedly contribute to a full explanation.
Arguably, the most important were the political difficulties of
specifying the location of preferred, major complexes of office
activities outside London. The embarrassment of having to
determine initial development priorities - to choose between
Manchester and Liverpool, or between Sheffield, Leeds and
Newcastle, for example - are all too apparent. They were
significantly compounded, however, by the persistence in policy
deliberations in both central and local government of major
factual uncertainties about the evolution of office activities,
and the very limited understanding of their locational
economics.

The formulation of office policy in the 1960s and 1970s
was consistently dogged by the lack of regularly updated
information, both on changes in the level of employment in the
office sector as a whole and on the shifts in the geographical
distribution of those jobs. It was noted in Chapter 3 that the
earliest policy initiatives in the 1960s were based upon a
false interpretation of developments in London's economy and a
gross over-estimation of the rate of growth in the total number
of office jobs in the Central Area. In consequence, policies
of that decade stemmed from a somewhat muddled understanding of
the problems which they were designed to alleviate. Even after
20 years of policy intervention, the amount and the quality of
information on recent office employment trends remained
depressingly poor. Only changes in those parts of the office
sector that are contained within industries which are almost
wholly office-based - industries such as insurance, banking and
finance - can developments be charted with moderate confidence
from official statistics, and then only with (at best) a five-
year time-lag and on the crudest of geographical bases. Even
with the availability of the full 1981 Census results, a detailed
analysis of the changes that took place in the previous decade
can provide only sketchy information on that component of office

110

activities which takes place within separate office buildings
(the component which policy in the past has sought principally
to influence), as compared with total office employment, much
of which is to be found in factories, hospitals, universities
and the like.

For a number of years attempts were made to remedy this
data deficiency. The South East Economic Planning Council sought
to persuade the Department of Employment either to add occupational questions to their Annual Employment Census, or alternatively to engage in other data gathering activities that would
provide up-to-date, spatially disaggregated, occupation data on
a more regular basis. The theme was also taken up by LOB, which,
in its *Annual Report 1972/73* noted that:

> There is an urgent need for some kind of annual employment return
> which clearly distinguishes office workers, including those in the
> manufacturing sector, from others and this can only be organised
> at governmental level. Despite the growing importance attached to
> regional economic policies and the increasing part that office work
> is playing in total employment the material available for the
> making of policy judgements is still totally inadequate (4).

The inadequacies of data was in fact a constant theme in LOB
reports. The Department of Employment, however, took the view
that any benefits from additional occupational data would not
be matched by their costs to both government and industry.
Taking note of representations made by the Confederation of
British Industry, that firms were already subject to more form-
filling and data provision than was desirable, the Department of
Employment judged that further additions to the information
already compulsorily collected from employers under the
Statistics of Trade Act would not be justified. In consequence,
students of office location trends and policy options in the
1980s find themselves equally constrained in their attempts to
understand the recent behaviour of the industry as they were
20 years earlier.

It might be noted in passing, of course, that many analyses
of the changing geography of office employment during the period
for which at least some detailed information is now available -
the 1960s - have not been as rigorous as they might have been.
For example, research has not generally taken into full account
such matters as the differential growth of public and private
sector office activities, the role of part-time work in the
changing patterns of employment, and alterations in the classification of industries. They have thus encouraged somewhat
erroneous impressions about the rate of growth in the demand
for office labour within the private sector, on balance tending
to exaggerate its expansion and to neglect the distinctive
characteristics and implications of part-time employment.

The cautionary lesson to be learned from these several
observations about office employment statistics - the frail
factual basis upon which office location policy was initially

based, the continuing inadequacy of data in this field, and the
weaknesses that characterise some of the published analyses of
the statistics that are available - is clear. Any attempt to
formulate policy in the future must be based upon an adequate
and, more especially, an accurate, understanding of recent and
current developments in the industry. It is arguable that the
Government's covert recognition in the late 1960s that office
employment growth in Central London had been seriously over-
estimated a decade earlier did much to reduce the political
impetus behind its policies. It certainly undermined any desire
that might have existed to develop a coherent response to changes
in the perception of the office location 'problem'. In the
absence of better data on the industry, therefore, any attempt
that might be made in future to specify an office policy faces
a major problem of credibility. One of the first tasks of any
renewed desire to influence the location of office activities
must be to establish the means whereby they can be monitored
with some geographical precision on an annual or biennial basis.
Initially this would allow the 'problems' and policy options to
be clarified. Subsequently, it would provide the means whereby
the effectiveness of government policies might be judged.

THE INSTRUMENTS OF POLICY

The several instruments employed to further office location
policy can only be properly understood within the context of the
considerable range of measures which were designed and adopted
by government to shape the economic geography, to alter the
pattern of regional development and to influence the pace and
the location of land use change in post-war Britain. The attempt
by central government deliberately to modify the evolution of
the country's economic geography dates back to the 1930s when
the Special Areas Act 1934 provided the first, tentative means
whereby the influence of market forces upon the balance of inter-
regional development might be challenged. For several decades
it was a policy directed essentially at the location of manufacturing industry, as government acquired an increasing number
of powers - such as the ability to deny the construction of
factories in particular localities through the refusal of an
Industrial Development Certificate, and the means to designate
the location of and provide the finance for New Towns, and then
to attract employers to them. In parallel and under the Town
and Country Planning Act 1947, local authorities (the then
counties and county boroughs) were given the responsibility of
supervising land use change at the local and sub-regional scales.
This role allowed them also to influence the location of manufacturing and office activities, although the adjudication of
major and contentious issues was placed ultimately in the hands
of a central government Minister. Upon these two bases, the
post-1945 years saw the progressive elaboration of arrangements
for public intervention in the location of new productive
investments and jobs.

Public supervision of the changing geographical distribution of office accommodation and office employment activities was for many years effected through the general planning system, and in particular through the granting or withholding of planning consents by local authorities. As has been seen, however, the emergence of a more formal set of office location policies resulted in the creation of three new policy instruments specifically for this component of the economy and built environment. These instruments were the Location of Offices Bureau, the granting or the withholding of Office Development Permits, and the Service Industry Incentive Scheme in the Assisted Areas. Each deserves a detailed review. In subsequent sections, some observations are also made about the contribution of relocated Civil Service posts to the broader objectives of office location policies.

The Location of Offices Bureau

Established under an Order in Council in 1963, the Location of Offices Bureau was initially given very simple terms of reference:

> It shall be the general duty of the Bureau to encourage the decentralisation and diversion of office employment from congested areas in central London to suitable centres elsewhere and to take such steps as may be necessary for this purpose, including without prejudice to the generality of the foregoing the provision of information and publicity and the promotion of research (5).

In 1977, the Order was amended and LOB's remit was changed to:

> It shall be the general duty of the Bureau to promote the better distribution of office employment in England and Wales and to take such steps as may be necessary for this purpose including, without prejudice to the generality of the foregoing, the provision of information and publicity and the promotion of research (6).

Although the LOB shared certain attributes with the Development Commission, set up by government to assist with the replacement and diversification of employment opportunities in rural areas, it was in many respects unique amongst the various public agencies involved in the management of spatial change. Certainly it had no counterpart in the manufacturing sector of the economy. Four features in particular characterised LOB.

First, it was small. Although during its lifetime it was able to respond to some 5 000 serious enquiries, and in some years it handled over 400, by the time of the Office Location Review in 1974 it still employed only 14 full-time members of staff. These comprised a Secretary (the administrative head), two location officers available to give advice to clients, two press and publicity officers, one information officer, two research officers and six support staff. The staff reported through the Secretary to the Chairman and (part-time) Bureau Members. The latter were originally three in number and drawn from the business world; in time, however, the membership was increased to four and their background was widened to reflect interests and experience in university research, local and central government (planning) administration, and the trades union movement, as well as business and commerce.

A second feature was the stress that it laid upon publicity, an activity which in most years absorbed approximately one-half of its budget. Designed to foster a climate of business opinion which was favourable to office decentralisation, advertisements were aimed at both office management and staff and an imaginative use was made of the national press, direct mailings to business and, for a number of years, tube cards and cross-track posters on the London Underground. The style and the humour of the advertisements gave it a considerable public visibility, even notoriety, especially in London (see Figure 7).

A third feature was its free advisory service to the business community and, save for a few special handbooks (7), its provision of free information. A considerable premium was placed upon having readily to hand the best available and most recent information on those matters which lay at the heart of a carefully considered office location decision. Geographically disaggregated data on the availability of office properties, on office rents, on commercial and industrial rates, on population and labour supplies, on wage rates, on communication and travel costs and on housing (*inter alia*) were all kept readily to hand, and were regularly updated. Information Sheets provided clients with national summaries of these matters and Town Sheets related to the data to particular places. In addition, it assiduously built up contacts with the many actors on the office location stage - the developers and agents, government departments, local authorities and Development Corporations, the postal, telecommunications and transport authorities, and office users themselves. By this means it was able to become a unique and highly valuable clearing house of impartial and well-judged information on office location affairs, a characteristic which increased the confidence of the business community in its opinions and advice.

A final characteristic was its commitment to research, a task specifically noted in its original terms of reference. Through in-house and commissioned work, and through the help that its research officers were able to give to academic workers, both directly and indirectly it was able to make an outstanding contribution to the advancement of the understanding of office location issues. It conducted and commissioned work on such questions as the economics of decentralisation from Central London, the characteristics of office activities in provincial cities, the shifting patterns of office communications following decentralisation, and the social response of staff to relocation and to new residential locations (8). All these topics were of interest to its clients. In addition, the LOB sought answers to some of the questions facing local authorities as they considered the impact of new offices on their local labour and housing markets and on their fiscal position (9). In consequence, within a very few years LOB had helped to fashion an impressive body of published, largely empirical research evidence on office location matters which was not available elsewhere to both management and public officials. Comparable evidence was certainly never available on anything like the same scale for the manufacturing sector, despite the much longer public involvement in its geographical management.

The free and impartial advice given to its clients was provided substantially through interviews with its location executives. The first such interview with a serious client was considered to be the most important. It was spent explaining what services the LOB had to offer, removing misconceptions and giving general advice. The discussion would range over what the firm was looking for, the kinds of offices it required, the sort of location best suited to its operations, the staff required, the necessary road, rail, air and telecommunications, any any other factors that might influence the firm's choice of area. The first interview usually involved a visit to the LOB's Map Room which contained illustrated information on the location and the amount of office space currently and prospectively available in Britain, as well as a property register which aimed to be - and, despite its limitations, probably was - the most comprehensive in the country. The Map Room also contained illustrated information on the country's communications facilities; maps and information about those areas in receipt of special government assistance, such as the Assisted Areas, the New and Expanded Towns, and the Inner Urban Areas defined after 1977; the locations of universities and polytechnics; and, of course, the distribution of population and, by implication, the labour force. Towards the end of the initial interview with the client, areas of possible interest were short-listed and fact sheets and other details provided on suitable towns. The LOB was in a position not only to arrange visits to these places, but also to set up meetings with local agents and officials. Occasionally it could arrange for an intending mover to meet the management of firms which had already made a successful move to one or more of the possible relocations. For places some distance away from London, this latter service was quite possibly the most effective means of persuasion. Having absorbed the information and advice made available by LOB, it was of course the firm itself which had to make its location decision. However, the LOB did provide a follow-up service once a decision to make a move had been taken. This included advice on all aspects of the move itself, from suggested timings for various stages of the operation to methods of informing the staff that would be involved and the public relations aspects of the move.

It was a service that appealed to firms of all sizes, from small professional partnerships to large multi-national corporations, even those employing their own consultants. It was estimated by one of the research officers that about one-half of all the office moves from Central London took place after some advantage had been taken of LOB's services (10). Any attempt to measure LOB's effectiveness, however, poses considerable difficulties, particularly since market forces increasingly endorsed its objectives. Nevertheless, a sample of the agency's confidential files on individual clients - selected in 1974 by the Management Services Organisation and Methods Division of the Department of the Environment, as part of the Office Location Review (11) - led to the conclusion that "LOB had played a significant part in many of the moves which had taken place". In general, of course, the smaller the firm, the greater the probability that it would call upon the LOB's resources. Once a firm was on LOB's books, the location executives and the research officers kept in contact with it until a decision had been reached either to proceed with or to reject a move. Through this monitoring of its clients' decisions, the raw information for the LOB's unique data set was acquired and provided a detailed record of office mobility from Central London between 1963 and 1979, a record that exists for no other large metropolitan area in the world.

LOB's success in decanting jobs from Central London, it must be repeated, can be attributed in considerable measure to the operation of market forces. However, it undoubtedly amplified and accelerated their effects by bringing home to Central London employers, more forcefully than might otherwise have been the case, the relatively high costs of operating office establishments in the heart of the capital. The pace of decentralisation, however, was very clearly affected by shifts over time in the strength of market forces, especially the rate of growth of office jobs and hence the overall demand for office labour, and the costs of Central London office accommodation compared with other locations. The LOB's effectiveness was consequently rooted in its ability to exploit the dynamic growth of office activities in the metropolis in the 1960s and 1970s. With reference to the future, therefore, some observers have predicted only a weak growth of employment in office activities in London as a whole. With the possibility that job opportunities may decline in the Central Area (see Chapter 8), it has to be recognised that the value of a purely advisory and propagandist agency like the LOB to serve a policy of employment redistribution is very much open to question.

At the same time, and this is another lesson of the LOB experiment, an important element in its success was its links with, but independence from, government. Policy effectiveness undoubtedly gained considerable advantage from the LOB's intermediate position between government and private business. By seeking to interpret public objectives and assistance to the latter, whilst taking every opportunity to remind government of the nature, the behaviour and the real locational options open to commercial concerns, LOB played a unique and valuable role. In the formulation of the 1977 inner area initiatives, for example, it sought both to ensure that proper consideration was given to office as well as manufacturing activities, and to inform policy with realistic assessments of what might be possible within a reasonable length of time. This intermediate position not only allowed a more effective exchange of ideas between government and the private sector, but it also generated unique information in its own right. Put crudely, the LOB sought to place and keep its finger on the office industry's pulse, and thereby to interpret current developments in such matters as construction activity, employment growth, locational fashions and trends, and the industry's emerging problems in a manner that was impossible from official statistics and sources alone, with all their deficiencies and delays. At the same time, it was sometimes able to assist private firms in their dealings with government and the nationalised industries, particularly with regard to the administration of ODPs and the speedy provision of telecommunication facilities.

Thus far, the discussion of LOB's role in office location policy has stressed the positive aspects of its activities. The practical reality of its day-to-day workings, however, were not without blemishes. In order to explore some of the problems associated with the style of operation, each of its main activities - the advisory service, publicity and research - are considered in turn.

Location decisions in the office sector tend to be taken over a relatively short period of time, often as a result of immediate stimuli such as a rent review, the expiry of a lease, or the sudden realisation of the difficulties involved in finding suitable space for expansion and the price demanded for such space. Occasionally firms wished to become owner occupiers but those prepared to construct their own premises were the exception rather than the rule. As a consequence the LOB had to build up a register of properties available throughout the country in order not only to advise clients on the general geographical availability of office space, but also to be in a position to provide them with details of specific properties which might suit their individual needs.

This property register was constructed by two different means. The first was a regular circular to estate agents asking for details of the properties for rent on their books. After the initial contact, the circular took the form of a six-monthly request to confirm that properties previously notified were still available and to add those that had appeared on the market in the interim. Local authorities who acted as their own agents were included in this process. The second was a careful scouring of the property press for information on any development that was mentioned there but which had not been notified to the LOB by any other means.

Although estate agents generally complied with requests for information, there were times when they were somewhat less willing to supply details of properties when they became available. This was particularly true in the case of office space that was judged to be easily lettable. Thus, properties that appeared on the market in the period between the six-monthly circularisation of the agents, and with which few letting difficulties were forseen, were unlikely to appear on the LOB register. For this reason, the property data offered a relatively poor coverage of small units (the most easily disposed of) in popular locations, particularly at times of business expansion and buoyant decentralisation demand. In these circumstances LOB had to resort to directing its clients towards estate agents in the localities of their choice, rather than being able to provide at first hand a comprehensive picture of space availability.

The other flaw in this system based as it was upon the voluntary notification of space availability was the delays that occurred between the letting of a property and its removal from the LOB register. Estate agents were understandably less eager to notify the fact of letting a property than their desire to market it. Although in the case of larger properties this problem was substantially reduced by reference to the property press in which major lettings were often reported, the accuracy of the LOB register as far as small units were concerned was once again affected. As a result of both sets of problems, therefore, LOB's information on office space availability could sometimes be up to six months out of date and incomplete as far as fast-moving, small unit properties were concerned.

The LOB also needed to be able to advise employers on the availability of staff in different locations. This was especially the case for those firms who were relocating for reasons of expansion and for those organisations for whom one of the major factors in the decision to decentralise was the need to escape recurring staff shortages and the extra costs of labour associated with a Central London location. The LOB, however, never achieved a really satisfactory mechanism for collecting this information. Official (Department of Employment) data are particularly unhelpful as a guide to office staff availability since a considerable proportion of office workers are found amongst married women who did not generally register as unemployed. The LOB commissioned an elaborate attempt to overcome this problem by deriving formulae which would produce estimates of office labour potential in particular localities from Census data (12). However, not only were the estimates of this methodology inevitably subject to considerable margins of error, but the Census data on which they were based were out of date even when they first became available.

In the face of these difficulties the LOB had to resort to a variety of unsatisfactory sources of labour supply information. These included local estimates of the numbers of school leavers likely to be seeking office employment. Such estimates were only available for those localities where the local authority was willing to supply information to the LOB (that is, those

authorities which had not set themselves against further office
development). Such estimates were supplemented by feedback from
clients who had already decentralised, so that firms could at
least be warned against moving to those areas where staff
shortages appeared to be developing. But LOB was often forced
into advising its clients that the only reasonably failsafe
method of ensuring that adequate levels of staffing would be
achieved in specific locations was to advertise a sample of
posts in the local press and then to gauge the response.

Thus, as a result of the voluntary arrangements into which
it was forced to enter, the LOB was faced with considerable difficulties in providing advice to its clients on the two main compo-
nents of the location decision. On other factors, however, such
as housing availability (at least until the demise of the
publication *Parker's Property Price Guide*), and physical and
telecommunications developments, the LOB did have access to
comprehensive and up-to-date information sources. All this
information was made available to clients on a necessarily
generalised basis, and it must be stressed that the location
officer dealing with any one client was heavily dependent upon
the firm's own perceptions of its location requirements. Staff
resources were never adequate, nor did LOB have the necessary
expertise, to offer firms a detailed locational consultancy
based upon an intimate understanding of their organisational
structure and costs. It has to be accepted, therefore, that
a considerable number of sub-optimal locational decisions could
well have resulted from the sort of generalised locational
advice that was provided. That weakness acknowledged, it is
equally important to reiterate that LOB's information was the
best that was available at a generalised level and that it was
regularly sought by management and location consultants engaged
in detailed, single firm studies.

The publicity activities of the LOB also had their flaws.
These activities had two functions. First, they were a propaganda exercise to promote the idea and practice of decentralisation. Second, they sought to attract as clients those
firms which were considering alternative locations for their
activities. The balance of the advertising activities tended
to favour the former function. This was partly because it
offered the possibility of simple and more imaginative advertising copy. The propaganda type of advertising was infinitely more
memorable in the public's mind than the 'bread and butter'
approach adopted in those campaigns that merely proffered the
range of LOB's services to individual firms. Propaganda
campaigns, however, inevitably tended to caricature the
decentralisation message. They portrayed decentralised locations
as having idyllic rural environments - the 'butterflies and bees'
approach - while Central London was characterised by images of
excessive costs and strangling congestion (Figure 7). A powerful theme in the promotion of office decentralisation, these
features came to be seen by some commentators as significant
amongst the attractions of a move 'to the country'. In reality,

"Your board has rejected £1,000 extra profit per employee."

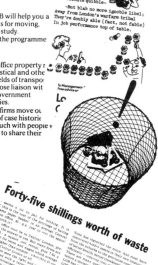

Figure 7. Some LOB advertisements

of course, the majority of firms opted for relocation in suburban and urban places, while some of those which decided (often against the LOB's advice) to accommodate their activities in a country house came, in time, to regret their relative isolation.

Vivid, memorable and successful though the propaganda campaign was judged by many to be, it came in the end to have a somewhat perverse effect upon the agency's credibility. It led some observers and especially politicians to the view that LOB had a pro-rural and, more damagingly, an anti-city prejudice. For example, when the LOB's future was being debated in the late 1970s, it found few supporters amongst London MPs of both major parties. Their perceptions of its role were dominated by such vivid images as were suggested particularly by the Octopus campaign which portrayed London's rising rents and mounting congestion in a particularly striking fashion (see Figure 7). This experience does not necessarily deny the legitimacy of the propaganda campaign, especially in the early years. It does underline, however, the failure of the Bureau to adapt its advertising to changing economic and political circumstances, and the difficulty of striking a satisfactory balance between attractive and memorable propagandist advertising, on the one hand, and the more factual copy of an information campaign on the other.

After 1977 it was necessary for the LOB to concentrate its advertising wholly upon the facts of its changed role. In particular, it needed to counter the widespread misunderstanding of its different tasks in Central and Inner London, and to challenge the notion that its role had in some way been reversed. The visual attractiveness of the advertisements inevitably waned as a function of the more factual message that had to be presented. This undoubtedly reduced their impact.

Two further lessons, however, can be drawn from experience during the last 24 months of LOB's existence. The first was the enormous difficulty experienced in attempting to counter a widespread misunderstanding of the altered role of the LOB, against the background of the simple propagandist image of its work that had been nurtured over the previous decade. The second was the herculean task of successfully presenting a set of relatively simple, but visually elusive, geographical ideas to the general public. The Assisted Areas could be portrayed starkly and clearly upon a map. The inner areas policy, on the other hand, did not admit to comparable illustration, especially when Central London (unlike central Manchester or central Liverpool) was properly excluded from policy assistance - whilst places like Blaenau Gwent, Bolton and Hartlepool were afforded Designated District status and became eligible for inner city funds! Although the LOB's new international remit was easily and clearly understood (albeit the role was *ultra vires*), its domestic activities after 1977 remained a matter of considerable press and political confusion until its closure in 1979.

The research activities, in common with the publicity function, also had a dual purpose. Initially, LOB needed to define and understand its market - the firms that might be persuaded in whole or in part to decentralise. A considerable proportion of the research resources in the first instance were therefore directed towards investigating the locational requirements of office firms and their attitudes towards dispersal. The reactions of staff to Central London commuting and the possibility of working nearer home were also extensively explored (13). It was only when these information needs were substantially satisfied that attention could properly be paid towards the second aspect of the LOB's research activities - the investigation of the wider implications and effects of office relocation beyond the individual firm. Only a small fraction of the research resources, which in any case were quite meagre (14), were devoted to this latter activity. Indeed, in retrospect, much too little attention was paid to understanding the impact of the decentralisation process on different parts of the country, especially the Assisted Areas and London's inner areas. The relationship between office development and sub-regional economic change, especially in the Outer Metropolitan Area and the Outer South East, and the links between indigenous office employment growth and the processes of decentralisation and spatial economic change, were also poorly researched. Greater efforts in these directions might have served to enhance the reputation of LOB as an impartial centre of information and understanding on office location matters generally.

Office Development Permits

Announced late in 1964 and legislated under the Control of Office and Industrial Development Act 1965, the Office Development Permit (ODP) was in effect a licence to apply for planning permission to build a new office. Modelled on the existing Industrial Development Certificate which applied to new floorspace for manufacturing activities, the ODP system required that every proposed office development (new buildings, rebuildings, extensions and changes of use) involving 3000 square feet or more of additional floorspace required central government permission as well as local authority approval. The control was administered throughout most of its existence by the Department of the Environment (although at the outset it was a Board of Trade responsibility). Its purpose was not only to impose a brake upon the process of office development in London and the rest of the South East - thereby reinforcing the local authority policies of Central Area restraint - but also simultaneously to steer developments and hence, in time, jobs into preferred locations elsewhere. In the first instance the latter were intended to be provincial towns and cities, especially those in the less prosperous regions; but in time the control was used, as has been noted, to support the accelerated development of the London New Towns and the growth areas of the *Strategic Plan for the South East*.

The ODP control was operated pragmatically in the light of both its legislative origins and the broad intentions of Ministers. Because it was not possible, even after 15 years of its administration, to produce comprehensive guidelines for its operation, it was applied on a case by case basis, largely by rule of thumb, but naturally constrained to some degree by precedent. Broad criteria were specified by Ministers for the adjudication of applications by civil servants and were set out in statements to Parliament and elsewhere. They can be summarised as requiring the applicant for a permit generally to name the proposed tenant of the new or substantially refurbished building; to demonstrate that the tenant had a commercial tie to the area for which the application was being made; to show that the tenant could not find suitable accommodation elsewhere in that area; and/or to demonstrate that the project was in some sense 'in the public interest'. The first three criteria, in particular, were clearly rather crude yardsticks for the day-to-day administration of the control. Civil servants and Ministers simply did not have the necessary knowledge or methodology whereby they could judge realistically 'the need' for a commercial employer, a professional firm or any other office user to be in a particular place. Indeed, to the extent that it was always easier for applicants to make a case for remaining in their present location rather than moving elsewhere, the control probably served above all to restrict intra-regional change in the geography of office employment.

Moreover, the notion of 'suitable space' had of necessity to be qualified by criteria of kind and cost, which in the last resort could only be matters of commercial and personal, but certainly not governmental, judgement. Consequently, it was only the criterion of 'the public interest' - in the form of, for example, the simultaneous provision of improved railway termini, interchanges and stations, or local road improvements in comprehensive redevelopments with a substantial office content - which could be more objectively interpreted by the Department, and even then in only a qualitative fashion. In such circumstances, it was inevitable that the administration of the ODP system appeared at times to be somewhat arbitrary and that it generated a good deal of criticism from property developers, politicians and the press.

From the mid-1970s the administration of the control was further complicated by a new willingness of government to waive the 'named tenant' condition and to allow in certain circumstances speculative office development. This was an understandable response to the criticism that the ODP system unfairly favoured the large firm which could guarantee to fill a new building, and the growing scarcity of modern, small office suites for professional users in particular. It meant, however, that the Department had to begin judging some ODP applications not against the characteristics of a proposed tenant but rather against the office development and office employment policy of the locality to which the permit applied. However, it was not every local planning authority that had already formulated an articulate office policy on both these counts; yet another opportunity for apparently arbitrary administrative judgements was thus created.

Disquiet about the management of the ODP control was further
heightened by the frequency with which changes were made to the
rigour of its application. Between the announcement of the
'Brown ban' in 1964 and late 1969 - years during which the control applied first to the London Metropolitan Area; then additionally to Birmingham; and then to the whole of the South East,
the West Midlands and the East Midlands (before it was rolled
back to apply solely to the South East, and then to the more
narrowly defined Metropolitan Region), the Government sought to
administer the control with considerable rigour. Its immediate
impact upon the behaviour of the development industry, however,
was inevitably limited as a result of the considerable number of
office planning permissions already in 'the pipeline', permissions
which had been granted before the control had become effective.
By the late 1960s, however, with the National Plan abandoned,
regional planning was in intellectual and practical disarray.
With the Government under mounting pressure from the property
and development industries, the Department of the Environment
began to adopt rather more flexible attitudes towards permit
applications, particularly those offering advantageous transport
planning gain, or in approved locations for formal overspill as
specified in the *Strategic Plan for the South East* (Table 9).
However, within a few years - in 1973, in fact - as a result of
the political climate that was engendered by several aspects of
the office boom of the early 1970s, the Government once again
declared a 'standstill' on the granting of new permissions.

Table 9. Office Development Permits issued, South East region,
1965-1979

	No.	Gross area	Relinquished	Net area
		(million square feet)		
1965-66	252	3.72	1.43	2.29
1966-67	481	5.82	2.12	3.70
1967-68	467	6.88	2.80	4.08
1968-69	633	13.22	4.65	8.57
1969-70	402	12.91	3.63	9.28
1970-71	682	28.08	7.08	21.00
1971-72	489	29.98	6.79	23.19
1972-73	488	25.64	4.59	21.05
1973-74	375	21.89	3.89	18.00
1974-75	241	11.40	1.04	10.36
1975-76	319	15.45	1.29	14.16
1976-77	232	13.74	0.97	12.77
1977-78	156	15.55	0.75	14.80
1978-79	182	18.14	0.62	17.52

Source: Annual Reports on the Control of Office Development, HMSO, London

The gross area permitted in 1974-1975 was just over one-half
that granted in the previous year. But the relatively severe
restraint lasted for only two years, and after 1975 the Department
of the Environment adopted more flexible attitudes once again.
In the economic circumstances then prevailing, however, and in
the wake of the office boom of the early 1970s, it is not sur-

prising that applications and permissions for ODPs remained at
relatively modest levels. The control was finally abolished in
1979.

As a result of these persistent shifts in the administration
of ODPs, considerable difficulties are immediately posed for any
evaluation of its effectiveness as a tool for shaping the geography of new office space. The control was never applied
strongly enough and for long enough for its full possible effects
- both good and ill - to appear. There is another problem in
interpreting ODP policy as well, that is, the nature of the
official ODP data.

The administration of the ODP system allowed the Department
of the Environment to publish an annual return indicating the
number and the aggregate floorspace of applications, refusals
and permissions granted. The Government's records also allowed
the Department to publish each year, for very broad geographical
areas within the control zone, the amount of space subject to
Government permission which was complete and vacant, which was
under construction and for which planning permission had been
given - office space 'in the pipeline'. Thus ODP data provide
an annual measure of the supply of new and refurbished office
buildings within Greater London and the rest of the Metropolitan
Area. Temporal and spatial variations in the amount of new and
refurbished space recently made available or about to come on to
the market can therefore be established with some accuracy. In
Table 10 it can be seen how new and vacant space in Greater
London in 1974 was about one-fifth of the 1964 level when the
controls were introduced, although the amount under construction
was, after several years of restraint, approximately the same.
In the rest of the Metropolitan Area, the amount of space 'in
the pipeline' by 1974 had exceeded that of the pre-control
period, but complete and vacant space remained at a relatively
low level.

Tendencies in the ambitions of the development industry can
also be detected from the ODP data. Thus, between 1965 and 1970
the number of ODP applications in Greater London averaged 490
each year: between 1971 and 1974, in contrast, the figure fell
to about 390. At the same time the average amount of floorspace
requested each year in the same two periods rose from 7.7 million
square feet to 33.2 million square feet. In the rest of the
South East by comparison, both the number of applications and
the amount of space requested rose between the two periods -
applications from an average of 220 to 270 each year, and the
amount of space involved from 4.5 to 14.8 million square feet
annually.

There is much in the ODP data set, however, that can be
readily misunderstood. The statistics exclude all smaller office
developments of both new and refurbished space; they are therefore by no means a complete measure of additional supply. Moreover, and of central importance in any analysis of the office
market, the data offers no reliable guide to changes in the

Table 10.　Office space in the pipeline in the London
　　　　　　Metropolitan Region*, 1964-1975

(million square feet gross)

	Complete & vacant	Under construction	Outstanding planning permission	Total
GREATER LONDON				
1964 (Nov., pre-control)	5.1	14.1	17.9	37.1
1968 (March)	3.8	5.4	2.5	11.7
1969	3.0	4.4	2.9	10.3
1970	1.4	4.3	6.2	11.9
1971	1.9	5.2	9.5	16.6
1972	1.6	10.9	9.0	21.5
1973	1.0	12.7	10.5	24.2
1974	1.1	14.1	12.3	27.5
1975	1.4	16.2	11.0	28.6
REST OF THE METROPOLITAN REGION				
1964 (Nov.)	1.1	4.1	5.9	11.1
1968 (March)	0.8	1.9	2.5	5.2
1969	0.6	1.7	2.5	4.8
1970	0.5	1.9	2.5	4.9
1971	0.2	1.8	3.7	5.7
1972	0.2	2.4	4.0	6.6
1973	0.3	4.2	5.2	9.7
1974	0.4	5.3	5.6	11.3
1975	1.2	4.5	6.3	12.0

* Greater London plus the Outer Metropolitan Area

Source:　Annual Report by the Secretary of State for the Environment
　　　　　and the Secretary of State for Wales (1974), Town and Country
　　　　　Planning Act 1971, Control of Office Development, HMSO, London

magnitude and geography of the demand for office space. It is
clear that many developers, having had an application or applications refused in a particular locality, very frequently decided
not to make any further applications for developments there in
the expectation that an ODP would not be granted. Further, in
the light of experience, some types of application were judged
to be more likely to obtain ODP consent than others; this
undoubtedly influenced the nature and the location of applications. At the same time, developers are known to have applied
for more permissions than they really needed, in the hope that
at least some consents would be given and their flow of activity
could be maintained. The ODP data therefore give no reliable
indication of what space might have been built in response to
market demands and in the absence of the control. It is impossible to tell for any one area and/or any one year the degree to

which the supply of office space was in fact suppressed by
central government policy.

In its analysis of the effectiveness of ODPs, the Economy
Group of the South East Joint Planning Team in 1976 (15) noted
that the amount of office space that received planning permission
in the control zone had in recent years been below that permitted by issued ODPs, even though the former would have included
premises smaller than the ODP threshold. They reported:

> Prima facie..... (the planning permission) net appears to have a
> much finer mesh than the ODP system. Between 1966-73 about
> 63 000 000 square feet of office floorspace in London was granted
> an ODP whereas only about 28 000 000 square feet received planning
> permission. The difference between the amount of floorspace
> granted an ODP and that given planning permission was especially
> great in Central London. (16)

The Joint Planning Team, therefore, cautioned against exagger-
ating the restraining effects of ODPs upon the supply of office
space. However, assuming that a significant number of ODP
applications were made in excess of real demand in order to
ensure a continuity of the development industry's activities,
this conclusion is less persuasive. Indeed, a closer inspection
of local planning authority decisions indicates that planning
procedures were in fact a less formidable hurdle than the earlier
figures suggest. Even though approval rates declined in the
early 1970s, it was still relatively rare for a local authority
to refuse planning permission for office development, taking
applications for the South East as a whole. Moreover, in examining the available data, allowance has to be made for lags between
ODP approval and an application for planning permission, and it
is clear that between the stages of obtaining an ODP and seeking
planning consent there was a substantial drop-out of development
schemes. The Joint Planning Team also noted that some planning
control takes place informally. Thus, developers who were made
aware of the fact that their proposals did not conform with
local authority requirements or ambitions very often did not
bother to submit a planning application, even though they had
obtained an ODP. The extent of such informal influences upon
the office development process is not, however, known. It cannot
be escaped, therefore, that ODP data offer only limited insights
into the effectiveness of central government policies of office
development restraint.

There can be little doubt, nevertheless, that ODPs did
serve as a significant restraint upon office construction in the
Central Area, and especially upon developments of a purely speculative nature because of their 'named tenant' requirements. In
two important respects, therefore, the control exerted a powerful
conservative influence over the geography of office activities
by favouring larger users and existing office locations. Since,
for a number of years, ODPs could be obtained only for named
tenants who could demonstrate a need to be in the South East,
the control operated with an in-built bias in favour of large

127

national and international concerns by comparison with smaller
firms, without any objective reference to real user needs.
Moreover, to the extent that the control was applied to new
buildings, the policy meant that new locations for office activities in the South East suffered most from both space shortages
and rent increases. The distribution of office space within the
region, therefore, was to some degree fossilised. In its *Annual
Report 1973/74* (17) the Location of Offices Bureau noted:

> Although some of the firms that would like to relocate in the
> South East are large, it is mainly the small firms that have
> sound trading and operating reasons for remaining in the region.
> These small firms neither wish to build for themselves, nor to
> commit themselves to some possible office development before a
> permit and planning permission have been obtained. Of every
> five jobs that LOB clients are thinking of moving, four want
> rented accommodation, and most of these want it in the South
> East. The overwhelming demand, therefore, is for so-called
> 'speculative' premises, designed for multi-occupation.

The LOB returned to the same theme a year later in its *Annual
Report 1974/75* (18).

> As stressed on many occasions in the past, the demand for office
> premises lettable in small units to accommodate (small) firms
> has not been met. The ODP system of control, whereby the con-
> struction of few speculative premises is allowed, has militated
> against the adequate provision of small premises. It is possible
> for developers to construct offices of less than 10 000 sq. ft.
> which do not require ODPs. There are, however, relatively few
> of these and one of the reasons may be the reluctance of Local
> Authorities to grant planning permissions unless they have a
> 'local users only' clause.....

By helping to create a relative scarcity of office space in
the South East, it is clear that the ODP control (along with
local planning constraints) both raised the average price of
space and lowered the overall level of office demand. Especially
during the early period, when the effects of the controls were
tending to increase, the demand for additional office space was
held back. As a result employers failed to find accommodation
in places which they preferred and reacted to rising rents by
making better use of their existing space. By implication,
working conditions for the office workforce were poorer than they
might otherwise have been, with floorspace per worker remaining
relatively small and the age of the occupied office stock somewhat older than might have been the case without government
intervention.

The full costs of the ODP system, however, elude measurement.
In so far as the control involved delays and inconvenience to
individual firms there were efficiency costs which it is impossible to estimate. In so far as the control added to the pressure on rents, there was a general cost falling on office
activities as a whole which would be carried through into the

Table 11.   Average office rents in major West European
            cities, 1977

                    (£ per square foot)*

     London (City)   13.45
     London (West End)   10.20

     Amsterdam   4.65
     Brussels   4.95
     Dusseldorf   7.25
     Frankfurt   6.36
     Geneva   6.90
     Paris   10.35

     * Air conditioned offices on prime sites

     Source: Economists Advisory Group (1979), *Factors
              Influencing the Location of Offices of
              Multi-National Enterprises in the UK,*
              Research Paper No. 8. London: LOB

prices of goods and services.   During the period of ODP controls,
the level of Central London rents generally, and City of London
rents in particular, were substantially higher than those of
comparable office centres in the rest of Western Europe (Table
11), and even North America.   Some of the differential might be
explained by the unique attractions of the City of London as a
financial and trading centre, and it has been suggested that
this factor could perhaps have accounted for a differential of
perhaps twice the rent levels in other metropolitan centres.
But London rents were several-fold those of elsewhere, and the
Office Location Review suggested that for every £1 per square
foot that Central London rents were raised by the control the
extra annual costs to firms there was £50 million.   This calculus
assumed that the higher rents affected only one-half of Central
London's office users, particularly of course the expanding firms
needing additional accommodation (19).

     The benefits to be set alongside these extra costs are
equally elusive.   The Layfield Inquiry on the GLDP doubted the
effectiveness of the control as a means of acting either on the
volume or the distribution of employment.   It applied to buildings and employment within those buildings and could vary quite
significantly.   When refused an ODP, London firms displayed no
tendency to seek accommodation outside the control area.   An
examination of all named-user applications in Greater London
(for the period 1965-1972, and for office developments over
50 000 square feet which had been rejected) revealed the following: of 41 such rejections, 11 firms had remained in the same
premises, 24 had subsequently obtained an ODP either on the same
site or on another site in London, and only six of the applicants
had in the event moved out of London.   All moved to sites within
the South East.   In consequence, the Office Location Review
took the view that, although ODP controls had undoubtedly imposed

significant costs upon many office activities, they had generated no demonstrable direct benefits in steering employment to the Assisted Areas for whose benefit the policy had originally been in part designed.

It can be noted, however, that indirectly some of the development activity which was delayed or denied in London and the South East in the late 1960s and early 1970s was diverted outside the region. In some instances, this was just across the boundary of the control area to such locations as Poole and Swindon; in others, it was further afield to provincial centres both inside and outside the Assisted Areas. The burst of central area redevelopment with a substantial office component in such cities as Leicester, Nottingham, Sheffield and Cardiff at this time was in part a response, of course, to the more general economic, planning, financial and civic circumstances of the day. However, the office content of those schemes, and the new interest of traditionally London developers in provincial locations can undoubtedly be associated with planning constraints in London and the South East. By providing new opportunities for office relocation, these developments undoubtedly influenced the redistribution of office activities to some degree, as well as allowing many indigenous firms in provincial cities to leave older Victorian and Edwardian accommodation and to take up modern and more efficient space.

Another indirect effect of the ODP legislation, however, was its impact upon the self-confidence of the development industry. After a few years, and especially for those developers with sites or land banks having ODP and local authority permissions in London and the South East, the controls inevitably came to provide a cushion of risk reduction in speculative office provision. By restricting supply, they ensured not only inflated rental values for all office space, but also a ready market for those developments which were able to attract ODPs in the area of control. Outside the South East in contrast, by failing to assess demand with reasonable accuracy the development industry created a substantial oversupply of offices in a number of provincial city centres, of which Leicester was an extreme example. The profitability of development in the provinces must in consequence have been generally rather low. In the post-ODP era, therefore, it was not surprising that developers began to display extreme nervousness about prospective investments in all but the most attractive locations, and began to concentrate their activities above all in traditional locations. The existence of ODP controls therefore could well have altered - for a time at least - the industry's perceptions of acceptable risk. Certainly, the provincial experiences of the development industry pointed to a need for rather more rigorous analyses than hitherto of the likely future geographical demand for office space.

In sum, therefore, although ODP controls had the merit of being administratively simple - and they were in fact handled by a mere 15 civil servants in the Department of the Environment - they were an unsuitable instrument of policy from the outset.

Carried over from legislation and practice in the manufacturing sector of the economy, ODP legislation was framed without proper recognition of the substantial differences that exist between the two sectors and especially in the way in which firms look for, decide upon and occupy buildings. Unlike manufacturers, office users in the main require space immediately available to rent, and only the larger firms are able and willing to commission and have constructed their own purpose built premises. It was with reference only to the latter that the control might have been both justified and successful. For most activities in the office sector, on the other hand, ODPs were too insensitive an instrument for intervention, and it was this insensitivity which lay at the root of the Government's inability to apply the control strictly and consistently over any length of time. In retrospect, the TCPA's early advocacy of a locationally variable payroll tax and supplementary rate levies might have contained a more appropriate answer to policy needs.

Regional Policy Incentive Scheme

The third instrument of intervention in office location was the Regional Policy Incentive Scheme, designed to attract office employment into the Assisted Areas. Introduced as late as 1973, and administered by the Department of Industry, its potential impact was immediately constrained by the almost simultaneous arrival of economic recession. This inevitably reduced the rate of growth of office employment and hence the pressure upon individual firms to contemplate moving to new premises and possibly new locations. Incentives in the Assisted Areas had in fact been advocated for some years by a number of observers interested in broadening the range of measures and increasing the effectiveness of policies designed to ameliorate the economic ills of the country's less prosperous regions (20). But prior to 1973, whilst service industries were in principle eligible for regional financial assistance under Section 7 of the Industry Act 1972, in fact office activities benefitted very little. This was because the grants available were related to the amount of capital spent by firms moving into the Assisted Areas, and this was usually quite modest in the case of office users.

Undoubtedly the most persuasive advocacy of a more deliberate approach towards the service sector in regional policy was that of Rhodes and Kan (21) in their 1971 study, *Office Dispersal and Regional Policy*. In that analysis it was argued that many firms were decentralising their activities from London sub-optimally by relocating only 10-20 miles from the capital. However, the authors also showed that there was no real economic incentive for office managements to move their activities beyond the 40-80 mile zone. They therefore proposed that the financial incentives should be made available to offset the measurable cost penalties that were involved in longer-distance movement from London, and also to counterbalance some of the imaginary disadvantages of locating in the less prosperous regions. By this means, they argued, office activities could come to serve for the first time the objectives of the Government's Assisted

Area policies in redressing imbalances in regional employment
levels. Rhodes and Kan also advocated the construction of
'advance offices' by central and local government in the Assisted
Areas - in the same way that advance factories had for long been
provided as an inducement to the growth of manufacturing employment there. They further urged that any financial inducements
made available to office employers in localities of economic and
social need should be related in some way to the number of jobs
they would create there, and suggested that the incentives should
be set at £1500 per job in the form of an immediate offset to
the transitional costs of movement plus a general grant payable
over a period of three years (22).

In launching its 1973 scheme, the Government accepted that
the basis of any financial inducements for office activities in
the Assisted Areas could not be related to capital investment.
On the assumption that one of the principal concerns of firms
considering longer distance movement was the need to retain key
staff, the original 1973 Incentive Scheme therefore offered
grants to cover both the cost of renting office space in the
Assisted Areas, and the expense of moving key staff there. The
latter element of assistance was linked to the number of jobs
that it was expected would be created, and was spread over
periods of up to seven years. Under these arrangements, the
average offer made by the Department during the first four years
of their availability was below £1000 per job, and the scheme
attracted only 99 projects associated with 4150 jobs. Since the
initial hope was to divert to the Assisted Areas about one-fifth
of the 25 000 or so jobs thought to be leaving London and the
South East each year, an early review of the Incentive Scheme
was necessary, and the incentives were substantially modified in
1979 in an effort to increase its attractions.

The 1979 package comprised two elements. First, there was
a negotiable 'job creation grant' with maxima of £2000, £4000
and £6000 per job in the Intermediate, Development and Special
Development Areas respectively. Second, there was an employee
transfer grant of £1500 per head payable directly to key staff
moving with a project, but the number of qualifying staff was
limited to 30% of the total number of jobs expected at the new
location. One-half of the total grant was paid one year after
the first job was provided, and the remainder either two years
later or on completion of the project. All of the grant was subject to evidence that the assisted project was mobile - in other
words, that it was capable of successful operation outside the
Assisted Areas. There is evidence that this second scheme bore
more fruit. Backed by a modest advertising campaign it attracted
119 projects in the financial year 1979-1980 (Table 12). However,
following the loss of Government interest in regional policies
in the late 1970s, and the cessation of advertising and promotion,
interest in the scheme declined sharply.

Reviewing the Incentive Scheme overall, between 1973 and
1981 over 400 office projects were assisted by the Department of
Industry. In consequence, more than 25 000 jobs were created in

Table 12. Office movement into the Assisted Areas, 1964-1979

(No. of jobs)

	NI	Scot	North	NW	Y&H	Wales	EMid	SW	Total	No. of firms
1964/65	14	-	-	3	-	-	-	3	20	3
1965/66	-	-	-	-	-	-	-	-	160	2
1966/67	7	100	29	248	9	-	-	-	393	10
1967/68	-	9	1024	263	912	-	-	-	2208	17
1968/69	-	54	58	726	2245	40	-	-	3123	16
1969/70	-	3	90	301	147	33	-	-	547	12
1970/71	-	50	-	15	-	-	-	63	128	3
1971/72	-	3	-	1140	8	10	-	170	1331	9
1972/73	-	-	305	53	-	10	-	-	368	5
1973/74	-	101	30	28	124	115	-	-	398	15
1974/75	-	22	185	1847	847	-	12	1?	2923	19
1975/76	-	180	-	127	952	202	-	-	1461	13
1976/77	-	24	3	190	113	-	9	-	339	10
1977/78	-	19	525	84	1004	14	-	-	1696	9
1978/79	4	9	2	143	88	18	1	-	265	13
Total	25	624	2254	5268	6509	449	22	236	15387	
(No. of firms)	3	22	21	58	30	16	3	8		156

Source: LOB records

the Assisted Areas, many of which came from or might well have
located in London and the South East. This annual rate of job
creation compares very favourably with experience before the
introduction of incentives. During the period 1963-1974, only
92 clients of LOB moved into the Assisted Areas, creating on
average less than 1000 jobs there each year. These figures represent, of course, only a very small part - 6% and 8% respectively - of total office movement associated with the LOB
throughout that period. In contrast, during the last five years
of LOB's existence, when the Incentive Scheme was available,
nearly 10% of the moves and 13% of the associated employment of
its clients went to the Assisted Areas. During those same years,
the Department of Industry scheme helped to create annually an
average of 3000 new jobs in the Assisted Areas, and in the
period 1977-1978 to 1980-1981 that average rose to over 4000.

On this evidence, therefore, and assuming all other influences bearing upon the geography of office dispersal and
growth remained substantially unchanged, it would appear that
the Incentive Scheme did leave an impress upon the geography if
not necessarily the magnitude of longer distance office relocation, to the benefit of the Assisted Areas. The average cost
to the Exchequer of each job created has been estimated at
£1657, a figure that compares very favourably with the average
expenditure of Section 7 and development grant aid given to

manufacturing firms over the period 1974-1980, which was £2383
per job. Moreover, the benefits of the new office jobs created
in the Assisted Areas undoubtedly went well beyond those recorded by the Department. Not only would their arrival generate
local and sub-regional multiplier effects with employment implications but, in addition, the moves drew attention to the office
labour reserves there and the possibilities of conducting at
least some types of mobile office activities in such assisted
locations.

The Incentive Scheme can nevertheless be criticised on
several counts. One is the falling level of grant in real terms
between 1973 and 1979, and the fact that it took six years before
the initial incentives were increased to offset (at least in
part) the effect of inflation. Moreover, it has been argued that
the level of the grants was not really high enough in the first
place. The firm moving into the Assisted Areas automatically
benefitted from the lower costs of office space and of locally
recruited labour - but only by comparison with Central London
and not necessarily when compared with **some locations in**
the London suburbs or in the rest of the South East. On the
other hand, it had to bear the recurring higher communications'
costs of a non-central location. Goddard (23) argued, therefore, that in addition to the incentives which were designed to
offset the costs of longer distance movement throughout the
settling-in period, thought should be given to subsidies which
would encourage firms in the Assisted Areas to adopt advanced
communications technologies and thereby reduce the recurring
disadvantages of relocation and peripherality.

A question also surrounds the quality as well as the quant-
ity of office jobs that were attracted into the Assisted Areas
under the Incentive Scheme. Data on this matter are elusive,
and any judgements must be based substantially upon anecdotal or
informal evidence, and by inferences from an analysis of total
office employment in particular less prosperous regions (rather
than by the characteristics of the incoming firms). Nevertheless,
it is all too clear that the proportion of non-clerical,
relatively highly-skilled office jobs that were attracted into
the Assisted Areas in the 1960s and 1970s was relatively small,
and that the number of higher managerial and professional jobs
in those regions was left substantially unchanged by public
policy. Indeed, it can be plausibly argued that the very limited
achievements of the Government's office Incentive Scheme in the
less prosperous regions were probably more than offset by other
developments in the economy, some of which were actually being
encouraged by the non-spatial policies of successive governments.

The tendency towards the merger and agglomeration of what
were formerly separate firms into medium and large corporations
- encouraged by the activities of the Industrial Reorganisation
Corporation, for example - strengthened a long-standing tendency
for the higher-order administrative functions of an ever larger
share of the economy to be concentrated in the South East in
general, and Central London in particular. A theme of some

geographical criticism, therefore, was that government intervention in the evolution of inter-regional employment opportunities should have been adapted so as to recognise and influence
the location of key administrative functions within large scale,
multi-site enterprises (24).

A further, and probably central, weakness of the Incentive
Scheme stemmed from the fact that it was grafted on to an
existing set of policies designed to influence the inter-regional
balance of manufacturing investment and employment. In consequence an identical map of assistance was adopted for office
policies and it had a number of perverse consequences. The map
represented, both in the extent of the areas eligible for
assistance, and in its differentiation into Special Development
Areas, Development Areas and Intermediate Areas, a statement of
perceived employment 'needs'. It was certainly not an indication
of office development potential. In consequence, Liverpool was
provided with larger incentives for attracting offices than
Manchester: moves to Newcastle received higher public rewards
than moves to Leeds: firms relocating in the Sheffield area
could claim only the limited rent subsidies of the Intermediate
Areas: and Birmingham, which had only a small number and limited
range of office functions and was set within the West Midlands
conurbation with its rapidly deteriorating economic base, was
offered no assistance at all. It is just possible that a case
could be made in broad regional development terms for the
priorities that were implied in the Assisted Areas map (Figure
8). There were many observers, however, who had reservations
about this declared geography of assistance for even the manufacturing sector, given the fact that it was principally the
criterion of high and sustained levels of unemployment that was
used in its determination (25).

Even more reservations, however, must be acknowledged from
the viewpoint of office location policy. When in 1980
it was decided to roll back the map of assistance from a spread
that embraced about 45% of the population to one that covered
only 25%, and thereby to concentrate assistance only upon those
sub-regions and localities experiencing the most acute problems
of unemployment, not only Birmingham but also Sheffield,
Manchester and Leeds were amongst major provincial centres in
the less prosperous regions which were excluded from assistance
(see Figure 8). The day when a few significant centres of office
employment outside London might have been deliberately encouraged
by public policies was thereby set back once again (26). In
theory, at least, the concentration of provincial office employment growth in such centres would have had many advantages.
It would have allowed a fuller exploitation of existing public
investments in their urban infrastructure, especially public
transport facilities; it would have allowed the associated
development of a wider range of supporting office services there;
and it would have offered a much greater choice of employment
opportunities in those same provincial centres. However, the
political will to make the discriminating, but necessary, choice
of preferred office centres in the provinces was not forthcoming
(27).

135

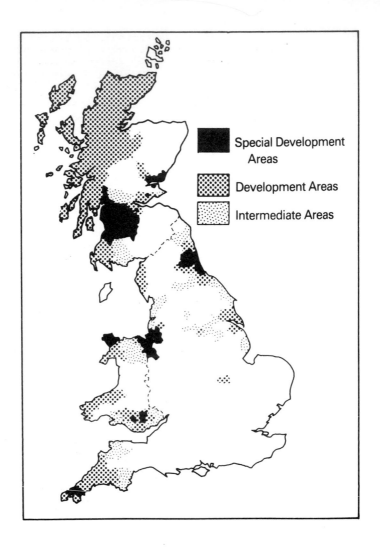

Figure 8. The Assisted Areas, 1982

Public sector relocation

Earlier, brief reference was made to the decisions which flowed
from the 1963 Flemming and 1973 Hardman proposals for the relocation of some Civil Service employment. Between 1963 and
1977 about 29 000 government posts were dispersed from Central
London to other parts of the metropolis, to towns in other parts

136

of the South East, and to the provinces; more than 65% of these jobs were relocated in the Assisted Areas. A further 19 000 new Civil Service posts were established outside Central London, nearly three-quarters of them being located in the Assisted Areas. In the latter year a further 39 000 posts remained to be moved; nearly 90% of them were destined to be in the Assisted Areas to conclude the Flemming and Hardman programmes. It is clear that these relocations reduced the scale of public employment in Central London from what it might otherwise have been, and supported the policies of decentralisation within the metropolitan region. In addition, they brought a wider range of jobs into the Assisted Areas, demonstrated the opportunities available to the private sector for longer-distance office moves, and benefitted both economic and social life in a number of major provincial centres through the increases they brought to local purchasing power. It has to be accepted, however, that the efficiency gains or losses of dispersing Civil Service functions in this way have not been the subject of a published review, and it would appear to remain an act of faith that the higher longer-term communication costs of dispersal are more than offset by the lower costs and more ready availability of labour outside London, by the lower costs of office space in the regions and by the wider benefits that have stemmed from the new geography of Civil Service posts.

It is important to acknowledge, of course, that the momentum of Civil Service dispersal in the 1960s and 1970s has not persisted into the 1980s. Past policies rode on the back of an expanding Civil Service payroll. But that payroll began to contract after 1979. Indeed, continuing fears that the economy's non-market sector of employment may have become too large, plus the substitution of many routine clerical posts by machines, suggests that Civil Service employment could continue to fall for the foreseeable future. They also suggest an employment environment within which the public sector unions are less likely to agree to further employment dispersal. What London civil servants have, they may want to hold (certainly within the metropolitan region). Indeed, in 1981 some dispersal plans were cancelled in order to make a short-term saving of £200 million.

Amongst the stream of office activities moving away from Central London, the nationalised industries, unlike the Civil Service, have been noted for their absence. Successive governments sought to encourage some dispersal of their administrative functions, and in a few cases they were successful. The decision to locate the headquarters of British Shipbuilders in the North East and the then British National Oil Corporation in Glasgow are two examples. These followed on the earlier partial dispersal of some National Coal Board management functions to Harrow and Doncaster, and decisions by British Rail and the British Steel Corporation to move some of their administrative activities to locations outside London. However, considerable difficulties have apparently stood in the way of a greater dispersal within the nationalised sector of the economy generally. The management of such nationalised corporations as British

Airways, British Gas, the British Transport and Docks Board and
the Central Electricity Generating Board consistently argued
that they needed to remain located in London - partly to allow
them to exploit its uniquely skilled labour market, partly to
take advantage of its specialised management services, and above
all to allow them easy, close and frequent contacts with government.

THE MANAGEMENT OF POLICY

Throughout its brief history, office location policy was the
victim of divided and ill-focussed administrative arrangements.
No one Department of State had overall responsibility for its
determination and implementation. LOB was originally set up
under the Ministry of Housing and Local Government; the Board
of Trade assumed responsibility for a short spell towards the
end of the 1960s; then in the 1970s its activities were sponsored
by the Ministry of Housing's successor, the Department of the
Environment. The Department of Economic Affairs throughout its
brief existence in the mid and late 1960s took an active interest
in office location policy, and it was the then Secretary of
State for Economic Affairs - George Brown - who announced the
introduction of ODPs; with that Department's demise, the Board
of Trade briefly took over ODP administration before it was
transferred in 1969 to the Department of the Environment (then
the Ministry of Housing and Local Government). It was the
Department of Industry, on the other hand, that had the task of
administering the regional incentives scheme from its inception.
The Civil Service Department has always handled the relocation
of Civil Service posts.

These changing and divided administrative arrangements did
little to promote a coherence in office location policies. In
some respects they simply served to push office location issues
into a 'no man's land' between other areas of policy making.
Considerations relating to the location of office employment
frequently had no clear voice in the making of land use and
regional plans, and considerations affecting the office sector
lacked proper integration into many broader spatial planning
initiatives. It has to be accepted, of course, that after the
1966 Census had revealed that the actual rate of employment
growth in Central London in the late 1950s had previously been
overestimated, any inclinations that might have existed in
government to forge a more coherent location policy were substantially reduced. Some examples will serve to illustrate how
this administrative confusion affected the nature and the quality
of policy making.

At the outset of policy in the early 1960s it was the
Government's intention to couple with LOB's exhortations to
Central London firms to disperse from the capital a more positive
strategy to encourage movement to 'preferred' office centres.
Indeed, the 1963 White Paper (as has been noted) went as far as

138

to mention the types of reception centre that the Government
had in mind. This aspect of intervention - the obverse of the
'origin of movement' initiative with which LOB was concerned -
was never properly developed, especially at the inter-regional
scale, for reasons that undoubtedly include the diffused nature
of office policy responsibilities within government. During the
1960s the Department of Economic Affairs initiated several
attempts to study the potential of major reception centres outside London and the South East, and argued for a strategy of
concentrated dispersal. But the necessary political will and
administrative coherence that might have ensured its adoption
and implementation was not forthcoming. Although,
therefore, government successfully encouraged some concentration
of office activities in the major and medium growth areas of the
South East, the absence of policy initiatives at the inter-
regional scale implicitly encouraged a general scattering of
decentralised office jobs throughout the rest of the country.
Any clustering that did occur - just beyond the western boundary
of the control zone (in Poole and Swindon, especially), in
Bristol and in a number of other provincial centres - was a
response to market forces.

A second example of the results of divided administrative
responsibility can be found in the relationship between policy
towards the location of offices and the development of the
country's international airport facilities. Had considerations
affecting the location of office activities been articulated more
decisively throughout government, the international tendency for
a large number of office activities to be attracted towards major
international airports would have been more widely acknowledged,
and decisions to make appropriate provision for such activities
- and even deliberately to encourage them - could well have been
taken. Instead, the substantially parochial and to some degree
vacillating policies of local authorities, generally upheld by
central government on appeal, resulted in a relative scarcity
of office space (and thereby raised its market worth) within
easy reach of Heathrow and Gatwick. The point is illustrated by
the 1980 rent contours in Figure 9. Simultaneously, the failure
of policy to encourage the upgrading and further provision of
appropriate office accommodation for airport-related and airport-
attracted activities near to the 'gateway' airports outside the
South East - in particular Birmingham, Manchester and Glasgow -
neglected an opportunity to promote inter-regional mobile employment in their direction. Initiatives of this type might well
have served better than the conventional 'carrot and stick'
methods that were adapted from regional policy practice in the
manufacturing sector, and they might have served to accelerate
the diversion of at least some international traffic generally
away from South East airports, and from Heathrow in particular.

The addition of office location responsibilities to the
existing briefs of several government departments militated
against the development of a coherent spatial strategy towards
the office location in another way. As has been noted, when the
Department of Industry was charged with the task of providing

139

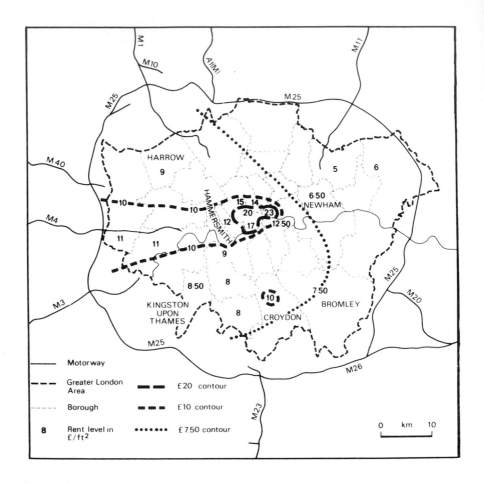

Figure 9. Greater London rent contours, 1980

incentives to office activities in the Assisted Areas, it decided
that the areas within which these subsidies might be claimed
should be identical to those already specified for the management
of location policy in the manufacturing sector. The contrasting
attributes of office activities - their different locational
needs and the distinctive qualities of their labour force by comparison with manufacturing industry - were consequently ignored.
As a result, when the policy was initiated in 1973, the West
Midlands - with only a limited range of office activities and a
regional economy beginning to experience an accelerating structural decline - was denied assistance. Meanwhile, Manchester,
the country's second largest office centre, but one badly in need

140

of new private sector activities, was afforded smaller government incentives to new office employment than Liverpool, which happened to have Special Development Area status for reasons that were in no way connected with an office development strategy for the Assisted Areas. Again, after 1980, when a revised map of the Assisted Areas was announced in a bid to reduce public expenditure, incentives were withdrawn from such major provincial office centres as Manchester, Leeds and Sheffield, to expose the essentially minor role that office location policy played in the strategic thinking of the Department of Industry. Such cities must surely have a central place in any serious attempt to re-shape the geography of office employment at the inter-regional scale.

Yet another example of the somewhat muddled approach of government to office location policy was the lack of coordination between measures designed to influence the location of private office employment and those affecting the Civil Service. The relocation of some of the headquarter functions of central government under the Flemming and Hardman initiatives served to demonstrate both the possibilities of moving higher-order activities further from London than hitherto, and the under-utilised resources of office labour in the Assisted Areas. The scale and the speed of the movement of thousands of posts to some provincial centres, however, reduced the likelihood of such places being able contemporaneously to attract significant private sector moves as well. This was for a variety of reasons.

First, a substantial proportion of the vacant and planned office space was often preempted for public sector use. Second, the speed at which an indigenous clerical labour force could be assembled for private employment was constrained by recruitment for the public service. At the same time, the fact that Civil Service labour is more highly unionised than that of the private sector could well have led some private employers to the view that a substantial government presence would adversely affect their interests in the local labour market. In consequence, any hopes that might have existed in the particular provincial centres to develop a mix of both public and private office functions were, at least temporarily, compromised. Meanwhile, the concentration of Civil Service moves upon certain cities in the Assisted Areas meant that office space and labour elsewhere that might on social grounds have been beneficially utilised were left unfilled and unemployed. As the LOB remarked in its *Annual Report 1976/77*:

> There are plans to move more Civil Service jobs, mainly to the Assisted Areas, (and) there are Government incentives to encourage the movement of private offices into the same areas....The Bureau has felt for some time that there is a requirement to monitor this public service and commercial movement more closely and to co-ordinate the information for the benefit of the receiving planning authorities and their developers, whether private or public. This might help to avoid in future some of the waste in time and money illustrated at present by potential Government moves to Scotland

and Wales where there is virtually no office space for their
accommodation and a surplus of just about the space required
sitting empty in the Midlands without any immediate prospect
of a client. Had this supply and demand situation been brought
together four years ago there would have been benefits all
round. (28)

Whilst there would have been little justification in the
Government steering office employment simply to lessen the adverse
consequences of inappropriately located and badly timed private
office developments, it so happened that the filling of empty
space in Birmingham, for example, could have been justified on
the grounds of a sound labour market policy, and the social
benefits that such employment would have brought to the ailing
conurbation.

The absence of a coordinated view of public policies towards
the location of office activities had a further adverse consequence. It meant that during the 1960s and 1970s successive
governments introduced measures that were designed to serve ends
other than an improved geography of office activities, but which
nevertheless had a significant but apparently unconsidered influence upon the behaviour of the office development industry,
upon the market value of office space and upon employment in the
office sector. Both the freeze on business rents in the early 1970s
and the introduction of the Development Land Tax, for example,
perceptibly restrained the activity of office developers;
they thereby affected the quality and the volume of the
country's office stock, and in consequence increased users'
costs. Moreover, even some government measures designed to influence the location of office activities - such as the establishment of the ODP system in 1960s and the standstill imposed upon
approvals in the 1970s - appear to have had as much backing from
those Departments of State wanting to deflect resources away
from office construction, as they did from those actually responsible for the coordination of the control.

In no circumstances, of course, could office policies ever
be considered or implemented as a separate and in some sense a
self-contained package. Nevertheless, it is a persistent theme
of this study that any attempt to intervene in the location of
office activities must be made within a broad and consistent set
of policies designed to shape the evolution of the urban and
regional system, and as part of a more general attempt to improve
the processes of land use and employment change. The management
of policy in the 1960s and 1970s by successive government departments, in contrast, meant that many decisions affecting the
location of office activities appear to have been taken in an
isolated and often ill-coordinated manner. The quality of the
intervention suffered as a consequence.

A further facet of policy management concerns not so much
the nature and the quality of policy but rather the timing of its
implementation. The record is once again less than impressive.
Looking back and, it must be conceded, with the knowledge of
hindsight, each major policy initiative in the 1960s and 1970s was

timed too late for it to have a substantial, let alone a maximum, effect.

Before central government's initial foray into office location planning, the London County Council and the TCPA had (from about 1957) been arguing the case for new initiatives to control office development in Central London. In Parliament itself, as early as 1959, during the discussion on the Local Employment Bill, the idea of introducing IDC-type controls over office development had been mooted. But, as we have seen, it was not until 1963 that the Conservative Government acted; and even when it did intervene it elected to do so in a limited fashion by creating LOB and rescinding certain rights to extend existing office buildings. It was the end of 1964 before a method of controlling office development was introduced and the ODP system established. By that time, however, it was in many respects too late. The demand for office space which had been created by London's first post-war office boom was beginning to abate and construction activity was on the wane.

The effect of controls, therefore, was merely to ensure that the surplus of office space which had begun to appear on the Central London market was soaked up quicker than might otherwise have been the case. Indeed, market forces by the mid-1960s had tentatively but clearly begun to set in train the process of major office decentralisation, and it can be argued that what was needed by 1963-1964 was a policy designed to shape that dispersal rather than merely to encourage it. Because of the surplus of office space in the mid-1960s, and the construction programmes and permissions in the pipeline, it was not until the end of that decade that ODP policy really began to bite and a situation arose in which it might have been possible to influence significantly the geography of dispersal. Ironically, it was just at this moment that the control policy was relaxed.

The next major initiative in the development of policy was the introduction of financial incentives for the office sector in 1973 in an attempt to assist the development of the country's less prosperous regions. As has already been noted, they were arguably too small at the outset. Certainly, they were too late. By the end of the 1960s it was apparent that, despite the substantial level of office dispersal from London relatively little inter-regional movement was taking place. Since there was little economic incentive to move far beyond the South East, however, it was recognised that some form of financial inducement was necessary to encourage movement into the Assisted Areas. Unfortunately, the actual introduction of such incentives in 1973 coincided with the peak year in the movement of jobs from London. After that year, the rate of decentralisation began to decline as employment growth slowed, as rent differentials narrowed and as the implementation of earlier decisions to leave Central London was completed. The potential for inter-regional movement was thereby seriously diminished.

It is possible that the mid and late 1970s, years during which there was an increasing substitution of machines for office labour, simultaneously saw a particular phase of decentralisation coming to an end. That phase was one during which many of the more routine types of office function relocated away from Central London, and one that was inspired especially by a search for additional supplies of labour. The poor timing of the introduction of the incentives, therefore, cannot be understated. Moreover, delays in the revision of the nominal worth of the financial incentives offered in the Assisted Areas, the real value of which fell steadily with inflation, further reduced their effectiveness. Of course, if the incentives were in any case insufficient to compensate for the higher operating costs of many types of office activities in the Assisted Areas, as Goddard has argued (29), then the delays merely exaggerated the policy's fundamental inadequacy.

The next phase of office policy began in 1977, when LOB's terms of reference were changed and included the brief to encourage the location of office employment in inner city areas. As far as the inner areas of the conurbations outside London were concerned - and there, quite rightly, little distinction was made between policy objectives as they affected both the central and inner areas - this represented little more than a slight change of policy emphasis. In the case of London, however, the LOB had been encouraging movement, not only from the Central Area, but also to some extent from the inner areas and the outer suburbs as well. The change in its remit thus involved a significant shift in policy.

Decentralisation in the 1960s and early 1970s had seen the outer boroughs gaining most from the exodus from Central London. The inner areas were generally by-passed by this wave of decentralisation; as has been seen, only Hammersmith - and to a lesser extent Lewisham and Stratford - managed to attract a significant tranche of office investment and of jobs. The failure of London's inner areas to attract office activities was partly a function of their labour markets, historically adapted to non-office employment opportunities, and partly the general indifference (and at times even the declared hostility) of many boroughs to the notion of office development in their areas. By the late 1970s, however, when action was taken to remedy these attitudes, it was probably too late to rely solely upon a package comprising exhortation, a shift in ODP policy and a more welcoming set of local authority attitudes as a means of encouraging new office employment in inner London. Those years saw only a relatively low level of demand for decentralised space, largely because Central London jobs were no longer increasing in aggregate but also because office rents had fallen significantly in real terms since the early 1970s and in consequence the rent gradient from Central London outwards flattened.

Firms deciding to decentralise were doing so increasingly for reasons other than the cost of space - reasons such as staff availability or the consolidation of separate activities - and were often seeking to escape from the London environment completely. Inner London was not an attractive alternative location

144

for most of these firms, since it shared many of Central London's problems but few of its benefits. Once again, therefore, the policy response to London's inner area problems, especially given the nature of the instruments used, was too late and too tentative. In just the same way as government initiates towards the manufacturing sector in the inner areas of the conurbations can be characterised as shutting the stable door after the horse had bolted, policies towards the office sector there were singularly badly timed as well.

A final point needs to be recorded with reference to the timing of office policy. The policy changes that have been described reflect in part shifting perceptions of the nature of the office location 'problem', changes in the central objectives of government, and shifting opinions about the most appropriate methods and politics of intervention. All occurred within a relatively short period of time. What government cannot claim is to have administered a consistent policy over an extended number of years. Yet the very nature of office activities, their normal accommodation in rented buildings, the distinctive role of the office developer in the provision of workspace, the time that it takes to get permission to design, build and equip an office building, and the number of development permissions that are invariably in the planning 'pipeline', all mean that it takes the best part of a decade for any policy to begin to have any significant effects. The very diversity and strength of market and institutional forces beyond government, therefore, demands that policy intervention, if it is to be attempted, should be firm and persistent, whether it is seeking to make good some deficiencies in the workings of the market or to reflect alternative social and political values. To be effective, policy must be designed not as a short-term expedient, but as a servant of longer-term objectives. This longer time-scale must be much more central to policy deliberations in the future than it has been in the past, and it is to these matters of future policy that the next chapter is devoted.

In conclusion, the characteristics and shortcomings of policy towards the location of office activities suggest one final lesson. The original rationale for intervention was rooted in certain perceptions of the Central London office 'problem'. Subsequent policy changes were merely tacked onto that original initiative, and on to a set of attitudes and initiatives towards manufacturing industry. It is not surprising, therefore, that the results of policy evaluated against even quite modest criteria of success were on balance quite modest. Undoubtedly, a central lesson of intervention in the 1960s and 1970s must be that old and unadapted policy vehicles should not be employed to secure new policy ends.

REFERENCES AND NOTES

1. G. Manners (1974), "The office in metropolis", *Economic Geography*, 50(2), pp. 93-110.

2. Compagnie Generale d'Economie Appliquee (1969), *La Decentralisation des Activites Tertiaires en France et en Grand-Bretagne*. Paris: CGU.

3. J. Goddard (1975), *Office Location in Urban and Regional Development*. Oxford: Oxford University Press.

4. Location of Offices Bureau (1973), *Annual Report 1972/73*. London: LOB, p.29.

5. Statutory Instrument No. 792 (1963), *Town and Country Planning, England and Wales, the Location of Offices Bureau Order*. London: HMSO.

6. Statutory Instrument No. 1296 (1977), *Town and Country Planning, England and Wales, the Location of Offices Bureau (Amendment) Order*. London: HMSO.

7. Location of Offices Bureau (1970), *A Wise Move*. London: LOB. Location of Offices Bureau (1972), *Moving Your Office*. London: LOB.

8. Economist Intelligence Unit (1964), *Survey of the Factors Governing the Location of Offices in the London Area*. London: EIU. M.V. Facey and G.B. Smith (1968), *Offices in a Regional Centre*, Research Paper No.2. London: LOB. M.J. Croft (1969), *Offices in a Regional Centre*, Research Paper No.3. London: LOB. S.J. Carey (1969), *Relocation of Office Staff*, Research Paper No.4. London: LOB. S.J. Carey (1970), *Relocation of Office Staff: Follow-Up Survey*. London: LOB. Interscan (1970), *Survey of Offices in the Central Area*. London: Interscan. British Institute of Management (1971), *Office Relocation*. London: BIM. M. Bateman, D. Burtenshaw and R.K. Hall (1971), *Office Staff on the Move*, Research Paper No.6. London: LOB. J.B. Goddard and D. Morris (1976), "The communications factor in office decentralisation", *Progress in Planning*, 6(1).

9. G. Yannopoulos (1972), *Office Decentralisation and its Impact on the Towns of Reception*, Research Paper No.7. London: LOB. G. Yannopoulos (1973), "The local income effect of office relocation", *Regional Studies*, 7, pp. 33-46.

10. R.K. Hall (1972), "The movement of offices from Central London", *Regional Studies*, 6, pp. 385-392.

11. Department of the Environment, Management Services Organisation and Methods Division (1976), *Review of Location of Offices Bureau*. London: DOE.

12. Economic Consultants Limited (1971), *Demand and Supply for Office Workers and the Local Impact of Office Development*, 2 vols. London: ECL.

13. Location of Offices Bureau (1967), *White Collar Commuters*, Research Paper No.1. London: LOB.

14. See the Annual Reports of the Location of Offices Bureau.

15. South East Joint Planning Team, Economy Group (1976), *Development of the Strategic Plan for the South East: Issues Report*. London: DOE.

16. *ibid.*, para.3.64.

17. Location of Offices Bureau (1974), *Annual Report 1973/74*. London: LOB, p.26.

18. Location of Offices Bureau (1975), *Annual Report 1974/75*. London: LOB, p.26.

19. Department of the Environment (1976), *Office Location Review*. London: DOE, para.6.7.

20. G. Manners (1963), "Service industries and regional economic growth", *Town Planning Review*, 33, pp. 293-303. E.M. Burrows (1973), "Office employment and the regional problem", *Regional Studies*, 7, pp. 17-31.

21. J. Rhodes and A. Kan (1971), *Office Dispersal and Regional Policy*. Cambridge: Cambridge University Press.

22. *ibid.*, p.102.

23. J.B. Goddard (1979), "Office development and urban and regional development in Britain", in: P.W. Daniels (ed), *Spatial Patterns of Office Growth and Location*. Chichester: Wiley.

24. G.F. Parsons (1972), "The giant manufacturing corporations and balanced regional growth in Britain", *Area*, 4, pp. 99-103. J. Westaway (1974), "The spatial hierarchy of business organisations and its implications for the British urban system", *Regional Studies*, 8, pp. 145-155.

25. G. Manners (1976), "Reinterpreting the regional problem", *Three Banks Review*, No.111, pp. 33-55.

26. *Financial Times*, 27th July, 1979.

27. Although service industries were more broadly included in subsequent adjustments to regional policy in 1984, the notion of seeking to develop a limited number of major provincial office centres was rejected by the Government once again.

28. Location of Offices Bureau (1977), *Annual Report 1976/77*. London: LOB, p.31.

29. J.B. Goddard (1979), *op cit.*

8

Postscript:

an office policy for the future?

The retreat from spatial planning in Britain - which began in
the mid-1970s with the collapse of the earlier, broad consensus
about the desirability of both anti-disparity policies at the
inter-regional scale and articulate strategic plans within each
of the country's major regions - has continued into the mid-1980s.
The retreat has occurred in the face of a widening gap between
the economic performance and employment prospects of the different parts of the country, and the representations of a number
of independent bodies to reconsider the desirability and the
possible dimensions of new regional policy initiatives (1).
Simultaneously, pleas have been heard for the reintroduction
of at least a minimum framework of strategic economic and land
use guidance at the regional scale within which the process of
statutory physical planning might be more confidently pursued (2).
Nevertheless, any concern with unemployment matters has concentrated on the overall volume of unemployment rather than its
regional distribution, and with job generation irrespective of
its sectoral and occupational mix.

This is no place to rehearse the debate on these matters
or to evaluate the likelihood of particular policy developments
in the next five or ten years. However, given the evidence and
the lessons of this study, it would be improper not to explore
briefly the contribution that an office location policy might
make in a changed political climate to British regional development and planning.

THE OBJECTIVES OF FUTURE INTERVENTION

The most likely central objectives of any future spatial policies
must be clarified first of all. In the late 1980s and into the
1990s it might reasonably be assumed that governments will

continue to be concerned with the need to improve national economic performance and to assist national economic growth. At the same time, there will be demands to arrest and if possible reduce what appear likely to be growing contrasts in the economic achievements, the social conditions and above all the employment prospects in different parts of the country. At the regional and sub-regional scales, it might also be assumed initially that public policies will seek to shape the detailed pattern of urban development and land use changes in such a fashion as will balance government commitments to the encouragement of economic growth with three simultaneous desires. These are, first, to shape the geography of development so as to take full advantage of existing public infrastructural investments and to minimise future infrastructural investment needs; second, to make certain that private locational decisions do not impose undue indirect burdens upon public costs; and, third, to ensure that due regard is paid to policies which seek to maintain and improve the quality of the social and physical environment.

Turning more specifically to policies which might be directed towards the location of office buildings and activities, it is highly likely that governments will be driven to consider more seriously than hitherto the contribution that intervention in this sector might make to the amelioration of the problems posed by major and persistent concentrations of local and regional unemployment. On the basis of past experience, government can legitimately assume that there will be occasions when the development industry will not necessarily anticipate the space needs of office users and - given the time-lag between market signals and the completion of new office buildings provided in response to them - will sometimes respond only slowly to those needs once they are recognised. Government can also assume that at times the perceptions of office employers with regard to their locational objectives and options may be limited by poor intelligence or prejudice, or both, and that their decisions about where to conduct their activities may in consequence be in some respects imperfect, even in terms of private costs. In theory, therefore, public intervention to influence the behaviour of the development industry and the location of office activities can be justified both as an attempt to offset the imperfections of market behaviour and as a reflection of social and political priorities.

It cannot be denied, however, that the public authorities responsible for the formulation and the implementation of policies can be equally badly informed about the nature and behaviour of the development industry, about the needs of office users, and about the markets in which they both operate. Moreover, past experience suggests that planning advisers and policy makers are capable of adopting intuitive and sometimes false, rather than properly researched, assumptions about the nature of particular land use or transport problems as they impinge upon office location decisions. Without systematic and up-to-date statistics on the activities of office developers and office users - and these are still not kept by any government department

150

- it is difficult to see how policies could be based upon a confident analysis of contemporary circumstances and future prospects. Moreover, governments and their agencies can too easily be indifferent to the wider costs that their policies sometimes inadvertantly impose, both upon the activities which they seek to influence and upon the economy in general. At times they can also be strangely blind to the distributional or social effects of their actions. Nevertheless, with spatial planning remaining one of the most valuable instruments that is potentially available to the community for adapting and improving the outcome of market forces - and for containing their less desirable consequences - such cautions argue for its sensitive use rather than its abandonment. Spatial planning can also be seen as a particularly useful vehicle for the collective assertion of alternative social values.

The lessons of the 1960s and 1970s suggest that, in the short to medium term at least, any intervention of the conventional type in the location of office activities can at best be only marginally influential upon the overall geography of employment in this sector of the economy. History also suggests that office policies must be directed towards clearly specified and well researched objectives, rather than being an intuitive and perhaps naive reaction to a perceived evolution of events. In the absence of a ready means of monitoring recent changes in the geography of the office activities, however, it could be some time before a really clear picture begins to emerge about the changes that are occurring and that are most likely to occur in the distribution of office employment over the next ten or 15 years in the absence of policy, and hence what those objectives should be. The case for resisting any desires to intervene in the changing geography of office location until such time as the existing spatial dynamics of office employment are more clearly established is quite persuasive. The first policy task of government, in consequence, must be to rectify this deficiency. Simultaneously, the best available evidence on recent locational dynamics of office activities needs to be vigorously explored. The difficulties involved in so doing are considerable.

SHORT TO MEDIUM TERM ECONOMIC PROSPECTS

A reasonably precise review of recent changes - or at least developments during the 1970s - in the magnitude, the mix and the location of office activities must await a full analysis of data collected in the 1981 Census, an analysis delayed and hampered by changes in its spatial and occupational definitions. Some indication of employment trends in part of the office sector, however, can be derived from annual Census of Employment data. This indicates that the Insurance, Banking and Finance (IBF) industries, for example, the only Order in the Standard Industrial Classification which can be regarded as wholly office based, grew throughout the decade in the country as a whole. In Greater London, on the other hand, the same industries expanded

their employment until 1974; they then experienced a three-year
decline; and then their workforce expanded once again in the
late 1970s.

Within the IBF Order nationally the story was somewhat
different for particular industries. Jobs in the insurance
industry in fact declined during the early 1970s. This was
partly because some of the industry's operations were computer-
ised; partly because some regional companies were taken over and
their employment structure was rationalised; and partly because
some large companies undertook major decentralisation and in
the process rationalised their use of labour. In the later
1970s, in contrast, employment in insurance activities grew once
again. This situation can be attributed to the development of
new types of insurance and new companies to market them, as well
as to the entry of some foreign insurance firms into the British
market for the first time. Even more vigorous was the growth of
jobs in other financial services from the mid-1970s. This reflected the rapid expansion of building society business and
branch networks; the extension of the clearing banks' branch
networks and credit card operations; and the inflow and expansion
of foreign banks, especially into Central London.

Whilst the Census of Employment indicates that other office-
based activities such as accountancy and legal services also
expanded throughout the 1970s, and in both cases employment grew
in Greater London as well as the country as a whole, it offers
no firm evidence on trends in the size and location of office
employment associated with most other industries in the economy.
The number of office jobs in firms concerned with the exploitation
and processing of natural resources, with the whole spectrum of
manufacturing activity, and with the provision of utility and
transport services, for example, cannot be abstracted from the
industry tables. It might not be unreasonable to assume that
the massive decline of employment in British manufacturing industry generally will have led in the late 1970s to a significant reduction of jobs in its headquarter offices and in its
corporate control activities. Whether in aggregate this has
proceeded at the same pace as, or much slower than, 'blue-collar'
job losses is simply not known. On the other hand, since the
early 1970s the further exploitation of North Sea oil and gas
reserves has undoubtedly generated thousands of new office jobs
nationally; of these, a large proportion - in oil companies,
oil service companies, consultancies and the civil engineering
industry - are located in the South East. Together with any
increase in office work that has been associated with a greater
centralisation in the ownership and management of transport,
distribution and retail activities, this growth could well have
offset, or at least substantially ameliorated, trends in the
manufacturing sector. Census of Production evidence, however,
casts no light upon this uncertainty.

Even if it was possible to monitor in some industry and
geographical detail the changing scale and pattern of office
employment, however, there would still remain major uncertainties

152

about the future. Recent years have witnessed poor and fluc-
tuating economic fortunes for Britain. It is impossible to tell
when, or whether, the tide will turn. It cannot be too strongly
stressed, therefore, that the recent past provides a singularly
frail basis from which to judge future job prospects - both in
the economy as a whole and in the office sector in particular.
Unless it can be demonstrated, argued or assumed with conviction
that the economic, social and political forces which produced
past trends are likely to persist for some time to come, historical evidence on employment change by industry and occupation
has only limited worth for forecasting purposes. With so many
uncertainties overhanging the national economy, and with office
activities generally facing the prospect of adaptation to further
technological change through the arrival of the micro-processor
and new communications technologies, the pitfalls of mechanistic
projections of employment trends has never been greater than
they are today.

Nevertheless, projections of employment change have been
made, and deserve some attention. Taking a short to medium term
view of prospective change in the structure of employment in
Britain, the Cambridge Economic Policy Group (3) and others have
suggested that jobs in the service sector generally, and by
implication office jobs in particular, will continue to grow
strongly throughout the 1980s. Whatever assumptions are adopted
about the evolution of macro-economic policies, the expansion
of private sector services appears likely to persist, and indeed
could grow from less than 6.8 million in 1981 to between 7.3 and
8.3 million in 1990. Such projections are based, of course, upon
the best and most recent statistical evidence available for employment analysis. It is evidence that requires cautious hand-
ling.

For example, future job prospects in the financial sector
will be strongly affected by the new technologies that handle
and transmit information, and which could substantially alter
the historic relationship between the growth of output and the
level of employment. As competition in the provision of financial services grows in the short to medium term, the pressures
upon individual firms to contain their costs will undoubtedly
increase and thereby encourage the adoption of the new technologies as well as other means of encouraging a more efficient
use of labour. Further, the high costs of the new technologies
could well lead to the merger of small and medium sized firms,
and an associated rationalisation of the labour that they employ.

Any expectation of a continuation of historical trends must
also be qualified by the knowledge that the expansion of much
office employment in recent years has been in the public sector
- in education and medical services especially. There are,
however, grounds for believing that this growth is unlikely to
be sustained in the forseeable future. In this part of the
public sector, of course, there is in any case relatively little
scope for the spatial manipulation of employment opportunities
since these are services which are substantially tied to the
distribution of population.

MEDIUM AND LONGER TERM ECONOMIC SPECULATIONS

Given the many uncertainties that flow from the national and world recession of the early 1980s, and the prospect of major changes in the international division of manufacturing labour as between the developing and the developed world, the nature of structural economic change is even more uncertain in the medium and longer term. Equally speculative is the likely magnitude of office employment and its geography.

Writers such as Daniel Bell (4) have drawn attention to the persistent growth of tertiary sector activities in mature industrial economies as manufacturing employment contracts both relatively and, in some regions and countries, absolutely. It follows from such a model of economic development, and more specifically from experience in the most advanced countries such as the United States and Sweden, that a further rise in the relative importance of office employment can reasonably be expected beyond the 1980s in Britain also. On the basis of national and international experience, a growing number of these jobs seem likely to be in the fields of information gathering and data processing.

Slightly at odds with this thinking, however, Gershuny (5) has observed that the growth of tertiary activities is strongly related in fact to the growth of manufacturing activities, and not independent of them. Even though employment in the manufacturing sector of the economy may decline, particularly as a consequence of the substitution of capital for labour, he has argued that a substantial level of manufacturing activity is in fact an essential prerequisite of many service jobs. These employments include both producer services to meet the needs of manufacturing activities, and jobs in consumer services to meet final consumer demands. In consequence, should British manufacturing industry exhibit a poor performance in terms of sales and output in the 1980s, the growth of service employments and, by implication, office jobs would be restrained. Gershuny has also made another point: whilst historical evidence, both national and international, indicates that higher income groups have been (and indeed still are) closely associated with higher than average levels of personal expenditure on services, and hence the generation of service jobs, employment forecasts should not press this relationship too far, by automatically assuming that rising incomes generally will inevitably generate additional service, including office, employments. Experience in most developed economies also indicates that rising living standards are widely associated with the development of the so-called 'self service economy' - the substitution of manufactured goods for many traditional forms of service provision and jobs, such as washing machines for laundry workers, or DIY tools for builders. Such a tendency naturally imposes a restraint upon the growth of service employments which forecasters cannot ignore.

154

Integrating these two schools of thought, several points can be made. First, since the demand for producer services is an important component in service employment growth, Britain's manufacturing output must increase above its present level if the growth of employment opportunities in associated producer services - such as marketing, product transport, advertising, designing, accounting, product testing and the like - is not to falter. An adverse indirect impact upon the demand for those consumer services that are purchased by the manufacturing work-force would also follow from a lacklustre performance of the manufacturing sector. On the other hand, office employment in the headquarters or regional offices of multinational (manu-facturing) corporations could continue to expand in Britain even if their manufacturing facilities were to be located increasingly out of the country. Moreover, some services in the trading sector of the economy are exported, and their scale is in some measure indifferent to the country's manufacturing role: banking, the commodity markets, insurance, international consultancy, some educational and health provision, computer software pro-duction, tourism and international transport services, for example, fall into this category. Again, jobs in some office-based services - such as motor and household insurance - are dependent upon owning and using goods in the UK and not on where those goods are made. There are, in other words, many office jobs in the service sector which are generated independently of the wealth produced by the country's manufacturing base. The insights of both Bell and Gershuny are thus both valid. Neither of their approaches, however, provides any practical guidance as to how many, and what sorts of, office jobs might be available in Britain in ten to 15 years' time.

Another contentious issue surrounding the future scale and nature of office employment in the medium to long term stems from the uncertain impact of recent and prospective technological change, particularly developments in information and data pro-cessing. Much of the published evidence on this subject is inevitably highly speculative, and it is still too early to make an objective assessment of either the qualitative or quantitative impact of micro-computers, text editors, electronic information storage and transfer and the like upon jobs. There can be little doubt that capital equipment is being substituted for labour in many types of office work, and will continue to be as the costs of the equipment continue to fall. The eventual impact of this process upon labour requirements, however, depends substantially upon the changing costs of, and the elasticity of demand for, office services. The relationship between increasing demands for services and any improvements in the efficiency with which they are produced is extremely elusive because aggregate service outputs are outstandingly difficult to measure, let alone fore-cast, and indeed they are commonly measured by service labour inputs! Moreover, whilst the growth of managerial, professional and technical jobs in the manufacturing sector would appear to be a likely result of the information explosion generated by the new technologies, the overall size of that sector is clearly heavily dependent upon the successful adaptation of the country's industry to a rapidly changing international environment.

The shifting relationship between the new technologies and
the location of office work is equally unclear. The distribution
of some office employment will clearly be influenced by the
geography of its related manufacturing facilities. Industrial
technology consultancies, however, which are likely to grow both
in numbers and size, can operate from a wide variety of locations
and increasingly reflect the changing residential preferences of
their workforce. In the service sector, as a consequence of
distributed processing, the new technologies will facilitate -
ceteris paribus - a wider geographical spread of activities.
This could mean in particular that fewer large blocks of centralised clerical work will be available for *en bloc* relocation.
On the other hand, the variable and uncertain relationship
between new information technology and other factors affecting
the location of office work - the availability of skilled labour,
suitable premises, corporate structure and the like - leaves the
likely tendency of locational preferences overall highly speculative.

Nevertheless, recent empirical evidence (6) suggests that
the process of decentralisation continues, although at a somewhat
reduced level when compared with the mid-1970s. But that evidence
also points to a substantial shift in the factors contributing to
relocation. Out of a total of 85 reasons quoted in a sample
survey, 25 related to firms deciding to integrate in a single
place those activities which had formerly been dispersed in
several locations. This proportion (29%) contrasts with only
12% of (the earlier) LOB movers who quoted the same reason. If
this recent 1983 sample is in any way representative, it
suggests that fewer current relocation exercises can be regarded
as being footloose in the sense of choosing between a wide range
of alternative locations.

A STANCE ON FUTURE POLICY

The future size and the prospective spatial dynamics of office
activities are sufficiently uncertain to advise any government
of the need for extreme caution before it once again embarks
upon a major programme of intervention in office location. The
first prerequisit of any policy initiative must therefore be for
the government to ensure that it is better informed on these
matters. An arrangement for measuring and regularly monitoring
the scale and the geography of employment in office activities
is, therefore, of paramount importance and should be instituted
at the earliest opportunity. Certainly, intervention must be
tentative until such time as the contemporary dynamics of the
industry, and its likely future development in the absence of
policy, are better understood.

In the short-term, given the continuing concentration of
office activities in London and the rest of the South East, plus

the relative lack of office employment opportunities elsewhere
in Britain, it would not be unreasonable for government to
continue to provide incentives for the encouragement of office
activities in those areas of employment 'need' where opportunities genuinely exist for the efficient operation and possibly
the eventual expansion of the firms taking up the incentives.
Indeed, the 1983 White Paper on *Regional Industrial Development*
(7) proposed, and the subsequent 1984 Cooperative Development
Agency and Industrial Development Act provided, that a much wider
range of service industries than hitherto would become eligible
for regional development grants. In the Assisted Areas, as well
as in parts of the South East, central and local government
policies together might also usefully encourage - by means of
fiscal or other incentives and through the due processes of land
use planning - the construction of new office premises in locations that particularly serve both private (user) interests and
the objectives of public policies.

The evidence of this study poses one central dilemma.
Government attempts to steer office activities into the Assisted
Areas during the 1960s and 1970s met with only limited success.
Yet during those years employment growth nationally was buoyant
and large firms in particular were looking for relocation
opportunities to ease their labour supply problems. In the
1980s and 1990s the employment needs of the Assisted Areas
(however those areas may eventually come to be defined) are
almost certain to be greater. In addition to the further
loss of jobs in manufacturing, employment in many of the existing
'routine' office activities in the Assisted Areas could also
shrink as a direct consequence of new office technologies. The
attractions to relocate there, however, may be very much reduced.
Firms may want to move for reasons of economy and efficiency.
They may see advantage, if their operations have come to be
relatively and inefficiently dispersed, in seeking to consolidate
at least some of their activities in one place as part of a
rationalisation programme. They may even decide to move as a
means of reducing their staff and introducing new technologies.
As a generalisation, however, they are unlikely to be moving in
search of additional supplies of labour. It is not unreasonable
to conclude, therefore, that even if generalised incentives and
controls designed to divert employment away from the relatively
more prosperous parts of the country were to be substantially
strengthened, in the light of experience their effects upon the
geography of office employment would, in all probability, be very
modest indeed.

It might be argued therefore that a more substantial impact
upon the broad geography of job opportunities must await the
willingness of government to intervene more directly in the
location of private sector employment, including that of office
firms. The reluctance of central government to take such a path,
given its lack of detailed knowledge about the choices that are
realistically open to individual firms about the location of
their activities and jobs, is all too obvious. Local authorities, on the other hand, may be able to develop the sort of

relationship with individual firms that such intervention might require, and this might have advantages at the borough or district and at the county or metropolitan scales. But a major question remains as to how such knowledge might to used operationally for the 'strategic' intra-regional manipulation of the location of office activities, let alone any attempt at the inter-regional diversion of office work.

It cannot be escaped, moreover, that international competition for the provision of office-based services is tending to grow. The London insurance market is being increasingly challenged by New York, for example, and stockbroking jobs in the City are vulnerable as the Wall Street market for shares in major British companies steadily increases. Government action to serve the ends of domestic spatial policy, therefore, obviously must not impose unnecessary inflexibilities and costs upon such office users, impairing their efficiency and reducing their international competitiveness. In this field, as in many others, there will always be a tendency for conflicts to exist between government ambitions to assist (individual, firm) efficiency and their desire to promote simultaneously (more general, social) equity. Yet choices have to be made between them. These choices can have a locational dimension in which, for example, the desire to ensure the continuing commercial success and to exploit the many advantages of Greater London, the Outer Metropolitan Area of the South East and the so-called 'Western corridor' of southern England has to be weighed against the problems facing other parts of the country. Similarly, at another scale, the desire to enable and even encourage spontaneous office employment growth in particular parts of London's wider region has to be measured against the need to revise the role and renew the economic base of some of the capital's inner city areas. Whereas in the 1960s office location policies could be, and indeed were, developed on the assumption that everyone would benefit from their implementation, throughout the 1980s such a happy coincidence of interest is unlikely to exist - and hard choices will have to be made.

The development of new policies towards the location of office employment must **acknowledge the constraints and** opportunities that follow from the broader framework of the country's economic and social goals and the spatial dimensions of both. Above all else, it must acknowledge the slow pace at which any adjustment in the broad pattern of office location is likely to be possible, and must be shaped with a 20 year view in mind. Unlike the situation faced by government 20 years ago, however, the choices that will have to be made can be measured against the experience of policy intervention in the 1960s and the 1970s. As has been demonstrated in this study, it is an experience that makes the choices better informed. It does not, however, make those choices any easier.